WOMEN OF A PROMISCUOUS NATURE

DONNA EVERHART

KENSINGTON PUBLISHING CORP.

kensingtonbooks.com

KENSINGTON BOOKS are published by
Kensington Publishing Corp.
900 Third Avenue
New York, NY 10022

All Kensington titles, imprints, and distributed lines are available at special quantity discounts for bulk purchases for sales promotion, premiums, fund-raising, educational, or institutional use.

Special book excerpts or customized printings can also be created to fit specific needs. For details, write or phone the office of the Kensington Sales Manager: Kensington Publishing Corp., 900 Third Avenue, New York, NY 10022. Attn. Sales Department. Phone: 1-800-221-2647.

ISBN: 978-1-4967-4072-4

ISBN: 978-1-4967-4073-1 (ebook)

First Kensington Trade Paperback Printing: February 2026

10 9 8 7 6 5 4 3 2 1

Printed in the United States of America

The authorized representative in the EU for product safety and compliance
is eucomply OU, Parnu mnt 139b-14, Apt 123
Tallinn, Berlin 11317, hello@eucompliancepartner.com

Outstanding praise for Donna Everhart and her novels!

The Education of Dixie Dupree
An Indie Next List Selection!

"Young Dixie Dupree is an indomitable spirit in this coming-of-age novel that is a heartbreaking and honest witness to the resilience of human nature and the fighting spirit and courage residing in all of us."
—*The Huffington Post*

The Road to Bittersweet

"You will fall in love with Wallis Ann Stamper as she meets the bitter challenges of her hardscrabble life, inspired by her sweet love for her family. Her grit and unfailing faith in herself will melt your heart, as it did mine."
—Sandra Dallas, *New York Times* bestselling author

The Forgiving Kind

"Reminiscent of the novels of Lee Smith, Kaye Gibbons, and Sandra Dallas, Everhart builds a firm sense of place, portraying the tiredness and hope of a dry Southern summer and voicing strong women."
—*Booklist*

Women of a Promiscuous Nature

"Both a cautionary tale and a deeply compassionate rendering of women wrongly imprisoned in a system designed to break them, Donna Everhart's propulsive story is filled with injustice, intrigue, and the determination to fight back. Book clubs will find themselves discussing *Women of a Promiscuous Nature* late into the night, and readers will long remember the remarkable women so aptly rendered within its pages."
—Lisa Wingate, #1 *New York Times* bestselling author of *Shelterwood*

"A remarkable fusion of research and imagination, all that we hope for in the best historical fiction, but there is much more to admire here—vivid scenes, compelling characters, perfect pacing—but most impressive of all is Everhart's creation of Dorothy Baker, a woman who, as her past is slowly revealed, becomes so multifaceted that even in her most appalling moments we cannot ignore her humanity. She is one of the most memorable characters I've read in recent fiction, and further proof of Donna Everhart's immense talent."
—Ron Rash, author of *Serena*

"Eye-opening . . . Everhart writes movingly about the American Plan (a real government program that tried to regulate women's bodies and sexuality) and its consequences in the first part of the twentieth century. With its strong women characters, the novel is a brutal but unforgettable read."
—*Library Journal*

Books by Donna Everhart

THE EDUCATION OF DIXIE DUPREE

THE ROAD TO BITTERSWEET

THE FORGIVING KIND

THE MOONSHINER'S DAUGHTER

THE SAINTS OF SWALLOW HILL

WHEN THE JESSAMINE GROWS

WOMEN OF A PROMISCUOUS NATURE

Published by Kensington Publishing Corp.

Dedicated to my grandmother, Lillian Mae Holliday Davis,
for your bravery and forward-thinking nature, and
to my Aunt Linda, a special, unique soul

We do not "cure" children—we train them.
—Elsa Ernst, psychologist and superintendent, from the Annual Report of the Board of Directors and Superintendent of the Caswell Training Schools for Mental Defectives. . . , for the Year Ending June 30, 1926

That the Secretary of War and the Secretary of the Navy are hereby authorized and directed to adopt measures for the purpose of assisting the various States in caring for civilian persons whose detention, isolation, quarantine, or commitment to institutions may be found necessary for the protection of the military and naval forces of the United States against venereal diseases.
—From the Chamberlain-Kahn Act of 1918

It is the philosophy they helped to cement: that women and promiscuous people are dangerous and morally inferior; that they need to be stopped, locked up, and reformed.
—From *The Trials of Nina McCall: Sex, Surveillance, and the Decades-Long Government Plan to Imprison "Promiscuous" Women,* by Scott W. Stern

Chapter 1

Baker

Eagle Springs, North Carolina
1931

Dorothy Baker's reputation is on the line. She knows this as soon as she peers into the depths of a hall closet, hands clenching in tight-fisted rage at the items tucked away. Cleaning supplies, linens, a mop and bucket, organized and ready for working hands sit innocently along with the *intoxicating materials*. She manages to conceal their effect on her even as a sensation like slipping into a tub of warm water overtakes her at the sight of them. Without question they're intended for mischief. Matches, wads of old newspapers, and a small tin of lighter fluid are hidden behind the sheets and towels. Her mind takes off on a rampage while her expression is restful, serene even. She's a striking, elegant woman, with a cool composure that contradicts her mental state at the sight of these attractions. She turns to Mrs. Libby.

"They think they can fool us, do as they please because they don't want to be here. It's unbelievable, really. Here is for their own good, they just don't realize it."

"Yes, Mrs. Baker. I wholeheartedly agree."

"This is alarming."

"Most definitely."

Reports of disgruntled girls complaining about punishment came by way of teachers and other staff who overheard their discontent at being locked in their rooms, the whippings and the meals withheld. Only days before, disciplinary measures were given to a couple of girls, aged fourteen. Sandra Haynes and Millie Wilson were whipped for running away. Those girls, with oversight by the housemother of Chamberlain Discipline Hall, Mrs. Libby, received what is standard protocol, punishment at the hands of other residents. The two girls had to lie down on their stomachs while six other girls struck them with a switch. This method is viewed as an ideal deterrent, providing a firsthand lesson of what not to do unless one wants a taste of the same.

And now, had it not been for the eagle eyes of Mrs. Libby spotting these items, there's no telling what might have happened. Baker resists the urge that comes at the sight of the accelerant and matches. The Incident, as she calls it, a terrible time from her childhood, sneaks forward as stealthy as an undiscovered flame. An involuntary shiver runs the length of her spine and she quickly raises her arm. She points into the closet to cover her momentary lapse, and instructs Mrs. Libby on what to do.

"Place those offensive items on the hall table. Have the girls line up."

"Yes, Mrs. Baker."

Baker paces while she waits. As superintendent, how far should she take this particular violation? Issues like leaving the hall without permission, rudeness, and uncleanliness are managed by assigning demerits. Ten demerits means a visit to Miss Walker, the Supervisor of Student Government. What about something as serious as possible arson? On the other hand, it didn't happen—it was only in the planning stage, an idea not yet executed. She is quite skilled at getting pertinent information out of even the most stubborn. Usually, a threat is sufficient, and she can go from there depending on the contriteness or contrariness of the guilty parties.

Baker hears a bell, and Mrs. Libby's faint commands. She places herself in front of the hall table, her hands folded. Like the rush of a mountain stream, they enter. Her girls, as she thinks of them, cheeks crimson from cold air and the exertion of preparing the fields for the spring planting of vegetables. This is how she wants them, vibrant, wholesome, and healthy. And, of course, obedient and polite. The flow of chatter stops as they conform to the code of silence once inside. They are to speak only if spoken to when called in front of the superintendent, as instructed upon admission to the reform school.

They file by Baker, and she studies each face, checking for guilt. Some are nervous, while those she views as bad girls flaunt their disrespect and boldly meet her gaze. This means nothing. The defiant are known to be shifty, and like to test her. The innocent meet her gaze because they're curious. She'll probably have to interrogate each of them, one by one. They line up along the length of the hall ranging in age from ten to sixteen. The older residents, those in their late teens to early twenties who're sent because of prostitution or other corrupt behaviors, aren't under her care. They're housed separately. She prefers training the age range standing before her, those still viable for alteration. She smacks her hands together, and a few of the younger ones jump. Her voice is stern as she addresses them.

"If you know anything about these items, say so now."

Baker motions toward the items on the table. The girls shift their attention there, then resume staring straight ahead. Shuffling feet, throat clearing, and the occasional huffs of impatience cease. Baker, in black lace-up shoes with two-inch heels, paces before them. Those heels strike the wood floor with a slight uneven bump as she walks down the line of girls, peering into thirty pairs of eyes. She removes her wire-rim glasses and polishes the lenses with a handkerchief she keeps tucked in the sleeve cuff of her blouse. She places them back on her face, tucks the handkerchief away again, and resumes walking. Everything is done with deliberation; she doesn't rush. She gets to the end of the line, turns, and makes her way back again. Midway, she stops and points at the table behind her.

"This is serious and I plan to get to the bottom of it."

The girls are frozen in time, the only movement the rise and fall of their chests as they dare to breathe. A few risk looking at her again, but it's fleeting. The door to the hall is open and a chilly breeze enters, ruffling the hems of their hand-sewn dresses, and the ends of their hair. Baker waits, but nothing is forthcoming from any of them. She'll have to do it the hard way.

"Mrs. Libby, I'll speak with them one at a time. For now, this half can resume their work. The rest will remain here. Send me one girl at a time."

"Understood."

Baker's office is in a different building next to Chamberlain Hall, and that's where she heads. The pines between the buildings are thick and surround the Samarcand Manor facility. There's a fresh, crisp scent to the air even on such a cool day and the ground is soft with their needles. She enters the administration building, turns left, and goes into her office. It's sparsely furnished, with only a large oak desk, two wooden chairs, and a lamp on a small table by the window. There are no family photographs. Baker has done nothing to brighten the space except every day she opens the heavy curtains to allow the sun to stream in. It's March and this helps warm up the room, at least with regard to the temperature. She stands in front of her desk and waits for the first girl. Before long, there's a knock.

"Come in."

It's Millie Wilson. Smart for Mrs. Libby to send the most likely culprit. She comes from a nearby area known as Vass where many of the girls' families work as farmers or in the Vass Cotton Mill. Millie is classified as a delinquent, the type of girl whose family consists of drunkards, moral degenerates, or the unemployed. Millie's not the only girl with this background, and a few have it even worse. Some of the girls, surprisingly, come from respectable, decent families, but have been sent because their parents believed they were engaging in immoral behaviors, or, as they put it, were "incorrigible." Perhaps they were seen as promiscuous, spending too much time running the streets, or contemplating matters of a sexual nature.

Whatever the reason, Baker's purpose is to restore them to the pristine nature of their Southern womanhood, to rid individuals of impure thoughts, and return them to their communities with a renewed outlook on their future. The government's initiatives to keep prostitutes from spreading venereal diseases, thereby protecting the military and armed forces, includes preventing juvenile delinquency and the downfall that comes with such behavior. Millie is on her way to a life of sin unless she changes. She sends Baker an insolent glare. The girl is undisciplined and feebleminded and Baker deems her as such, as she does many of her charges. Decent, intelligent girls don't end up here. Baker sets her shoulders and raises her chin.

"What do you know about the items found in the cleaning closet?"

"Nuthin'."

"Excuse me?"

"Nuthin'. Ma'am."

They go back and forth for several minutes. The girl doesn't back down. Of course, Millie would deny any knowledge. Frustrated, Baker sends her out, and the next girl is sent in, and the next, and the next.

This goes on until Baker, by the end of the day, has all but given up. Each remains silent, plays dumb, is dumb, or innocent. It's more than disappointing and she feels like she's lost because she even resorts to threats and those didn't work. If there's one thing she can't stand, it's losing. She goes to bed that night feeling like a failure and she doesn't like it. Her mind, gone haywire from the events of the day, eventually slows its frenzied processing, and she drifts off. It seems she's only entered into a deep sleep when she wakes again, a sharp, acrid smell filling her nose. Half asleep, a bizarre, out of place incessant clanging makes her sit up and look about. Why is the dinner bell ringing? There's a strange orange glow filtering through the window of her room, creating unusual shadows on the walls. Her legs play an old trick and become uncooperative, like she's in one those nightmares, unable to move, except this is no dream. They did it. They somehow succeeded, despite themselves. Someone bangs on her door and then Mrs. Libby, as if conjured by the oddness of it all, appears by Baker's bed.

"Get up, get up! Chamberlain Hall is on fire!"

Baker's chest tightens. Recollections of limpid orange flames fill her mouth with saliva. Mrs. Libby tugs on her while Baker's uncanny attraction attempts to control her once she understands what's beyond her window. Behind Mrs. Libby comes a familiar crackling sound that goes with fire consuming wood. Baker's vision blurs, realizing that even at thirty years old, it grips her the same as it did when she was seven. Mrs. Libby's cries finally get to her.

"We need to get to the girls!"

Baker swings her legs over the side of the bed and Mrs. Libby gapes, speechless. Baker yells at her.

"My robe! I need my robe!"

Mrs. Libby recovers from the disturbing sight of thick burn scars going every which way down Baker's legs. She grabs Baker's arm.

"We don't have time!"

There's a tremendous noise, a pop, like fireworks. They rush out of Baker's door and outside, where an expanding mass of gray smoke boils upward into the night sky. Once they're near the dormitories, they're exposed to a devastating sight. Amber swirls reach for the sky out of every window. It's an ominous, surreal scene. Chamberlain Discipline Hall isn't the only burning structure; Bickett Hall is ablaze and girls from both dormitories stand in clusters some distance away. There's a loosening in Baker's gut, the sensation not unpleasant, but she has the presence of mind to ignore her impulse to get closer. Mrs. Libby coughs, sputters, and gags and she refocuses herself and slaps the woman's back. She is uncomfortably aware of her state of undress, the exposure of her legs. No one knows about her old injuries because, as her mama taught her, she keeps her legs covered in black stockings no matter the time of year. Even Ed, her ex-husband, didn't know until their wedding night. She believes it's the real reason for his leaving her.

She turns to Mrs. Libby and in a rare moment of weakness, says, "They can't see me like this." She gestures at her legs. "They'll use it against me somehow. You know how cruel they can be."

Mrs. Libby immediately removes her own robe, which reaches

the ground, and gives it to Baker. Grateful, she puts it on, and it's just in time because Mrs. Howard, the housemother for Bickett Hall, joins them along with a handful of teachers, their distress and fear apparent.

"Can you believe this?"

"It's utter insanity!"

"They've gone and done it now."

"How will Samarcand ever recover?"

While they wait for the firetrucks, thirty minutes away in Carthage, they watch sparkling embers float and dance around them. Baker tries not to think of the shaky future the school might have because of this. Some of the girls nearby are crying, others gape in silence, while a few cling to one another and whisper. Baker watches them, furious at the knowledge the guilty ones stand among them. She can hardly stomach the thought of the repercussions. The two dormitories are sure to be a complete loss. She wants someone, anyone, to explain. She faces the teachers and housemothers.

"Given what we found earlier, we know this was intentional."

There's a general murmur of agreement. Baker keeps an eye on the girls who glance their way every now and then.

"We need to see if anyone's willing to confess. Let's see what they say."

She leads the staff over and speaks in a firm voice.

"If you had nothing to do with this, then you should stay out of it. Those of you involved, step forward."

She's stunned when a dozen or more girls boldly step away from the others without hesitation. It's not only because they do so and quickly, but because there are so many. One of them is Millie Wilson. She smirks at Baker, as if proud of getting something over on her. Baker instructs her staff.

"Keep them separate from the others."

The group is vocal. They don't hesitate to boast as to why they did what they did, declaring it as a form of protest.

"Y'all are treatin' us worser'n dogs."

"It ain't right to be whipped or locked up."

"Look at my hands. I'm sick of workin' in them fields, day in and out."

"My own mama works long hours at the cotton mill and fares better'n this."

From a distance the sound of sirens grows loud and everyone's attention shifts as firetrucks come quick and fast down sandy paths followed by the sheriff and a deputy. The girls who claim responsibility are arrested and Baker watches as they're taken away to face unknown consequences. She turns to Mrs. Libby.

"This will be my ruination."

Mrs. Libby frowns.

"How? You certainly tried to stop it."

"This is only part of the trouble."

"What do you mean?"

"It'll be about the punishment and who knows what else. It won't matter about the ones who've gone back home restored to decent and productive individuals, a help to their families instead of a burden. Nor will it matter we're not the only school in the country operating likewise. There's one in Montana that made residents stand with soap in their mouths for an entire day. At least we didn't do that, but once they know they've got the ears of those above me, they will say what they want."

Mrs. Libby shrugs.

"There will always be those who are irredeemable. Perhaps this lot is just that, and we get our say too, don't we?"

Despite Mrs. Libby's rationale, Baker's mind bleats *failure, failure, failure.* The smoldering structures take her back to her beginning with this job. Only two years ago she became superintendent, right after she'd caught Ed, her husband of less than a year, spending time with the very type of women she wanted to ensure these girls didn't become. Because of her personal situation, it became her mission to rid society of delinquent, troubled young girls who could become philandering females. Over her dead body would she allow them to turn into the sort who ruin marriages, like the one who ruined hers.

Samarcand is her dream job, where the troublesome are taught how to run a decent, clean household and receive a bit of education. This is where instilling virtue and goodness takes place. Active work, meaningful work. It's the chance of a lifetime, and a tremendous reward for her dedicated years within the Federation of Women's Clubs and other worthwhile organizations. Why, even Ed never recognized it was she who was the one to almost single-handedly gather hundreds of signatures petitioning for the reclamation of young Southern white women. By her measure, it's been a success and her biennial reports prove it.

The unfortunate fact is, this fiasco will outweigh the good and nothing she's accomplished will be viewed favorably. The girls will talk. The meaning behind her methods will be lost. Her efforts will be wasted because it's impossible to think such a catastrophic event under her watch would enable her to remain. This fire is the catalyst and what grips her with fury more than anything is how these girls, those she deemed low-class degenerates, bested her. She must face this truth, and somehow overcome it. Baker shuts her eyes as the roof of Chamberlain Discipline Hall collapses and her dreams of saving the very girls standing nearby collapses with it.

In the following days, she gets wind of letters from some of the parents and a couple of teachers. She turns to Mrs. Libby in distress.

"Have you heard what they're saying? Have you read these accusations?"

"I have. It's a disgrace. An out-and-out disgrace."

Newspapers are filled with claims about the punishments, carrying various details far and wide. The *Chapel Hill Weekly, Rocky Mount Telegram*, and *Greensboro News*, to name a few, bang the drum of alarm and shock. They have a field day, criticizing the abysmal treatment and conditions. Everyone screams for an investigation. Girls, but in their tender years, it's reported, were subjected to the same horrors as the strictest institutions the state has to offer—the prison system. Is this the intent for these young women, asks one journalist? Perhaps there's justification, some suggest. Nevertheless, Baker's oversight at the school is highly suspect, and out of the blue, others come forward against her, to include, of all people, Mrs.

Libby. Baker is stunned, even as she realizes the woman is only trying to save her own job.

The Board of Directors makes their decision and Baker is out. A mental hygienist with extensive training toward the mentally deficient replaces her. The day she arrives, Baker can barely manage to speak as she's quizzed by her successor.

"Mrs. Baker, you're leaving me your files? All of them?"

"Yes, they're in my . . . your office. I've organized them according to name and date."

"Thanks, but that wasn't necessary. I have my own system."

Dismissed, disgraced, Baker leaves Samarcand. She has no prospects, and so she goes home to help her ailing mother, to wait and see what happens. Her father passed years before, so it's only the two of them. She eventually returns to assisting the Federation of Women's Clubs in whatever way she can, while her enthusiasm and hope for another position as superintendent dims. News travels fast. She's cut off from direct, hands-on involvement in reform. She can raise funds, but her chances of working in such a capacity again doesn't look encouraging. She no longer sees her future as she once did, filled with accolades and appreciation for her efforts and what she accomplished.

Five years go by. She continues raising money on the sidelines for reform and other efforts. After her mother passes, a big piece of how she kept herself preoccupied, what with the daily chores and tasks required of elderly care, ends. Her brother, Tommy, is married, living in Raleigh and doing well. The same goes for her younger sister, Suzanne, who recently sent Baker a picture of her new baby, a boy named Dwight, after her husband.

Baker studies the photo dispassionately. Maybe it's just as well she and Ed never had children, even though she'd always thought of it as a natural course to any well-mannered, respectable woman's life. She'd have been a good mother, she's certain of it. After all, look at how she cared for her charges at Samarcand. Was that not a foundation for what some called a natural instinct to nurture? Even so, two reasons why her solitary outcome turned out for the best, whether a stroke of luck, or God's divine hand, eliminated any regret.

For one, how horrible it would've been if she'd found out about Ed's sordid pastimes when it was too late, while trying to raise children. Such an environment would've required quelling her anger and disgust at his cheating ways, perhaps even allowing it in order to keep the family together. Maybe she would've taken it out on the children, or would've grown to resent them for keeping her trapped with a cad. Second, her own weakness. It's possible she'd have borne a child with the same propensities she had, tempted by the same irrational, illogical desires, and perhaps that child would have suffered a similar injury—or worse. No. It had been for the best to be alone, living in her childhood home, with all of its ghosts, memories, and—she could still swear—a distinct odor of smoke from The Incident. Perhaps this served as a just reward for that.

One day her longtime friend Eloise Belle asks her to lunch. They do this on occasion and for Baker, it's a much-needed outing. Eloise works as the secretary-treasurer at a local church, and is also a member of the North Carolina Equal Suffrage League. They've gone to their favorite diner and their talk is the usual, catching up on this and that. In a quiet moment, Eloise takes a sip from her coffee cup, dabs at her lips with a napkin, and regards Baker with a serious look.

"One should always have a plan, Dottie."

"Hm. Well. At the moment that's rather like trying to cook a meal when the pantry is empty, you understand."

Eloise lights a cigarette and sits back, her expression thoughtful.

She says, "Have you by chance heard of the State Industrial Farm Colony for Women? It's a facility located in Kinston, about three hours east of here."

Baker shakes her head.

"I don't think so."

"They need a superintendent."

Baker, not wanting to get her hopes up and not wanting to come across as desperate, says nothing. She takes a casual sip of her coffee.

Perhaps Eloise is applying for the position, or it could be Winnifred DeLong. Although Winnifred doesn't live close, the three women have come to know one another through their reform efforts. Eloise continues.

"I contacted the chairman, told him I'd known you for years. As to what happened at Samarcand Manor, I explained you tried to stop it, but those girls were bent on burning the place down. After all, everyone saw the truth of this since they set fire to their jail cells as well. The facility in Kinston is in dire need of someone to oversee it. I didn't know if you'd want to give it a try? They mostly deal with women, not younger girls. The youngest might be seventeen. I told them I'd ask you about it. Would you be interested?"

Baker clasps her hands together, joyful. At last, after five long years, the second chance she believed would never come is here, as unexpected as Ed Baker's proposal.

"Yes. Yes, of course!"

Chapter 2

Stella

Deep Creek, North Carolina
1941

At fifteen years of age, Stella is whisked away by a life event some call bad luck. In the long run, what happens saves her, at least that's what she believes. Later on, once she finds out what's been done to her, how she'll never be the same again, it's too late. But. Before all this, she's with her parents, Alice and Cordell, and this is where her trouble begins. Her father works as a foreman at McCall's Cotton Mill. He's gone all day and Stella is too, traipsing up and down the harrowing halls of school, a misfit because everyone knows the Temples are a curious lot.

Stella's a loner, and often pretends she's chatting with her classmates, answering questions she overhears them ask their friends as if they're engaging with her. Her lips move in silent conversation until the whispers start about how she's going crazy like her mother. Mortified, she stops. From an early age she's taken care of herself, and can only invent in her head the way other children might live. Mothers who cook hot meals, bake cookies for after school, wash clothes, and keep a clean house. Fathers who help with homework, make sure the grass is cut once a week, and take their families to church on Sundays, then ice cream afterward.

When her classmates arrive at school, they're in clean clothes, cheeks pink with good health, and their solid, robust frames speak of regular meals. Most important, they appear happy. Stella's reflection in the cracked mirror on the door of the medicine cabinet in the bathroom shows her truth every day. Dull brown hair, sallow cheeks, and brown eyes with an edge.

At home each morning she's awakened by the smell of coffee brewing and cigarette smoke, indicating Cordell's up. When the front door slams and he's left for work, only then does she come out of her room. She rifles through a laundry basket, hunting for something to wear that isn't dirty, or needs mending. She eats whatever she can find, brushes her teeth, and hollers goodbye to Alice, who will not hear her and who will stay in the bed until she feels like getting up. Stella walks to school, taking her time. The closer she gets, the slower she goes, her insides a mix of anticipation and anxiety. She enters the building and first has to contend with a gauntlet of taunting classmates, but once she's in class, she's in her element. She's curious and entranced, learning all she can.

This is her routine. It never alters. She does the same things, the same way, every day. Routine, or structure, isn't how she thinks of it. For her, it provides comfort, if only in her mind. When school is out for the day, she dawdles along the dirt road heading back home, feeling a different sort of dread as she approaches what should be, by all rights, her haven. Though she may have taken solace for a few hours outside those walls, once she's back within them, anything positive she took in, like getting the answer to a question right, thereby earning an approving nod from one of her teachers, disintegrates.

Stella skirts around the house and enters the back door where she finds her mother at the kitchen table, still in her nightgown and housecoat, her hair a chaotic, wild clump on top of her head. Her mother has spent the day chain-smoking, the evidence a mound of cigarette butts in the ashtray close by her elbow. Alice sips hours-old coffee left over from the morning. They regard one another, Stella assessing her mother's mood, while Alice offers the usual complaint and request.

"Had me a real bad night. Heat my coffee up, will you?"

Stella dumps the ashtray first. Pours more of the black liquid from the pot on the stove into the cup. She takes small peeks at Alice, who's busy pulling at a thread, unraveling the sleeve of her gown. Stella creeps away to her room where she'll spend as long as she can before she's expected to go and fix something for supper. She remembers a different mother and she has proof she once existed. Every now and again she retrieves the Park Lane shoebox sitting at the top shelf of her closet and goes through old photos of her mother maybe looking like other folks. Maybe normal.

The first time she understood her mother wasn't well, she was ten. Alice started going away for a couple of days, and when she returned, there were curious marks on her wrists and ankles. Sometimes her tongue was bloody. If she and Cordell stayed gone longer, and Stella got hungry, she went across the street to Mrs. Beale's house. She didn't like going, especially if Mrs. Beale's kind but work-worn face appeared extra tired. Mrs. Beale didn't need another problem. She already had five, but she always answered Stella's polite little *tap, tap, tap*.

"What's up, shug?"

"Alice—rather Mama—she's sick and Daddy took her somewhere."

"Oh? How long they been gone?"

"A while."

"I got a bit of supper. You hungry?"

Stella always is. Very. Mrs. Beale's five young'uns gawk at her through the screen door, the oldest a seven-year-old boy with a bad haircut, the youngest a baby of about six months.

"We got beans and hot dogs for supper. If your folks ain't back by the time you finish eating, you can sleep in yonder till they get home."

Stella never cared what they had. It's more than she would get and she also didn't mind sleeping on the dilapidated couch with their stinking basset hound named Humphrey, who she loved despite his odorous self. The Beales taught her she had it worse than most, maybe worse than anybody. It gave her a hollow feeling knowing, yet there she was, begging at their door. There were the times Mrs. Beale couldn't feed her, and wouldn't let her stay, even when Stella said she didn't need to eat. Mrs. Beale would gaze at her sadly, explain the assistance check hadn't come; she didn't have enough, not even for themselves. She was real sorry.

Eventually, Stella's mother stopped going to the place that changes her, so much so that when Stella stares into her eyes, she's staring into nothingness. Cordell refuses to take her. Sick and confused, Alice stays in the bed and the woman who was once Alice Temple is no more. Stella keeps her distance, listening to Cordell often lecture her "no good" mama as he stands in the doorway of the bedroom.

"Dammitall to hell, Alice! I can't keep taking off'n work to take you to something that ain't working."

"It'll work. Eventually. You got to."

Alice, head lolling, her coordination as good as a newborn's, fumbles trying to tap a cigarette out of her pack. Stella scoots around her father and goes to her mother's aid. She gets the cigarette out, sticks it in Alice's mouth, and strikes the match to light it. Her mother sighs, and grunts her thanks. Stella bends down to look at her. Nobody home. Cordell isn't right about much, but he's right about this. If anything, Alice is worse. She moves less, eats more, has gotten big. Clothes no longer fit. She wears only nightgowns and housecoats. Her old clothing, the bright reds, pinks, and yellows, hang in the closet, shoved to the back, and the woman who used to inhabit them retreats into her own murky corners.

Stella turns eleven, then twelve, and each day is much like the last, until out of the blue, Cordell takes a notion to stand in the doorway of her bedroom at night. Stella is confused by this sudden attention. She fakes sleep, cracking her eyes to slyly watch him as he watches her. His glowing cigarette travels to his lips, then back down. The hall light behind him makes him a silhouette, like a nameless nobody. Maybe he has something to say. Sometimes she thinks he's going to speak, but he never does. She wouldn't mind a conversation with him. They never spend a lot of time together because he's always working. Many nights she's almost asleep only to find him leaning against the doorframe, the tobacco odor from the warehouse wafting into the room. She drifts off, comforted by the thought he's watching over her.

One night, she learns the reason he's there. It's a horror so unexpected she could've never have dreamed it. She fights. She scratches and kicks. She screams and he smothers the sound with a pillow to keep Alice from hearing. Stella almost passes out. It's over quick, except he keeps coming back and her goal becomes to get through it, get it over with. He leaves her little favors. A barrette for her hair. A piece of candy. A flower, once. There are ways to shield herself from the awfulness of it. She pretends it doesn't happen and for three years it works. Nobody knows. Then, she's fifteen and something does happen. Alice isn't aware much of the time, but this can't be hidden.

"You sick again, this morning? What's going on?"

Stella is paralyzed with fear.

"Nothing, Mama."

"Git over here."

Stella moves closer to Alice, who grabs her arm, and presses her other hand to Stella's belly. She briefly shuts her eyes, opens them to gape in disbelief at her daughter.

"I knew it. I can't trust you to do right, it don't seem, not even when I'm sick in the bed. Why're you giving me something else to worry about? Who're you messing around with?"

Stella wants to tell her the truth, but it's so upsetting, so humiliating, she can't. Cordell comes in, and Alice points at her.

"She's gone and got herself knocked up."

Cordell's eyes dig into Stella's, coded with a message.

"You done what?" he says.

Stella whispers, "Liar."

He ignores her and starts arguing with Alice. Alice is adamant.

"She's got to see a doctor."

"Only one she's going to is one who'll get rid of it."

They bicker, sporadically, into the night. Stella goes to bed and when she gets up the next morning, Alice is waiting.

"No school today."

"I want to go to school."

"I ain't hearin' no sass, let's go!"

They set off walking, no easy feat for Alice. The route takes them by Stella's school, and she sticks to the right side of Alice, putting her mother's bulk between her and anyone who might observe the Temples going wherever the Temples are going. Cordell smokes and meanders behind, as if he's ashamed to be seen with them. Alice stops every ten minutes, to catch her breath. Cordell cusses under his. Stella wishes herself anywhere but here. Somehow, they make it into town, going straight to the one and only doctor's office in Deep Creek. They're shown into a small room where Alice goes on a rant, telling the nurse she can't believe what Stella has "gone and done." Cordell leans against the wall, his foot propped, leaving a streak of dirt. He distances himself from the conversation, as if he has no claim to any of it. Him. Guilty as they come, Stella thinks. She stands in a corner, refusing to look at anyone. She can hear the doctor and nurse discuss her just outside the room, and what they say makes her utterly ashamed. The doctor enters the room and speaks to them like they're barn animals.

"What's going on here? There is no excuse for this young woman to be left running wild."

Her mother and father shift about. The doctor pins his steely gaze on them, and points a thumb over his shoulder at a trembling Stella.

"Her troubles can be taken care of and I can arrange it. She's salvageable. She can be fixed."

Like she's a wrecked car. She folds her arms. She's a wreck, all right, no doubt about it. He's not done.

"Her virtue must be restored at all costs. Society demands it. All it takes is one phone call."

Alice makes a bold claim. Sniffling into a soiled hanky, she talks about the shame this will bring, perhaps to improve the doctor's view of them as parents. Cordell watches the doctor with guilt-ridden, glittery eyes as Alice bemoans the situation.

"I seen it coming, I reckon. Can't be keeping an eye on her, sick as I am. Can't you see I ain't able? Can't get outta of the bed most days. She's done gone and got loose, is what it is."

Everything in front of Stella goes blank as she takes herself off to some place outside these walls. She's to blame, it seems. She's no good. The way the doctor and his nurse act solidify what she overheard earlier, *she's as common as they come.* Maybe she is. She doesn't know enough about herself to deny it. Alice, ankles bloated and covered in broken veins, sits on the single chair in the room, and shifts her bulk. She can crush furniture like she's crushing Stella's soul and Stella fears for the chair's safety. Furniture plumb gives out on her at times. It's happened before, like at the Squat and Gobble. Alice pulls at her housedress, and wheezes.

"Gallivanting about, is what's going on. I'm sorely disappointed in you, girl."

Stella would like to express her own disappointments. Cordell faces the doctor spraddle-legged and defiant. His voice is borderline hostile.

"How long is this going to take? I got to get to work."

Stella smells his sweat and it makes her want to gag. The doctor holds up a finger.

"Do I have your permission to make the call? That's all I need."

"Hell yeah."

"Give me one minute."

He leaves the room to arrange for Stella to go and get "fixed." She's glad to be going someplace else, if only for a little while, and she doesn't care where it is. She's contemplated running away before, if only to escape Cordell. Apparently, the problem has been solved for her. Not much later, a Mrs. Todd arrives and Stella, after a truly awkward goodbye with her parents, is on her way to Kinston. Mrs. Todd smokes on the ride, sips on a Pepsi, and talks about Stella's future. How does Stella feel? Does she know she's getting a second chance? Does she understand that?

"You're very, very fortunate," she says.

She explains she's a caseworker for the state. Stella doesn't pay her much attention. She's thinking about the doctor and how he practically demanded she be taken to get . . . what was the word he'd used? Reformed? They arrive at a two-story redbrick building similar to Stella's school. There's a sign out front, THE STATE INDUSTRIAL FARM COLONY FOR WOMEN. She gets out, a hand pressed to her stomach where the small knot of firmness barely the size of a pear has betrayed her. She doesn't think of it as a baby. She thinks of it as a bad thing that must come out. Like a tumor. If they, whoever they are, can do this for her, she'll be grateful, even happy. She can start over. The next step toward that would be to never go home again, if she can help it. They enter the building, Mrs. Todd almost tripping on her heels, like she believes Stella might run. Stella stares at a large wooden sign that hangs on the wall straight in front of her.

It says, LET THE LESSONS BEGIN.

The next day, Stella's on a hospital bed with a sheet over her. She doesn't much care that something is about to happen to her, something only girls like her have to go through. Shameless girls. Bad girls. That's what she was called, a bad girl. A nurse with blond hair in a messy bun comes over and peers down at Stella's arm where an IV drip pierces the skin and the tape holding it in place makes her skin itch. The nurse isn't the one who called her that, it was another woman. She isn't here at the moment, only the nurse whose face is half-covered with a surgical mask that does little to inform Stella anything about her because she keeps her eyes averted. Stella understands this much: you have to look into a person's eyes to see *them*. Even though the nurse's mouth is covered, Stella smells peppermint and her stomach rumbles. The nurse pulls at the sheet.

"I'm Nurse Crawford. This won't take long. I'll give you something to relax and it'll be over before you know it. I'll get you something to eat when you wake up, if the anesthesia doesn't bother you."

Stella knows the word; it won her first place in a spelling bee when she was eight. She closes her eyes, what she does when she wants to block out what scares her, or to avoid seeing something, or someone. Moments later she begins to feel warm, a bit woozy, and right before she enters a twilight sleep, a strange man's voice comes from her left.

"She's how old?"

The nurse answers him.

"Fifteen. She's been asked some questions and wasn't very forthcoming. A complete alteration is recommended."

"Well, we're about to take care of her problem." Stella wants to hear more of what is said, but the drug works magic on her and she falls down a dark tunnel.

A finger snaps near her ear. She's in a completely different room with a headache and a funny, crampy feeling in her stomach. Her mouth is dry, and her throat hurts too. After a moment, she glances about. This room, like the other, has stark white walls, a window too high up to see out, and a metal bed across from hers with no one in it. That bed has a strange crisscross of broad straps over it, like they want to keep someone from getting out of it. This puzzles her, but since her bed doesn't have them, she isn't terribly concerned. She locates the same nurse who was with her earlier. She's standing by the door, writing on a chart. Stella sounds hoarse when she asks a question.

"Is it over?"

Nurse Crawford stops writing, and approaches her.

"Yes, it's over."

Stella tries to sit up and reach for the water and Nurse Crawford offers her hand.

"Here, let me help."

Once Stella is sitting up, she gulps and the nurse says, "Whoa. That's enough for now. You'll throw up."

She lies back against the pillow while her blood pressure is taken and the next steps are explained.

"After you've recovered, we'll begin some other tests and then, depending, you might be allowed to join the others."

"What kind of tests?"

"One is a blood test. The others are questions. Like in school. Now, you should rest."

Stella, ever obedient, relaxes, and begins to think about what might happen while she's here. Mrs. Todd said the people here will teach her things, and her life is going to be so much better now. She said she can be like other girls, perhaps. Go to school and learn to be whatever she wants to be. She suggested maybe she'll even make some friends. Wouldn't she like that? Certainly, she must have hopes and wishes? She must have dreams? Sure. Stella has all those things, and maybe what this means is, for once, they'll come true.

A week later, she feels better. She's given a brown uniform dress to wear and Nurse Crawford lets the doctor in to check her over.

"We got you fixed up good as new," he declares.

Stella nods agreeably. The following day, the lady who said she was a bad girl comes to the quarantine room. Stella knows authority when she sees it and immediately straightens up. There's another woman with her, who was perhaps tall at one time, but because of the progressive curvature of her back, she's lost a couple of inches and stands bent forward. The lady with the curved back speaks in a hushed voice to the tall woman.

"She's a special case."

Stella likes that the word *special* is used in association with her. And Mrs. Todd, the day she was brought said something fancy too.

"She's like a vessel adrift, charting her small section of the world with no guidance, a boat without a sail."

It was her way of describing the sordid backstory of Stella's life and sounded a lot better than what went on in Stella's head. The two women whisper for a few more minutes and then the tall, commanding woman approaches her and speaks in a calm, firm voice.

"Hello. I'm Dorothy Baker, Superintendent of the State Industrial Farm Colony for Women. We call our little abode the Colony. And you are . . . ?"

Surely she must know her name already, but because Stella's eager to get along she answers promptly.

"Stella Temple."

Eyes like black ice in winter assess her, sending a tickle of warning. *Be careful*, her internal voice prompts.

"Call me Mrs. Baker. This is Mrs. Maynard; she'll be your housemother."

"Yes, Mrs. Baker."

Mrs. Maynard, of the crooked spine, sorts through papers, signs something, and hands them to Mrs. Baker. Stella would like to read what's been written about her, but maybe it's best she doesn't. She'll have a good idea based on how they treat her anyway. That's what official papers created by those in charge tend to do, make people treat you this way or that. Mrs. Baker scans the first few pages.

"Her condition has been handled, and she's free of disease?"

"Yes."

"Excellent. She's the youngest here?"

"Yes. Frances Platt is a year older."

"Stella? You're fifteen?"

"Yes, Mrs. Baker."

"Hm. She's not much bigger than a twelve-year-old."

Mrs. Baker comes closer and Stella wants to shrink away. She wants to vanish, to become small, inconspicuous. *I'm nothing. Don't mind me.* It's the same feeling she had with Cordell, the desire to become invisible.

"Come along with me."

Stella trails Mrs. Baker, who moves quickly, although with a bit of a limp, but certainly not like Mama, who could only shuffle along. She's led into a room similar to the other one.

"Sit there, please."

Stella sits and picks at a fuzz ball on the dull brown dress she'd been given. Mrs. Baker claps her hands and Stella jerks.

"There will be a response. Always."

An icy shot of alarm runs along Stella's back. Already she's made a mistake.

"Yes, Mrs. Baker."

"Always. Understand?"

"Yes, Mrs. Baker. I'm sorry, Mrs. Baker."

"Good, good, but don't fawn. It's unbecoming."

"Yes, Mrs. Baker."

Stella barely breathes and even though she'd like to look around, she doesn't. What she does is look up at Mrs. Baker only to see the edges of her mouth curve up. It's a spontaneous miracle, like the unexpected appearance of the sun from behind dark clouds while rain still falls, resulting in a rainbow that softens and brightens the atmosphere, no matter how thunderous the storm.

"Why don't you tell me about yourself?"

Stella wants to keep that smile on this woman's face. She plows ahead, understanding immediately if she does everything she's asked, things will go along fine for her, and Mrs. Baker's mood will reflect that.

"I live yonder a ways, in Deep Creek, with Alice and Cordell. Alice, she don't get around so good, and Cordell is . . ."

She stops and shudders.

"Yes?"

"Mean."

"I see. Alice and Cordell, they're your parents?"

"Yes, Mrs. Baker."

"Why do you call them by their first names?"

"I ain't ever called them by nothing else."

"Not even when you were young?"

"I don't remember, ma'am, no, I don't think so."

"You understand why you were brought here?"

Stella hesitates. Mrs. Baker has to know, and she hopes she does because it's not something Stella cares to talk about. She has to answer, though, and keeps it simple.

"Yes, Mrs. Baker."

"Do you want to tell me how that got started?"

"Not really, no, ma'am."

"Dr. Greene is here to help you with that, but, don't worry for now. You'll have a schedule which provides expectations of what you'll do at any given time of the day. Do you understand?"

"Yes, Mrs. Baker. I like to know where all I'm supposed to be and what all I'm supposed to be doing."

"You should do fine, then. Rising bell is at six, breakfast is at six thirty. From seven to eleven, some do the farm work, while others work within the facility on housekeeping, and then attend classes. You get two free periods a day in which you may write letters home, play a game, or read, whatever. It's your time. Dinner is at twelve. In the afternoons, the schedule begins again, and groups rotate the assignments. Supper is at six. We go to chapel every evening at seven. We require residents to help run this facility, but more importantly, to gain knowledge and skills that will serve them once they leave. This is the schedule and it's to be followed at all times. Any questions?"

"No, ma'am, Mrs. Baker."

"Good. We have rules and they are to be obeyed. You want to be sure to never deviate, or intentionally create mischief. Punishments for violations can be severe if repeated. You get demerits for breaking them, and those can quickly add up. After ten demerits, you can expect to receive punishment. Is this clear?"

Stella grows ever more troubled as she listens to the drumbeat of do's and don'ts. She goes to respond, but her throat goes dry, and she wishes for some water. Mrs. Baker waits and she resorts to nodding vigorously. Mrs. Baker frowns and strikes the table with her hand. *Smack!* Stella manages to croak a reply.

"Yes! Yes, Mrs. Baker."

"Forgetting so soon, I see."

"No! I'm sorry. My, my throat's dry, is all."

"Now, the number of demerits for not adhering to instructions is specific. These are relatively minor. There are worse things you can do. Would you care to guess as to what those might be?"

"I don't believe I could, ma'am."

"Any sort of disgusting behavior between you young women or running off. Those two alone will insure swift and harsh action. *Effective action.* Questions?"

Stella, despite what Mrs. Baker has laid out is still glad to be here instead of home.

"No, Mrs. Baker. I only want to do what I'm supposed to and be what Mrs. Todd said I could be."

"And what is that?"

"Restored to proper womanhood."

"Ah, well. For some it's an easy path, others struggle but eventually make it, while some never learn. Mrs. Maynard should be on her way momentarily to take you to Building A. That's your dormitory. The other is called Building B. See? We aim to keep things simple here. Take this booklet to help you keep track of everything I've told you."

"Thank you, Mrs. Baker."

Stella is handed a small handbook and on the printed cover it says, *Everyday Rules and Guidelines for the State Industrial Farm Colony for Women, Kinston, North Carolina, created by Mrs. Dorothy Baker, Superintendent.*

"All residents receive a copy of this handbook to help them learn the rules. You should know everything in here within a month. I'll test you on this occasionally in the following weeks."

"Yes, Mrs. Baker."

"No excuses not to know expectations here."

"No, ma'am."

Then Mrs. Baker does the magical thing where she turns into someone else, someone who resembles a kindly person. She beams at Stella as if she's pleased with her. Stella instantly holds a preview of her future, one where Mrs. Baker looks upon her with approval, just like this. Stella wishes her transformation were already complete, and Mrs. Baker was bragging about the new Stella, the reclaimed Stella. For now, she can be glad she's seen another side and Stella smiles back readily. She's filled with a willingness to do whatever she's asked. Surely, Mrs. Baker has a good heart because God wouldn't give a smile like that to just anyone.

Chapter 3

Ruth

La Grange, North Carolina
1941

On a brisk morning in February, twenty-four-year-old Ruth Foster walks to work, when the local sheriff, Luther Wright, materializes from out of nowhere and approaches her. He's a thin man with a large nose, small eyes, and aggressive attitude. She's never paid him much attention, but lately he's been hanging around her neighborhood more than usual. He begins a conversation with her in a random, harmless fashion.

"Where you heading to, Miss?"

She could take his question as general curiosity, except his manner puts her off because his way of asking carries a command. Ruth crosses her arms in a defensive gesture, her distrust emanating from the fact she saw him speaking to a couple of other young women who, as far as she could tell, were minding their own business too. He went up to them this same way and what was strange was the more he talked, the more distraught they became. Cried, even. Both ended up in his patrol car and off they went. Ruth observed this from a window of the second-floor apartment she rents above the local hardware store. She believed then the sheriff was up to no good, but if those young women went along with him, who was she to question what was going on? An hour later, she'd forgot about it.

Now, he's stopped her. She points down the road toward The Daily Diner.

"Just yonder. On my way to work. Why?"

Her hand is held to her brow against the rising sun. She sounds suspicious and has every right to be, given her observations. Sheriff Wright doesn't bother to look where she points and doesn't bother to meet her gaze either. He clears his throat and aims his words at the ground as if dropping seeds that will sprout and grow into something that makes sense.

"I'm required to get you checked out. For public safety."

Ruth isn't sure she heard right, and even if she did, she certainly doesn't understand what he means.

"What're you talking about?"

"I'm authorized to take you to the local health official, make sure you don't get others sick."

He's turned jumpy and his eyes dart hither and yon, as if tracking a gnat. Ruth tosses her hair back. She's no ingenue. She challenges his ridiculous demand.

"I feel fine. I'm not sick."

Sheriff Wright's tone changes along with his expression. He turns his attention to her and his tiny eyes have gone hard and unfriendly. Maybe they weren't friendly to begin with.

"It's not up to me. All I'm supposed to do is make sure you go. It's required. You live alone?"

"Yes."

"Shouldn't you have a husband?"

"No, thank you."

"Don't get sassy with me. You don't want to get on my wrong side."

"I'm answering your question."

"Listen here, missy. Your habits, such as they are, could put others at risk. I've seen you, going out and all. Others say . . . you have friends over."

"How is this any of their business, or yours?"

"My job is to keep this community safe. If you don't comply, I can arrest you for civil disobedience."

Ruth was having a bit of fun with him, but now her face gets hot, and her neck damp. Her stomach tightens with uneasiness and a vague queasy feeling because she can see he means it. She had an innocent little kiss with her date the other night. Maybe someone saw that, and now this sheriff is making noises about her lifestyle.

"Is this what happened to those other girls? Those women you drove away with?"

"It's mandated I oversee the public's safety."

Ruth grips her purse and wishes her mother were there. She would stand up to this nonsense. She's close, an easy walk of about two miles. She would vouch for her, explain how she came to live on her own. It was innocent enough, something Ruth always wanted to do, and even more so after reading Marjorie Hillis's bestselling book, *Live Alone and Like It*. During her last visit, while playing their favorite game, Lexico, her mother took Ruth's hand.

She said, "Honey, you're doing so well. I'm proud of you."

Ruth doesn't want to think how this will trouble her mother once she finds out. Sheriff Wright heads for his vehicle, making the assumption she'll follow obediently. She doesn't move, and when he checks and sees she's still in the same spot, his hand drops to the handcuffs at his waist. She doesn't want to be arrested but she doesn't want to go with him either. She fiddles with the latch on her purse. Maybe if she does as he wants, she can get on with her day. This is going to make her late for work, but best get it over with. It will amount to nothing, anyway, and confident of this, she approaches his car.

Sheriff Wright opens the back door for her. She drops into the back seat and swings her legs inside, feet primly together. She sits back, purse on her lap, and as he shuts the door, the decisive *click* sounds like she's been locked in. She stares over her shoulder toward the diner, hoping her employers, the Buncombes, aren't watching. La Grange is a small town of about 1,600 people and you can practically see everyone's movements by glancing out a convenient window. How would she ever explain this? Ruth doesn't speak as he drives her away. She keeps her head down in case anyone on the street wants to see who's been picked up so early. After a moment, he lights a cigarette and offers her the pack over the back of the seat.

"No, thank you. I don't smoke."

She notices a couple of people getting their morning papers off their front lawns and she envies them this normalcy while she feels trapped and headed toward some unforeseen disaster. Sheriff Wright slows down and pulls the cruiser alongside the front of a small brick building with a large picture window at the front. They're on the outskirts of town. A sign in the window says MARVIN TYNDALL, HYGIENE AND PUBLIC HEALTH SERVICES. Ruth sits until Sheriff Wright comes around and opens her door. After she exits the vehicle, he holds his hand out, gesturing for her to go ahead of him. At the door to the building there's a medical insignia painted on the entrance. Whoever this doctor is, hopefully he'll sympathize with her, realize it's a mistake.

A nurse at the front desk speaks to a receptionist. Both are about Ruth's age, and they give her a questioning look. Sheriff Wright appears by her side and both women's expressions immediately go from polite inquisitiveness to an air of disapproval. The pit she's had in her stomach since the sheriff stopped her grows. Clearly, being with him automatically puts her in a different light. She doesn't care. She only wants to get whatever this is over with, and get to work. The receptionist reaches under her desk and hands her a clipboard.

"Fill this out, and be quick about it. You *can* write, can't you?"

Ruth shoots her an incredulous look as she takes it.

"Of course," she says quietly.

She tucks a strand of hair behind her ears. The nurse scrutinizes Ruth's appearance, but Ruth is used to this from other women. She's always stood out given her almost black hair and olive-green eyes.

"Cover Girl" was her nickname in high school. She sits in one of the scratched wooden chairs by a window where the early morning sun filters through a smudged glass window. For a moment, she doesn't move, but the receptionist taps her pen like she's waiting, so she begins to fill in her information. It's a standard form: name, age, address, and some medical history.

Sheriff Wright says to no one in general, "Reckon my duty's done if y'all got this handled now."

The receptionist glances at Ruth, then him.

"Will you be bringing any more?"

Ruth is done and takes the clipboard to the receptionist, who points her to the side door where the nurse waits. She waves Ruth through. As she goes through the doorway, she hears Sheriff Wright.

"Nah, hopefully no more today. Call me if transport is needed for this one."

Ruth is led quickly down the hall and into a room. *Transport? To where? Maybe to her job.*

The nurse says, "I'm Nurse Moore. Remove your shoes, hosiery, and your underwear. You may keep your bra, slip, and dress on. Cover yourself with that sheet. When you're ready, tap on the door."

"What did he mean by 'transport'?"

"Don't worry about that for now. Let's take this one step at a time."

The nurse leaves and Ruth moves stiffly, slow to do as she's told because she's so nervous. She's never done this before, but she's heard the details from her friends and tries to prepare herself. She wishes her mother were waiting for her in the lobby. Just her presence would help. After she's done as the nurse instructed, she taps the door, and uses the small step stool to get on the table and puts the sheet over her lap. The nurse returns.

"First, I'll get your temperature and blood pressure."

The nurse completes these steps, and jots the information down. Ruth stares at the wall as Nurse Moore adjusts the sheet, then she opens the door and motions to someone on the other side.

"She's ready."

Dr. Tyndall bustles into the room smelling of cigars, antiseptic, and to Ruth, vaguely like mothballs. He's an elderly man with a heavy jowl, messy white hair, and he whistles under his breath as he moves about the room. The nurse motions for her to lie on the table, and her unease grows.

After a moment he acknowledges she exists with a cursory glance, then says to the nurse,

"Get me two slides."

Ruth is startled when, without any warning, Dr. Tyndall flicks the sheet back. She shuts her eyes to block him from her sight. He turns on a lamp. He begins and Ruth endures. To her great discomfort, he rummages around as if he's selecting a cut of beef at the butcher counter. She withstands what he does without a sound, except for a sucking in of her breath when he leans forward, one hand on her abdomen, and what feels like his fist inside her, pushing and shoving at her innards. Ruth gets this strange twinge that shoots to her navel. She jerks, and the doctor mumbles to himself as if he's discovered something. Finally, he's no longer touching her. Water runs in the sink, and Nurse Moore hands him a towel before she helps Ruth sit up. Again, he only addresses the nurse as he leaves, like Ruth is invisible. Fine with her. She's intent on getting out of there and forgetting this happened.

"Show her to my office as soon as she's dressed."

Nurse Moore gives Ruth a sympathetic pat.

"All right, dear?" And without waiting for the answer, she says, "Dress yourself and open the door when you're done."

When the room is empty, Ruth hops down. She grabs some tissues, dabs at herself, and comes away with a reddish tinge on the paper. It isn't her time yet. This worries her, along with the dull ache deep in her middle, different from her monthlies. She gets dressed, smooths her hair as best as she can, and reapplies her lipstick, which always gives her confidence, the color a bold red called Cherry Drop, and one of her favorites. She opens the door and peeks out.

Nurse Moore is waiting.

"Follow me," she says.

After opening the door to the doctor's office, Nurse Moore points to a chair across from a giant and ornate wooden desk.

"It won't be long."

Ruth sits, but can't relax. She's perched on the edge of the leather chair, with its hammered nail heads, detecting the scent of stale smoke, and that other musty odor she likens to that mothball smell she detected on the doctor. She fidgets and wishes for some water. Her abdomen has a pulsing dull ache and between her legs it feels as if she's been violated. She grips her small purse in sweaty hands. At last, the doctor comes in.

"Do you work?"

"Yes, at the diner in town."

"Hm. And you live alone?"

"Yes."

"How do you feel? Any sort of symptoms over the past few weeks?"

"No."

"Miss Foster, are you aware of the effort to keep women from running the streets?"

"I don't know what you mean by 'running the streets.' I work. I go home. Sometimes I go to a movie with a friend. My mother comes to visit. I go to church . . ."

"Why aren't you married? Having children? A girl with your looks should be thinking about getting married. I suppose I shouldn't be surprised by the outcome here. You're the sort that ends up infected, and infected you are, at least moderately."

Ruth is doing her best to follow what he's saying. Moderately infected? What does that mean?

"I don't understand. What do I have?"

"A venereal disease."

"But, how? I'm . . . I've never . . ."

"There are many ways to get it. You're required to go for treatments. No question about it."

"Treatments! What kind of treatments?"

"They're for your own good. And the good of the community.

There's a nice facility just down the road in Kinston. Sheriff Wright can take you."

"Wait a minute. Can't you be more specific? What do I supposedly have?"

"Syphilis. And there is no supposedly about it."

Ruth almost laughs.

"Impossible."

"Are you doubting my medical expertise? I assure you, I know what I'm talking about and we can't have you running around with that. I'm sorry, but these are serious matters, Miss Foster. I'm doing what I need to do to protect the public, and specifically, our servicemen."

"Servicemen? I've not been around any servicemen. This has got to be a mistake."

"I assure you. It's no mistake."

"I'm not going. There's no need for it."

"Miss Foster, it's not like you have a choice. If you refuse, I'll be forced to quarantine you within your residence, as well as notify the public by placing a sign on your door stating your illness. It will stay there until I have it removed. It's up to you."

Ruth is appalled at the thought of this.

"But what about my job and my apartment?"

"The real question is, are you willing to do what's necessary to keep the public safe?"

"Wait, wait. I need time to think. My mother? Can't I stay with her?"

"She'd have to be quarantined as well and a sign would have to be placed on her door."

Ruth tries to process what she's being told, while the doctor looks at his watch impatiently, rushing her, wanting her to hurry up and make up her mind.

"I need your answer so I can make the arrangements. It's your decision, Miss Foster."

No matter what she chooses, the small life she's made for herself is bound to be ruined. While reluctant to go, she's compelled to keep everyone she knows out of this, and more importantly, prevent her mother having to live with the stigma.

"It seems like I don't get much choice in the matter."

"I've given you two."

"Fine. The facility."

"You'll go?"

Ruth nods. Even as she makes this decision, she's filled with doubt.

"Wise choice. The sheriff will take you."

Sheriff Wright had to have been around the corner because he reappears in no time, and she's quickly escorted from the doctor's office, her face blazing with humiliation. He holds her elbow, but she pulls it from his grip. She yanks open the car door for herself, drops into the seat, and slams it shut, then sits in a daze. She can't believe what just happened, but it's real, very real. Her thoughts jump about, one to another, as if her brain has short-circuited. She's unable to think in any logical way. There's a part of her that wishes she could argue more effectively, or turn the decision around, but in this moment, she shuts down. As the sheriff drives her away, the faces of the nurse and the receptionist ogle her from the window. Like she's some sort of zoo animal.

During the twenty-minute ride Ruth grows anxious. She worries about her mother not knowing where she is. It's been hard for the both of them because her father's passing two years ago was so unexpected. In the heat of summer one afternoon, he collapsed at the cotton warehouse where he'd worked for as long as Ruth could remember. One of the last things he said to her was a warning, of sorts.

"You best be careful about who you're seen with, and the like. People tend to talk, Ruthie."

He didn't like her decision to live alone because he thought she was setting herself up for gossip around the neighborhood. She didn't understand him, although she and her mother discussed it more than once. Her mother was pragmatic about her father's views.

"Oh, honey, he thinks women ought to get married soon as possible, and once the wedding bells stop, start having babies. He's old-fashioned is all."

Ruth knows enough about marriage to know it's not for her, at least not right now. Her best friend in high school, Patty Sullivan, now Patty Campbell, married her Howard right after graduation from La Grange High, had two babies in two years, and told Ruth recently, Howard wanted another. Patty, drawn about the face, and the same age as Ruth, could've been a decade older.

"Look at you," she'd said. "Living alone with nobody but yourself to look after. Huh."

The sheriff's car slows and a sign, THE STATE INDUSTRIAL FARM COLONY FOR WOMEN, comes into view. He turns into a drive that leads to a two-story brick building. He pulls up to the front and Ruth gets out before he's barely stopped. She boldly goes up the steps and enters the building. A tall, thin woman, her hair in a bun, wearing a light blue dress and sensible brown shoes, is there. Her back is curved, as if under some tremendous weight. The sheriff comes in before Ruth has a chance to say anything, and he and the woman, while keeping their eyes on Ruth converse in low voices.

"Bringing us someone already this morning, I see. Second one this week."

"Yep, been keeping watch. When I seen her this morning, I got her here pronto. Good thing too. Obviously."

Ruth is offended they're discussing her like she's not present and the idea he's been watching her as if she were a common criminal is disconcerting.

She goes over to them, and with a firm tone, she says, "I'd like to speak to whoever is in charge, please."

The woman in the blue dress offers a weary smile and holds up a finger. She steps over to a desk, and in seconds, speaks over an intercom.

"Dorothy Baker, new admission at the front."

The woman in the blue dress doesn't speak after this and the three of them stand in an awkward silence until another woman, so thin she appears to live off of water and air, enters the area from some other part of the building. Ruth turns and her gaze is met by dark, unblinking eyes behind round, silver-rimmed glasses. Sheriff Wright tips his hat.

"Mrs. Baker. She's all yours. Have fun."

No one acknowledges him as he leaves the building. The woman in the blue dress also leaves, exiting through a side door. Ruth is left with the thin woman with the silver frames, who pauses for a long moment and finally addresses her. Her voice is soft, almost melodic.

"What is your name?"

Ruth, still coming to terms with her situation, is slow to answer and the woman arches a brow.

"Is it a difficult question for you?"

"Ruth Foster."

"I'm Dorothy Baker, superintendent of the State Industrial Farm Colony for Women, or the Colony as we call it. Welcome." She points at a sign just over her shoulder. "I'm assuming you can read?"

Again, there's that question regarding her education, as with the nurses at the local health official's office.

"Yes. I can even write."

She can't resist adding on the last part. If Dorothy Baker notices, she chooses to ignore it.

"Wonderful. Take note. Today begins a new way of life for you."

Ruth unleashes what she's been holding back.

"I like my life just fine. There I was, not but an hour ago, minding my own business, going to work until that sheriff insisted I go to that doctor and endure *that* humiliating experience. Now I'm here, supposedly carrying some sort of infection. I had no choice but to come, no matter what I said."

Dorothy Baker continues on as if Ruth is complaining about an item she purchased that didn't turn out as she liked.

"I'm sorry for your troubles. We'll start the process to admit you and see how we can help. How does that sound?"

"Crazy. That's how it sounds."

She spins about on her heels and walks out the door. She hears nothing behind her. Maybe that's all she had to do. Put her foot down and tell them how it was. She's outside and walks rapidly down the long drive, gets an urge to run until that voice makes her think twice.

"If I call Sheriff Wright, and if he has to pick you up again and bring you back, your start here will be very different than it might have been."

Ruth stops. Baker continues.

"Don't make this any worse than it needs to be by making a bad decision. You look too smart for that."

Ruth looks back at Baker, her face squinched, incredulous while the superintendent continues.

"Let's call it an opportunity to get started on a positive note. I will help you, if you'll let me."

"I haven't been arrested, have I?"

"No."

"In that case, you have no right to keep me here."

"Yes, I do. In case you forgot, the sheriff was involved. If you come along with me, I can explain how things are going to work here. Who knows, perhaps you'll be out on parole quicker than you think."

"Parole? What is this place? A prison in disguise?"

Baker points to the fields where, in the distance, the small shapes of women working under the sun paints a favorable scene. As if on cue, there's a faint sound, a burst of laughter from those working the fields.

"Miss Foster, does this look like a prison? Do you see guards? Gates? Fences?"

Ruth takes in the grounds, the women out in the field, the formidable brick buildings.

"What happens here?"

"Transformations, Miss Foster. Character building and improvement. Education. It begins with quarantine while we confirm the clinic's test. If you need medications to treat your infection, you stay there until the tests come back free of disease."

"What if I don't need it?"

"You'll be allowed to join the other residents and start your training. My program allows you to become an upstanding, contributing member of society. It's proven quite successful."

The superintendent offers a slight smile, as friendly as a rabid fox, fixing her with a stare as hard as the concrete sidewalk they're standing on. Ruth backs away.

"I'm already an upstanding member of my community. I'm certainly not sick."

Displeasure creeps in when the superintendent speaks.

"Denial is common. You'll come to understand the good intentions meant here."

Ruth doesn't want to hear anything more from this woman. She spins about and walks fast, her leather shoes brisk and businesslike on the pavement. The more distance between herself, that woman, and this joint, the better. Behind her comes a demand, the soft voice no longer a lilt.

"I'm warning you to stop."

Off in the distance, those same women who laughed earlier turn to watch Ruth half run down the drive. Is one of them motioning at her? A shrill whistle blows. Ruth glances their way again, and whoever it is in the field repeats the hand movement. This time in a more frantic gesture. Panic shoots through Ruth as she understands the signal. She runs.

Chapter 4

Baker

If every incoming resident were like Stella Temple, her job would be much easier. Ruth Foster, now in the process of fleeing the premises, has decided to be difficult. Baker goes back inside where she accesses the intercom.

Pressing the button with authority, she says, "Code R. Code R. Entrance area, Administration Building."

She created a process after they began experiencing a high number of individuals who weren't partial to the Colony's teachings and revealed their distaste in a similar fashion. Each staff member has a part. The housemothers, Mrs. Maynard and Mrs. Dillard, as well as the teachers of both classroom and vocational areas, are to keep the other residents busy and from interfering. Mrs. Maynard's additional responsibility is to contact the local authorities for backup. The facility psychiatrist, Dr. Greene, is to be on hand in case a resident becomes volatile, hysterical, or otherwise difficult to manage so he can talk to them and help calm them down. Dr. Graham or Nurse Crawford is to prepare and provide crucial medications as needed.

Baker previously met with her staff, and obtained their approval on how they would handle the difficult ones. She made them vote on it. She did this so no one could say any particular incident was her fault and hers alone. They all agreed on this process. The only one who doesn't have an active part is the budget officer, Wanda Perkins. Baker returns outside hoping Ruth changed her mind, but she's nowhere to be seen. Sometimes her efforts to persuade these older women they're here for their own good, to do as they must, is as complicated and difficult as trying to straighten her scarred leg, meaning impossible. She emits a tiny noise of irritation. Mrs. Maynard is back now, and Baker barely listens as the housemother's breathless voice updates her.

"The sheriff's office was called."

Baker makes an agitated gesture in the direction Ruth disappeared.

"He's not going to like it. He dropped her off no more than ten minutes ago. I can hear him now, running his mouth, telling whoever will listen that we don't have things under control over here."

Dr. Greene, Dr. Graham, and Nurse Crawford appear, the nurse alarmed and the doctors perturbed. They've had runners before and, as expected, Dr. Greene makes known his opinion.

"I was in the middle of a session. I thought we made progress against this happening."

Dr. Graham offers no support either. "Aren't your deterrents working?"

Baker grits her teeth at his choice of word: *your.* They do it every time. Manage to get to her, but she never shows it. She speaks in monotone and anyone standing nearby would never have guessed her level of irritation.

"It's a new drop-off. A young woman named Ruth Foster the sheriff just brought in. She's in denial. It's always good to test *our* process, I suppose. As to deterrents, she'll experience them soon enough. In this line of work, such challenges arise. No way around it."

Dr. Greene shakes his head, and checks his watch.

"I hope the matter is sorted out quickly. I was about to have a breakthrough with my patient. It's a moment that may well be lost at this point."

Dr. Graham, not to be outdone, complains equally.

"And I was on the phone with the medical director of Mary Elizabeth Hospital in Raleigh."

Both look at their watches, an action synchronized tighter than time itself. Baker would like to point out they're not the only ones with important work to do. She doesn't trust Dr. Greene, not after he suggested she's the cause of some of the residents' stress and unhappiness. Obviously, a few (a lot?) are bringing their petty little gripes to him. It's that, or he's intentionally quizzing them. Dr. Graham, on the other hand, has a swollen head of self-importance that drives her batty. It's reminiscent of the professional relationships at Samarcand, the underlying noncompliance while smiling to her face and making snide remarks behind her back. As much as she hates it, both doctors must be "kept in the loop," as the chairman of the board, Dr. Ralph Woodall, reminded her at the last annual meeting.

She's casual about her updates to the board, intimating the Colony is running efficiently and as it should. She will not mollycoddle these women. She intends to instill self-control, good manners, and a decent work ethic. She ensures their health is looked after. She keeps copious notes of what she receives from the weekly reports of the staff, including both doctors and Nurse Crawford. They've filled dentist visits for cavities and dental plates, as well as the handling of incoming residents and any discharges, and the necessary health tests required. Tests for Vincent's infection—pyorrhea—Wassermann tests for syphilis, testing for gonorrhea, hookworms . . . the list goes on. Then, there are re-checks after the shots. These are the basics aside from the structure of reform work. If there are unhappy people, she's ready to remind anyone who needs it, they're not running a resort. Reform isn't meant to be easy, for pity's sake.

She puts her attention back to watching and waiting. Soon enough, the sheriff's car reappears, approaching at an excessive speed. He stops with a little screech of tires, leaps out, and stomps around to the back. He extracts his passenger, her face shiny with sweat, handcuffs dangling off her thin wrists. She stares at her feet, allowing her hair to cover her face, a tactic Baker views as either evasive, or submissive. Sheriff Wright jabs his thumb in Ruth's direction.

"Y'all reckon you can you handle her now?"

Baker bristles at the sheriff's high-handed attitude.

"She's not the first one to explore how far she could get. I'm sure she'll cooperate now."

"If you have to call me again . . ."

Baker cuts him off. "I *know.*"

Apparently, he wants to be sure Ruth understands because he bends so he's right in her face, even though she's yet to lift her head. "You listen to me, now. Don't pull that dumb stunt again 'cause if you do, I ain't bringing you back here. It'll be straight to jail. And let me tell you, this place is better than there."

In response, Ruth sticks her hands out for him to remove the handcuffs. He doesn't right away. He makes her wait. Actually, he makes them all wait and Baker's about to suggest he should get on with it when he reaches for his keys.

As he unlocks the cuffs, he repeats himself. "You understand what I'm saying. *Jail.*"

"Yes."

He clicks the cuffs onto his belt, points his index finger in a silent warning before going back to the patrol car. Baker waits until he's driving away before she and Nurse Crawford approach Ruth. Nurse Crawford takes Ruth's arm and Baker is pleased to see this is accepted. Nurse Crawford leads her toward the entrance of the building, and Baker turns to the doctors and Mrs. Maynard.

"Such incidents, while an inconvenience to schedules, can be helpful. Did you see how docile she is now? In the end, this is the outcome we want and it will further disincentivize such actions." She then addresses Mrs. Maynard. "Thank you for your help."

Everyone disperses and Baker goes into the main building where Nurse Crawford is waiting for her alongside Ruth Foster. Baker's voice is modulated as she talks to the Colony's newest resident.

"I'm sorry to say all you've done is create a stir that lasted less than thirty minutes, while insuring your beginning here is going to go harder on you. This is inconsequential to everyone but you. In other words, we'll go along as usual—but you? You'll spend time in meditation and I imagine once that's over you'll understand. You'll be placed in a room by yourself, a carefully managed environment, but nonetheless meant to encourage you to become a good citizen of the Colony. Nurse Crawford, put her in Room Two; Rooms One and Three are still occupied. Provide her with our standard issue."

"Yes, Mrs. Baker. And, what is the recommendation?"

"Seven, and limited. Then, we'll see."

"Yes, Mrs. Baker. I'll get what's needed."

Baker prides herself on having fashioned these cryptic instructions. If Ruth Foster understood them, she'd likely run again. Baker has experienced plenty of that in the past, women falling to pieces once they understand the repercussions of their actions, neglecting to think of how they bring it on themselves. Lucille Griffin, for instance, a prostitute who continues to be brought back to the Colony because she refuses to change her ways, threw what was tantamount to a tantrum, creating more physical and emotional turmoil for all to witness after Baker laid out the punishment. This was before Baker made the changes. If there's anything positive about this incident, it's that Ruth is now exhibiting the signs of an individual coming to the realization of the circumstance she's in. Perhaps she won't be as difficult as she first thought.

They traverse the rest of the hall lined with doors on either side. Behind those doors, the good work of the Colony is underway. She can hear the whir of sewing machines, the sound of reading, a teacher's voice giving instruction. Dr. Greene's office is next and Baker knows it's nothing but clutter and disorganization. He has stacks of books on mental health all over the room along with overflowing ashtrays, and bottles of liquor kept in his desk drawer. His secret, so he thinks. Dr. Graham's office is neat, but it bothers her worse than Dr. Greene's. It has a hospital smell to it, and takes her back to the pain and trauma she endured as a child. She's not sure which is worse: the smell, or the fact he keeps a big jar filled with formaldehyde on his desk holding a human brain. She's certain Dr. Greene covets it. Nurse Crawford's examining room is after Dr. Graham's, then the tiny room they use for surgeries. Next is her own office, the dining hall, and at the very end of that hall, steps that lead to the basement and the three rooms designated for meditation. They descend the steps and stop at the middle door with a large number 2 painted on the front. There are no windows on it.

"And here we are, Miss Foster."

Ruth appears a tad bewildered while Baker's feeling congenial. She pulls the large metal ring from around her waist that holds several keys. She has to sort through a number of them and catches Ruth Foster staring. She twists her body to block her view. She's not so dumb as to reveal which key works what door, not after Frances Platt pulled a Houdini-like move. That imbecile came waltzing into the dining hall one evening during supper when she still had four days left after having one of her spells that put her in this very room. It was only discovered later on that a spare had been swiped at some point. They never did find it, and Frances's way of responding to questions was to bark when they pressed her for an answer. Baker learned two things from that spectacle, which involved dragging the kicking, biting, and screaming Frances back to the room, and adding on more days as a lesson. One, she now keeps *all* the keys on her. Two, never let the residents see which is used for what door, wily creatures that they are.

She finds the right one, but doesn't open the door immediately. No need for her to see the inside of the room, not until Nurse Crawford returns. An uncomfortable silence descends, and unlike other residents, Baker is somewhat impressed by the determination of the young woman before her. Most would start talking, wanting to fill the air with nervous words, maybe to cover anxiety, or fear. Ruth Foster acts content to gaze about, even allowing a brief glance at Baker, but nothing significant registers in that look. Baker could've been a piece of furniture for all she seems to care. Finally, Nurse Crawford returns with items stacked in her arms.

Baker opens the door and leads the way. It's dark as night, and she reaches up, feeling about for a second, then finds and yanks on a chain. A bare bulb overhead flickers, and mercifully stays on. There are no windows here either, and because it's an interior room within the building, without the ceiling bulb, it could be midnight for all the inhabitants would know. This is intentional, as are the meager furnishings, but probably the most obvious characteristic might be that the room feels cold and damp. It doesn't matter the time of year. From Baker's viewpoint, it's the perfect environment for self-reflection. It offers a direct contrast to what the Colony provides otherwise, such as bright, clean rooms. Warmth when needed, and the benefit of a good breeze when days are hot, when they open up the windows and doors, and fresh air flows through. They have fans when Mother Nature doesn't provide. There's plenty of food, hot, nutritious meals so as to encourage a solid effort as they work.

After a few days in one of the meditation rooms, those suffering from ill-natured dispositions, a propensity for mischief, disobedience, and troublemaking are always ready to get to work. Most don't want a repeat visit, either, except for hardheaded Lucy with her scarred face from syphilis sores. That one isn't even grateful for the injections she's received, which worked fairly well to eliminate them. Baker gives Ruth a moment to soak in the ambience. She's quick to see what lies ahead and her features are overcome with despair. Baker has no sympathy. She shouldn't have taken off, so she has no one to blame but herself. Baker takes pride in being intentionally subtle with her approach, much in the way the soft green grass covers and conceals a compact and unforgiving ground below.

"Miss Foster, I'm sure you have much to think on, which is, of course, the point of your time in this room. When I next meet with you involving a decision as to your future, I imagine the time in here will benefit you, and encourage you to consider what you say and do going forward. Nurse Crawford will schedule your intake exams once your time in here concludes."

For the first time in the past half hour, Ruth speaks.

"How long will I be in here?"

"That depends."

Baker nods at Nurse Crawford and both leave without a backward glance. Once Baker's in her office, she allows herself to collapse in her chair. She leans back so she can stare at the ceiling. This initial introduction certainly went different from the one with Stella Temple, who showed up with her wicked bulging belly created by the most abhorrent of state of affairs, yet oh so eager to please. After Stella's assessment, and once the pregnancy and other critical matters were seen to, the girl fell under the spell of the Colony's program, adjusted to routines and is, so far, a model resident. Stella's future is on the right course toward becoming redeemed, whereas Ruth Foster's is uncertain. As fallen women go, she's going to be a challenge, but Baker's willing to give her a second chance. The little hellcats at Samarcand provided plenty of experience in dealing with the difficult. While she knows adolescent girls are often more amenable to change, although prone to wild mood swings, they're still impressionable and can be swayed, molded as Baker sees fit. Regardless, her aim is to restore each one handed over to her, even the difficult ones like Ruth Foster. It's her mission to turn her into an exemplary citizen, one way or another.

Chapter 5
Ruth

Meditation is Ruth's first lesson in Baker's ability to mask reality and facts. It's a smoke screen, a fancy word for what is actually solitary confinement in a hellish little room with no sunlight, no comfort, and certainly no hope. The first few seconds after the door is closed and locked, Ruth can barely comprehend where she is. Paint peels off the walls and hangs in sad little slivers. Scratch marks by the dozen exist on almost every surface. It's clear this is how those who'd been here before her kept up with their days, or only wanted to leave a mark of existence. *I am here. I still live.* A rusted, decrepit little cot covered with a mattress and a pillow in no better condition is the only place to sit aside from the floor. A blanket, frayed around the edges, covers the mattress. She picks it up, intending to wrap it around herself because the room is damp, except it carries an off-putting odor she's unable to determine. She tosses it back down, but eventually retrieves it, and decides if she breathes through her mouth, it's bearable.

There's a small sink mounted to one wall and it bears an orange stain around the drain hole, courtesy of the perpetual leaking spigot. It looks like a smear of blood. By the door is a small, warped table. She stares here and there in alarm. How will she . . . and then she sees it, tucked in a corner. A galvanized metal bucket, and a roll of toilet paper beside it. There's no soap on the sink. She sits balanced on the edge of the cot as hot stinging tears form. She tips her head back to stop them, and her attention is drawn to a thing creeping along the ceiling. Gripping her elbows, she watches a large millipede, its ladder of legs flowing like a curtain in a breeze, navigate its way into a crack where the ceiling joins the wall.

And there she stays, her thoughts directionless, on a trip of their own without a map. She doesn't want to think about how long she might be in this room, or at the Colony in general. She's been provided no information. She's been told nothing except some test they call a Wassermann said she's infected. She worries about her job. Mr. Buncombe will think she's skipped out on him. He might try contacting her mother about her not showing up for work, who won't know where she is, or what to say. And what about her apartment? Mr. Ellerby will want his rent. Ruth needs to get word to her mother as fast as she can to let her know where she is, and she can get help. Her thoughts are on these issues when food is brought.

"May I have some paper? A pen? I'd like to write my mother."

The tray of food is left and the door slams shut. Ruth doesn't get to see who put it there, only the set of hands dropping it unceremoniously. What's on the tray isn't very appetizing. The meal is served on a sectioned, beige plastic tray like a hospital uses. Ruth picks up a fork to poke at a grayish piece of meat, tests the lump of plain mashed potatoes to find them stiff and the roll dried out. She needs to put something in her stomach, so she nibbles the roll, then puts the tray back on the table. She can't eat this nauseating mess. Curling onto her side, she tries not to breathe the stink of the pillow. Her only escape is sleep, and this is what Ruth does.

Meal deliveries become the only break in the day-to-day monotony. Three times a day her door is unlocked, and another tray with unappetizing food is placed just inside the door. When Ruth finally gets to see who's leaving it, her initial thought is, they're the same age. The young woman is an inmate too, because she wears a plain brown dress like Ruth's. She appears miserable and refuses to speak or look at Ruth. Maybe she's not supposed to. When Ruth doesn't have the tasteless food to preoccupy her, she tries to figure out what Baker meant by "seven, and limited." Limited is solved for her within a couple of days when, as usual, food is brought. The door shuts and Ruth ogles the scoop of white hominy and a biscuit. This is breakfast. She's ravenous now, enough to eat whatever she's given, no matter how bad it is. She plows through everything fast and wants more. She taps on the door when she's done. Someone approaches. She assumes it's the young woman who brings the food, but whoever it is doesn't open the door.

"What is it?"

"Can I have more?"

"Nope. You're limited."

So that's what that means. It takes a bit longer to figure out the number. On her sixth day—and she knows it's the sixth because she's been making her own marks on a wall—she has an epiphany. She's eating a breakfast of watery grits and plain toast and thinking how after today is over, she will wake up to the seventh day. Her brain revs into a higher gear. Seven. Seven might mean seven days and if so, hopefully she'll be let out of this repulsive little room. She preoccupies herself counting steps from one direction to the next. She eats her meals, then resumes, going from one wall to the other, counting under her breath. The seventh day arrives. Everything happens exactly like the days before. She's pinned her hopes on this number. She won't let herself think beyond getting through the day.

The eighth morning arrives. She doesn't know what to expect, but it's certainly not a tray laden with scrambled eggs, fat sausage links, and a biscuit dripping with butter. She wolfs everything down, chewing frantically, her fingers holding in what tries to fall out of her mouth. She has a sudden image of herself and makes herself chew slow and careful, eyes closed, jaws bulging, regaining some self-control. It's strange realizing she'd forgotten how good food could taste. Even if she's wrong, the improvement in this morning's breakfast must mean something is going to change. She finishes every morsel and feels full for the first time in a week. She sets the tray aside, rinses her hands and face, uses her fingers to brush back her dirty hair, and then she waits to see what might happen.

She's not sure of the time, but maybe an hour later, there's noise outside the room. Ruth jumps to her feet when Baker's voice resonates through the door. It swings open and Baker stands for a moment studying her. Ruth knows how she must look. She's not been able to bathe properly, wash, brush her hair or her teeth. The brown dress they gave her the first day, along with a pair of white bobby socks and black Oxford shoes, are stained and dirty. Baker doesn't enter the room, but addresses her from the doorway, her voice so low Ruth strains to hear.

"Meditation is intellectual and spiritual purification. That's what I think. What do you think?"

Ruth isn't sure how to respond, but she wants so badly to leave the room, she drops any hint of pride and kowtows.

"Yes, ma'am. That's a good way to put it. I've been given this chance to do a lot of thinking, and it was wrong to try and leave."

"Excellent. I take it you're ready to begin again, a fresh start?"

"Yes, Mrs. Baker."

Baker acts pleased, maybe even happy if that's possible.

"Did you enjoy your breakfast?"

"Yes, ma'am, very much. Thank you."

"Nurse Crawford works with a state dietitian who periodically visits and plans the meals so everyone gets the best nutrition. We aim to not only strive toward correcting deviant behaviors but to build up your health as well. It's plain but good food, intended to serve that purpose."

"I worked at a diner before; maybe I could work in the kitchen?"

Mrs. Baker looks at her in such a way she wishes she could gobble the words and swallow them down like the breakfast she just enjoyed. She hates to sound desperate, so servile, yet getting out of Room Two makes her willing to do whatever is necessary—even groveling. Mrs. Baker motions for her to follow and Ruth does so, gladly, and as she steps beyond the door she gulps cleansing breaths of fresh air. They reverse the path down the dark narrow hall, go back up a small set of stairs and into the main section of the building. Here bright sunlight spills through the windows and doors. She squints as one would expect after being kept in a dank, dim interior for a week. She can tell it's chilly outside because a couple of women working near the building exhale small puffs of vapor as they move about under a tree, raking leaves. They aren't dressed for such cold weather, and yet they're smiling. She does a double take and realizes the stretch of their mouths is a grimace of agony as they stop for a second to blow on reddened fingertips. Baker tips her head in their direction.

"They complained one time too many, were rude and disruptive to the staff. That's what that gets you. Work detail outside. It builds character."

"Yes, Mrs. Baker. How long has this building been here?"

Baker doesn't hesitate to share background information that leaves Ruth speechless. She details a law called the Chamberlain-Kahn Act, otherwise known as the American Plan.

"It's been around for decades to protect society and, more specifically, our men in the armed forces, but the government is ramping it up again. Prostitutes, fallen women, those with loose or no morals and with diseases of the most intimate sort must be kept away from military bases, not to mention the rest of the population until they're well and taught new behaviors. Our facility was built in 1927, and reeducates women in these matters. I've requested many times, mind you, for my program to be called a personal betterment program, but for now, the term *reform* is used. So, you see, Miss Foster, it's not just here, or in our state, but for the country."

Ruth is digesting the enormity of what's she's inadvertently become involved in as they enter a different wing where there are four doors, two on the left of a short hall, and two on the right. Nurse Crawford is there with a clipboard beside one and Baker gestures at Ruth while speaking to the other woman.

"Will you see to her, Nurse Crawford?"

"Yes, of course."

Thus begins Ruth's second week at the Colony. Quarantine. It's nothing like meditation because for one, there's a window in this room, and the first thing she's allowed to do is bathe, which is heaven in and of itself, as is brushing her teeth. She's given two additional dresses, a nightgown, a bar of soap, several pairs of underwear, more white ankle socks, and last, her black shoes are taken away to be polished. This is the wardrobe of every inmate at the Colony. She's told to settle in, and then, aside from a supper tray, she's left alone for the night, and she slowly begins to unwind from her ordeal.

Nurse Crawford returns to her room early on her second morning and with her is Dr. Graham. She's taken to a small exam room and asked a couple questions by him.

"You're Tammy Ruth Foster?"

"Yes, sir."

"Your birthdate is January 25, 1917?"

"Yes."

His demeanor is that of Dr. Tyndall's, no-nonsense and the bedside manner of a toad. She's glad Nurse Crawford is there, because she's efficient and businesslike, and Ruth is more relaxed because of her. Dr. Graham explains he must dissolve the medicine in a special solution, and then he'll inject it into the vein in her arm.

"The process to mix the solution used to be much more dangerous with the first medication, called Salvarsan 606. Nowadays, you gals have it much better."

Ruth is glad he thinks so.

He opens packages, mixes what's necessary, and says, "Ready?"

Ruth believes she is.

"Go ahead."

She feels the sharp pinch, and as the medication is injected, Nurse Crawford talks about next steps.

"You'll need to rest for the next twenty-four hours. You might experience some nausea, headache, fever, et cetera. This means it's working."

Dr. Graham says, "Done. Now, following this, we give you other shots too. Those start after the twenty-four-hour period."

The door shuts, and Nurse Crawford says, "There you go, first one over with."

Ruth's arm has a distracting, dull ache and as the day progresses she experiences nausea and a headache. All she wants to do is sleep. The next day, Dr. Graham returns to give her the other shot, as mentioned. The fact she's given adequate, if plainly cooked, food doesn't matter because she's unable to eat. After a few days, she's more coherent, and begins to eat a little. She watches out the window, studying the other inmates going about their various activities and the atmosphere of the Colony looks mostly peaceful. If she didn't know better, it's as if the women are working on a neighbor's farm. There's even a burst of laughter now and again.

Nurse Crawford comes in one morning and Ruth is almost herself, at least well enough to be curious.

"What's in it, the shots I'm getting?"

Nurse Crawford's expression is guarded. "You had your initial test at the local health official's office?"

"Yes."

"Records state you likely had syphilis. The drug in the first shot is called Neosalvarsan. The second one is mercury."

"It's just I've never, you know, done anything to catch something like that."

"You've never kissed a man?"

"Yes, but . . ."

Nurse Crawford's tone changes to matter-of-fact.

"They can get it from you from kissing *and* otherwise. I need to know everything in case we need to alert the authorities."

"All I did was kiss someone after a date."

"And?"

Ruth's face grows warm at what Nurse Crawford is insinuating.

"No. I've never . . ."

Nurse Crawford plows ahead.

"You can have it and not know. Have you noticed sores anywhere?"

"Sores? No."

"You might not. They're painless. Have you had a rash? Felt sick? Fever? Sore throat? Muscle aches?"

"Not that I recall. I'm hardly ever sick."

"It's a complex illness. Symptoms are similar to other illnesses. You can have it for years and not know. That's why it's known as the Great Pretender."

Ruth, dismayed, says, "I didn't know."

"Most don't."

Dubious about the diagnosis, Ruth doesn't want to argue with the nurse who's treated her with consideration, so she changes the subject.

"Is there a reform program for men? If they test positive, are they sent to a facility like this one?"

Nurse Crawford pauses writing in her notes.

"No."

"But if *they* get it, what happens to them?"

Nurse Crawford doesn't answer at first. She takes Ruth's pulse, her temperature, has her leave the room to step on a scale, asks about her bowels and urine output. She makes notes in her charts and finally answers in a roundabout way.

"Listen, you'll be cured. This is a standard, effective remedy. As to your question about infected men, I'm here to administer your medications and see to your overall health. You should speak to Mrs. Baker, if you're so inclined, with these types of questions."

"All right. Maybe I will. How long will it take for the shots to work?"

"You'll have several courses while you're here, but in general, it can take eighteen months to two years. They'll continue outside of the Colony for those who make parole. It's Mrs. Baker's intention to only keep individuals for as long as is necessary. After all, we don't want anyone becoming institutionalized, and unable to adjust to living on the outside."

Nurse Crawford gathers her things and leaves, shutting the door quietly. Sinking down to the bed, Ruth stares at the wall. She's unsure which part is worse: the idea of being here, or what she's just learned. She doesn't ask any more questions, and actually, doesn't speak much at all as she bears the quarantine period. Mrs. Baker checks in every now and again, and Ruth wishes she wouldn't. The woman unnerves her with her intense and commanding ways, but that soft-spoken voice makes her especially nervous. It's slick, persuasive, like a salesman with a gimmicky tool. Ruth presses for more details about her time at the Colony and the response is less than satisfactory.

"Begin the program, achieve certification, and you'll be free to leave on parole. You'll appreciate the time here, I guarantee it."

"Yes, Mrs. Baker. I'd like to write to my mother. She has no idea where I am. May I send her a note?"

"Of course. We'll get you what you need."

An hour later, Ruth is brought paper, an envelope, and a pen. She sits at the small table by the window, and begins. Her eyes fill as she churns out a long saga of her ordeal, attempting to soften words and facts.

Dearest Mama, she writes, *the most important thing for you to know is where I am and why. I've been sent to Kinston, to the State Industrial Farm Colony for Women.* She goes on from there detailing all she's been through, from the moment with Sheriff Wright, to the visit to the local health official, the arrival at the Colony, and on and on, including the misery of meditation and beyond. She's satisfied she's conveyed her dire situation as best as she can, so she folds the paper, and puts it into an envelope. As she's adding her mother's address to the front, Nurse Crawford enters the room. Ruth is about to lick the adhesive, and Nurse Crawford waves her hand.

"Wait. Don't seal it yet."

Ruth lowers the envelope, puzzled.

"All correspondence from here is read before it's sent out. Incoming letters too."

"What? Why?"

"Some tend to fabricate their experience. Some get things sent that aren't allowed."

"I'm only telling her where I am and what's happened to me."

"Are you accusing anyone? Are you being critical of the facility? Staff? Basically, are you complaining?"

Ruth squirms and her face grows warm.

"I suggest you rewrite it. Let her know where you are, that you're being cared for and are doing well. The letter will not get sent otherwise."

Ruth slumps. She has to let her mother know something, so she must accept what Nurse Crawford suggests, or leave her mother in the dark, and that won't do.

"All right. Fine."

She rips up the page and jots a much shorter note.

> *Dear Mama,*
>
> *I've been sent to Kinston, to the State Industrial Farm Colony for Women because they say I'm sick with an infection. They're treating me for it. Please don't worry. I hope to be home soon. Love, your daughter, Ruth*

She hands it to Nurse Crawford, unsealed, not even in the envelope. She doesn't care anymore because it's a lie. While her mother is bound to become alarmed, Ruth doesn't expect she'll act immediately. No. Instead, if she knows anything about her mother, it's that she's always been a bit timid, and will spend endless hours analyzing what it means, rather than taking immediate action. Without a doubt, she'll be mortified her daughter is in such a facility, and she'll wonder why she's there, and how it could've happened. Then she'll try to hide the shame of it from those she knows. Ruth is alone in quarantine, but at this thought, her face burns.

Chapter 6

Stella

The dorm is empty because everyone at the Colony is working on getting reformed and very soon, she'll be one of them. That's what Stella thinks as she follows Mrs. Maynard through the building and enters the dormitory for the first time since her operation for the tumor. The room is longer than it is wide and all white. Like a hospital ward. There's a long stretch of windows down one side and lots of beds. They're set in a row, twelve up one side and twelve down the other. She's in awe at the scale of it.

"Gosh, how many sleep in here?"

"How many beds do you see? I've assigned you that one."

Mrs. Maynard is a no-nonsense sort, Stella can tell. The housemother points to a bed in the middle of the row not by the windows, but against an expanse of bare wall so white it hurts Stella's eyes. She isn't used to sleeping in a room filled with other people. Plus, she'd rather have an end space and a window. She doesn't dare ask to be switched as her good common sense tells her it's highly unlikely. Stella's hopeful feelings take a tiny nosedive, thinking ahead to how she's going to get along with whoever's in here, what they'll say to her, if they say anything at all. She worries it'll be like at school.

She'll be ignored, or they might make fun of her. She would like to ask questions, but decides to wait and see what she's told.

Mrs. Maynard hands her a stack of supplies and indicates she's to put the items away in a small wooden box at the foot of her bed. She's been given two more of the ugly brown dresses and she can tell someone else must've worn them before her, because though they're clean, there's some sort of spot on one and a frayed edge to the sleeve of the other. There are two more pairs of white socks, underwear, a toothbrush, towel, washcloth, and a plain white cotton nightgown. She does as Mrs. Maynard directs, sticks everything in the box, and when she's finished, the housemother begins to talk about what's next. Stella likes this. She likes to know the expectations others have of her.

"Now, I need to see about getting you assigned for work detail and vocational classes. We have nine work courses offered. You need to complete at a minimum five to get your certificate. I think you'd be best suited for laundry, homemaking, cooking, sewing, and character education. The other four are charm, physical education, kitchen supervision, and canning, but canning is mostly done in the summers. We won't send anyone out of here unable to help support themselves, or their families in some way. Work details include any one of the following: kitchen work, farm work, and housekeeping. As you can see, you'll be kept very busy working to improve yourself."

"Yes, Mrs. Maynard."

She doesn't mind staying busy because it'll keep her preoccupied so she doesn't have to think about Cordell. The person who ought to get to work improving is Cordell, but of course she keeps this thought to herself. She does miss her mama though, despite her faults and her accusations. So far, no one's mentioned the real reason she's here. She'd just as soon they didn't. It's bad enough trying not to think about it. Maybe Alice and Cordell are relieved, although she thinks her mother will miss her help. Mrs. Maynard gives the room a quick assessment and evidently finds something not to her liking. She makes this little sound of disapproval, a sort of grunt. Stella spies a bed with a wrinkle in the top cover, and a trunk that's not quite as straight as compared to the others. She can't say if these are the problems Mrs. Maynard is unhappy about, except her own habits are those of orderliness and alignment. Mrs. Maynard bustles out the door and down the hall while Stella is still staring at the crooked box.

"Come along!" Mrs. Maynard calls out in an impatient voice.

Stella kicks the box straight and tugs the top cover in place and hurries from the room. Mrs. Maynard leads her outside where she shows Stella the areas of the Colony intended as part of her reform. Stella absorbs everything, from the vastness of the facility and the grounds to the distant voices of women she can see working in a field.

"Mr. Lumley's in charge of the farm buildings, the work, and the equipment. You'll take your direction from him when you work outside." Mrs. Maynard points out the dairy barn, and the cows in the pasture. She moves along fast while Stella would like more time to look around. She hurries toward the chicken houses and smiles at how the birds take off in a flurry of feathers, scuttling to the other side of the enclosure where they stand grouped. There are several pairs of beady eyes turned in her direction. Everything about the outside part is appealing, and where she might do better than working alongside someone who might not like her.

"I wouldn't mind doing farm work."

"You ever milked a cow before?"

"No, ma'am."

"Fed chickens? Gathered eggs? Hoed a row?"

Stella's enthusiasm withers because she's never done any of those things, but she's willing to try. Mrs. Maynard doesn't prompt her for a response like Mrs. Baker, but she doesn't come right out and say no either.

"For now, I'm going to have you help with laundry. Later on, since you're close in age to one of our more troubled girls, I might pair the two of you together. She can be a little skittish with those she doesn't know. We'll see."

Stella is curious about who the girl might be, but doesn't ask and only provides the standard obedient answer.

"Yes, Mrs. Maynard."

"All right, then. Come along to the kitchen. We're about to serve dinner in the dining hall. You can eat and then begin your duties."

"Yes, ma'am."

They reenter the building and Mrs. Maynard points her to a table in the dining hall and Stella sits. Soon women fill the expansive room, and they remind her of Alice with looks that speak of a hard life. Five approach her table. Three ignore her, but two ask her name. She tells them and they share theirs.

"Lucy Griffin, prostitute at large."

Stella's eyes grow big and round, and so does her mouth.

"She's proud of that, can't you tell? I'm Josephine Littles."

Mrs. Maynard and the lady who must be Mrs. Dillard, along with three other staff, keep watch over the dining hall. After everyone is seated, the staff point at tables individually, giving residents permission to go and get their food trays. Glasses with water or sweet tea are on side tables, and picked up after they get their food. The women get to their feet, some groaning, and shuffle along in a line to a window where sectional trays filled with food are slid toward reaching hands from a tiny window. It's tightly controlled, efficient, and well run. Stella's table is waved on to get theirs. Once she's back, she's impressed with what she sees. It's adequate and there's a variety. Today it's chicken, rice and gravy, green beans, and peaches. Sliced bread stacked on small plates and dishes of butter are on the tables, along with salt and pepper.

Everyone eats as if they've had nothing that day and the noise from utensils scraping across the hard plastic is rhythmic and constant. There is a low volume of conversation among them, and it creates a hum that fills Stella's ears and is strangely soothing, like a big family enjoying a meal. Stella observes the others as she eats. There are some who sit with a blank stare and don't pick up their forks. This is a problem, evidently. A staff member goes and stands right behind the individual. No words are exchanged; none are needed. The reluctant eaters always pick up their forks and begin, even if it's small bites.

Stella is content and even at ease until a screech interrupts the rather peaceful atmosphere. Mrs. Maynard whizzes by, aiming for two women arguing over some unknown issue. It escalates as they push their chairs back and lean across the table, their faces close enough one has to wipe spittle off her forehead. That woman's next reaction is swift. She grabs a handful of the other woman's hair and yanks repeatedly. Stella sees strands come out and the one whose hair is being pulled bellows. Those sitting with these two grab their trays and move away, still watching as they continue to cram food in, as if it's entertainment. Several staff join Mrs. Maynard and before a full-blown fight erupts the arguing women are separated and escorted from the dining room.

Stella wonders where they're being taken, and what strikes her is they seem to know because anyone with ears can hear as they plead and beg, "No, no, no."

Their voices fade. Stella, disturbed, turns to those at her table for an explanation.

Lucy half whispers to Josephine, "Meditation, for sure."

Josephine snorts. "Maybe group punishment."

Stella is highly disturbed.

"What's meditation? What's group punishment?"

She looks into a pain-riddled face. With a flick of her wrist as if to brush off unpleasant thoughts, Lucy, owner of the face, provides the answer.

"Both are something to avoid at all costs. Trust me. If you're stuck in this hellhole for too long it *can* get worse, and it ain't where you want to end up. They think of ways to make you not only regret how you messed up, but you'll be second-guessing if it was worth it. Personally, I say yes. Yes, it is. They ain't got no right to do what they're doing, and that bitch, Baker, she knows it."

Stella drops her eyes to the food on her tray, flustered by the information, but more so from the hate spewing out of the prostitute. Maybe those women shouldn't have acted like they had, so whatever they get, it's their own fault. A bell sounds and chairs are shoved back in one movement. Amidst more groans and moans, trays are dropped into a large plastic bin by the exit door and the residents go back to work or class. Mrs. Maynard magically reappears at Stella's elbow and she's escorted to the laundry room and left to work with, of all people, Lucy. Lucy talks. She doesn't seem to care Stella doesn't have much to say. Lucy tells Stella she entertains men and provides details.

Stella, before she's able to think of any appropriate reaction, shivers, repulsed, and says, "Why would you want to do *that*?"

She's folding towels, the scent of soap and bleach familiar because her mother had a bad habit of using too much of the latter when she was in the mood to clean.

Lucy smirks and says, "Shocked?"

"No, ma'am."

"'Ma'am'? Please. I ain't *that* old."

Lucy lets out a peal of laughter and Stella doesn't know what to make of her. She folds and folds and still folds. It's like she's folding all the clothes ever sewn by humankind and when she comments on the never-ending pile of towels, Lucy explains burdensome work.

"When you work here, you do it all, both dorms, the kitchen, whatever, we wash, hang, fold for everyone."

It turns out Lucy's highly particular about washing, drying, and folding. Sheets, towels, and washcloths must be done a certain way. She mostly points at what she wants Stella to do, shows her, then leaves her to do the work, periodically checking and making her do the job over if it's not up to her standards. Stella observes Lucy's meticulous methods. Before washing any items, they're sorted by what Lucy calls needs. Items go into different piles she's designated as needs soaking, needs mending, or needs replacing. The sorting comes first. Stella is slow, Lucy is fast. She must've been at the Colony a long time, or so many times it's like she never left. The wash gets done and Lucy wrings the clothes, feeding rinsed pieces through the roller and out the other end, tossing them into a basket. Lucy holds up a dress she's about to feed through the roller.

"Look'a here. I'm picturing this ugly old dress is Baker. Wouldn't you just love to run her through this wringer? Like she does us?"

Stella's uncomfortable with the constant badmouthing of Mrs. Baker. She doesn't want to make anyone mad, but she also doesn't want to end up in meditation, whatever that is, if someone overhears.

"Maybe we shouldn't talk about Mrs. Baker."

"Oh, don't be little Miss Goody Two-shoes. Believe me, she doesn't care about you even if she acts like it. You're here, so something's wrong with you according to her and them so-called experts who help her run this place."

"It ain't that. Maybe someone will hear. We could end up in trouble."

"What's your name again?"

"Stella."

"Huh. Ain't you a sweet little thang. Well, Daffodil, I do love innocence. You're proof it still exists and hallelujah for that."

"Stella. It's Stella."

As to innocence, Stella also knows better. She's ruined, which is why she's here. She changes the subject.

"Do I get to hang out the clothes?"

"Get? Hell, this is work, not a privilege, and we do it all, honey. Come on, you crank for a while."

The afternoon is endless, stuck in this dank room with the rusty, clunky washer and this unusual woman who occasionally bursts into laughter for no apparent reason.

They've been at it for a while when Lucy cocks an eye at Stella and asks, "Ever seen a man's . . . member?"

Stella's neck and face flare a deep red. She knows more than she'd ever admit, more than she ought to know. It's like Lucy's trying to get a reaction, especially when she forms her mouth into a circle and makes an appalling motion, then proceeds to tell Stella what she gets paid for that service. Stella is about to feed a towel into the roller, but drops it back into the basket in a sloppy heap. She stands stiffly, hands clenched, head averted, shut down mentally. Lucy lets out a loud breath in exasperation.

"Lord, Jesus, help me. Innocent *and* a prude! All right, Miss Goody. Hand me that towel so I can rinch it. After, we'll go outside and you can hang these clothes, every last one, to your heart's content. Me? I'm gonna have me a well-deserved smoke."

Stella extends a stiff arm with the towel and Lucy takes it, shaking her head. Outside, it's cool, but the sun is bright. Stella carries one of many heavy baskets to the clothesline. Lucy is the same about hanging out clothes as she is about folding. She shows her how to clip the clothespins to the corners of the sheets a certain way, the same for the pillowcases, and the towels until they hang in perfect order, going from big to small. This orderliness speaks to Stella too. They return to the laundry room to get more baskets of wet things, and after a while, she's so tired, she can't hardly think of lifting another item of clothing into the air. They're done anyway, and just in time.

The bell rings, and Lucy singsongs, "Oh, golly gee, Miss Goody! It's suppertime for you and me!"

Lucy kicks the laundry baskets across the floor so they bounce against the wall and walks out of the room. Stella doesn't like the soap powder spilled over the work counters, or the puddles of water left on the floor, and the mess nags at her. Her instinct says she can't do anything about it and risk being late for supper. She goes up the stairs to the main floor and falls into step with women from all points around the facility. They flood the hallways, exhausted and one day closer to redemption. Supper is like dinner. Same food served. Same sounds. Same recalcitrant eaters persuaded by the presence of a staff member at their elbow. After supper is the thirty minutes of free time. She doesn't know what to do with herself, so she stands just outside the room designated for the evening prayer service—she wouldn't want to be late.

That night after Stella's finally in bed, her arms ache and her back hurts. She's exhausted but she's also aware of the other women.

Unlike with eating, here the noises from clearing of throats, sighing, rustling of sheets, and other sounds won't allow her to relax. Soft conversations are slowly replaced by light breathing while some snort or snore. It's a long night, and at every flap of a sheet, squeak of a spring, or hacking cough, she wakes up.

When the six a.m. bell rings, Mrs. Maynard opens the door, emits a blast off the whistle around her neck, and shouts, "Time to get up! Wake up, now!"

Stella is sitting on the edge of her bed with bleary eyes, bed neatly made, nightgown folded and tucked in the box. She's already been to the bathroom down the hall, washed her face, brushed her teeth. She's already dressed. Mrs. Maynard gives her a strange look. As the other women make haste to get ready, there's a bit of orderly chaos until the clock strikes six twenty-nine and Mrs. Maynard returns. Somehow, everyone is dressed, beds made, faces washed, hair and teeth brushed.

"All right, let's go!"

They fall into a line starting with the two women nearest the door, and one by one like worker ants, they obediently file out of the dorm.

Mrs. Baker is in the hall and stops Stella. "How are you coming along learning the handbook I gave you?"

Unnerved, but with the entire pamphlet already stored in her head, Stella begins to recite every regulation in it. She repeats them, including the number of demerits for each and the page number each is on. She's only halfway through when Baker holds up her hand and stops her.

"You memorized it. All of it."

It's not a question, but Stella answers as if it is.

"Yes, Mrs. Baker."

Stella doesn't say it only took her a couple of days. She waits for the praise to come. She did it because she's supposed to, but also, and maybe more so, to impress the superintendent. The corners of her mouth turn up in a small smile of hope, believing this will prove she's ready and capable of turning herself around. She's always done well in school, despite all. Now, this very important lady will see she's quick to learn. Except. Mrs. Baker's eyes narrow, and darken, transforming her into a menacing presence. She doesn't take them off Stella and Stella's gut tightens with fear. Did she sound like she was showing off? Fawning? Was that the word? She didn't mean to. She doesn't know what to say, and the moment passes.

"Hm. We just might find a special job for you, yet."

Mrs. Baker resumes making her way down the hall toward her office, and for the first time, Stella is aware of a deviation in the otherwise firm step—a limp. She wishes the superintendent was pleased with her. Maybe she is, but can't show it. Mrs. Maynard waits at the door to the dining hall, and wiggles her hand at Stella to hurry. Despite her slight delay, she arrives at exactly the time printed in the booklet. This makes her want to check it off as an accomplishment. Those who come in late, like Lucy, are chased into the dining hall by a staff member smacking her hands together, *clap, clap, clap!* It only makes Lucy laugh and sashay her way through the door. Stella goes through the line, picking up a tray of food, and settles down at the same table she sat at the day before. What she can rely on is the food is decent. She can rely on order and the schedule. This is better than what she had at home, better than what she was able to carve out for herself.

She bites into a boiled egg, and looks up in time to see a young woman enter who doesn't fit the mold of anyone there. The fact she's a minute late is wiped from Stella's thoughts as she watches her hesitate just inside the entrance to the dining hall, like she's unsure of what to do. Her black hair glistens and Stella envies her for it. She plops the rest of the egg in her mouth, chewing, fascinated as this person crosses the room. She walks like she's modeling for a fashion magazine—not that Stella would know a thing about that, but this must be how it would look, this refined walk, sophisticated and elegant, chin up, looking straight ahead. This person's got quality looks, for sure.

Stella touches her own hair pulled back in a messy, half-wet ponytail. She'd like to have hers cut the same and gosh, to have them cheekbones too. Stella keeps her attention on the intriguing person throughout the rest of the time they have for breakfast, which is easy to do because the woman sits near Josephine and Lucy. Even though Stella's distracted, her ears are tuned to what she hears. Many are grumbling about one thing or another.

She hears a variety of chatter. "Given a chance, I'd stab her with this here fork," and "I'd lock her in one'a them rooms for twice as long as she done me, see how she likes it," followed by "I hate her."

Stella swings her head sharply in the direction of the comments, but can't determine who's saying these things. Unexpectedly, the dining hall noises surge in her head, and what she thought was comforting yesterday shifts so that the chewing and smacking make her want to put her hands over her ears. It reminds her of Alice's eating, all the slurping and other noises that come with consumption of food and drink. It must be because she's tired. She nibbles on a biscuit, pushes the sausage around her tray while her breakfast companions hunch over their plates, shoveling food in so fast, sometimes it spills out. They scoop it up and stick it back into their mouths. Most eat with a spoon, ignoring the fork beside the plate. Raucous laughter bursts forth. The bell rings just in time, right before she was about to take her hands and mash them over her ears.

She makes sure to push the chair back under the table neatly before taking her tray to the plastic bin. After she drops it off, she turns and the striking woman is right behind her, holding her own tray. Stella looks at it and wonders how she got away with not eating everything. There's a dullness to her features, as if she isn't alive. How did she miss her in the dorm room?

The woman murmurs a soft, "Pardon me," before moving around Stella, who can't seem to budge.

Stella blurts out, "You're supposed to eat everything."

The woman has no reaction; it's like Stella didn't speak. This new woman places her tray in the bin and then leaves the dining room. *Well. I tried.* Stella goes back to the laundry. Two others are there, meaning Stella doesn't have to listen to just Lucy. They complain about everything from their red, roughened hands, to how long they've been there (one's been to the Colony three times!) to the mandated medication and how it makes them feel. Lucy joins in with their complaining while Stella feels lucky. She's not receiving the shots. She reckons she can't blame them for their ill-temperedness, given they're suffering so many side effects. For instance, one woman has loose teeth, and her tongue constantly probes inside her mouth. The other offers to look and after she does, she shakes her head.

"You got to get them pulled, Doris."

Doris, of the bad teeth, shrieks.

"Do you know what that's going to make me look like? Like that cartoon character, Popeye!"

Her friend grumbles.

"Is that who I look like?"

Lucy interrupts their conversation about dental work.

"Teeth ain't the issue. Who're they to keep us here, and make us to take them shots anyway?"

This gets the other two worked up. Stella would never admit she likes being at the Colony, and doesn't mind the work. Here in the laundry, the smell of soap powder, the steam from hot water, the very act of taking something dirty and cleansing it, is soothing, and it feels right. If only she could do the same for herself. She's bad, rotten maybe, inside and out. They could throw her out like dirty laundry water, but instead? They say she's redeemable. She's worthy of saving. Mrs. Baker even reaffirmed this, but Stella can't quite rid herself of the notion she's fouled and she's of a mind Mrs. Baker just can't see it yet.

Before the day is done Lucy has the others calling her Miss Goody too, which means it's already started. No different from school. During her free time, she doesn't join in playing games, or reading. She watches to see how the rest act with one another, observing their interactions and comradery, how they nudge one another, or roar with laughter together. She hopes to see the pretty young woman, but doesn't. Instead, this one girl in particular catches her attention for the oddity of her looks. She has a severely wandering eye, and is extraordinarily tall. Stella guesses she might be the same age, or maybe a bit older. This girl's prone to doing what Stella used to do—talking to herself.

She goes over to Josephine, who's playing checkers. Josephine herself is interesting with her flaming red hair gone gray at the roots and freckles across her nose.

"Who's she?" Stella asks, pointing at the strange girl rocking back and forth and twiddling her fingers.

"Her? That's Frances Platt. We call her Freaky Frances."

"Why?"

"Just you wait."

Chapter 7

Baker

No one is allowed to buzz the superintendent's cottage for any reason unless it's an emergency. An intercom connects it to the other buildings, but every other weekend, Baker is considered off-limits for mundane employee or resident issues. It's her sanctuary, the place where she doesn't have to wear the suffocating black stockings, where she can sit out on the small brick patio if the weather is nice and do as she pleases. On this particular weekend, Baker isn't enjoying her off time. She's brooding over Ruth Foster. She'd never admit she harbors a grudge against her type, attractive without knowing it, strong-willed, intelligent, and knows her own mind. Each aspect of a woman's time at the Colony, from coordinating testing for disease and competency, to treatments, to training, all are carefully considered per individual. The mental acuity tests provide what she and her staff need so they can be placed into strict but appropriate programs that she takes full credit for developing. Her role is to show them what society expects, and in turn, prove her own worth. When they leave on parole, it's a win for both. If they return, she counts it the same way, a loss for both.

Samarcand, which to her mind is as she left it, nothing but cinders and soot, was a hard lesson, but she's certain most who work in this field have a restored faith in her efforts and trust her to do what's necessary. Since coming five years ago, she counts herself fortunate and she'll always remain indebted to dear Eloise for guiding her here, God rest her soul. Her friend's untimely death some months back was terrible news to receive. Eloise, her one true friend, although Winnifred DeLong can't be discounted, was who Baker had turned to during her most difficult times when all was coming to an end. Her job. Her marriage. She and Eloise came to know one another through their work with the Woman's Club of Pine Hill, where many with such backgrounds as those in child welfare, public health, and other services eventually turned to the work of reform. Eloise had never minced words. For instance, she'd been forthright in her assessment of Ed Baker long before their marriage ended.

"You know, Dot, you shouldn't let him treat you like a leftover sandwich."

"I think he's seeing someone. I've tried—you know. To keep him interested. Ever since"—and she gestured toward her legs—"he saw this, it's like a switch flipped off."

"Good heavens. Since your *wedding* night?"

Baker blinked. Eloise put a hand to her cheek, and gave her a wide-eyed sympathetic look.

"How despicable. Was he like this before you got married?"

"It's hard to say. We hadn't known one another very long. The truth is, I wasn't having much luck meeting anyone. I intimidated most men. Not Ed. He came right up to me while I was browsing through magazines at the store, struck up a conversation, and asked me out. We dated a few times. It was rather sporadic. He didn't call for a while, and I believed he was drifting away. Out of the blue, he came by and proposed. Father said I should agree, although he's always told Mother, 'Never shoot at the first thing that flies by.' "

Eloise gave her an amused look. "Most times we only get one proposal, unless we're Scarlett O'Hara, or immoral. Why *did* he propose, do you think?"

Baker looked hurt and Eloise patted her hand. "I only meant given the way things went in the beginning, with his erratic calls and all."

Baker fiddled with a napkin and couldn't meet Eloise's eyes as she gave a one-word answer. "Money."

"Money? I don't understand."

"My father."

"*Paid him?* Like one of those old-fashioned dowries?"

Baker shifted in her chair, and stared out the window, noting it was fall, and how the leaves looked like bright spots painted against the dullness of a gray sky. She spoke with resolve.

"Not exactly. Ed owed debts. He likes to play cards. My father thought I should already be married. I guess he and Ed made some sort of arrangement . . ." At Eloise's expression, Baker became a bit defensive. "I don't dwell on it. I try to be a good wife."

Eloise was there for her when Ed Baker lived up to the other side of his reputation. Baker recalls the day with a wince, still uncomfortable after all this time. She wasn't supposed to be home for hours, but she'd forgotten her notes for a meeting. She went back to the house and walked in on him and his floozy flouncing about on the bed she'd made with clean sheets only that morning. There wasn't any perfunctory scrambling to make themselves decent; there was only Ed glaring at her over his shoulder as he lay on top of his paramour, as if wanting her to hurry up and get what she needed so he could finish. She'd fled to Eloise's house, upset and angry. Eloise, pragmatic as always, took her by the hand and gave her the best advice ever.

"Leave him. He won't expect it."

And she had. This is why when someone like the Foster woman crosses her path, the memories come wholly unwanted, with the same urgency as an out-of-control fire. It becomes personal. Baker knows the type. She's the kind who steals husbands. Coercion, threats, and if required, harsher measures, are what works best with women like her. She'll always have to contend with those who claim they're there by mistake, but they're always wrong, and she likes proving it to them. It takes time for some to accept what experts and local authorities know. Diseases spread by the ignorant can't be left unchecked. It's her responsibility to do what she can in the name of the public.

She's one cog in the process, but an important one. In addition, for those who make probation, she's obligated to safeguard against them returning to a corrupt way of life. A formidable task, indeed.

As she ruminates, her attention shifts to the puzzling enigma of the youngest inmate, Stella Temple. Only a few short days ago the girl exhibited an uncanny memory. She also scored well on the IQ assessments, better than most who come, except for the troublesome Ruth Foster. Miss Foster's above average intelligence irritates Baker. If she were an imbecile, her presence wouldn't bother her so much. Her only issue with Stella's intelligence is it doesn't align to the typical background for sterilizations, that of imbeciles, morons, and degenerates who are typically chosen for additional correction. No need to encumber the general population with more of that sort. Stella's the exception with regard to her aptitude, not that it matters now. If she returns home at least there's no worry the issue she came with will happen again.

Baker's experience with girls of this age is that they sometimes behave in a wanton fashion, seeking attention. They don't understand the power they wield. If not held to account for their actions, they mature and what do they do? Steal husbands. It's most upsetting, sickening in fact, how a father could do such to his own daughter. It's not unheard of, though. Issues like this usually crop up in the homes where a wife has failed in her own duties of intimacy. Given Mrs. Temple's disabilities, this is more than likely what happened. Baker scrutinizes the notes from the physician who saw Stella originally. It's a shame the girl's so smart only to waste it with unbecoming and licentious behaviors that got her into trouble in the first place. No matter. She's at the Colony now, and Baker can correct her course, and possibly influence her future. She'll address it first thing Monday. Now that she's decided, she can relax and she meanders out onto her patio Sunday evening to enjoy the birdsong with a snifter of whiskey, her secret pleasure, and the guarantee of getting a good night's sleep.

Early Monday, she's back at work, seated at her desk, and implementing her plan.

"Bring Stella Temple to my office."

There's some static and then the voice of Mrs. Maynard crackles through.

"Stella Temple? Now?"

Such a birdbrained question. It makes her impatient and gives her a hot flash.

"Precisely what I said."

"She's—"

"Mrs. Maynard. I don't care where she is or what she's doing. Bring her to my office. Now."

"All right."

Baker swivels in her chair to face the door leading to the main hall where she can hear two women conversing as they mop. There's an antiseptic smell reminiscent of a hospital and it makes her legs itch. She reaches down and strokes along the backside of her calves—the sensitive, tight patches of scar tissue beneath the thick stockings urge her to rub, rub, rub, but she stops herself. From past experience, this only makes it worse. She told the girl she might find her a special job and this might give her a much-needed dose of self-worth as well as build her self-esteem.

Baker rises and drifts around the room while she waits. She passes by the window and as is her habit, she looks out, and catches a glimpse of something going on in the fields that causes her to rush over. Her forehead presses against the glass, mouth agape. Mr. Lumley is in the process of directing a group of women in the finer art of farm work, and to her disbelief this morning's activities involve a highly restricted task. Mr. Lumley has a long stick with a cloth wrapped around the end. He's dousing it with a clear liquid from a red container with white letters painted on it in a haphazard fashion, spelling "Gasoline." He sets the container down, steps away from it, and flicks a lighter, holding it to the soaked end, which catches fire quickly. Black smoke rises from the homemade torch and he sets off, motioning for the cluster of women to stay back as he dips the flame here and there at the edges of the field where stubble and weeds gone dormant have become overgrown in the area.

She'd made it clear no tasks of this nature were to take place around her or the residents. She needs to do something, but can't move from the window. She bites at a fingernail as her brain engages with the torch in Mr. Lumley's hand, and she's entranced as spot by spot, the flames kiss the ground and spread. It's been so long. She's enthralled and the knock at the door startles her out of her trance. It makes her angry. She wishes she'd seen this before she requested Stella be brought to her office. Now she has to respond when all she wants to do is to watch the beauty spreading out below her. The knock comes again, and to Baker, it has the sound of impatience. Her reaction is to speak in a harsher tone than she intended.

"Come in!"

She immediately goes back to what she was doing, turning her back to Mrs. Maynard whose voice is also impatient.

"I've brought Stella. As you requested?"

Baker grips the windowsill. It's a monumental effort to disengage with the goings-on in the field. She moves from the window, assumes an authoritative position behind her desk, and composes herself.

"Ah. Stella. Yes."

"Is that all?"

Baker slants her gaze toward Mrs. Maynard. The housemother stammers.

"I-it's just that I was in the middle of addressing a situation, and I left it to do as you asked."

"A situation? Is everything under control?"

"Of course, but as you know, constant supervision is necessary and I can't be everywhere."

"Exactly why I wanted Stella brought to me."

"Oh. An idea, then?"

"Perhaps. Maybe you'd like to hear my proposal."

Baker doesn't wait for a reply. She concentrates on Stella.

"You did well to learn the rules in the handbook so quickly."

"Thank you, Mrs. Baker."

"I want to give you that special responsibility. It's a secret job, meaning you'd have to be careful, but I need someone who's smart."

Ah. That's the hook. The girl's back straightens, and then there's a smile pulling her mouth upward, altering it from its perpetual downward shape.

"Yes, ma'am, but how could I help?"

"Our job, all of the staff, is to ensure everyone follows the Colony's rules and guidelines. We have them for a reason and they're important. Don't you think so?"

"Yes, ma'am."

"Good. We also can't be everywhere and hear or see everything that goes on. These women get to talking about one thing or another, and it would be nice to know if someone is thinking of stirring up trouble. That can't be tolerated. It could be dangerous."

"Yes, ma'am."

"You'll do your work as you're assigned, but as you go about your day-to-day duties, all you have to do is pay attention to the ones not doing as they should, or if you hear something that might be a problem, you're to immediately let Mrs. Maynard or Mrs. Dillard know. Everyone is required to do what we ask of them, otherwise they fail. If they fail, I fail. You can see it's very important."

"Yes, Mrs. Baker."

She appears amenable, yet Baker senses a reluctance. She sweetens the pot.

"This is part of your reform. It will show me what you're capable of, meaning able to accept additional responsibilities. Of course, you'll be rewarded for this work. Perhaps extra privileges, like an outing. You might even make parole quicker."

Stella appears enthusiastic until the mention of an early parole. At that her face collapses into disappointment. Baker offers a rare smile of encouragement and a warning.

"To refuse jeopardizes your success here."

Stella nods in understanding.

"Yes, ma'am. I done seen some things."

This admission infuriates Baker. The very idea these fallen women are getting away with breaking rules, as if thumbing their noses at her back, is intolerable. Baker shoots a nasty look at Mrs.

Maynard, but even as her ire is kindled, she's levelheaded in her response.

"We won't worry about what's already happened. Going forward, you're to let one of the housemothers know. And, Stella, be discreet about it, you understand? You're not to confront anyone, or say a word."

"Yes, Mrs. Baker."

"Good. Mrs. Maynard, I hope this will enable you to be more efficient in dealing with those who have devised ways of circumventing your authority."

The older woman wilts at the criticism. Baker's goal is to produce parolees, to focus on receiving only new residents with no returns. That's her objective, along with the possibility of expanding the Colony. She waves her hand, dismissing them.

"That's all. You both may go."

Mrs. Maynard leads Stella away, and as soon as the door shuts, Baker hurries to the window. She comes close to crying at the sight of only a blackened field—the controlled burn is out. Mr. Lumley has several women turning the smoky soil with hoes and shovels, while others rake here and there to carefully mix in the ash left behind. Baker's brief encounter plays with her mind. Like a match strike to an unknown source within her, she recognizes the resurgence of something gone dormant. It's troubling and she wishes she hadn't picked that moment to look outside. She needs to set old Mr. Lumley straight once again as a vision of fields ablaze consumes her. Her mouth fills as she battles the buried craving. She has to divert her thoughts. There's a map of the Colony on the wall tacked up where land for new dormitories might one day exist. She focuses on it. *To go backward is a sign of weakness, of failure. You must step forward.* She wraps a scarf around her neck and puts on a coat. By the time she's outside and tramping across the field, she's got herself worked up, but it will do no good to rant. She will maintain her composure because the women are always searching for a crack. A weakness. A way to circumvent authority. She knows how they are.

She spies him standing off to the side, smoking a cigarette. She raises a hand.

"Mr. Lumley, a word, please."

Everyone stops working to gaze at her with curiosity.

He yells, "Keep working, you got the whole field to tend to!"

There's a pause as he watches them bend to their task. Only then does he make his way over to her. He doesn't hurry and this adds to her aggravation. It's difficult but she talks to him in a manner befitting her station—cordially, and carefully.

"Mr. Lumley, I made a request to not burn around residents. I thought I made myself clear when I did so."

"Oh, I know, I know. But I thought if I did it this way, it'd be quick-like, it'd be done and that's that."

"As you know, it can be dangerous. I'm sure you can appreciate these women get all kinds of ideas in their heads. It might entice them to do something."

"Oh, I was real specific about why we were doing what we were doing. I told 'em, this is a way to clear the ground quick. I said it's this or they had to do it by hand and that might take a good week or two. It's done now."

"Mr. Lumley, fieldwork serves a purpose. Work is what they're here for, not to have their jobs made easier. As I've also made clear in the past."

"Right."

It's a less than satisfactory response. Mr. Lumley has shown himself to be as obstinate as Mrs. Maynard at times.

"From now on, they need to put their backs into it. This is how we wear them down, calm their state of mind, quell their urges. I want them exhausted. This is not a request."

She glares at him and leaves, every single pair of eyes on her along with whispers. She hears a derogatory name or two. She could turn around and confront them, except that would produce nothing and that would be one of those cracks. They'd know they got to her. They always know.

Chapter 8
Ruth

After the cryptic note to her mother, Ruth waits to see if anything might come of it, though it's highly unlikely. April arrives, dreary and rainy. She sees the business of the Colony go on from her quarantine room window. The weather brings her mood down and she starts to think it's like her father said: She brought this on herself in some way. She isn't oblivious to her appearance, which has been described as arresting. When she attended La Grange High, she didn't wear anything different from her peers, though she favored solid dark colors like navy or black, along with a shade of deep red lipstick that made her lips the color of blood. She's kept her hair as it was back then too, the cut as precise as a paper's edge, the color like glossy black paint. It's a standout trait, the same as her father's. He said they had Cherokee blood in them somewhere down the line.

She confronts the cloudy, cracked mirror in the quarantine bathroom when she brushes her teeth in the mornings and evenings, noticing how her eyes now have red threads laced over the whites from lack of sleep. There's a new line between her brows that wasn't there before, and while she's not vain, she does notice. She's gone through several injections. Nausea, headaches, and other maladies linger, hampering her sense of well-being. She's lost weight somehow, despite the mandate they clean their trays. One morning she gets a visit from Baker. Nurse Crawford is there too, and Ruth, who's been waiting on the results of her latest Wassermann, is impatient.

"Am I okay now?"

Baker doesn't answer her question directly.

"You're being released from quarantine. You'll be under Mrs. Maynard in Building A dormitory."

"Yes, Mrs. Baker. But, what about the results of my test? Can't I see them?"

Baker snorts.

"Those are kept confidential and only viewed for therapy planning and for the state's medical records. What you should concern yourself with is the next step, which is to make an effort toward achieving parole. Do as instructed and you'll be well on your way. I assume that's your heart's desire. I am a strong believer in the concept a sound body results in a sound mind. Please understand, making parole is your goal here, and to do that, you'll need to get your certifications. All of this will be explained."

"Yes, Mrs. Baker. Will I continue the shots?"

Baker defers to Nurse Crawford who says, "We'll have to see when we retest."

The superintendent signals Ruth to follow her. She obediently trails Baker again, observing a few women they pass in the hallway with sluggish and dull looks about them, like they're drugged. As they continue on, Baker points out various parts of the property.

"There are two dorms, Building A and Building B, which is overseen by Mrs. Dillard. You can see it out that window there. We're on four hundred eighty-eight acres of land with one hundred and six of those acres managed by residents along with the farm help, Mr. Lumley. We grow our own fruits and vegetables, harvesting some for use in our kitchens here, and selling others to help with expenses. Have you ever done any work on a farm?"

"Not much, Mrs. Baker."

"Learning hands-on is best. You'll get plenty of that here. Ah, there's Mrs. Maynard. She can help get you settled in. Now, after that rough beginning, I can properly welcome you to the Colony. I believe you'll find your time here valuable, and anticipate it will set you on the correct path society expects. This booklet helps everyone familiarize themselves with the rules and guidelines. Please study it. Learn them so you know what is expected of you at all times."

Ruth takes in her surroundings. It's so clean, and bright, like waking up in a different place altogether. She's encouraged by this bit of freedom and obediently takes the booklet.

"Yes, Mrs. Baker. Thank you."

"Mrs. Maynard, you remember Ruth Foster? She's released from her quarantine and ready to begin the program."

"Excellent."

Mrs. Maynard grips Ruth's upper arm, fingers digging deep into the muscles.

"You've obviously never done any heavy physical work. That's fine. Before long, you'll be stronger, healthier, a better person, and ready to leave us, I guarantee it."

Mrs. Maynard's prodding fingers are intrusive. Ruth, in her new quest to remain agreeable, doesn't protest. Her goal is directly in line with Mrs. Maynard's. She wishes to get out of here.

"Yes, Mrs. Maynard."

Mrs. Maynard releases her arm and continues.

"Mrs. Baker's program is top-notch and her work enables a high percentage of women to reenter society with success. Mind you, the goal is to not return."

Ruth smiles politely. "Yes, ma'am," she repeats.

Ruth is skeptical since she ended up here without cause. How can she know whether or not the same thing won't happen again?

Mrs. Baker steps back and says, "I'll leave it to you two. I'm sure you'll get along just fine."

And with that, Ruth is transitioned to the housemother, and hopes from this point on it won't be necessary to see much of the superintendent. Mrs. Maynard holds a clipboard and turns pages while running a pencil down a piece of paper with names, checkmarks, and other information. She taps her pencil on the page.

"I think I'll have you work in the kitchen. We'll start you off washing dishes. Can you cook?"

"Yes, ma'am. I know how to cook. And bake—cakes, pies, cookies, whatever is required."

"Bake? We don't allow such as that, other than biscuits or cornbread. But we might use you to cook at some point. Let me show you to the dorm where you can put the things you've brought."

"Yes, ma'am."

Mrs. Maynard is rather brisk in all she does, despite her physical limitations, and as she leads the way, Ruth has to speed up or get left behind. This sudden movement after receiving her shots makes her dizzy, but she doesn't complain. She's assigned a bed in an enormous room, and barely has time to place her clothes in the box at the foot of it before she's escorted to the kitchen. In minutes, she's doing dishes alongside an older woman with red hair mixed with gray. Ruth introduces herself.

"Hi. I'm Ruth Foster."

"Josephine Littles. That's Freaky Frances yonder. She usually dries if she's in the kitchen. She has a thing about dishwater, or something. Can't tell with her. She's an oddball, that one."

Ruth takes a look, but all she can see is the backside of a gangly girl. They're tasked with confronting a mountain of plates, bowls, utensils, glasses, cups, pots, pans, basically anything used in the kitchen or dining hall from the earlier meal. It's more dishes than Ruth's ever seen and the scraping, scrubbing, and rinsing seems to go on without end. If nothing else, there's a couple windows to look out as they work. Josephine points to three women through one of windows.

She whispers, "Them out there? Them's my boarders, or they used to be. They stayed at the house with me, and worked at the mill. That's the truth, but nobody would believe me when I tried to tell 'em that. That's Natalie Watts with the blond hair, Melissa Taylor with brown, and Paula Akers is wearing the glasses."

Ruth's curious to know every woman's story who ended up at the Colony.

"What happened?"

Josephine glances around, ensuring she can talk without being heard.

"Well, there we was. I run a clean boardinghouse called the Orion, after the knitting mill where many of my girls work. Them gals rented rooms from me, nothing more. Between the three'a them, they been with me anywhere from six months to a couple years. One day, here comes this uppity police officer nosing around. Says to me, says, I'm running a dirty house. Asks me if I'm married. I say I ain't married, and, no sir, I ain't running no dirty house. Been there all of ten years and ain't never had no problems. He says, 'Somebody complained.' Arrested me right there on the spot, and before I was taken off, got them three as they were coming off their shift. Can you believe it? It was a setup, if'n you ask me. Anyway, we been here a couple of months now."

Ruth tells her own story. Josephine shakes her head in disgust.

"You mean to tell me you got picked up because you were living on your own?" Josephine gawks at Ruth. "Here you had you a job, minding your own business, and he just come along and demanded you go to that doctor?"

"That's the gist of it."

"They don't care. If they're suspicious, that's all it takes. How long you been here?"

"About a month. I was put in meditation for a few days. A nice name for solitary. Then I was in isolation starting on those horrible shots."

Josephine picks up a plate and dunks it into hot water. "Oh yeah. We're all going through it. That first one, and then the mercuries. I been getting mine, and can't hardly lift my arm, much less do what they expect us to do given how I feel. What'd you do to get put into solitary?"

"Tried to leave soon as the sheriff let me out of his car. Nothing seemed right about it. I saw someone working in the field motion to me, like she was telling me to run. It scared me, so I did. I've never been in trouble before. The sheriff picked me up again and brought me back. Mrs. Baker said because of that, I'd have a different start. I was put into a rotten little room where food tastes like it's made of paste. By the time a few days pass, you'll eat anything because there's so little of it. It was terrible, never mind they expect you to take care of your personal business in a bucket. I don't ever want to go back there, if I can help it."

"So, you been Bakered already."

"Bakered?"

Josephine lifts a pot of hot water and dumps it into a washtub sitting on a table. "It's just something we call it 'cause she's the one who decides what happens, and if she's involved in a decision with anyone here, I can tell you now, it ain't ever good."

"She makes me nervous."

"Honey, she makes us all nervous. And drop the Mrs. She ain't worthy of that kind of respect, not amongst us chickens."

At that, Ruth smiles.

Three days later, after she's had the opportunity to listen and learn a little more about the day-to-day operation of the Colony, she quickly comes to a conclusion. Their fancy term of *reform* is nothing more than utilizing them as maids. Each day after breakfast, they're divided into three groups: indoor work, outdoor work, and training or class work. Indoor work is what she's been doing, washing dishes, otherwise it's cooking, cleaning, or laundry. The vocational training is weaving, sewing, or learning how to budget and run a household. Outdoor work ranges from gathering eggs, milking cows, gardening or fieldwork, or repairing something. Personally, Ruth would prefer the outdoor work. She could enjoy fresh air and the sun. Even so, the last thing she wants to do is sit on a stool beside a cow and squirt milk into a bucket.

A week after washing dishes, new assignments are given. Ruth gets her wish for an outdoor job. Weeding. Ruth is a worker, but this whole setup seems like a sham.

"How will this improve me as an individual?"

Mrs. Maynard looks up from her clipboard.

"I see you haven't figured it out yet. It's about discipline and obedience. You need to accept authority, follow instructions, and see a task through to completion. Remember, Miss Foster, this is for your own good. It's to turn you into a good and decent citizen."

Ruth would like to inform anyone who'll listen her life *was* good and decent. What would happen if none of these women did a thing? Held a mutiny? Those in charge go on about "their girls," and how their singular goal is to help them return to society by teaching them appropriate skills. They're doing nothing more than menial labor and, to Ruth's opinion, this serves no one and nothing except those running the Colony. The inmates keep the place functioning, yet to balk means no parole. There's only one way out and that's to do what they're told.

One day an incident occurs that reveals the sincere desperation of some. It's true that not a day goes go by when they're not distracted by a brazen act of one of their own. If something's going to happen, it's always fast, as if the person gets a sudden urge and decides right then to see it through. Ruth is outside with Josephine and several others. They're moving slowly, their bodies sore and stiff as they weed around the dormitory buildings. The odd girl, Freaky Frances—her funny name stemming from her strange tics and outbursts, and skewed stare—takes off running pell-mell across the grounds. Not a sound is made by any of them who watch her go, mainly because most aren't sure what she's up to, but a few seem to know. There's whispering.

"She's gonna do it."

"Damned if she ain't!"

"Again."

"Ain't she ever gonna learn?"

"She thinks she's Lucy Griffin."

Ruth says, "Who's Lucy Griffin?"

Josephine answers. "The prostitute. She's been here several times. She's the best on escapes. She's right over there."

Josephine points her out and Ruth recognizes her and the young girl with her, the one who told her she had to eat everything, but it's Lucy she focuses on. She's the one who signaled her to run the first day she arrived. She might be close to Ruth's age, but looks twice that. The treatments and punishments take a toll. Her condition is the embodiment of months of time in isolation, food deprivation, and the shots, and newcomers, like Ruth, get an unfortunate vision of themselves in the future. Lucy has bruises along her neck, and the back of her arms. If Ruth understands nothing else, it's that in the short time she's been here, intimidation is mighty powerful.

The women straighten their backs, place hands to their foreheads against the sun, and watch Frances, mentally encouraging her. She arrives at the ditch, jokingly called the Clap Trap, because if you can't find a little humor in here, you might as well give up and die. Ruth learned Mr. Lumley filled it with barbed wire years ago at the behest of Baker to discourage this very thing. Ruth saw it for the first time when she was on her way to gather eggs from the hen house, its reputation for snagging unsuspecting victims and holding onto them a thing of legend. It doesn't seem like the best way to escape. Out of nowhere, Mrs. Maynard lets go a distinctive bawl, not unlike the cows they milk, followed by short blasts on the whistle she keeps around her neck. Frances pauses, suddenly unsure.

Mrs. Maynard hollers, "That's right! You better think twice, Frances Platt!"

Frances gawks, her irregular eyes agog, as if she can see every single one of them at once even though they're dispersed about the grounds. She raises her arms above her head, and lets out a strange chortle. She jumps up and down a couple times as if excited. Being the center of attention appears to galvanize her actions. Mrs. Maynard blows her whistle with the fury of a hurricane and proceeds rapidly toward Frances. Her curved spine doesn't hinder her. The women cheer Frances on. Ruth doesn't. She's afraid for her as she runs again, picking up speed. She gives it her all, legs churning, and then comes the great leap of faith. It's not enough. She isn't going to clear the ditch, and her legs stiffen in realization, giving her the appearance she's been electrocuted. Ruth figures it's easy to misjudge distance when you don't have time to think. Frances lands right in the middle, and a few of the women give a collective groan.

Someone says, "Oh no."

Frances tries to lift one leg out of the wire and loses her balance. Down she goes and out comes a little yip of pain. Mrs. Maynard reaches the edge of the ditch and stands there, hands on her hips. She shakes her head while Mr. Lumley, without being told, goes to the tool shed to get the wire cutters. Everyone, including Ruth, goes back to work. No one wants to see what comes next. Most have seen it before and even though Ruth hasn't, it's bad enough listening to Mrs. Maynard berate Mr. Lumley, while Frances whimpers and occasionally squeals like a little pig caught in a trap. Mrs. Maynard has no sympathy for the plight of Frances.

"Serves you right!"

Her usual efficient and controlled manner is knocked for a loop in this high-stress situation that makes her jabber on.

"Dear Lord, it's always something with you! How're we supposed to straighten you out if you keep pulling stupid stunts? What is wrong with you? Why won't you learn?"

Finally, Frances is freed. As she goes by the other women, Ruth cringes at the wet, red scratches decorating her thin arms and legs. Frances snarls at Mrs. Maynard, who grips her arm.

Josephine watches as they go, then continues her story of Lucy. "Lucy, she used to be a real beauty, so some of the others say."

Ruth looks at Lucy again. She's got hair similar to Ruth's, but blue eyes that have gone gloomy and without life. Regardless, the combination is as striking as Ruth's own coloring. Lucy, however, no longer cares much about her appearance. She refuses to take care of herself. Her hair hangs in greasy strands, and her teeth are loose so she's constantly probing about in her mouth with her tongue. Ruth sees nothing of the emboldened behavior described by the others.

"How long has she been here?"

"Only a few months. This time around."

Only? That's a lifetime in a place like this.

Two weeks go by before anyone sees Frances again, and when they do, she's a testament to what happens when someone is taken away for what the staff call *additional rehabilitation*. Ashen, she wanders about the grounds aimlessly, shrugging and jerking oddly. Her lazy eye circles the yard while the other remains fixed and dull, without interest. Ruth begins to assess the others. Some who've been there longer don't look or act much better than poor Frances. It's as if they have no minds of their own. Their hair falls out in clumps, their teeth loosen, their arms and legs are puffy and fat with fluids. They shuffle when they walk like they're ancient, and many appear as if they've lost their way, and are removed from their circumstances. Later that night, in the dorm room, Ruth gazes at her reflection in the mirror, wondering when she'll start to look like them.

Chapter 9

Stella

Mrs. Baker thinks she's a person of worth, one who can reclaim herself, and because of this, she takes the special job ever so seriously, memorizing names with ease, the same way she did the handbook. She's honed in and no one knows. When their talk is boring, she entertains herself concocting little scenes that are exciting to think about. Most are where she impresses Mrs. Baker in some way. Sometimes she imagines the future, where's she's fully redeemed. In her daydreams Mrs. Baker gushes over her, giving her praise, and always in front of the others. These make-believe visualizations run around in her head like mice through the walls of a house, but her best is the one where the superintendent holds her up as an example, bragging about her ability to understand the intentions of reform. *Can't you be like her?* she asks, sweeping a hand toward Stella, who demurely stares down at her spotless brown dress and polished black shoes.

Her special job proves easy because no one suspects her. She takes advantage during free periods and while it's not always good about the housemothers, it's alarming most comments are about Mrs. Baker. Stella quickly learns who the mouthy ones are, like Lucy who thinks the staff are nothing but pawns of Mrs. Baker. What's fascinating is not everyone is necessarily upset at being there. They discuss the Colony in terms of fine, okay, good, and in some cases, say it's better than being at home. Stella agrees on this. After all, she *is* better off. Maude Turner shared her story during their free time the night before.

"My husband, he can't hold a steady job, but let me tell you what he *can* hold: his rotgut liquor. I can't begin to count how many jobs he's done lost. He's hotheaded, which don't help matters none. We have to keep moving around. It ain't been nothing but one thing after another. I guess it won't right for me to get into his drink. 'Cept, law, I was so sad 'bout having no money, again. Drink makes him right happy and I thought to myself, I'd like to be a little happy. I had a bit much, though. Found myself in someone's house. They called the police on me, and next thing I know, I'm getting charged with breaking and entering, and public drunkenness. Fred was fit to be tied. And embarrassed. The cops asked what he wanted to do with me. He told 'em I needed to get brought here. Said someone needed to fix me so I'd do right, be a good wife. Since then, he's sent me here twice. What he don't know is I ain't here 'cause it's what he wants, but 'cause being here is better than being with him."

Several women lean forward in their chairs.

"How'd he learn about here?"

"Prob'ly one'a his drunk friends."

A woman named Gloria says, "Ain't there no place to sort out good-for-nothing husbands?"

That got a round of laughs, while Stella pictured Cordell getting sent somewhere to fix his problem. Maude, with her large brown eyes that peek out from behind pink-framed cat-eye glasses, finishes her story.

"When I get outta here again, I'll find a room to let, and take in some wash, or some sewing. Or I can watch someone's young'uns. I can do housework for some rich lady. I don't need no man telling me what for. After I come here again, I got to thinking, huh, maybe here is the best thing ever to happen to me 'cause I can learn to read, and then do for myself. He'll be sorry when ain't nobody there to get supper on the table, wash his dirty drawers, or mend his shirts.

Sending me off like I don't matter. Like I'm trash to be taken out. He'll see. He'll know when it's too late I *was* a good wife. Can't a woman have sorrows of her own she needs to drown?"

The women sit back, their expressions filled with approval at Maude's plan, and they encourage her.

"That's right, honey."

"He don't deserve you."

"You got some backbone."

Maude gets up.

"I'm going to have me a smoke. Talking about that sonofabitch gets me riled up and in need of a drink, and since that ain't coming, I'll take what I can get."

After Maude leaves, a few women talk about how they were sitting in jail or possibly heading for a workhouse. Some, like Lucy, were suspected of prostitution, or of nothing other than being suspicious-looking. Many complain of sorry husbands and no money to buy food for their families. Most weren't doing anything except living their lives, only to find themselves accused of depravity, disease, or both.

"I was eating supper by myself."

"I won't doing nothing 'cept going down the road to see a friend."

"Me and my friends saw some soldiers near Fort Bragg. They called us over and all we did was talk to 'em."

They complain they aren't being treated fairly, weren't allowed to defend themselves, weren't seen by a judge and given due process. Stella listens carefully. She needs to get past the complaining about how they came to be there, the resentment over work, the moaning about how sick the mercuries make them. She wants to hear the type of information Mrs. Baker needs, or witness something against the rules. What Lucy says next gets Stella's attention.

"Baker needs to spend time in that hellhole she calls meditation. If I could figure out a way to put her in there, I'd sure do it."

Lucy challenges the others, staring at them one by one to see if anyone is willing to join her in this crazy scheme. Some shift about in their seats, and others look away. She gets frustrated.

"Come on! There's more of us. We could grab 'em one by one and stick 'em in those little hellholes."

A few question her logic.

"Then what? Do we stick around or do we leave?

"Wouldn't that make it worse for us in the long run?"

"Yeah, and if we leave, who'd let 'em out?"

Lucy waves her hands around.

"Well hell, I don't know, but I still think it's a good idea. Give 'em a taste of their own medicine."

No one is in agreement on this.

"No way."

"Not if it means worse trouble for me."

"I aim to get out, not stay longer."

Everyone's too nervous, sick, or resigned to do much. Despite their poor home life, many want parole, and they'll go right back to what they had. Only a few mumble they'd love to see Lucy's idea happen. After this, they begin to swap stories of being in the meditation rooms, comparing their experiences as if they're competing who had it worse. What they share about the food, the cold, the condition of the room makes Stella wonder if it's true or an exaggeration. Josephine hasn't said anything, just listened. Stella whispers in her ear.

"You ever been in one of them rooms?"

There's a group setting up the checkerboard and one empty chair left. Someone waves at Josephine and she gets up, moving toward the table.

Over her shoulder she says, "Who hasn't? Everyone gets a turn at some point."

"Not me."

"You ain't been here long enough, and unless you plan to found out, I say don't worry about it."

Before Stella can ask anything else, Josephine calls out, "I'm coming," and hurries away.

Stella sits back, unhappy with nothing to report. No matter what everyone else thinks, she believes in this place, and what she's been told. She believes it's a good thing, and this has become her new gospel. Who else? She looks about. Everyone is absorbed by some activity, or talking with others. She feels conspicuous, self-conscious, left out. She decides to go outside when the woman with the pretty black hair walks in. They come face-to-face and each speak at the same time.

"Excuse me."

"Pardon me."

Stella goes right as she goes left. The dark-haired woman lifts a hand to indicate Stella can go first.

"Please. Go ahead."

Stella slips through the door and as she does, she blurts out, "My name's Stella. Stella Temple."

The woman stares for a split second before she speaks.

"I'm . . ."

Stella interrupts.

"Ruth Foster."

Neither move. Ruth stares at her curiously. Now she's embarrassed because Ruth Foster doesn't seem to know what to think of her. Stella breathes out slow.

"I know everybody's names. How long you been here?"

"I'm not sure. About a month, I think."

"Me too."

She waits to see if Ruth will keep talking, maybe even invite her to sit with her. Ruth doesn't move away, but doesn't extend an invitation either. Stella can't think of anything interesting to say. She's too self-conscious, knowing her hair probably needs a better wash and brushing, and her color is downright ghostly. How is it possible despite wearing exactly the same thing as Stella, Ruth comes off like she does? How can that brown dress look so much better? It's more than that, though. It's her striking green eyes and black shiny hair that's never messy.

Ruth says, "You seem . . ."

The scrutiny by Ruth is intense and Stella's embarrassed for herself. What does Ruth think of her? She cares, but she can't explain why.

Ruth completes the sentence. ". . . young."

Stella's breath escapes, relieved it's not a criticism.

"I was told I'm the youngest one here."

"You're thirteen, fourteen, maybe?"

"I'm fifteen. I'm small for my age."

"Still. That's young. Why're you here? What could you have possibly done?"

Heat builds inside her. She's never been a good liar, but shares a little bit of truth.

"My parents sent me."

What would Ruth think if she knew? Would she think she was repulsive? Sick? *Promiscuous?* Ruth has no reaction. She moves into the parlor and as she does, she states what most everyone has said at some point or another.

"We're going to get out of here. One day. Right?"

Stella dips her head.

"I guess so."

"Of course we will. They can't hold us forever."

She drifts off and begins looking at some books stacked on a table. Stella knows one thing is certain: that might be the goal everyone has, but it's not hers. Hers is the opposite. She wants to be redeemed, stay as long as she can, help Mrs. Baker and make friends. That's her wish list.

The following day she has her first experience reporting something to Mrs. Maynard. She's on her way to the dining hall for breakfast. The same two women who were in the hair-pulling fight from before, who she now knows as Maude and the other is Patsy, are testing one another. Stella can spot trouble brewing because she's always been on the periphery, an observer. Patsy cuts in front of Maude in the food line. Suddenly, they're not single file but shoulder to shoulder, and war is about to erupt. Everyone ignores them, not wanting to become involved, hurrying by to grab their trays and get to a table. Stella walks calmly over to Mrs. Maynard, who's preoccupied talking with a resident. She finishes and gives Stella an icy stare.

"What is it?"

Stella keeps her head down as she discreetly explains.

"There's a problem in the food line."

In seconds, she's back in line and looking anywhere but at the troublemakers. It was exciting because it felt daring. Like those radio shows her father liked to listen to about undercover cops pulling raids on warehouses of liquor. She glances about to see if anyone noticed. No one did. They're watching Mrs. Maynard, who approaches the two women. They stop struggling against one another and Mrs. Maynard speaks to them. Patsy loudly denies she started it. Mrs. Maynard jots something into her tablet, and walks off. She doesn't acknowledge Stella. A fight was surely diverted, and Stella feels important, and helpful.

Above the usual sounds of the dining room, she can hear Lucy at the back of the line. She's complaining about the food they're about to eat, but then she complains about everything, so no one is paying her any mind. Lucy doesn't care who hears her opinions about the Colony, or Mrs. Baker, or the staff in charge of them. Stella doubts she'll ever have to say anything to Mrs. Maynard about her because Lucy says whatever is on her mind, sometimes right to their faces. Stella can't conceive of doing this. She inches forward, her stomach growling with hunger. In front of her are Josephine, Natalie, Melissa, Paula, and Ruth. Lucy continues to gripe about everything under the sun.

"I got more learning in this noggin of mine about life than any of them teachers who've got us in there reading out of children's books."

Lucy's voice is loud and Mrs. Maynard returns.

"Miss Griffin, is there a problem—again?"

Lucy answers the question with one of her own.

"Mrs. Maynard, how many times I been here?"

"There's two answers to that: too many and not enough."

Lucy makes a face at Mrs. Maynard's supposed wit.

"Every time I show up, what happens?"

"What're you getting at, Miss Griffin?"

"I'm making a point."

"I'm not one for guessing games. Humor me."

Lucy juts a hip out and tosses her hair before she turns to see who's around and hearing what she has to say. She gestures with her thumb over her shoulder.

"Baker says it's about improving ourselves."

Mrs. Maynard interrupts.

"You'll speak of our superintendent with respect. It's *Mrs.* Baker."

"Fine."

Lucy doesn't correct herself; she merely picks up where she left off.

"She talks about doing this, that, and the other. Says it'll change us. What would *you* say? Is it working for me?"

Stella sees a transformation when Mrs. Maynard allows her expression to show her repulsion as she moves close to Lucy.

"Some are dumber than a stick and that can't be helped. Some are delinquents, degenerates; others are feebleminded. Some are all of the above, and that makes you a rare case, Miss Griffin."

For once, Lucy doesn't come back with a sassy remark. Stella looks anywhere but in her direction. Lucy's prideful and Mrs. Maynard just put her in her place. When Stella does take a chance to peer over at her, the flush of color to Lucy's cheeks gives away her embarrassment.

Stella wants to get away from Lucy's humiliation and hurries to get a tray of food. This morning it's oatmeal with raisins, orange slices, and coffee. She goes to her usual table and sits in the same chair she's sat in since she arrived. Others come and drop into seats at the same table, but never beside her. It's only when there's no other choice, does anyone ever sit with her. She spoons oatmeal into her mouth and swallows, eating mechanically, her gaze flickering here and there, long enough to observe, never long enough to catch anyone's unwanted attention.

Stella imagines how she appears to others. Dr. Greene, for example, when he meets with her—which isn't as frequent as she thought it would be—pays attention to what she says, but he never responds to her answers, or really looks at her. And here, in this room full of women, no one sees her. They ignore her, a young, small, plain girl with slouched shoulders, holding tight to a little notebook and sometimes chewing on the end of a pencil, as if in deep thought. She's as harmless as they come, a new fixture in their midst, no more obvious than the bowl of flavorless, beige oatmeal she consumes. Maybe less so. She scribbles from time to time, some of it nonsense. If anyone were to peek over her shoulder, they might be a bit curious about some of the cryptic notes they would see, but no one ever does.

Chapter 10

Baker

The American Plan is on the up and up, once again. Oh, she'd seen signs of it back in 1939 when she'd read in a newspaper about the Germans bombing a Polish village, and after France and England began to move troops about to prepare for war. Roosevelt pronounced the United States neutral, only the communication that followed declared a "limited national emergency." This enabled his armed forces to add one hundred thousand men to its ranks. It didn't take long for various government branches to grow concerned over new recruits becoming infected with venereal diseases. It happened in WWI, and it could happen again. It's Baker's mainstay, her focus to do her part in keeping their community free of disease. It's job security.

As it is, with the heightened awareness of the ever-escalating conflict overseas, she's assured of her role continuing. She's quite proud of the part she plays. An important one, to be sure. She's required to report to the North Carolina Board of Corrections and the Colony Board of Directors, not to mention the governor and General Assembly, meaning influential people know of her and what she's about. After her first biennial report with its showcase of frugal expenditures and appropriations, she had a chance to brag on her sharp accounting skills and savvy savings knowledge. It impressed the board, so much so she was allotted the funds she'd requested to build the superintendent's cottage.

With that success in mind, it's her plan to take another bold risk and request funds to support the building of two new dormitories. From Baker's perspective, it's not an unreasonable request. How is she to keep dangerous women off the streets if she doesn't have enough space? Her capacity to persuade is notable and while it's exciting to think of doubling the Colony's size, there's a lot of work to do to get everyone in agreement. This is why, for the staff meeting this morning, she's trying to sweeten the pot by putting out refreshments. Her staff meetings are generally very quick, all business and nothing more. Today, she'll see if she can persuade them to agree to her expansion idea. The challenge is each of them has made their own demands about what they want and she'll probably have a fight on her hands. The last meeting ended in a stalemate. She wipes a smudge off the table holding coffee and pastries, paid for out of her own pocket. Mrs. Maynard and Mrs. Dillard are the first to arrive.

"Good morning," Baker says pleasantly.

"Good morning," responds Mrs. Dillard.

"Oh, this is nice," says Mrs. Maynard as she helps herself to coffee and a raspberry tart.

Mrs. Dillard does too, and then they seat themselves. Nurse Crawford comes in, followed by Dr. Greene and Dr. Graham, and last are two domestic sciences instructors and two classroom teachers. Greetings are repeated, and everyone appears pleasantly surprised by the refreshments.

Baker points at the food and says, "Please, help yourselves."

Jericho Lumley arrives last, smelling of manure, and Baker casts a distasteful glance at him. Without hesitation, he grabs a pastry, a cup of coffee, then sits in her finest chair, and she cringes at the thought she'll smell manure for days on end. She stands by her desk and opens the meeting following *Robert's Rules of Orders*, the well-regarded guide to parliamentary procedures. They proceed with minutes, read by Mrs. Dillard, the treasurer's report read by Wanda

Perkins, and then it's on to old business. This is what Baker must suffer through, a litany of their old requests. Mrs. Maynard is first.

"As stated before, we could use some additional linens, towels, and such. We need new dresses, underwear, socks, and shoes. Even though our girls do a wonderful job to mend and repair the current stock, everything is becoming quite worn out. On the maintenance side we need work done on one of the lavatories on the first floor. We have a slow toilet. We don't need it to overflow and cause damage to the floor. Last, we had one make parole and one return."

Mrs. Dillard stands and provides a list much like Mrs. Maynard's, with similar requests for clothing. She preens a little at her next update.

"Two residents made parole and no one has been sent back."

Baker holds up a finger.

"This means we have capacity for two more?"

"Yes, Mrs. Baker."

"Well, the county will be happy to hear that."

The rest share their reports. Everyone repeats the list of their needs. Dr. Graham insists a small onsite operating room for abortions and sterilizations is paramount. Dr. Greene demands more office space. The teachers need additional supplies to include paper, pencils, textbooks, and notebooks. Nurse Crawford lists medical supplies, cough syrups, aspirin, bandages, and other medications. Mr. Lumley talks about the farm equipment falling apart, the need for additional storage buildings. The vocational teachers want newer sewing machines, canning equipment, not to mention a cold storage room. Finally, they've exhausted their demands. Baker circles the floor, wondering how to begin. The only way is to simply state facts.

"New business? Anyone?"

The staff glance at the floor, at one another, and no one speaks up with anything new to present. Mr. Lumley's offer is to persistently belch under his breath. Baker moves on.

"I have something I'd like to propose. Let me repeat what I've said before because it's worth it. I'm quite pleased with our residents' overall progress. I feel confident, whatever their downfalls, they're on an honorable path. Whatever might go wrong with an individual's life can be fixed, it *will* be fixed as long as they choose to learn and listen, to follow the guidance given them by those of us here. It's quite simple. Our methods utilize practical experiences meant to lead them to successful reentry into society, and the more we can offer this service, the better."

Here she pauses, waiting for agreement. She doesn't expect anything other than that because it's common sense. Glances are exchanged, but she doesn't let that stop her.

"I've seen it, you have too, how a damaged individual becomes an asset instead of a hindrance. Why, it's almost guaranteed. They can emerge as a reclaimed individual made whole again, like being reborn, some have even said. Here's what I propose. I'll request certain residents write letters about the training and education they're receiving. These missives can go into a special report, outside of the usual biennial submission. It's important the higher-ups hear of our successes straight from the horse's mouth, so to speak. Does everyone agree?"

At this, heads wag in affirmation. She beams at them and plunges ahead.

"These letters will fortify the earlier request I made for the appropriation of funds for two new dormitories. After all, wouldn't you agree it's best women aren't sent to jail for nonviolent crimes? In my opinion, placing them into that environment is doing them a great disservice. If my request is approved, there should be enough for what most of you want and need. There are ways to ensure that, if you understand my meaning?"

Now their eyes are wide, unblinking. She doesn't miss how they each gauge the possibility of her proposal and their own needs. Baker tenses when Dr. Greene shakes his head.

"It would seem more realistic to make a request that's less costly, perhaps, instead of that. Like office space instead of something so extravagant, for God's sake. They've been tight-fisted the past few years."

Baker pushes back.

"I think if we make the case with the successes through the letters, they'll sit up and pay attention."

Dr. Greene is bent on making a point.

"What's the total population now?"

"At last count we had forty-four residents, after two went out on parole. It's always fluctuating, with some leaving, and some returning. With today's report, it appears we have forty-two, and space for two more."

Dr. Greene raises his brows.

"The letters mean nothing. It's the numbers and unless there's a higher turnover and no returns, I don't see how it matters."

Dr. Graham adds his opinion.

"Actually, the real number is how many were here in total from the beginning of this establishment, how many new have come in, how many returned from previous times, and how many didn't. That's the real picture."

Baker is forced to establish her view, which won't matter to them.

"Everyone works at their own pace. Some need more time. We're not dealing with the most educated people here, remember."

They nitpick over the best way to present success. She grows frustrated. They sound like a bunch of squabbling hens. Can't they just agree with her and move on? No one understands the magnitude of what she's attempting to accomplish. Dr. Greene ought to know as he's involved almost every day with the minds of these women. Even a single success is better than none. It doesn't matter how long it takes. Every promiscuous, diseased, and immoral woman is worth the effort, even if they somehow manage to find themselves right back at the beginning. Baker has steadfast faith her way works. She shuts down the meeting by going around to her desk and taking a seat. She looks at her watch, and interrupts the debate.

"Thank you for your time and input on this matter. Have a good week."

She's so abrupt, they're uncertain of what just took place. One by one they get up and file out. When the room is empty, she goes to her window. Her gut bubbles uncomfortably. Sometimes working with staff is as complicated and difficult as dealing with residents. The individuals who return for additional training certainly frustrate her. You'd think they'd do everything in their power to avoid coming back after she's done with them. She tries to make sure nothing appears out of line, or off-kilter, a method that might push boundaries and end with a result like Samarcand. That consistently looms before her, a specter she can't exorcise.

She stares out at the women working in their neutral-colored uniforms. It presents such a bucolic scene, she's reassured once again what she's doing is right. To the casual observer, the wholesomeness of such a view where backs are bent over rows of vegetables is evidence their minds are healing, as well as their bodies. The Colony's mandate is to teach these women how to keep a proper home, clean and organized. No slovenly behaviors. Manners are a must. There's vocational work like canning and preserving, gathering of eggs and milk, a multitude of tasks to position women for success in their own households.

If there's a forlorn, melancholy air about the place, it's because she expects each to take their time here seriously. They need to approach this as a chance they've been given. In the end, the betterment of broken lives comes at a cost, both physical and mental. Oftentimes someone like Ruth Foster must learn the hard way, through force. Through deprivation. Through pain. It takes commitment to reshape stubborn thinking, to hone the habits that build character. Sometimes, it takes form through control. Perceived cruelty. An impression of calculated coldness. Unbending meets the unwilling. Being "Bakered," the residents call it, of all things. They don't understand her, or her efforts, but surely they must know that in the end, all she wants is what's best for them.

Chapter 11

Ruth

Every morning Ruth awakes, it takes a second before she remembers where she is. Her reason to get up is to get through another day and put herself one step closer to getting out. Mrs. Maynard comes to the door, blasting her whistle as usual, but on this morning, she gets their attention when she makes an unusual request.

"Ladies! We have a few disciplinary issues to address. Line up and be quick about it!"

They do as asked and with haste because everyone is always extra-obedient when something out of ordinary happens, especially if it means trouble. As soon as they're standing at the foot of their cots, she begins reading through a very detailed list of infractions. The list includes names, what they did or didn't do. It involves tardiness to meals or other time-driven tasks, as well as beds with sheets not pulled tight and smooth, instances of rudeness, not completing chores to standards, and more. Some of the same names have multiple offenses and demerits add up.

The women look at one another in disbelief. There have been slips in behavior before and they've gone undetected. It's expected because housemothers can't keep a watch over every single person at every single moment, so inmates get a little lax from time to time.

Desperate glances bounce around the room. They wait for what's to come, already defeated before the day has begun. Mrs. Maynard eyes the mass of despondent and hopeless humans. She points one by one to those who've earned enough violations to be punished while warnings are issued to those pushing their luck. As the worst of the wrongdoers are separated from the rest, verbal protests begin. They complain it's underhanded, sneaky, trapping them unaware. Many thought they'd got away with a little slipup or two, or, that they were doing fine.

"I didn't know I had that many."

"Why wasn't I told like before?"

"It sure don't seem fair to me!"

The last remark is from Lucy. Mrs. Maynard clucks.

"You best watch out, Miss Griffin. You're getting close to being one of those who needs discipline."

Mrs. Maynard claps her hands again, her manner all businesslike.

"The rest of you, get yourselves ready for your day. No one is to be late to breakfast, or to your assigned work or classes. Remember, ladies, doing what's necessary is how you earn parole!"

Josephine leans in close and whispers to Ruth.

"This is crazy. We're not children with no say-so. Who do they think they are?"

Mrs. Maynard smacks her hands together and raises her voice.

"Hurry it up and no talking!"

Ruth mentally agrees with Josephine, and sends Lucy a look, admiring her devil-may-care attitude. Ruth's days in meditation keep her from being so bold. Those whose names were called follow Mrs. Maynard out of the dorm. Melissa, one of Josephine's boarders, is among them, and she casts a tragic look over her shoulder at Josephine, Natalie, and Paula. Freaky Frances is also in the group, and begins to obsessively pull at the skin of her cheeks. Ruth is nervous for this group, especially the odd girl who's barely had the chance to get over the debacle of her attempted run. Her distressed behavior bothers her and Josephine shakes her head as she watches Melissa disappear.

"I done told Melissa she won't making her bed good enough for drill sergeant Maynard."

"What do you think will happen?"

"Maude Turner told me she had to hold someone down from Dorm B for a whipping. Said it's intended as a lesson so no one else makes the same mistake."

Ruth can't believe this happens too. What else goes on in this place? They can hear Mrs. Maynard yelling at Frances. Josephine finishes making her bed and hurries over to the dorm door.

"They went left, to the basement. That's where they do it."

Ruth frowns at her.

"That's where the meditation rooms are too. I can't believe they'd beat people."

"Ask Lucy."

Lucy is pulling on her sheets with rough, quick motions. She's two beds away from Ruth, and she tugs and straightens and smooths. When she's done, she stares across the space at Ruth.

"I saw you that day. When you first came. You sure didn't get very far."

"No."

"I hate this place more'n I can say. I'll run again, and next time is the last time, one way or the other."

"How many times have you done that?"

"Least half a dozen. Sure, they're gonna whip 'em. And yes, they done it to me. Here's something you can tuck away for your sweet dreams at night. Mrs. Maynard? She likes it. Sometimes she does the whipping. Sometimes she stands off to the side and watches. She likes watching, it excites her. After all, I know what lust looks like."

Lucy raises the hem of her nightgown to reveal a few healing pale pink streaks along the back of her thighs. Ruth is sickened by something so debase, as well as the brutality of Lucy's scars. Lucy lowers the material and spins around, startling a loitering Stella.

"What're you doing? Git! Git over there!"

Lucy claps her hands loudly in Stella's face and Stella backs away, flustered.

"I . . . I . . ."

She holds out a pair of white socks. Lucy shoves her hand away.

"Those ain't mine, and you well know it. I have mine. Git on away from here!"

"Oh. I . . ."

"Git. Over. There."

Stella scurries back to her side of the room and busies herself making her bed, face hidden by her hair. Lucy throws a hand in her direction, watching with squinted, suspicious eyes. She returns her gaze to Ruth and speaks in a low voice.

"Be careful 'round that one. I don't trust her. I've seen her listening in and acting like she ain't."

"Stella? She's so young. Why is she even in here? What on earth could she have done?"

"That soft heart won't get you nowhere, and being naïve won't neither. Haven't you heard a word I've said?"

"Naïve? I don't consider myself that."

"You ain't been out in the world, not like me, anyway. There's all kinds, and you don't know what anyone's capable of when they're only looking out for themselves. I've seen it all, believe me. As to little Miss Goody, I work with her in the laundry. Sure, she's young, and she also thinks Baker means well." Lucy steps closer to Ruth, blue eyes gone flinty. "Do you think Baker means well?"

"I don't know. I guess she's only doing her job."

Lucy gapes, then she starts laughing. She lays her hands on her belly and guffaws. Several women glance their way and Ruth gets offended.

"What's so doggone funny?"

"Doing her *job*? Exactly what is her job? Superintendent she ain't. This is a prison, though they want to make sure it's not called that. I guess they can toss me into the slammer for what I do, but you? What did you do? What do you reckon most of these women did? Look at 'em. You ask 'em how it happened to them and what they'll say is they did nothing wrong. They're ordinary women, somebody's mother, wife, sister, daughter, aunt." Lucy softens. "Listen.

That's what we are, ordinary women, although I do count myself as a bit exceptional."

She swerves her hips in an exaggerated manner, spins on her heels, and her nightgown floats about her form, diaphanous, and Ruth sees not only her beauty as it once was, but the danger—or threat—she would pose to someone like Baker. Lucy resumes her lecture.

"One day you're going about your business and next thing you know, you're here because you're 'diseased.'"

She isn't saying anything Ruth doesn't already know, but Ruth's goal is to get along best as she can until she's allowed to leave. Lucy sighs and waves a hand at her in a dismissive way. The dorm is a beehive of activity as hurried footsteps move along the hardwood floors on the way to the bathroom and back. Low-level conversations, questions of how someone slept and other routine interactions, albeit subdued, resume. Beneath the mundane chatter, judgments are made by each individual in the dorm room. The women are filled with suspicion about who among them is the betrayer. Ruth is careful as she studies Stella. Is Lucy onto something about Stella, or is it someone else eavesdropping and spying on behalf of the staff?

Ever since Ruth spent those first few days in meditation, she's made it through the subsequent days unscathed. She's made sure to blend in, their identical dull-brown dresses easing the effort while robotically following orders, demands, and routines. She feels lucky to be excluded from punishment because she knows of a time or two when she *was* late, if only by a few seconds, to a couple of meals. There was another time she forgot to drop her dirty clothing down the laundry chute. She remembers now it was returned to her by Stella, washed and folded, with a timid smile. Maybe Lucy is right and it's Stella, but there are others ripe for causing trouble given the constant undercurrent and apparent competitiveness for favoritism. She's been privy to some heated arguments, and even a discreet pummeling a time or two, after lights were out.

For the most part, everyone tries to get along. It's no easy feat when the majority of them aren't feeling well, are distraught or disgruntled given the workload they're mandated to do, as if they're healthy and without ailments. Some are depressed about how they're somehow considered flawed and a danger to society, while others see it as an opportunity to get away from desolate households and hateful husbands. All are expected to participate with amity, project happiness, and to act grateful for this "opportunity" to better themselves. The results are mixed.

After last-minute adjustments to their bedmaking and with faces washed, teeth brushed, and dressed so they represent what is expected by the Colony staff, the women file out and head to the dining hall. Each of them is compelled to double-check the state of their personal area as they leave the dormitory, praying nothing of theirs is out of place whenever Mrs. Maynard returns to inspect it herself. Ruth falls in behind Lucy and they file down the hall alongside Mrs. Dillard, who shows up to escort them. Ruth feels like she's back in grade school.

"While Mrs. Maynard attends to the problem at hand this morning, I'll be keeping an eye on you, so please mind yourselves, ladies. Let this be an example that we take every action of yours very seriously, as you should. Reform won't happen if you backslide."

Ruth gets her tray of food, but her appetite isn't there. She nibbles at a biscuit, and picks at the scrambled eggs. She's required to eat everything, somehow. Close to the end of the thirty minutes they're allowed for breakfast, she's managed to swallow most of it down, but the food remains unsettled in her gut. There's a commotion near the entrance of the dining hall as those who were taken away file back in. Melissa's face is tear-streaked while Frances has stopped pulling at her face, but is now making strange noises, her distress bubbling out of her mouth in snorts and gasps. The others, two women Ruth doesn't know, have flaming faces filled with fury.

This group is handed their trays of food and Ruth takes note Stella is the only one not paying attention to them. Her head is down and she's intent on tracing her empty tray with a finger. Mrs. Maynard addresses those who were punished.

"You have five minutes to eat. I suggest you hurry it up."

The housemother dabs a handkerchief at her upper lip. She looks different somehow, her color high, her eyes bright. Ruth turns in her chair and finds Lucy staring at her from across the room. She dips her head, as if to say, *See?* Melissa sits gingerly beside Josephine, and across from Lucy and Ruth. Her face is pale and her hands shake as she picks up her fork. Josephine rubs Melissa's arm.

"You okay?"

Melissa shakes her head. A sudden, loud racket to the right of their table causes everyone to turn as one. Scrambled eggs and grits slide down the wall. Frances, her chest heaving up and down, her hands clenched, is near the mess. She begins wailing, the sound escalating until many cover their ears. She begins hitting herself, punching her forehead, her chest, her stomach, and her thighs. Her arms flail, and she behaves as if she's become infused with uncontrollable energy. Her fists strike her body creating a dull *thump*, growing faster and faster. The sound is as bad as her yowling. But when Frances digs her fingernails into her cheeks and drags them down her face, leaving vivid red scratches, every single woman in the dining hall reacts.

"No!"

"Somebody stop her!"

"Frances! Don't!"

Mrs. Maynard rushes toward the stricken girl, blowing her whistle. In between the shrill blasts, she yells Frances's name.

"Frances Platt, control yourself! You're going to get more demerits! Frances! Frances Platt!"

There is no controlling Frances, not when she's gone out of her mind. Frances lunges at Mrs. Maynard, hands extended, fingers curved into dangerous little weapons that can tear someone else's skin instead of hers. Everyone jumps to their feet as Frances lurches toward the housemother. There are whispers that Frances has really gone off her rocker this time, and no one knows what to do. There was a time before when an inmate attacked another inmate with a fork and a few of them jumped in to help, which only escalated the situation. They were told never to do that again, so they stand by and watch, and Ruth does the same.

Frances plows into Mrs. Maynard, whose bent posture makes her move awkwardly. The impact sends her stumbling backward. Her balance thrown off, she comes close to falling, but reaches out at the last minute and saves herself by bracing a hand on a table. Frances comes for her again. Mrs. Maynard whips a chair in front of herself to keep Frances from reaching her, like how an animal tamer would manage a wild lion.

She yells at the bystanders, "Do something!" perhaps forgetting the rules she implemented herself.

Frances, quick and agile as a rabbit, gets around the chair and Mrs. Maynard bends and covers her face with her hands. But it's not Mrs. Maynard's face Frances is after, or to even hit her. She lunges for the gold chain hanging around Mrs. Maynard's neck. Ruth reacts to Mrs. Maynard's screech to "do something!" and gets behind Frances, but as soon as she touches her shoulders to pull her away, Frances turns her head and tries to bite her. Ruth jerks her hands back and emits a little squeak of fear. Frances turns back to Mrs. Maynard, who fights to keep her from getting hold of the chain where the cherished whistle is attached. Frances, her hair half in her face, her reddened eyes giving her an extra-demented look, stretches out her thin arms, reaching, reaching, reaching. Her thin, bony body defies its appearance and is actually very strong. She gets hold of the chain and begins to haul Mrs. Maynard around the dining hall.

The women yell and it's hard to tell if they're cheering or shrieking for Frances to stop. A crowd of them follows while others continue to sit at the tables finishing up their meals, as if this is entertainment. Those trailing behind the fracas can't do much. No one wants to get near the girl, and some mumble how they know from past experience France needs to unwind in her own way, and woe to anyone who doesn't allow this. Mrs. Maynard stumbles along in a wide circle, until, with a vicious final yank, Frances manages to get the chain over Mrs. Maynard's head, and in doing so, snags her hair—which turns out not to be her hair, but a wig.

Mrs. Maynard emits a little "Oh!" and claps hands over the frizzy white hair on her scalp.

Meanwhile, Frances morphs into a nymph, a renegade Pied Piper. She frolics and skips out of the dining hall, blasting little tweets on the whistle while waving the wig over her head before slapping it on. She chortles with glee. Ruth is first out of the dining hall and the first to see the strutting Frances blasting erratic tweets from the whistle, the wig riding low and crooked on her head. She disappears around the corner. Mrs. Maynard, semi-recovered from her ordeal, pushes by Ruth, who thinks the poor woman looks every bit like an ostrich. Mr. Lumley, tucked away in a back corner of the dining hall, eating his breakfast and reading the newspaper when pandemonium broke out, whizzes by Ruth to assist with the contrary Frances.

Before they get the chance, Baker shows up, holding Frances by her arm, and Ruth witnesses something she won't ever forget it. First of all, Frances is as docile as a senior cat. She's no longer fighting and when Mrs. Baker releases her arm and holds out her hand, Frances blows one last little soft "tweet," and calmly hands the whistle over. Mrs. Baker takes it and waits. Without any prompting, off comes the wig, and that too is handed over meekly. Mrs. Baker returns the items to Mrs. Maynard, who tries to explain the incident. The superintendent shakes her head as if she'd prefer not to know. And then, of all things, Frances grins at Ruth and winks. Ruth is startled by this conspiratorial behavior, but her response is to bestow a hesitant smile toward the quirky girl. Mrs. Baker dusts her hands off, and calmly speaks as if nothing out of the ordinary has taken place.

"Mrs. Maynard, get these women working or in their classes, and then report to my office."

"Yes, Mrs. Baker."

As they disperse to their appropriately assigned areas, Ruth whispers to Josephine, "I don't think Frances is as nutty as they think she is."

Josephine smiles.

"She's not. She goes nuts like this every so often; it's her temper she can't seem to control. I heard it's why she's here. Her parents couldn't handle her."

"That's so sad, but why here?"

"No room at the insane asylum, I guess."

"How did you find out all this?"

"Frances told me. She'd rather be here than in that place. But don't say nothing."

Ruth is so astonished words would fail her anyway.

Chapter 12

Stella

Stella suffers a bout of terrible guilt for what happened to the ones she reported, but this is quickly overshadowed when Mrs. Maynard informs her she's to meet with the superintendent.

"I'll take you to Mrs. Baker's office. You're to be there at three sharp."

"Yes, Mrs. Maynard."

"Take that, that little pad thing you scribble in."

Mrs. Maynard sounds mad at her, and Stella is certain she must be in trouble. She opens her mouth to ask if she is, but Mrs. Maynard doesn't give her a chance.

"Back to work!"

Stella hurries away and when she enters the steamy, soap-and-starch-scented basement area, Lucy spins around and glares at her. Stella goes to work, but she can feel her watching. The hairs rise on her arms and neck as she starts going through the dirty clothing, towels, sheets, and whatever else the housemothers think needs cleaning, and toss down the laundry chute to land in the big bin in the basement where Stella now sorts. There's anger in the silence and Stella gets hot around her neck, and actually doesn't feel so great. Her belly's been aching a bit. Maybe her monthly is finally coming on.

"You're late."

"I am?"

"Jot that down in your little notebook, why don't you."

Stella flushes and lowers her head to concentrate on the dirty underwear. Lucy goes on a tangent.

"Here's something that'll interest you. One day you're gonna wake up and it'll be, 'Where's Lucy Griffin?' Make a note of that."

Stella drops underwear into the basket intended for extra soaking, and turns to the dresses. She focuses on an imaginary spot, or thread, or wrinkle she needs to fix, though there's nothing in particular she sees.

"You hear me?" Lucy persists.

"Yes."

"Go on, then. I want to see you write it down."

"I'm not . . . What do you mean?"

"What do I mean. What do I mean. You *know* what I mean."

Stella is terrible at lying, but she tries.

"No, I don't."

"Well. Who could've guessed? Goody's a liar *and* a snitch. I can see it in your face. I can't stand liars. Or snitches. Maybe Goody's not the right name for you."

"I'm not a liar."

"It's Baker, isn't it? She put you up to being her little snitch? That would be like her. I might be more inclined to understand, if so. But after what happened to Melissa and the rest, I ain't so sure it's a good enough excuse."

"Wh-what happened to Melissa?"

"You know. You saw. You heard. Ask yourself how you feel about being the one to cause it."

"I didn't do nothing."

"Sure you did. They got group punishment, thanks to you."

Stella fidgets with a dangling thread on a hem. Lucy exhales loudly and Stella tries to explain her ignorance again.

"I ain't heard nothing. I saw them leave the dorm, but you made me stay on the other side of the room when y'all was talking."

"Listen up, then, to what you caused. Baker's creative in her ways to remind us what can happen if we don't toe the line. Those in trouble get beat by those who're borderline in trouble. If they don't do it, then they get it too. It's a warning."

"That ain't true."

"You think I'm lying? I ought to know, but I'd rather take a licking than be the reason someone else gets it, especially if they've done nothing to me. I seen you creeping around with that little book of yours, always listening in, pretending innocence."

Stella has to make up something, anything.

"It's a diary."

Which is sort of the truth. Lucy snorts with derision.

"A diary, huh. Prove it."

"I don't have it. I keep it hid away. Ain't nobody supposed to see what's in it 'cept me. That's how diaries work."

Lucy rolls her eyes. She seems tired all of a sudden and drops the subject. She resumes her work, mumbling under her breath. From that point on, she ignores Stella, who moves to her own worktable. She doesn't like what Lucy told her. She's not sure she believes her either. That's not what the handbook says. If anyone gets demerits, they do extra chores. Or maybe get deprived of a meal. If they do something worse, like try to run away, they're sent to meditation. Meditation means you sit and think about what you did wrong. None of those things seem so bad.

The best thing she can do is keep to herself, and not talk to Lucy until she gets over her mood. Mrs. Baker asked for Stella's help and it makes her feel important, like she matters. Also, it's part of her reform, so she has to do it. Mrs. Baker believes in her, wants her to get redeemed. She said so. The new Stella will be able to live a normal life, meaning maybe one day she'll get married, have children of her own. The more she thinks of this, the more she believes this is her destiny, to have a good family to make up for how her own turned out. She might even allow Alice to visit, but she won't have anything to do with Cordell. She'll live her life differently, loving her children with all her might, and her husband will love her and cherish her. He won't be mean and say hateful things. Lucy comes near and Stella's dream fizzles. She hunches her shoulders, waiting to see what she's going to say next.

"See that pile of dresses?"

With relief, Stella looks to where Lucy points. In the farthest corner of the laundry room is another worktable with the dresses stacked on top.

"Yes."

"Can you sew?"

"I know how to sew buttons on, and I can do hems and tears."

"Go over there and fix them dresses."

Stella walks to the table in the corner. Here, she's as far as she can get from the prostitute while still in the same room. She's certain it's intentional. Lucy's temper makes Stella tense, similar to the way she was at home when Alice was out of sorts, or when Cordell wanted to pick an argument. Her parents shaped how her days would go. Good days were when she was ignored, especially by Cordell. Bad days were when they argued about Alice never doing anything, her health, or when Cordell descended on Stella. It's an atmosphere she hated, and for the first time since coming to the Colony, she's fearful. She bends her head to the work. As she goes through the morning, she's aware she hurts all over, mainly in her lower abdomen. There's no clock in the laundry room, but the door to the outside is open, even if it too is on the other side. At least she can see the sun shining. She sits in the corner shivering, wishing she had a sweater to put on.

Lucy appears to entertain herself with her private thoughts, laughing out loud periodically. Stella would like to ask what's so funny, but she doubts the prostitute would tell her. Stella's used to fading into the background and this is what she does. When it's time for noon dinner, she waits until Lucy leaves the laundry room before rising slowly, her entire body aching. In the dining hall, she goes through the line, then finds a spot where the sun is coming in through the windows. Josephine, Melissa, Natalie, and Paula watch her, but mostly Melissa. She shifts on the hard chair as if sitting is uncomfortable. Lucy's nearby, and sits by herself, radiating rage that discourages other diners—that, or she's told them to sit somewhere else.

Stella places herself in the warmth of the sun beaming in through the windows. Her shivering doesn't stop, but it's not as bad. The smell of the hamburger patties, rice with gravy, and peas waft up to her nose, making her stomach gurgle in a funny way. She begins to eat, ignoring her misery. It tastes all right, but when the food is half gone, her entire body starts to react, from the aches to the shivering to her stomach rebelling. She fights to keep a normal appearance, to act as if nothing's the matter. The atmosphere isn't helping. The dining hall is quieter than usual. She can sense them, everyone. Staring at her. She continues the motions of chewing, swallowing, and repeating out of necessity. Mrs. Maynard wanders by and stops directly behind her. Stella's right arm turns to wood, her movements unnatural. Her midsection is in turmoil. It wants to reject what she's eaten. Mrs. Maynard doesn't go away and Stella gives up. She places her fork beside the tray, and puts her hands in her lap. She's sick. She can tell.

Mrs. Maynard says, "Pick that utensil up right this minute and keep eating, or you'll get demerits."

Stella does as she's told, and Mrs. Maynard stays behind her. Stella breaks out in a sweat. It's as if the food she consumes is expanding into an enormous, unappetizing mass. She stops again, presses her hand over her mouth, like a dam holding in water. Mrs. Maynard erupts, her voice tight with irritation.

"What're you doing? Eat. Eat! Clean that plate, or that's more demerits and no supper!"

Stella intends to speak, to respond verbally because that's what's mandatory, and instead of words coming out, it's a forceful spew of icky lumps. The regurgitated food lands in a sickening mess on what's left in her tray, and in her lap. Mrs. Maynard zips around to the other side of the table to face her. The dining hall descends into a tomblike silence. Mrs. Maynard stammers in horror.

"Wh-why didn't you say you were unwell?"

Stella can't decide if it was Mrs. Maynard and her disagreeable, hostile presence, or something else, but whatever the cause, her stomach rejecting the food offers no real relief. There's a sour odor rising up from her lap and it doesn't help either. She grabs her napkin in a futile attempt to rid her dress of the rank smell.

Mrs. Maynard says, "Stop! It's useless to clean it that way. Turn your tray in, go change, and report back to me here." Mrs. Maynard holds up her arm with the wristwatch. "You have five minutes. Do *not* be late."

This time Stella's able to get the words out.

"Yes, ma'am."

She stands, picks up the disastrous tray, and crosses the room. As she maneuvers around the other tables, every woman watches her and there's a low hum of voices. She refuses to slow down, much less look at any of them. She has five minutes. She drops the tray off and hears a reaction from those in the kitchen.

"Yuck!"

"Who did this? Is this a joke?"

Stella hurries out, runs across the yard and into the dorm building. In the room she lifts the lid of her storage box and gets out a clean dress. She has to pull the soiled garment over her head and gags at the smell. She does what she can to avoid her hair, yet ends up with some of the gunk in it. She drops the dirty dress on the floor and slips the clean one over her head. She buttons it up, and picks up the soiled one and carries it with her out of the room. Does she have time to get to the bathroom to rinse her hair? Should she drop her dress down the laundry chute? She can't stand the smell coming off her, but doesn't dare take the time. If she gets any demerits, Mrs. Baker might think she's not worth the trouble anymore. She could send her back home, a lost cause, beyond redemption. She can picture Mrs. Maynard standing in the doorway of the dining area. Waiting. Timing her. She's seen a similar scenario before. It didn't take her long to learn Mrs. Maynard's ways.

The Colony's clocks, and there are plenty, are reminders of the importance of punctuality. She passes one and has less than a minute. She dashes down the steps of the dormitory, across the yard, to burst through the door of the main building. As she hurries along, her stomach is still in knots, and those knots cinch tighter at the sight of Mrs. Maynard, who is staring at her wrist and shaking her head. A cluster of women wait behind her at the door, unable to return to work or their classes because she's blocking it, most likely on purpose because Mrs. Maynard loves using opportune moments as examples.

". . . three, two, one," she counts down.

And yet, Stella isn't quite there. She isn't standing directly in front of the housemother. She didn't make it, and her lower belly pounds in time with her heart, the odd discomfort rising to the point she feels the need to double over. She places her hand over the spot and stops before Mrs. Maynard, out of breath and sweaty.

"Miss Temple. You're late by fifteen seconds. That's three demerits, and another three more for the vomit I can clearly see still in your hair. This will go on your record, and I'll make certain Mrs. Baker knows."

"Y-yes, ma'am."

Mrs. Maynard spins on her heels and without a word leaves the women to do as they're scheduled. Stella creeps down to the basement, dirty dress clutched in her hand. She goes to her corner, tosses it under her chair and begins sewing a hem, the garment swimming before her eyes. Lucy comes in and Stella doesn't look up, or speak. She sits in a tight ball, shoulders hunched, giving a bit of relief to the dull ache rising and ebbing in the lower half of her stomach. She dreads three o'clock. Lucy bangs around the room as usual and before long, the washing machine is going. Stella breathes deep the smell of soap, which is almost strong enough to overtake the stink in her hair.

"Gimme that nasty dress."

Stella looks up.

"What?"

"Gimme your dress!"

"I can wash it."

"Maybe, but I know how to get it clean."

Stella reaches down to pick up the dress from where she dropped it by her chair. She hesitates, embarrassed to hand it to Lucy, who makes an impatient gesture. Stella gives it to her and watches as she takes it to the utility sink and drops it in. She runs cold water, and then pours in some baking soda, and vinegar. She waves Stella over.

"C'mere. I'll teach you somethin'."

Stella walks over and looks into the sink. There's a bubbling foam, and the smell of vinegar clears her head and she slowly inhales deeply. Lucy gets the wood stick she keeps propped by the large utility sink and stirs the dress about like she's cooking a vat of soup.

"It's how I clean lots of things. Nothing better'n good old vinegar and baking soda."

Stella learned long ago to stay quiet when Cordell would get to talking. This was how she found out things she needed to know. It works like this with Lucy too. Lucy continues sloshing the water about and after a few minutes she lifts the dress out.

"That ought to do it for a bit of a soak. Now, I'll go on and wash it regular."

Stella wants to go sit down, and get back to the mending because she's not herself and she doesn't know what's wrong. Lucy, ignorant to this fact, apparently wants to talk.

"I ought to remember you ain't so old. You ain't nuthin' but a young'un, yet."

Stella, ever suspicious of unexpected kindness, has no reaction. Lucy slaps a hand against the washer when it starts making a loud squeaking sound. She stands with her hands on her hips and cocks her head, studying Stella, who has gone back to shivering.

"Ruth said you're like a little hungry puppy, lookin' for scraps."

Stella doesn't care. She's going downhill quick and searches for an adequate response.

"Miss Ruth said that?"

"Yep, and I reckon she's right too."

Lucy's piercing gaze centers on Stella, who begins to feel as if she's all knowing, like Jesus being able to see her every move. She presses her hand to her forehead. It's flaming hot.

"I need to get back to my hemming."

"Fine. But first, how'd you come to be here?"

Stella doesn't want to talk about that. She wants the safety of her previous obscurity, overlooked and ignored.

"There's got to be a reason," Lucy insists.

Stella fidgets and fusses with the waist of her dress, plucking at the rough material. Her breathing escalates and she quickly becomes lightheaded. She shifts off one foot to the other, while her middle suffers a setback. She feels trapped and looks at the open door in desperation. Can she make it if she has to throw up again? Lucy's oblivious to her discomfort.

"Good golly, Goody. Was what you done so bad? Surely it can't be worse than what they accuse me of. Of course, they're right maybe to look down on what I do, but it's my business. It ain't theirs."

It's hard enough as it is for Stella to face what she knows about her own circumstances, that deep, dark secret she hides within herself and from others. To admit it to someone she barely knows doesn't seem right, but another part of her thinks, *Why would it matter?*

She whispers, "It was him. It won't me. I sure couldn't stop him."

"What? Who?"

"Cordell. My hateful, mean daddy."

She can't say anymore. She pushes past Lucy, stumbles out the door, and collapses in the grass.

Chapter 13

Baker

Baker reassures herself she's in control. She pauses to stare out the second-story window at the residents in the fields; a sight that usually makes her happy but in that moment, the sun breaks through the clouds and sets them aglow, as if God finds them favorable, a wholesome lot radiating golden purity like angels. It's a momentary illusion and rather mesmerizing until Mr. Lumley yells at someone. The vision warps back into reality and they're restored to their dull, wrecked, ordinary selves, and she lets out a breath. Look at how they act. Coarse and uncouth. There's so much work to be done on them, yet. She moves away from the window and begins to rehash her meeting with Mrs. Maynard earlier. It requires two doses of antacid before she allows herself to think on it. It went something like this.

For one thing, Mrs. Maynard was extremely upset her wig was ripped off her head by an unstrung Frances Platt, and she was made to look a fool in front of everyone. She came to Baker's office in a dither while Baker was anxious to hear about the recent group punishment, realizing Stella's work triggered it. Mrs. Maynard admitted the violations were recorded by Stella. The problem? It was an unusually high count. Mrs. Maynard hinted Stella's information might be suspect. At that, Baker wasted no time and began to ask questions. She was more inclined to believe an innocent Stella because she didn't think Mrs. Maynard was all that efficient at times. The conversation was . . . how would she put it? Touchy, for the most part.

"So, five were sent for group punishment."

"Yes. I almost sent Lucy Griffin since she was getting like she can be. Always trying to start some kind of trouble. She must be getting the picture because this time she didn't push her luck."

"We need to be sure everyone does as they should so they don't acquire the demerits to trigger that process. In reality, we should only initiate group punishment when it's absolutely necessary, Ethel. We don't need someone talking about this once they're paroled. Trust me, I've had experience with this sort of thing backfiring."

She used Mrs. Maynard's first name as a way to make her command a little friendlier, let her think they were in this together. She can allow her that because she has an ace. She knows about the housemother's dirty little secret. Residents have whispered how she gets excited during the beatings and if—or when—the time comes, this knowledge might become very useful. Indignation gets in the way of Mrs. Maynard's caution.

"I know that much."

"Of course you do. The disobediences were reported by Stella?"

"Yes. I admit I was quite shocked at the number she turned in. She keeps that notepad with her at all times, and constantly writes in it. Who's to say? She could be making some up. She's got as many problems as the rest, maybe more. I'm not so sure she's being truthful."

"You're questioning the integrity of what she provided?"

"I think she might be lying because she assumes this is what you want."

"Did you question her?"

"Well, no, because I didn't want her to think she'd done something wrong."

"Did you have anything else to report?"

"No."

"Why not?"

"I've been busy, of course, but I've not seen any problems. That should be viewed as encouraging."

"Perhaps. I find no reason for the girl to lie, however."

There was an indignant snort. Baker had ignored it and made her point.

"It's like this, Ethel. You're around these girls as much as anyone. Mrs. Dillard is just as busy, yet she submitted plenty of demerits for Dorm B without someone like Stella helping out."

"Again, I think not having any to report is good news. Perhaps my girls are doing better than those in Dorm B. They're learning, and doing their work, and what we want is improvement, don't we?"

"Excuse me?"

"It's what we want, to not make daily mistakes, to improve. Do better. Not incur violations."

"We also don't want them thinking they can get by not adhering to rules, thinking we're not paying attention. Perhaps you're not as observant as you need to be, or think you are."

And then Baker had given her a chance to respond and while she waited, Mrs. Maynard adopted a put-upon air, and drew up, a nearly impossible feat since her back is as crooked as the handle of the cane she uses. They faced one another and the woman's head appeared to free-float on her person; her eyes rolled upward for a view of her boss's face. Honestly, she gave Baker the willies and Baker had turned away to face the window.

"Please bring Stella to me at three sharp. That's all for now."

There was no sound from Mrs. Maynard, but Baker had refused to turn around. After a few seconds where she visualized Mrs. Maynard in the act of a very childish action, the sound of her shuffling out the door allowed her to let out her breath. That was hours ago.

She can't put her finger on why the woman causes her such consternation, except it's the truth certain people rub her the wrong way. Mrs. Dillard, for instance, is wonderful. And Baker gets along in an acceptable manner with Nurse Crawford, and sometimes even listens to her opinions. Dr. Greene and Dr. Graham are tolerable, as long as they don't get too uppity, but because they're men, of course they know better than anyone, so there is *that* to deal with.

In thirty minutes, Mrs. Maynard will bring Stella. Unbeknownst to the housemother the discussion regarding Stella restored Baker's spirits. She's pleased with how the girl proved herself valuable in a very short amount of time, as she expected given her intelligence. She's more helpful than the insipid Ethel Maynard. Baker taps her fingers on the desk, and watches the clock. At a few minutes before three, she drinks a cup of coffee to fortify herself. Next, she steps into her private bathroom, fluffs the hair she wears cut short and gets styled once a week at the beauty parlor. She adjusts her blouse and skirt, and then settles in behind her massive desk. At precisely two fifty-nine, a knock comes.

"Come in!"

Mrs. Maynard and a terrified, pasty Stella enter. Baker motions at the girl to take the one solitary seat in front of her desk. Mrs. Maynard frowns and Baker has a moment of internal glee at her puzzlement.

"There you go, Stella, please sit. Mrs. Maynard, I can manage this meeting. You go on about your duties, and please remember our earlier discussion."

"Before I leave, I have something to report of interest to this meeting."

"Something we haven't gone over already?"

"Yes. Since we met this morning, Stella has, unfortunately, accrued demerits. Six to be exact."

Baker is caught off guard by this news. She stares at Stella, then Mrs. Maynard.

"Please explain."

She takes in the girl's white face, and her ill-looking appearance.

"She stopped eating at dinnertime. As the guidelines state, this is unacceptable. *Waste not, want not.* I told her to clean her plate. She never said she felt unwell, and threw up, making a disgusting mess of the tray and herself. I gave her five minutes to go back to the dorm to change into a clean dress. She was late, and when she returned, she still had vomit in her hair. It's a lack of respect for the orderliness of this institution. As we all know, and there are reminders of this in several areas of the facility, 'Cleanliness is next to Godliness.'"

Baker moves around the desk and bends down to peer closely at Stella. She takes in her thin shoulders, arms, and legs, that she's underweight, and her strained features exhibit a high amount of stress.

"How do you feel at the moment, Stella?"

She peers into the girl's dark eyes, smudges of purple beneath each, and this has Baker wondering if she sleeps. The shadowed eyes glance at her, then go back into hiding, aimed at the crummy shoes the state issues. Her feet don't quite touch the floor as she answers in a soft voice.

"Not so good, ma'am."

"Mrs. Maynard. I do wonder if you're not deliberately obtuse or perhaps blind. Can't you see the child is sick? It's either a case of the nerves, or she's got a stomach bug, but scaring her isn't helpful."

"If she won't speak up for herself, I can't read minds!"

"Tone!"

Mrs. Maynard's shoulders twitch. She retreats, her lips pressed tight like they've been stitched.

"That will be all, Mrs. Maynard. I'll have a chat with Stella here, and we'll move forward. Please remove the demerits. They couldn't be helped."

Bitterly, Mrs. Maynard replies, "As you wish."

Mrs. Maynard shuts the door a little harder than necessary. Baker decides it isn't worth taking up at the moment. Instead, she smiles down at Stella.

"I have some soda crackers, perfect for an unsettled tummy. Do you think you can eat some? I'll call Nurse Crawford, as well. She'll get you back to feeling better in no time, but it might take a bit of time in confinement."

At Stella's expression of fear, Baker says, "Only for a day or two, to let you rest, and make sure you're not contagious. We'll see what she thinks. You sit right there, and don't worry about a thing."

Baker picks up the intercom, presses a key, and speaks into it.

"Nurse Crawford, you're needed in my office, please."

The speaker crackles, and the nurse replies. "Two minutes."

Baker opens her drawer and withdraws a sleeve of saltines. She opens them, and offers the package to Stella, who reaches forward with an unsteady hand to extract one.

"Please, take more, if your stomach will manage?"

"Yes, Mrs. Baker."

Stella takes two more, and Baker finds a napkin so she can place them on the desktop. She returns to her window, while Stella nibbles on the crackers. Baker muses out loud, her back to the girl.

"This place, I believe in it. I really do. Most importantly, I believe in you, and the rest who're sent here. I think of each of you as being lost on your journey in life. There are so many varying paths we can take as we go along. We're presented with certain facts at that time, and we make decisions. Sometimes we make mistakes because we don't know any better. Sometimes we have all the facts and still manage to choose wrong. To my way of thinking, if we do so, it's important to start over. Begin again. And then, once you realize the right way to go, your life changes and becomes more pleasant and you'll want things to stay that way."

She turns to see Stella finishing the last cracker, but Baker can tell she's listening.

"What do you think of this?"

Baker watches the young girl carefully. She hopes Stella's as strong as she thinks she is. She's searching for a weak point, a mar that will alert her to the girl's true disposition and whether or not this sweet and docile behavior is only a front.

"I don't know, ma'am."

"Well, I do. I think you're proving yourself to be very helpful to me."

Stella takes a shaky breath and admits a truth.

"I don't think Mrs. Maynard likes me much."

"Don't worry about that. You keep doing exactly as you've been doing. If you continue to work as you have toward your reform, I have another special plan for you."

"You do?"

"Yes. I want you to write about your experience here. It will be sent to some very important people."

Baker decided Stella's missive will be the first and easiest to collect. She widens her eyes at Stella to hint it's a big deal. This brightens the girl's spirits. She straightens up with a flush rising from her neck to her face, improving the shade of her sallow skin. The older women are too streetwise, too worldly and coarse for something of this nature to be viewed as rewarding, or important. For them, it will be as meaningful as a glass of water. Baker needs to make headway on the dormitory funds. She's heard nothing, so persuasion is next, a way to influence those recalcitrant board members. Proof will get them to take a closer look at her request. A quick rap on the door signals Nurse Crawford has arrived. Baker lets her in, and points to Stella, explaining why she asked the nurse to her office.

"Our Stella here has been sick. She threw up her lunch and isn't feeling well, yet."

Nurse Crawford approaches the girl, and places a hand on her forehead.

"She's very warm."

"Maybe isolate her for a couple of days, to ensure she doesn't give whatever it is to anyone else?"

"I'd say so, yes."

"Make sure she's given special care. Her restructuring is critical, given her background."

"Of course. No resident should have otherwise."

This remark sets Baker's teeth on edge, hinting the nurse might not fully agree with certain methods. She's another one Baker doesn't fully trust. Nurse Crawford is solicitous as she helps Stella to her feet.

"Don't worry, hon, we'll get you feeling better in no time."

Baker crosses the room to open the door. Keeping her hand at Stella's elbow, Nurse Crawford starts down the hall as Baker reminds the nurse of her requirements.

"Please keep me updated on how she's getting along."

"Yes, Mrs. Baker."

Once Stella is out of sight, she shuts the door, satisfied. Stella will regain her good health, and resume her reclamation with little, if any, time lost.

In the meantime, Baker has other priorities in getting the housemothers to select a few more to write the letters of commendation relaying their experiences at the Colony. She could flood the board's offices by having every resident write one, except she's decided certain individuals should do it, and in turn, the board will have a highly favorable impression of the residents here. She's decided those who can read and write will be the primary ones to contribute. She envisions her Industrial Farm presented as a model for others to follow. Imagine that. Dare she? If her efforts are finally recognized, and result in receiving the Jennie Award, it would be an extraordinary achievement.

She must ensure there aren't any major issues of behavior, no backsliding. Not from residents and definitely not from staff. She'll have to make an extra effort toward the irritable and insecure Mrs. Maynard. She needs another Mrs. Dillard is what she needs, a highly efficient individual who's resourceful, and creative with her interactions with residents. Mrs. Maynard having Dr. Woodall as a friend is surely why she's still here. It's why she gets that snooty demeanor. Baker doesn't want to upset her to the point she says something to a board member, much less Dr. Woodall. It's best to see if she can't try—and that's the key word, *try*—to work with the housemother. It's not ideal, but it could be worse.

Chapter 14

Ruth

Ruth is about to receive another series of shots and the thought of what comes with this overwhelms her with dread. When she brushed her hair this morning, clumps of it stayed in the bristles. Her reflection is something she's come to avoid because therein lies the truth of what's happening to her. Dull eyes, a rash that's developed, and she's constantly checking her teeth.

The question she comes back to time and again: Why are women the only ones locked away? Ruth knows better than to ask this question again. The reaction from Nurse Crawford told her all she needed to know. What she's gathered is if a woman's behavior is outside the boundaries of society's beliefs or expectations, it often falls under the label of promiscuous, or suspect. Women pose a threat. If this weren't so infuriating, she'd have a hard time controlling her amusement. At least in jail, those incarcerated know when they'll be released. Not that she thinks being in jail is better, it's the fact if she knew *when* she could go home, it would give her something. An end to this madness.

The more she considers this, the more she wants an answer, so she risks approaching Mrs. Maynard. The housemother must have some idea and Ruth keeps it impersonal.

"Mrs. Maynard, I'm just curious if you could tell me approximately how long women are held here?"

"Absolutely not."

"Might I ask why?"

"Because, Miss Foster, it's entirely up to you. There are certifications, testing, both physical and mental. Bottom line, when we determine someone is ready, they're ready. We can't predict when that might be."

Discouraged, Ruth says, "Thank you," and walks away.

She sees her days expanding into endless toil. She could be here indefinitely, based on the whims of staff and those they work with on the outside, like that sly Sheriff Wright, Dr. Tyndall, and who knows who else. During their free time after supper, she approaches Lucy. The prostitute is having a smoke at the fence by the cow pasture. She's the most knowledgeable in the ways of the Colony considering her history.

"Hey, Lucy."

"Hey."

Ruth lays her arms across the fence and stares out across the field.

"I'm curious. You got any idea how long we're kept here?"

Lucy exhales a plume of blue smoke into the cool air.

"First time? It took me about six months before they let me go."

"*Six months?*"

Ruth's voice rises in alarm.

"Well. It depends, you know."

Lucy glances at Ruth, before crossing her arms and leaning on the fence too.

"They won't tell you because no one has any real idea. I think it hinges on Baker's mood, most of the time."

"That's discouraging."

"Huh. Tell me something I don't know."

Ruth watches three Holsteins resting on their bellies, chewing cud. The sunset behind them draws her attention to the horizon's strip of orange spreading like melting butter. The color deepens to bloodred and there's the end of the world, Ruth thinks. Elsewhere, this would be her favorite time of day. She takes a deep breath, smells hay, manure, and the detergent used to wash the uniforms they wear. Lucy stubs out her cigarette on the fence rail and flicks it into the grass, but she doesn't leave. Ruth is tired and ready to go in. She turns to walk back toward the main building, commenting over her shoulder as she leaves.

"It's time for chapel."

"Hey."

Ruth stops. Lucy considers her for a second, and then, her voice low and secretive, she tosses a nonchalant question into the air.

"You wanna come next time? It's easier with two."

In an instant, Ruth knows her answer, but is curious why Lucy would ask her.

"Why would you want me along?"

Lucy smiles.

"Two brains and all that. You seem pretty sharp."

"What if we're caught?"

Lucy sniffs with derision.

"All they'd do is stick us in solitary. It's worth the risk, ain't it? Look at us. They're pumping poison into us. Ain't none of us like we were when we first come here. It's like they mean to make us ugly. Besides, I ain't been caught running from here. Only reason I'm here now is because one of them underhanded cops picked me up off the street. Every time I run, you can count on it I'll make it out."

Ruth pictures how it would go: the chances she'd have to take, and the likelihood she'd end up back here. A rule follower by nature, even thinking about running makes her nervous, and edgy. She prefers legitimate release from the facility because she's done what she was supposed to do even as she resents having to earn her liberty.

"I don't know. Let me think about it."

Lucy spins in a carefree circle, arms up as if reaching for her future.

"Anytime you're ready, but if I decide I'm ready? I'll go with or without."

"I understand."

They walk back inside where the hall is filled with women moving in a large, exhausted mass, most not talking and those who are keep their voices down. Lucy disappears somewhere in their midst while Ruth searches for Josephine, Melissa, Paula, and Natalie. When she spots them, she goes over, and they sit together. At the end of the service, she's surprised to hear the preacher, a local man who donates time to the Colony, make a special prayer request for Stella.

"Lord, we ask that you lay your hand on Stella Temple, and restore her to good health."

Ruth turns to Josephine, puzzled, while Josephine shakes her head and raises her shoulders. The service is over minutes later, and they're dismissed.

Everyone asks one another, "What's wrong with Stella?" And, "I wondered where she was." Or, "I didn't even notice she was missing."

Melissa shakes her head, her mouth downturned.

"I ain't one bit sorry for her."

Ruth can't blame those hard feelings. The next morning, Mrs. Maynard sounds the wake-up call, then claps her hands. Ruth tenses, believing another round of punishment is coming.

"Attention! We're due for a schedule change. Get yourselves ready and then I'll give you your new assignments!"

There's the usual mad rush to prepare, and once everyone is dressed, and standing at the foot of their cots, Mrs. Maynard begins.

"Listen up, ladies. I'm only going to call out your name once, and where you're to go."

She goes through the list and when she gets to Ruth's name, she yells, "Ruth Foster, cooking duty!"

Ruth is relieved and so are her tender hands, although she'd hoped to work outside again where she could enjoy the warm weather. Still, cooking is better than what she's been doing.

It's hard to believe Mrs. Maynard took her experience at the diner into consideration, and that's what she thinks until Josephine says, "You'll get farm work next. Probably milking or cleaning out the barn and hen house."

"Is that what they do, rotate by the same order each change?"

"Pretty much."

After breakfast, Ruth joins Opal Finch and Sally Timmons from Building B. Opal has done the cooking before, and knows the kitchen. She tells Ruth to take inventory of what's in the pantry, and to write down what's needed. They use a well-worn list with notes on the amounts of dry goods and staples to keep on hand for the inmates plus staff. Ruth goes shelf by shelf, jotting down the list of supplies they need to replenish. Next, she's given the menu to study.

Opal says, "For today, I'll have you make the biscuits for dinner, but you can see what all they got planned for the week on the menu posted there."

Ruth looks over both. If she has anything complimentary to say about the Colony, it's that their diet is adequate, if a bit bland. Opal watches Ruth as she reads the recipe.

"You can make biscuits, cain't you?"

"Yes."

"All right, then, ain't got no time to waste. Go on."

Ruth gets out bowls, and then goes to the pantry. She believes food ought to taste good, and can be a way to offer comfort. To be fed with care and thoughtfulness instills a sense of well-being. Her mother was an excellent cook, and Ruth grew up eating food cooked with attention to small details. For this first task, she makes a couple small adjustments to the biscuit recipe. They're not significant, or even all that creative, but might help make a difference. She wishes she could make sawmill gravy to go along with them, but she's been told what to fix and she's too new to be so bold.

She follows the measurements from an old scrap of paper that's about to fall to pieces, adds the one special ingredient, and digs her hands into the mixture, folding and folding again, but not overdoing it, just like her mother taught her. That's the second secret. She rolls the dough out and cuts the biscuits larger than normal, using the rim of a large drinking glass dipped in flour. She's making catheads. After brushing the top with melted butter, she slides the baking sheets into an industrial-size oven. Opal is frying sausage and Ruth hurries over to help Sally crack the dozens upon dozens of eggs needed to feed the Colony population.

After the allotted time, she checks on the biscuits and sees rows of beautiful, golden, and perfectly risen disks. She removes the heavy pans carefully and stands back to admire her work. Her arms tremble because the shots make her muscles sore, but she's happy with her efforts. She cuts out enough for two more pans and while they're baking, she selects a biscuit that's had a chance to cool, bites into it, and knows the instant her teeth sink into the warm, fluffy center they're better than the crumbly, dry, tasteless versions that have been served so far. Opal comes over and looks at them with longing.

"My my, they sure do smell good."

Ruth, her mouth full, responds by moving her head up and down in agreement. She swallows and points at the pans.

"Have one."

Opal doesn't need any encouragement

Just before she bites into it, she says, "Ain't had one made like this in a long time."

Opal's got thin brown hair pulled back in a limp ponytail. There's a long narrow scar across her left cheek, and another one under her eye. She's slender, so much so, Ruth can see hip bones jutting through the material of her Colony dress. She could use a bit of fattening up. Opal is losing her hair, and her teeth. She takes a bite, and her features smooth out, savoring the taste as she chews with care. After she's swallowed, she smiles, covering her mouth self-consciously. She points to the small square of paper on the table Ruth used to make the dough.

"You followed *that* recipe?"

"More or less."

"I don't know what you did, but they definitely taste better, to me anyway."

Opal takes another nibble and though her mouth is full, she yells across the room to Sally. "You got to come taste these!"

She continues to consume the biscuit. Crumbs fall freely to the floor, which is generally clean, except in the corners. Sally hurries over, a short and bulky woman with a hoarse cough. Ruth is of a mind she ought not be in the kitchen preparing food, but it's not for her to say. Sally stares at the pan of large biscuits and grins.

"Gee. You sure don't look like you been eating these all your life. Not like me no how."

Sally smacks her ample backside to emphasize what she means, and chuckles while grabbing a biscuit. She takes a bite and has a similar reaction as Opal, her eyes rolling like marbles as she chews vigorously. She hasn't swallowed the first bite before she's cramming more into her mouth, and then the biscuit is gone. She clasps her hands, eyelids fluttering and her cheeks bulging.

When she's able to speak, she says, "Glory be. I know it ain't nothing but a biscuit, but some people just know how to make 'em. That one tasted like my gramma's. It's certainly the best I've had since I got here."

Ruth grins.

"Thanks."

Opal leans in close.

"Hey, you still got all your teeth!"

"So far."

"Shoot. Well, that's lucky."

"No one's said when it happens."

"I can't remember when mine started coming out." She points at the biscuits. "What did you do different?"

"Not much."

"You got magic in them hands then, don't she, Sally?"

"She sure does. You done a lot of cooking?"

"I worked in a diner where I had a job as a waitress mostly, but sometimes I filled in for the short-order cook. And Mama, she's a good cook. She never measured anything, and it always came out just right."

Opal and Sally bob their heads as one.

"That explains it. I ain't ever had bad diner food."

"Or from mamas."

Together, the three of them discuss the menu briefly and Ruth makes mental notes along the way on how she'll adjust whatever they give her to do. They move on to begin filling the breakfast trays, forming a short assembly line with Opal dishing out eggs, Sally adding the sausage, and last, Ruth, plopping her biscuits on the tray before sliding it out the serving window where by six thirty a.m., one by one they're taken up quickly. After everyone is served, they fix their own and join the others in the dining hall. Ruth crosses the room to sit with Josephine and the rest. She pulls out the chair beside Melissa, who's still pale and suffering from lingering pain. She hasn't spoken about the incident or what happened and Ruth doubts she ever will. Melissa picks at the biscuit, then actually takes a bite. She chews slowly, and Ruth tries not to stare. She takes another bite and Ruth smiles to herself. She actually made a couple other secret adjustments she didn't share with Opal. A good cook never gives out their secrets is what Mama always said.

When Opal went to grab another dozen eggs thinking they didn't have enough, she said, "Here. Stir these."

Ruth took over the stirring and while she was gone, she added a big blob of the Colony's homemade butter to the large skillet and mixed it in with the half-cooked eggs. She added in a splash of milk. Opal returned, and thanked her for helping, none the wiser. She takes a bite of her second biscuit and peeks about. Lots of jaws move vigorously. The room is hushed as the food is eaten with more enthusiasm than usual. She sets her sights on the table where the housemothers and Mr. Lumley are eating. She can't tell if they're enjoying their meal more than usual from so far away. Josephine finishes, leans back in her chair, and gives a sidelong glance at Ruth.

"That sure did hit the spot. Better'n usual."

Paula and Natalie murmur in agreement and Melissa's tray is empty for a change. Ruth smiles with pleasure, and experiences a momentary bit of happiness. The others finish their meals, and dining hall noise picks up. Minutes later, chairs are shoved back and everyone moves on to their daily assignments. Ruth, Opal, and Sally go back into the kitchen. On the menu for the noon meal is vegetable soup. Opal explains to Ruth there can never be any waste, none whatsoever. The kitchen has a budget and they've been reminded time and again, when there's an excess of leftover vegetables, they're to make soup. She drags out containers of leftover vegetables from the past week's dinners and suppers.

Ruth says, "I can make it, if you'd like? I know a recipe from the diner because we used to serve vegetable soup and cheese sandwiches every Friday."

Opal and Sally glance at each other. "Suits me," they say.

They go to work with Ruth taking over and Opal and Sally helping, doing what she tells them. At dinnertime, the vegetable soup is gobbled up along with the corn muffins Ruth decides to serve along with it. Supper is next, and Ruth adds her touches to the meal of meatloaf, topping it with a piquant sauce, suggests they cook what her mother called country-style potatoes and slyly adds a good splash of vinegar and some sugar to the chopped onions and tomatoes to go on top of the black-eyed peas. Supper trays are emptied as fast as the other two meals.

After a couple days of cooking, Mrs. Maynard, Mrs. Dillard, Nurse Crawford, Mr. Lumley, and a few teachers glance her way several times in the dining hall. The conversation at her table is about Stella, and how she's still sick, and while Ruth listens, from time to time she looks toward the staff table where a rigorous conversation is taking place. They sit with their heads together and the glances come every few seconds, or maybe she's imagining it. Singling out an individual is always unsettling because it implies something was done to draw their attention, and usually it's not because of anything good.

Ruth didn't expect to enjoy the kitchen work as much as she has, but cooking gives her a sense of normalcy and getting creative with the meals is rewarding. Even though she's required to rise thirty minutes earlier to do this work, she has no problem because she has trouble sleeping, anyway. And, while it would be nice to be outside again, farm work would do more to remind her of where she is than a kitchen. Ruth gets into the rhythm of this new assignment, but, as expected, Mrs. Maynard makes her weekly appearance for the schedule, including a speech as usual.

"Time to rotate. Remember, ladies, everything you do here is to expand your knowledge and your skill sets. This is about your training, and the achievement of your certifications. Treat it seriously, every day."

There's one or two groans quickly squashed as Mrs. Maynard sends her beady eyes around the room for the culprits. Ruth was already up and ready to go to the kitchen as usual. In her peripheral vision, she spots Mrs. Maynard heading toward her and she straightens and drops her hands to her sides.

"Miss Foster, Nurse Crawford updates Mrs. Baker regularly with a health report of the residents. Some residents have gained weight and this is considered an improvement. As well, there've been a few remarks here and there about the quality of cooking. Mrs. Baker wants you to remain in the kitchen until further notice. Keep doing as you've been doing. Everyone appears to enjoy your efforts, including the staff."

"Yes, ma'am."

"Opal and Sally from Building B will continue to work with you since the three of you do well together. You've set an example of what solid working relationships are, along with an exemplary work ethic, and by that, I mean creativity and ingenuity."

"Yes, Mrs. Maynard."

Ruth reveals nothing, one way or the other at this news, while the tension she's had since she first set foot in the place loosens a little. She waits for Mrs. Maynard to leave, but she's not done yet.

"Also, Nurse Crawford has been given instructions from Dr. Graham about a special diet for Stella Temple. As you heard in chapel, she's taken ill."

"Yes, ma'am."

"Nurse Crawford expects you this morning. Report to her directly after breakfast is taken care of. Miss Foster, please consider this a positive step forward. After your less than stellar beginning here at the Colony, it's quite the achievement and a wonderful example to all."

Mrs. Maynard nods at her curtly and leaves the dorm. Ruth digests this little speech. Her spirits lift, feeling as if she's taken a step toward her freedom, which she wants more than ever. On the other hand, she doesn't want to be an example. She's doing as she's told because she has to, that's it. Her cooking isn't for those in charge, but for the women here who need something, a tiny bright spot in their day. God knows it's all they've got—that and each other.

Chapter 15

Stella

Glassy-eyed and disorientated, Stella shivers. Something's gone wrong with her insides. Something's definitely not right. She knows this as sure as she knows what Cordell did wasn't right. Her fingers find her midsection, barely grazing the length of rippled scar tissue and the surrounding area of skin. It's tender to the touch, and warm. She stops the self-examination and instead takes note of her level of misery, concluding she's sick as she's ever felt. Nurse Crawford peers down at her with concern before placing a cool hand on her forehead.

The worry Stella sees makes her want to turn on her side and curl up, but Nurse Crawford says, "I need to get your temperature."

She leaves the bedside, and returns to stick a thermometer in Stella's mouth. Stella catches the faint scent of alcohol, which she's always liked, though she doesn't know why. She slowly breathes it in. It's what she smelled right before she was given something to make her sleep while her tumor was removed, the moment her life was turned around. A brisk rap on the door startles her and she ducks down under the covers, wishing whoever it is would go away. Nurse Crawford crosses the room, opens the door, and Dr. Graham enters. He approaches the bed where Stella ogles him with fear and fever-flushed cheeks. He removes the thermometer from her mouth, and Stella shrinks against the pillow, reacting in an unlikely way. She switches from docile to anxious.

"Don't! Don't touch me!"

Dr. Graham, still holding the thermometer, glances down at her with a frown, and takes a step back. Exasperated, he looks at Nurse Crawford.

"What's this about?"

Stella clenches the edge of the sheet and her panicked breathing fills the room. Nurse Crawford is as surprised as the doctor.

"I don't know. She took ill and spiked that fever. This isn't like her, not from what I've experienced." Nurse Crawford approaches the bed. "Stella. This is Dr. Graham. Remember? He helped you when you first came here."

Stella grows emotional.

"I'm sorry. I'm sorry. I—I don't know why I said that."

Dr. Graham returns to the bedside and Stella allows him to get her pulse even though she's unable to prevent the almost imperceptible flinch at his touch.

He says, "Do you hurt anywhere?"

"My belly. Where the scar is."

He places a stethoscope on her chest, and Stella turns her head. She doesn't like him looming over her; it's too much like Cordell. He puts the instrument back around his neck and, to her great discomfort, pokes and prods her abdomen and she cries out. He grunts at her reaction, and bobs his head as if this was expected.

He turns to speak to Nurse Crawford. "I'll need to see the stomach area."

Stella stares at the ceiling after Nurse Crawford exposes her abdomen. To Stella's relief, Dr. Graham doesn't touch her. He shakes his head as if he's greatly disturbed and has Nurse Crawford adjust Stella's gown to close it. She pulls up the bedsheet while he strokes his chin. Stella hopes he knows what's wrong with her. He moves toward the door, and with his hand on the knob, he explains.

"It's an infection, likely from the procedure, an unfortunate turn,

I'm afraid. We need to begin treating it immediately. Hot and cold compresses to start. Clean the area, particularly the incision site with hydrogen peroxide, followed by alcohol. The incision isn't healing like I expected, but let's try this first. Repeat these steps three times a day, just prior to her meals. I'll put together a diet for you to share with the kitchen. She's to rest for now. Nothing else."

"Yes, Doctor."

"We might have to drain it and start her on sulfathiazole, but I'll wait to see if there's any change after a day or so."

"Yes, sir."

Dr. Graham and Nurse Crawford step out of the room, leaving Stella alone. She's never been sick other than a cold and she finds herself thinking of Alice. If she were at home and sick, would her mother take care of her for a change? Would she cook for her, give her aspirin, and check in on her, the very things Stella did for her when Alice would return from her treatments? These thoughts vanish when Nurse Crawford comes back and begins to move about in a way that makes Stella nervous. She moves quickly, very business-like, and appears to be in a mood, setting a tray down on the small table beside the bed hard enough the items rattle. She begins dabbing at Stella's stomach while Stella would like to go to sleep, but she's too miserable, and the nurse's demeanor is unsettling. Nurse Crawford continues to clean the wound area, and Stella's not used to being uncomfortable around her. The nurse lays a warm compress over the area, and after a bit of time has passed, she puts on a cold one. Stella hates it all, not because of how it feels, but because they don't speak.

For the next two days, she's subjected to this as well as Dr. Graham coming to poke at her abdomen. He taps his chin as if he's staring at some unknown part of her anatomy. His scowl tells Stella he isn't happy with what he sees. No one is ever happy when they look in her direction, not even here. He leaves and Nurse Crawford comes over, and Stella can't read her expression. The nurse appears impatient. Or offended.

"He's got to drain the area."

Stella's mouth drops and she sits up too fast, which causes her pain. She winces and Nurse Crawford tsk-tsks, fluffs her pillows, and eases her back to a reclining position.

She says, "You shouldn't be in so much discomfort this long after the procedure. It's not normal." Stella could swear she mutters something like, "And I told him he should start medication, but who am I?" Nurse Crawford sighs and with her voice more normal and reassuring, she says, "This will make it better."

Dr. Graham returns with a black bag he drops with a *thud* beside the bed and he proceeds to dig about in it before looming over her with a long needle and syringe raised in the air.

"I'm going to numb the area. Ready?"

Stella doubts it would matter if she said no. He bends over and there's a sharp prick to her center that's uncomfortable only for a second. Whatever is in the shot works quickly, and she relaxes.

"There. That's the worst of it."

The numbing medication works on the soreness and she can only sense every now and again a bit of pressure as he explains what he's doing.

"I'll just poke a tiny hole, and next, I'll insert this drainage tube," which he holds up so she can see. What he shows her looks like macaroni, only longer. He's bent to his task, and again humming under his breath as he works. After a few minutes, he straightens up.

"Nurse, I'm leaving the tube in. I'll tape it good, and come back in a couple days. We should also start her on some medication."

"Yes, Dr. Graham."

The doctor, for some reason, assumes Stella's interested in seeing what he extracted.

"See here, young lady. This is what's making you feel bad."

He holds up a small jar of cloudy, yellowish fluid with a foul odor near her face. She immediately begins retching, which makes both him and Nurse Crawford scramble: him to get out of the way, and Nurse Crawford to stick a bowl under her chin to catch what may come. Stella grows sweaty and uncomfortable. Dr. Graham snaps his bag shut, and hands the nurse a brown envelope.

"Give these to her as directed. Be aware of side effects. We sure don't need her straining her belly area too much."

"Yes, Doctor."

After a few days, Stella is sick of being sick. Once again, it's like her body isn't hers. She lies in bed in a dark mood like she fell into after Cordell left her room. She blames him and her mother for her current miseries. Dr. Graham comes more than she'd like and while she understands what he does is necessary and intended to help heal her, after being poked, prodded, and jabbed, she wants nothing more than to get better. She wants out of quarantine, to return to her restoration. Mostly, she wants to be left alone. She dabbles and sips and procrastinates over what's brought to her from the Colony's kitchen. Watery broth, plain toast, and other forms of what she considers "sick food" aren't part of the usual fare; it's nourishment dictated by Dr. Graham to "ease" her stomach back into eating. Her belly, already unreliable, objects. She struggles to eat, and Nurse Crawford says it's a combination of the infection and the medicine. Stella might agree to some extent, but the food might as well be plastic. As she picks her way through breakfast, dinner, and supper over the next few days, Nurse Crawford grows concerned.

"You have to eat to give your body the strength to fight back."

Stella shudders. The meals are about as appealing as that poison that came out of her. That's how she thinks of it. Poison caused by Cordell. After the doctor removed what her body made from the bad he'd done, they must not have got all of it. Left behind was the taint, the pure evil in the form of infection. Maybe it's God's punishment. She's never spent a lot of time thinking about God, or Jesus, but going to the Colony's chapel services gives her a new way of thinking about herself. She's a sinner and God isn't done punishing her for her wrongdoings.

Her appetite continues to lag. Her weight drops. Nurse Crawford warns if she doesn't eat on her own, they might be forced to take extra measures. Stella, anxious enough as it is, squeaks out a question.

"What do you mean?"

"They might force-feed you."

"You'd let them?"

Nurse Crawford shakes her head.

"*I* wouldn't, but I have no say." She places a hand on Stella's forehead. "Hm. You don't have a fever."

No matter what the nurse or what Stella want, she can't bring herself to eat. She's helped to a scale each day and continues to drop weight. Her incision remains tender, but at least the wound quits draining and Dr. Graham is able to remove the tube. One afternoon he props his hands on his knees and scowls at her. Stella shrinks from him. Without a word, he walks out of the room. Less than an hour later, Dr. Greene comes in, followed by Dr. Graham. The two of them together are a formidable force, and she's shaken by their presence, particularly when they send Nurse Crawford out of the room. *Go get some air. Come back in five minutes.* Nurse Crawford hesitates until Dr. Graham holds the door open for her. Dr. Greene lowers himself into a chair.

"Why won't you eat?"

"I'm trying. Nothing tastes good."

Dr. Graham says, "If you'd eat, your stomach would adjust. Food would become something you want again."

Stella doesn't know what to say. She hasn't got the answer they want.

"When's the last time you had a full meal?"

"I don't remember."

He and Dr. Greene put their heads together. They ponder over her chart, and point several times as they scan pages and have a hard to hear conversation. There's shared glances back at her, and lots of head shaking. She must be a real disappointment to everyone. Dr. Greene hangs the chart back at the end of the bed and with one last look, he leaves the room. Now it's just her and Dr. Graham. She swallows, and tries not to show her fear as he speaks to her in a stern voice.

"Young lady, I'm afraid you leave us no choice. You'll have a meal by the end of the day. If you won't help yourself, then matters are out of your hands. It's for your own good."

Nurse Crawford reenters the room, and hears the last part.

"What's for her own good?"

Dr. Graham leads the nurse to the other side of the room and speaks to her privately. She crosses her arms, and Stella is unable to read her expression, not because she can't see her, but because there's nothing there. It's devoid of emotion, as if the nurse is no more in charge than Stella. It doesn't get past Stella this is often how it is between men and women. Women give in. Alice did with Cordell, once. Stella too, although on the rare occasion she tried to fight. Her uneasy stomach clenches and she drops her eyes so she doesn't have to watch as they make their secret decisions. Nurse Crawford approaches the bed as if to coax Stella, her manner almost desperate.

"Listen. In order to get back to your reform work, you need to take in a bit of nourishment so you can feel better and continue your training. I know that's what you'd prefer, isn't it?"

The nurse's gaze pleads with her, and she truly wants to do what she's asking, but the very thought of eating turns her stomach inside and out.

"I do want to get better, it's just . . ."

Her voice is weak, and she feels exactly like she sounds. Dr. Graham's demeanor is abrupt. He grumbles with impatience and gives her no sympathy.

"It's no longer up to her. Dr. Greene and I agree, our way will result in a better outcome. She's failing. Her health. Her mental state."

Stella wants a choice, a say-so.

"I try to eat a little, but the food isn't good."

Dr. Graham gives her an uncanny look. She presses on, hopeful he'll leave her alone.

"I try, I do."

"You won't need to try anymore."

The words are ominous. They might get rid of her. They could send her back home to Alice and Cordell, declare her untrainable, and not worth the effort.

"I'll be back in a bit."

Dr. Graham leaves the room, and Stella's heart begins to race.

"What's he going to do? Where's he going?"

"It's going to be fine."

"Tell me! Are they going to do what you said?"

"It does you no good to get worked up. Lie back now, try to rest."

Stella lies back against the pillows, her heart racing. She jerks upright a few minutes later when Dr. Graham returns and trooping in behind him come Mrs. Maynard and Dr. Greene. Dr. Graham carries a few instruments. One item is a copper funnel, and the other is a tube, similar to what he put into her abdomen to drain the fluid, except longer and a little thicker. Mrs. Maynard is shaking a mason jar of pale-yellow liquid.

She sets it down and as soon as she does, Dr. Graham says, "Restrain her."

Stella has no time to react. Her legs are grabbed by Dr. Greene and Mrs. Maynard while Nurse Crawford takes a hold of her hands and grips them, giving her a look intended to calm her. The nurse nods at her in a reassuring way and she's okay until Dr. Graham fastens leather straps like oversized belts on each leg. She's too startled to react and then her wrists are attached to the metal frame of the bed. Struggling does no good. Her head is all that's free and she whips it left, then right trying to find Dr. Graham. She can't see him because he's moved to the head of her bed where he grabs her chin expertly and tips her head back. She opens her mouth to scream and he jams a metal contraption into it, pinching her lower lip as he does so. He turns a knob and it cranks her mouth open. Stella searches for Nurse Crawford, who's against the wall and has her hands up to her cheeks like she's about to cry. Dr. Graham grips Stella's chin again and inserts the long tube down her throat. She gags. It's like she's being choked. She can't breathe and makes a guttural sound and her legs spasm against the mattress.

Dr. Graham yells at her, "Breathe through your nose!"

Desperate, Stella does, but it doesn't ease her panic, and her brain gets confused. Dr. Graham attaches the other end of the tube to the copper funnel. Mrs. Maynard hands him the jar and he begins to pour it into the funnel.

"Here we go. Easy. Easy. Easy."

Stella squeezes her eyes shut. She can feel the coolness of the liquid in her chest and in her stomach. She starts retching again, and forgets to breathe through her nose. Tears run into her hair and ears.

Dr. Graham yells again. "Breathe! Breathe like I told you!"

And then it's over. He's no longer pouring the liquid in. He sets the empty jar down and cautiously extracts the tube. He appears very satisfied with himself because he begins to hum as he releases the metal contraption and takes it out of her mouth. He even takes the time to dab at her lips with a cloth and she sees blood. Her arms and legs are released. Mrs. Maynard and Dr. Greene leave. Stella lies without moving, even though she's no longer restricted.

Dr. Graham says, "Now. Maybe this nourishing blend of milk and eggs will restore some balance to your stomach. I'm sure you must feel better already."

Stella's stomach is out of whack. It rumbles. There's a lot of churning. She sits up suddenly and ejects a violent stream of milk and eggs that happen to go in the direction of the doctor. Dr. Graham gawks in disbelief as the mess drips down his pants and shoes. His face turns red, then an even deeper shade, akin to a beet. He seems to have lost his capacity to speak. Nurse Crawford steps forward.

"Dr. Graham, if I could make a suggestion?"

He ignores her, fixated on his clothing.

"Hand me something to clean this up, for God's sake!" he yells.

Stella puts a hand to her head. She still feels sick and she knows she's about to do the same thing again. She glances about, desperate for a bowl, a cloth, something.

"I have to . . ."

She turns her head, and out comes the remainder of the milk and eggs onto the floor. A few more spatters land on the doctor's pants. He snatches the dampened cloth Nurse Crawford hands him, and without another look at poor Stella, he hurries out of the room.

"Dr. Graham, I'm due to give Mrs. Baker the weekly medical report, should I . . ." Nurse Crawford calls after him.

From down the hall comes, "I'll handle her!"

Stella lies back against her pillows. Oddly, she feels a bit better. Nurse Crawford places a cool cloth on her forehead, then busies herself cleaning the floor.

As she cleans, she says, "I'm sorry that happened."

Stella whispers, "I didn't mean to throw up on him."

"Serves him right. Well, it's over and done with and we'll just forget it ever happened."

Nurse Crawford closes the blinds and turns on a lamp. Stella feels safe again and falls asleep. She wakes up at the sound of utensils rattling to her right and turns her head to see Nurse Crawford placing a tray beside the bed. Apprehensive, she eyes the solitary steaming bowl and sniffs the air like a feral animal. To her surprise, the bowl offers a tempting scent. Stella's stomach emits a wary little gurgle. Nurse Crawford raises the back of the bed so she can sit up and she leans over to see what's in the bowl. It holds a pale-yellow liquid. There's rice and tiny bits of chicken, but mostly rice.

"I asked Ruth Foster to fix this for you."

Nurse Crawford arranges the tray so Stella can easily get to it. Stella lifts the spoon and sips a little broth. Flavor fills her mouth, and to her surprise, she dips the spoon in again, and she keeps eating and doesn't stop until the bowl is empty. She even eats the saltines set on a saucer, dunking them into the buttery broth so they're soft, and so good she wishes there were more. She drinks the sweet tea with the sunny little lemon sitting on top and, for the first time in days, Nurse Crawford smiles.

Chapter 16

Baker

Baker is provided updates on Stella's progress by Dr. Graham, and the fact he suddenly takes care to do it daily raises her suspicions. The doctor has always claimed he has other matters to attend, and she's relied on Nurse Crawford. Another issue: his updates tell her very little. They're quite basic considering the seriousness of Stella's illness; plus, it doesn't go unnoticed there's a sudden shift in his usual demeanor, meaning he's more congenial. Unbeknownst to her in these recent and rather mundane reviews, he conveniently leaves out the incident of force-feeding. Baker always goes by her gut, and her gut says investigate. Who best to ask questions but the patient herself. She raps on the quarantine door and Nurse Crawford answers.

"I'm here to inquire about Stella Temple. How is she doing?"

"Isn't Dr. Graham. . . ? Never mind. See for yourself."

The nurse steps back so Baker can enter, and as soon as she does, there's Stella sitting up in the bed, rosy-cheeked, her hair neatly brushed and held back loosely with a pink ribbon. She is thinner, but otherwise looks much better. Baker turns to Nurse Crawford.

"Can I speak with you privately?"

"Certainly."

They step out of the room, and Nurse Crawford draws the door closed. Baker's approach is to credit the doctor and see where it goes.

"I see Dr. Graham's recommended sulfathiazole and bland diet are working quite well."

"More or less, Mrs. Baker."

"More? Or less?"

"Once Stella was off the medication her stomach settled down and that certainly helped. It's known to cause nausea. The diet was another matter."

"His reports didn't have much detail about that."

"I gave him my notes and I can assure you, the report I produced was extensive, as always."

Baker is careful as she progresses with the conversation, knowing Nurse Crawford and Dr. Graham must work together. She can't afford to have either of them quit.

"What was the reason for her illness?"

Nurse Crawford stares at her in the way someone does when they're not sure they heard the question, and looks puzzled at Baker's ignorance.

"She developed an infection from her surgery. He had to drain her abdomen area."

"There's no mention of either."

"I can't speak for why he'd leave that out."

"What did you mean, 'the diet was another matter'?"

"The medication made her nauseous and the infection didn't help. She began losing weight and she certainly didn't need that. I would bring her the recommended food he prescribed, but she picked at it."

"I see. Can I see her chart, please?"

They reenter the room. Stella hasn't moved. She sits on the bed, wide-eyed, her gaze shifting from one to the other.

Baker says, "Hello, Stella," but focuses on the chart Nurse Crawford retrieves from the foot of Stella's bed.

She immediately sees the nurse's notes are much more thorough and comprehensive compared to what Dr. Graham has reported. His barely had anything more than temperature taking and medication dosages. Baker scrutinizes the pages and zones in on a particular entry made a few days before.

"What's this here? What's 'FF at three o'clock'?"

"Dr. Graham didn't tell you."

Nurse Crawford's voice comes out flat, with a hint of anger.

"As I've said, his information told me very little. Nothing about bowel habits, meal or liquid intake, the patient's disposition, or any of the information you typically provide. He certainly didn't mention whatever this is." Baker's finger taps the spot again and she gives Nurse Crawford a probing look. "No secrets, Nurse Crawford."

Nurse Crawford moves away to stand near Stella. Baker's agitation builds because there's something being kept from her. She's certain of it. Nurse Crawford adjusts her cap, and pushes her hands into the pockets of her uniform as if to keep them still. Baker ambles around the room. She wanders by the sink against the back wall where there is a mirror and its reflection frames Nurse Crawford and Stella in the background. Baker meanders back and forth, picking up this and that, and as she passes by the mirror again, she catches Nurse Crawford signaling Stella, placing a finger over her lips, and giving a subtle shake of her head. For heaven's sake, she's cueing the girl about something.

Baker spins around and Nurse Crawford quickly lowers her arm, flustered. Stella grips the bedsheets like they're going to be ripped off. Baker's patience is thinning. She holds the chart up and taps a finger on the suspicious and troubling *FF*.

"I know how he is, his way or no way, but this is your writing, Nurse Crawford, so you know what it means, and your cooperation is expected."

Nurse Crawford, typically stoic and pragmatic, slumps in defeat, but it's Stella who tells Baker what she wants to know.

"He forced me to eat."

"Forced. What do you mean, 'forced'?"

"Quite literally that. He force-fed her," says Nurse Crawford in a lowered voice. "That's what *FF* stands for."

Baker brings a hand to her chest, which begins to rise and fall rapidly, as if she's just finished running laps. The acid in her gut is a volcano ready to erupt. It sets the center of her chest ablaze and she snaps at Nurse Crawford.

"*When?*"

"A few days ago. Dr. Graham and Mrs. Maynard assisted."

Baker's entire body goes rigid, incensed by the audacity.

"Unacceptable and certainly not part of our protocol. Why wasn't I told? Why didn't you stop him?"

Nurse Crawford is incredulous.

"He's my *superior.* It doesn't matter. It didn't work."

"What do you mean? It must have worked. She seems recovered."

Nurse Crawford nods at Stella.

"Go on. Tell what happened."

Stella avoids looking at her. She begins to explain, her face pale, the tremor in her hands obvious as she straightens her sheet.

"I was strapped to the bed."

Baker puts a hand to her forehead and presses her fingers there, massaging lightly. She drops her hand, and with what she hopes is something like an encouraging smile, she nods.

"Go on."

"He put something in my mouth to keep it open, and stuck a long hose down my throat with some sort of funnel on one end. He poured milk and eggs from a jar into the funnel. I threw it up. On him."

Baker's coloring goes wild and her face takes on a scalded appearance. She stares with intensity at Stella as red splotches around her neck expand and shrink, like her blood is having trouble figuring out what to do. Her voice is knotty and hard as she addresses Nurse Crawford in a way she doesn't do often when it comes to internal issues with other staff.

"By God. What does he think we're running here? A dungeon set in ancient times? This is a modern facility. I ensure it operates under thoughtful educational and corrective direction. Wouldn't you agree?"

She waits for Nurse Crawford. Is it her imagination Nurse Crawford's reply is too quick?

"Of course, Mrs. Baker."

It sounds insincere. Conciliatory, perhaps.

"Has this ever happened before? Were the same people involved? Mrs. Maynard and Dr. Graham?"

The nurse's answers to these questions raise Baker's hackles even more.

"This is the first time I've ever seen it, but I've only been here a year. It's possible it happened before, maybe before my time? I don't know."

Baker relents, because for one, Nurse Crawford, like herself, must work with the man and was put in a situation she couldn't control. She moves on, following with a question born of genuine curiosity.

"Despite this, she's obviously improved. How did she turn the corner?"

"At my request, Miss Foster prepared some soup, and it appealed to her. Since then, she's been eating. Puddings. Scrambled eggs. Cinnamon-sugar toast. We've only just started her on more substantial choices to include larger portions of protein. Miss Foster certainly has a knack in the kitchen."

Baker stares. "Her cooking is directly responsible for this miraculous turnaround?"

"Clinically? I have no idea. All I know is it was the first time Stella ate with any sort of enthusiasm and she's been eating ever since. She gained a pound this week. Miss Foster puts to good use what's available to her. Everyone is enjoying their meals more than before. As you know, I've actually recorded weight gains."

Baker says, "Yes, I've heard as much," then puts her attention back on Stella. "It's good to know you're feeling much better."

"Yes, Mrs. Baker. Much better."

"Nurse Crawford, if you think she's ready, let's get her back to her training tomorrow."

"Yes, Mrs. Baker."

Baker's fury at what she's learned propels her down the halls as she leaves the quarantine area. Her mind sorts through various approaches of what to say and not say to Dr. Graham, never mind Mrs. Maynard. She'll deal with her too. Administrative changes like suspension or firing can't be managed without the board's knowledge. They have to be apprised on these matters, and if this weren't the case, she'd tell Dr. Bradford Graham to pack his things and hit the door. She would send Ethel Maynard packing as well. She turns right, and then left again, passes her office, then Dr. Greene's—his door is closed . . . Was that the clink of a bottle against glass? God help her, another problem she must somehow handle. Seconds later, she's standing at Dr. Graham's door. She tugs at her dress and smooths her hair. She raps hard and fast on the wood with authority, although she knows she'll feel diminished as soon as she enters.

"Come in!" he yells from the other side.

Baker rolls her eyes. She opens the door briskly, practically launches herself into the room and shuts it decisively too. Dr. Graham is behind his desk, the ugly gray brain in the jar to the right and stacks of dusty medical journals to his left. There are a lot of papers here and there, and the clutter is something she has trouble with. How can he possibly know what he's doing? How can he keep up with anything? He looks perturbed by her presence. All fine and good, because she's no happier to be in his.

"Mrs. Baker."

"Dr. Graham."

"Would you care to sit?"

"No. This won't take long."

She waits, refusing to explain why she's come. He steeples his fingers and peers over his glasses at her. She observes his hair looks like a chicken nested in it, and there's an obvious stain of some sort on his tie. Aside from posture, one's personal hygiene and appearance matter. If one can't respect oneself, then who will? He gets up from his chair and moves to a cabinet where he retrieves something. When he faces her, she knows immediately what he's holding given Stella's description. It's the force-feeding kit. He dangles the long rubber tube from his fingers while he balances the funnel on the finger of his other hand. His manner is so lackadaisical, so nonchalant, the anger she experienced since first hearing of it returns.

"Is this the reason you're here?"

"You bet it is. Who gave you the approval to administer this . . . this utterly barbaric method of treatment?"

"Are you the physician now? Last I was in your office, I don't recall seeing a medical degree anywhere. And speaking of barbaric, I'd be cautious with that phrase given some of your procedures."

Baker's insides clench, and her chest smolders.

"*My* procedures? They're standard and used at many facilities. I don't think you understand. *I'm* the superintendent. *I'm* the one in charge here, *not you.* This wasn't a decision to make on your own."

"And I didn't. Dr. Greene concurred."

"The both of you should have requested a meeting to advise me of this recommendation. I don't recall ever—and I emphasize *ever*—using this method before and quite truthfully, I would have said no."

"You do realize, Mrs. Baker, the professionals must step in and take matters into their own hands when there is a need. I don't see how you would've had any sway. What would you have done if I'd said if she doesn't eat, she'll die?"

"Oh, please. Don't take me for the fool, Dr. Graham. No need for the dramatic. Once she was off the medication and allowed decent food, she ate. Force-feeding could've done more harm than good for her psychologically, and I would've thought between the two of you 'experts' you'd have known this. That's an aside. Given the structure of this institution, and the protocol, every action taken by staff requires the superintendent be fully apprised. These individuals are my responsibility, ultimately. You're here to provide medical expertise, not make broad and sweeping decisions without my approval."

"And I'll remind you, again, I know more about it than you."

"I can see this is going nowhere. I've a good mind to report this to the board as an act of insubordination."

"Do what you must, Mrs. Baker, although I highly doubt the outcome of your complaint will be as you expect."

"What's that supposed to mean?"

"Are they even paying attention to you? Did you get the funds yet for your illustrious expansion? Maybe there's a reason?"

He offers a congenial smile, one that sends a warning zipping through her. This is a cat and mouse game he's introducing, as if he has an upper hand. With head held high, she walks out the door, her limp betraying her attempt at a graceful exit. Back in her office, she collapses in her chair. Oh, how she wishes she could reach out to Eloise. Eloise Belle would have known how to manage the sort like Dr. Graham, who believes himself morally superior and smarter than anyone, with the exception of Dr. Greene. She can't even rely on Mrs. Maynard because she's just as guilty for her participation, and for all she knows they're in it together.

Surely Dr. Graham should be reprimanded, at a minimum, but putting that into motion means actually going before the board, which she never intended to do. Not to complain, anyway. If she did, it reveals a less than smooth operation. Her earlier threat was only intended to keep an upper hand. Everyone should be working like a greased engine, or it jeopardizes not only the funding request, but opinions can form as to her ability to manage the facility. After all, the State expects her and her staff to deal with their problems without causing them any. She actually prefers it this way, because the less they know, the better. She doesn't need inquisitive busybodies searching for weakness in the institution's workings. Ten years is a long time since the fire at Samarcand, but all it takes is one incident to bring scrutiny back on her, no matter the good she's done since.

She needs an advocate and, unfortunately, that brings her back to Ethel Maynard. The testy nature of their relationship is a challenge, but if nothing else, diplomatic and honest conversations can work wonders. She punches the button on the intercom.

"Mrs. Maynard, please come to my office . . . when you aren't busy."

She stops herself from saying "immediately." Now she must wait, which she despises. Another flaw, impatience. At least she recognizes her shortcomings. Now, how to handle things once she arrives? She has little time to consider the problem because a couple of minutes later, there's a soft tap on her door.

Baker, her voice equally soft, says, "Please come in."

She's always abrupt with those on the other side of the door, but today she isn't *and* she says please. She's got to begin somewhere. Baker can already tell these small—and yes, forced—conciliatory gestures have done nothing to help the housemother's disposition. The woman's stiff manner indicates she's still in a snit about group punishment and their disagreement regarding Stella. For the sake of continuing to play nice, Baker extends her hand in a gracious manner toward a chair.

"Please, sit down."

Mrs. Maynard doesn't do so immediately. She stands, the *C* of her posture annoying Baker as it does. They analyze one another, an assessment driven by avoidance in how to not concede to the other if they can help it. Baker does as usual, and goes to look out her window and stations herself there. After a moment, she begins speaking, addressing the housemother with a delicate touch.

"I realize our relationship is one of a professional nature, and that we don't always agree on how to manage a situation."

Behind her comes a rustle. Mrs. Maynard has chosen to sit, but doesn't rush to speak as she normally would. The housemother has the upper hand, and knowing this is like donning wool underwear, a major irritant, but Baker forges on.

"It would do us both good to come to some understanding when it involves our residents, so that perhaps we can work to resolve matters between ourselves. What do you think? For the good of the women and the Colony, of course."

Mrs. Maynard begins, but her voice cracks. She stops and tries again.

"I always do the best I can."

"Yes, well, I've called you here because of the situation with Dr. Graham."

"About what took place with Stella."

Baker pretends ignorance regarding Mrs. Maynard's participation.

"Oh good. You know about that?"

"I was there with Dr. Graham and Nurse Crawford. I assisted."

"I see."

"From what I understand, it was absolutely necessary, so said Dr. Graham. He's such a professional and I have to say, we're lucky to have him, considering he could practice anywhere, at any level. Even Ralph—I mean, Mr. Woodall—said as much the other day, that he's the absolute best, and I agree, not that I have that sort of background. All's well that ends well, don't you think?"

Woodall. She wondered when Mrs. Maynard would slap that card on the table. When Baker first came to the Colony, the chairman at the time was Mr. Thaddeus Gray. He hired her immediately and Baker, not one to like many, had liked him. Sadly, two years later, Mr. Gray became ill, and Dr. Woodall replaced him. Dr. Woodall golfs with the governor and Mr. and Mrs. Hubert Maynard socialize in the same circles. Mrs. Maynard, a Woodall loyalist, tends to wax poetic whenever he's mentioned. Baker finds this a higher hill to climb than expected. For her, the meeting has quickly turned into a lost cause.

"I suppose so."

A sneaky smile spreads over Mrs. Maynard's face.

"Was there something in particular you wished to discuss with me? Some concern, perhaps?" she chirps.

Baker gets a dull ache behind her eyes, the sign of a migraine. She waves a hand in the air and fibs, making up an excuse for calling Mrs. Maynard into her office.

"I thought you might provide me with Stella's update since the medical staff is sometimes busy with other patients. I know you care about the residents as I do, so that's what I wanted and you have done so, with Mr. Woodall's own opinion included. Thank you."

"Very well, then. Is that all?"

"For now, yes."

The housemother whips a finger in the air as if she's just thought of something.

"Mr. Woodall's supper party is next weekend. I'm sure Hubert and I will see you there?"

Baker didn't know there was a supper party. She feigns busyness, shuffling papers on her desk and opening drawers, acting as if she didn't hear. The door shuts and she props herself against her desk, her head pounding. She yanks a desk drawer open, grabs the bottle of milk of magnesia, tips it up and gulps it down. She puts the cap back on and shudders. She sinks into her chair and doesn't stir when the dinner bell rings, or when it sounds again to return to work or class. The Colony goes on about its business while she's wrestling with the idea those she manages might get the best of her. Memories of the delinquent girls and disloyal staff at Samarcand rise from the ashes. Baker fears her character is once again under threat, and a similar disgrace could repeat itself. She keeps to her office all afternoon, watching from the window how the women work together, their comradery a thing to be admired and envied.

Chapter 17

Ruth

Ruth is outside, nauseous and weak-kneed from Neosalvarsan. She thought fresh air might help before the noon crowd fills the dining hall, so she leans against the brick wall, eyes closed, and tilts her face to the sun. To her right, she hears voices. She looks and sees a figure in a familiar cloche hat with a flower, peeking into the window of the front door of the Colony. Nearby a taxi sits, the engine idling. The woman straightens up and raps on the window like she's visiting a neighbor.

"Hello?" she calls out.

It's a voice she'd know anywhere. Ruth, filled with more energy than she's felt in a long time, rushes across the grass.

"Mama!"

Mr. Lumley appears at that moment from the back of some field, pushing a wheelbarrow of manure to the garden area. He stops and sets it down, looking from her to her mother, then points, as if to say, *Hey, look who's here.* Ruth waves both arms in the air and yells again.

"Mama!"

Her mother turns as Baker launches herself out the door, throwing it open with the force of a strong wind. Mr. Lumley picks up the handles of the wheelbarrow and makes himself scarce. Her mother's attention shifts from her to the superintendent and Ruth is close enough to hear the Colony's regulations coming out of Baker like a machine gun. She's in a full-blown tirade.

"You're trespassing! No visitors! This facility isn't open to the public!"

Ruth has never heard Baker raise her voice, and though this registers, it doesn't matter because as soon as she reaches her mother, she embraces her. There's nothing Baker can do in that moment even as she attempts to reassert control.

"As you well know, Miss Foster, this is *absolutely* not allowed."

As if Ruth sent an invitation. She ignores the superintendent, reveling in the feel of her mother's arms as they return her embrace. She inhales the familiar brand of curling spray she uses, a mix of rose water and oil. That scent and her mother's warm hug is all she cares about because it's what she so sorely needs. Baker puts her hand on Ruth's arm and pulls, attempting to forcibly separate them. They hang on to one another even tighter. Baker stops trying, and instead threatens.

"Miss Foster. Be cognizant of repercussions. The rules of this institution do not allow for visits and there are reasons for that. This is a clear violation and it's a punishable one."

Ruth mumbles into her mother's shoulder.

"As if I could forget."

"Your mother must leave or I'll be forced to call law enforcement."

Ruth backs away but keeps a grip on her mother's arm, and begins to lead her toward the waiting taxi. She speaks fast, telling her what she's been unable to write. Her mother, still in shock at the sight of her daughter after all these weeks, listens, dumbfounded about the events that took her away and put her here.

Ruth is about to tell her about meditation, and the horrors of the shots when Baker, who's followed them, speaks again in that forceful way of hers and says, "That's enough, Miss Foster."

Ruth stops walking.

"I would like to go home."

Her mother grows confused as she transitions from happiness at seeing her daughter to dismay at what she's learned. Baker's unfamiliar hostility is foreign and unusual to her.

"What kind of place *is* this?" her mother asks, turning on Baker. "My Ruth is a good girl. A hard worker. What right do you have to hold her here? Look at her. She isn't at all like herself. She's underweight. Her face is puffy. What in heaven's name has happened to her? There must be some mistake."

Baker rises up to her full height of five feet seven.

"I beg your pardon, Mrs. Foster, but this is no mistake, you can mark my words."

"What proof do you have?"

"Tests, Mrs. Foster. Positive tests, from reputable doctors."

"Tests? What sort of tests?"

"For disease."

"Please explain so I can understand."

"All right. Venereal disease."

Ruth's mother visibly startles. Her eyes travel from Baker to Ruth and back.

Ruth starts to argue, "I don't think they're accurate, I think—"

Baker puts a hand up, stopping her. With efficiency and precision, Baker explains to her mother what Ruth first heard after she left meditation, about the Chamberlain-Kahn Act. She also explains her own personal history in less than thirty seconds, a history she's proud to share.

"Please understand, Mrs. Foster. I've been part of these efforts since the early thirties, almost a decade now. I assure you I know what I'm doing, and the governor of our great state knows exactly what this place is about, as do many, many other important people. Ruth is leading you astray with her less than accurate descriptions, and her apparent ignorance. Likely because she'd rather you not know the truth. Women of a promiscuous nature often don't want their families to know of this behavior."

Doubt slips over her mother's face. The questions are there, vague and not fully formed, but there.

"Promiscuous? What on earth?"

Ruth shakes her head in denial and with urgency. She holds her hands out, imploring her mother.

"Mama, you *know* me better than that. I'm not what she says. They've no right. I didn't break any law, and this place is nothing but a prison under a different name. They say I have this disease, but it's impossible! They won't let me see my test results, and they're giving me these shots that make me feel horrible. That's why I look like I do."

She's too emotional and overwrought while Baker's calm demeanor makes her sound like she's having a tantrum. Baker sighs, conveying exasperation and despair. She inclines her head to Ruth's mother and speaks directly to her, as if they share the weight of raising her strong-willed daughter.

"Oh, these young folks. Oftentimes, the hardest thing for them is to accept responsibility for the very behaviors that get them into trouble. This is the most difficult but necessary step if there's to be any improvement." She tsks and, in a conspiratorial fashion, leans down to Mrs. Foster. "I can understand your daughter wouldn't want her mother to know about her private life. That too is perfectly normal but when she becomes a danger to society, it becomes essential she's managed in a way that will put her back on the right track."

As if Baker knows her, or the sort of person she was before she arrived at this facility. Frustrated, Ruth hears herself sounding like a child, blurting out words in an effort to say something in her own defense.

"'Behaviors.' 'Private life.' 'Danger to society.' You don't know a thing about me, and you don't know what you're talking about."

She and Baker shoot dirty looks at one another until Ruth's mother begins to speak in a hushed voice, reflecting on past conversations she and Ruth have had.

"I've always worried what people might think with you living off on your own instead of getting married. Remember what your father said. People talk. Word gets out. They make assumptions. I don't know what to think!"

"Mrs. Foster, you can trust I know what's best here. Even the president of the United States has declared it a national emergency, and all we're trying to do is keep the men of our armed forces safe, healthy, and able to fight, should they be called to do so."

Her mother's face fills with even more confusion.

"Armed forces? National emergency? Ruth. Are you dating a serviceman? You haven't told me."

"No, I'm not. That's the problem. I've done nothing wrong."

Baker interjects quietly.

"Yet, here you are."

Ruth can see her mother shifting her thoughts, arranging them to try and accept what she's been told. It happens in a matter of seconds, but to Ruth, it's a slow, tortuous, and inevitable outcome. Baker is skilled at presenting her in a light her mother has never considered. With regret and her eyes filling, she grips her purse, uncertain and torn. Ruth can't believe the direction the conversation is taking.

"Mama, listen to me. You've always been *proud* of me for being independent. What people say shouldn't matter as long as you know I'm not doing anything wrong. It's nothing more than gossip."

"Gossip is one thing, Ruthie, but if a doctor says you're ill with some sort of questionable disease, I don't know. This sounds awfully serious."

Baker grabs at this opportunity to drive her point home.

"Mrs. Foster, I can assure you it *is* serious, but Ruth is coming along, and importantly, she's being treated. She's among others who're also working to change their habits and behaviors. What she does once she is out on parole will determine what happens in her future. It's as simple as that."

"I see. And when will that be? When can she come home?"

"It's up to each resident, Mrs. Foster."

Her mother has no choice but to accept what Baker tells her. She's the authority. She's backing down and Ruth realizes she never stood a chance. No one does. She still tries to argue, while knowing it's futile, as useless as trying to persuade Mrs. Baker she shouldn't be there.

"Mama, you've got do something to get me out of here. It's no different than a prison!"

"Oh, Ruthie. I'm sorry. There doesn't seem to be any way. Who would I talk to? If the law is involved, doctors, and my word, the governor? What can be done? You're going to have to do as you're told, and work hard to . . ." And she pauses, as if she isn't sure exactly what it is Ruth has to do.

Baker provides clarity.

"Restructure her way of thinking and living."

Her mother makes a face at this and squeezes Ruth's hand.

"You'll come home soon."

Baker is almost beaming with positivity.

"Indeed, Mrs. Foster. That's the goal, I assure you."

Ruth is in disbelief at how this has turned out even as her mother, albeit reluctantly, appears to accept what she's told.

"I don't like it, but it's what must be done. Now, come give your mother a hug. The taxi is costing me a fortune."

Ruth wants to scream. To run. She wants to jump in the taxi and instruct the driver to take her far, far away. Of course, she does none of these things; instead, she turns and walks away.

Her mother says her name with a hint of alarm. "Ruthie?"

Ruth ignores her and refuses to look at Baker, who must be feeling immense satisfaction at how she's managed to handle this. She doesn't stop.

"Ruth!"

She's still close enough to hear Baker cajole her mother, speaking with a regrettable air. "Oh, Mrs. Foster, this is how it is. She'll be good as new in an hour or so. Don't worry. We're taking good care of your Ruthie."

Ruth enters the door at the side of the building, and goes into the kitchen.

"Goodness gracious, where have you been? The bell sounded to serve several minutes ago!" Opal exclaims.

They're scrambling to fill trays with glazed carrots (Ruth used brown sugar), creamed English peas and spring onions, and fried chicken. Their foreheads are shiny with sweat and Opal is panicking when she sees the line in the dining hall forming.

"Come on, we got to hurry and get caught up."

Ruth hears the housemothers calling for the women in line to settle down. Mrs. Dillard sticks her head into the kitchen.

"What's the holdup?"

Opal and Sally reassure Mrs. Dillard they're getting things straightened out as Ruth begins working mechanically, quickly sliding food trays out the window. Her thoughts churn, and her chest is tight, constricted like she's climbed a thousand flights of stairs and can't catch her breath. The belief her mother could somehow help had given her something to hold on to, and now she has nothing. She must do as they say, bend to their ridiculous rules. Don't argue. Admit guilt, even if there's none. *Give up.* The serving done, she dumps food onto a tray for herself, not that she's one bit hungry. She goes and sits down with Josephine and the rest. No one at her table notices how quiet she is at first. After a few minutes, and with barely any of her food touched, which would be counted as another strike against her in one day, Josephine taps her arm.

"Bad morning?"

Ruth sits back, crosses her arms, and admits what's troubling her.

"My mother came and it didn't go well."

Josephine spins about to face Ruth, her face serious.

"Oh, no. What happened?"

"I was outside taking a break and saw her. I'd barely had time to hug her when Baker—you know she misses nothing, or very little—came outside. She convinced Mama I'm here of my own doing, and there's nothing she can do. My mother was intimidated after she threw out that the governor, the law, and doctors are part of this. Whether we like it or not, we're stuck here until they let us go and that's all there is to it. We'll never be completely free of this place. Even after we're out they'll always be watching out for the first wrong step. Look at Lucy. She's been brought back time and again."

"Did someone say my name? What're y'all talking about?"

Lucy flops down in the chair across the table from Ruth and leans forward, elbows on the table, chin in her hands. Ruth waves a hand about in a tired, annoyed manner.

"About how we can never be free of this place. How they say it's parole, and what that means is any one of us could be brought back again. Like you."

"You're just now figuring this out? You ask me, we might as well be wearing something like that scarlet letter."

Ruth is momentarily distracted.

"You've read that book?"

"Geez. Why so surprised? I can read."

She nudges Ruth jokingly.

Josephine says, "I haven't read it."

"Me neither."

This from Melissa, Paula, and Natalie.

Lucy says, "The story takes place several hundred years ago." She makes a derisive noise. "Not much has changed, if you ask me."

Ruth snorts in agreement and explains the rest.

"A married woman whose husband has been missing for a while falls in love, gets pregnant, then refuses to tell the townspeople, who're Puritans, who the father is. She's publicly humiliated, and forced to wear a red *A*, for adulteress, on her clothing the rest of her life. She's shunned and so is her daughter, eventually."

Several voices cry out, including from Maude and Gloria.

"That's so sad."

"How mean."

This gets everyone talking all at once, but the conversation ends abruptly when Baker appears to speak in an animated fashion to Mrs. Maynard. Ruth and the women sitting with her watch because Baker's presence can never be ignored. In seconds the only noise is the clatter of utensils. Baker and Mrs. Maynard periodically turn toward Ruth. Her mother's visit is going to cost. Baker leaves and Mrs. Maynard approaches her table as everyone in the dining hall busies themselves with eating while still paying attention.

Ruth looks down the length of her table at the others, and says, "Here goes."

"Miss Foster, if you could come with me."

Ruth doesn't move.

"Why?"

"I think you probably know why."

Slowly she stands while Mrs. Maynard, her expression neutral, leads the way out. There's a hush throughout the dining hall, but as soon as they're beyond its walls, Ruth begins to protest vigorously.

"I had nothing to do with my mother coming. I know it's not allowed. She came on her own. My letters to her were read and there was nothing in them except where I was, and that I was being treated."

Mrs. Maynard breathes out heavily. "Miss Foster, that very well may be so, but it happened, and because it did, Mrs. Baker heard some statements from you that cause her great concern. All you can do is face the consequences brought on by the choices you make. You know this."

Ruth shuts down. She might as well accept the defeat. They arrive at Baker's office and the door swings open before Mrs. Maynard can knock. Mrs. Baker retreats into the interior and they follow, Ruth's heart an internal fist beating on her chest wall. Baker goes behind her desk and sits in her chair, then motions with an impatient hand at Mrs. Maynard.

"Shut the door."

Mrs. Maynard retraces her steps to shut it firmly. Ruth chances a peek at the housemother, who delivers a rancid look at the superintendent, but Baker's too busy scribbling in a notebook to see. Not for the first time, Ruth has the impression these two don't get along. The superintendent finally sets her pen down, and folds her hands on top of her desk.

"I suppose there's no need to explain the reason why I've asked to see you."

"No."

Baker's pause has Ruth correcting her response.

"No, *ma'am.*"

"I need something from you, Miss Foster. Do as I ask and you can go on as you have been, working toward your parole as well as continuing the vocational work you seem to enjoy, cooking. If you choose to help with this request, there won't be any repercussions for what took place earlier today."

Ruth is silent and Baker doesn't make a point of it.

"I want you to write a letter describing how your life is being turned around. You'll write about the improvements with your health and you'll explain how your future, now that you've come here and received excellent training and guidance, will give you opportunities to live a moral life once you're out on parole."

Ruth cringes. Doing this would be like bragging how nice the enemy is, and she struggles to keep her face expressionless. Baker continues on.

"A few select residents will contribute. In your case, it will stand as a correction toward what I heard from you today about the earnest endeavors undertaken here. That's not what we want our residents sharing once they're out on parole."

It's blackmail. She doesn't want to do this at all. It will go in her record, and will seem like she had no issue being here. As if she agreed.

"What purpose will they serve?"

Baker glares.

"Ma'am," Ruth amends.

"My, aren't you the inquisitive one? You can rest assured these letters of commendation will be read by individuals who're at the very top of this institution. I suggest you do yourself a favor."

"I . . ."

"You agree, I'm certain, this is an easy request."

"What if I don't agree?"

There's a sharp intake of breath from Mrs. Maynard, while Baker goes still. Her eyes are on Ruth, dark, impenetrable, and cold. Ruth could swear the room temperature drops by a few degrees, yet she refuses to look away. Baker comes around to stand beside Ruth. She's close, too close.

"I wouldn't think you'd refuse, Miss Foster." Baker's breath is wintergreen scented. "After all, it's not as if you actually have a choice. Not delivering on a direct request results in consequences, a little time spent in a place I believe you're familiar with? I expect it tomorrow before the evening chapel service. Give it to Mrs. Maynard. Is this clear?"

"Yes, Mrs. Baker."

"Good. That's all."

Mrs. Maynard escorts Ruth out. As they walk down the hall, the housemother chastises her, glancing at her now and again in disbelief.

"Don't be a fool. It's been going along well for you these past few weeks. You should consider this an honor. Like she said, only a few are getting a chance to tell a bit about their experiences here."

Ruth can't believe what she's hearing.

"An honor?"

Mrs. Maynard takes her out of context.

"Absolutely. That's how you should write it. You're fortunate to be here and don't worry, it doesn't have to be a long missive. Short and sweet is best, Miss Foster."

Mrs. Maynard points toward the kitchen, dismissing her, and Ruth gladly makes her way there. To write such a letter would be filled with nothing but lies and would turn Baker and her staff into do-gooders, saviors, even. Baker's request is to remind her who's got the upper hand. Ruth wants to refuse, but the meditation room looms fresh in her mind. What if it's group punishment instead? She shudders at the idea of Mrs. Maynard watching it, enjoying it, or even worse, administering it.

She enters the kitchen breathing in the scent that comes with cooking, reminding her of better times and better places, not unlike her cozy, small apartment where she would have Sunday dinner ready for her mother's afternoon visit. Her mother. She grows despondent at how things were left between them, and the uncertainty of when she'll see her again. Opal and Sally raise their voices in greeting, grinning at her from across the room, each of them looking like they've seen better days too, but in this moment, those are the sweetest faces she's seen all day. She goes toward them, grateful at least for their friendly, warm presence.

Chapter 18

Stella

Stella enters the laundry room where Lucy, cigarette dangling from her lips, feeds just-washed linens through the rollers of the washing machine. Stella's state-issued dress hangs loose on her frame and she exudes a new fragility, more a wisp of a girl than ever. Even so, it's also true she appears healthier and she feels better too.

She sends a tentative smile to Lucy, who stops working, and with her usual dryness, says, "Well, if it ain't Miss Goody returning to her duties. Can't say you look great, but you sure do look better than last time I seen you."

"Yeah. I feel all right, now."

"What was wrong with you? After you fell in the yard out there, geez, I thought you were done for."

"I had some kind of infection from my operation."

"You had an operation?"

"Yeah."

"When?"

"When I first come here."

"What kind of operation?"

"I had a tumor."

"A tumor."

Stella points at her belly and Lucy gives her a funny look. Sage, and doubtful at the same time.

"Okay, if that's what you want to call it." She lifts a basket of wet sheets and goes toward the door. "You want to hang these, or would you rather sort through that pile over there for the wash?"

"I can sort."

"Suit yourself."

Stella moves to the mound of dirty clothes, which is bigger than usual since Lucy didn't have any help. She begins to place them into appropriate piles. She works quietly, sunk in thought over something that's been bothering her since quarantine. It's the power she thought Mrs. Baker had at the Colony. Wasn't she supposed to be in charge? She said as much time and again, but Dr. Graham did what he wanted anyway. Given this experience, she concludes Baker is no different from any other woman. Dr. Graham has more sway. Men in general have more sway, if not all the authority.

She vaguely remembers one of her teachers in school talking about feminism and women's rights. At that time, she listened in disbelief and not a little incredulity at the idea of women having an equal say in important matters. How is that even possible when women can't own bank accounts, secure loans, or much of anything? She knows this because of conversations her parents had, more like arguments. Alice wanted her own checking account, and Stella remembers all too well her father's derision, reminding her of all the ways a woman couldn't have that, and more. She didn't bring this up in class because the teacher insisted it would eventually change, but Stella is sure if she ever met the likes of a man like Cordell, or a Dr. Graham, her certainty would suffer a setback. She can still see Dr. Graham in her mind, standing near the top of her head, his expression as he snaked the tube down her throat impatient and unsympathetic. She grits her teeth and looks outside at Lucy as a way to erase that mental image.

Out the laundry room door, the sun is shining bright and the sky is that deep vivid blue it is in spring before the haze of summer turns it flat and dull like aluminum. Realizing the kind of day it is, she regrets turning down Lucy's offer to hang the sheets. There's a slight breeze carrying in freshness along with the fetid scent of turned soil. She speeds up. If she finishes, she'll go help. She picks through the clothes and stops at the sight of an undergarment that bears a monthly stain. These are always removed from the main wash for Lucy's special soaking treatment. She can't recall the last time she had hers. It had stopped before the predicament that sent her here and she assumed it would've come back by now. Maybe it takes a while, after going through that kind of operation. That must be it. It'll return, and when it does, she'll be wishing it would go away because she hated how it always made her feel, bloated and grumpy.

She drops the item into the special soaking bucket and as she works, voices from outside draw her attention. It's Mrs. Baker and she's with Lucy, who points toward the door of the laundry room. The superintendent crosses the yard and Lucy trails behind her. Stella gets to her feet, feeling the pull of the scar left over from the drainage tube. Mrs. Baker enters and considers her for a moment before speaking.

"Stella, you appear well, I see."

"Yes, Mrs. Baker."

Lucy leans her shoulder against the wall, glaring at Mrs. Baker's back, but only Stella sees this. She and Lucy are both surprised by what she says next.

"Miss Griffin, Stella will no longer work laundry. We'll find someone else to help. Come along with me, Stella."

Stella gives Lucy a bewildered look as she follows Mrs. Baker out of the laundry room. Lucy folds her arms, then appears to remember something. She mouths words at her, but Stella can't make them out. She glances back, and Lucy repeats herself in a more pronounced way and Stella understands this time. *Don't tell her what I said.* This is about Lucy saying she'd run again. She glances once more and Lucy is back to hanging clothes, the sunlight shining over her in such a way it reminds Stella of a painting she once saw in a textbook at school. It was by an artist named Charles Courtney Curran called

Hanging Out Linen. It was a beautiful painting, and she deems the prostitute pretty until the sun goes behind a cloud, turning the scene before her dreary.

She hurries to keep pace with Mrs. Baker, feeling lucky, luckier than Lucy. It's plain to see, even to her, Lucy isn't one of the redeemable. Not like herself. Some people, like her father and mother and others she's observed, they don't want to change. They're set in their ways and no matter what gets said or done, they go back to doing what they want. Stella, though, she learned a long time ago it's best to be malleable, to submit as needed, to try and do better. That's what she wants, which is why she wants to please Mrs. Baker. Mrs. Baker's uneven gait makes their progress slow. Stella glances down a time or two at the older woman's legs as they walk toward the front of the building. She's embarrassed when Mrs. Baker explains.

"I was injured badly as a child. I misbehaved and paid for it. Dearly."

Imagining Mrs. Baker as a child is difficult, but mostly Stella's interested in this childhood mistake. She herself has made lots of mistakes—which is why she's here. This intrigues her that Mrs. Baker did too.

"And then they sent you to a place like this, to redeem yourself?"

Mrs. Baker studies Stella for a long moment and Stella's about to apologize when she replies.

"No. My parents' disappointment and my injury taught me what I needed to know. Some of us learn from our mistakes, others can't. Or won't."

They enter the administration building and walk down the main hall. Instructions are being called out from a classroom. What's being taught, Stella already learned a long time ago. She realizes most of them don't know how to read, much less how to conjugate a verb. They don't know the chart of chemical symbols like she does.

"You're to keep that to yourself."

"Yes, Mrs. Baker."

"I only told you for one reason and that's because I believe we're alike in some ways."

"You do?"

"Yes. We've both made significant mistakes and we've both paid a price, a permanent price. Do you understand?"

Stella nods, although she's not sure she does.

"Yes, Mrs. Baker."

"You haven't grown close to anyone since you've been here. You feel as if you don't belong. Is that right?"

"Yes, ma'am. I ain't ever fit in much, nowhere."

"Again, a similarity."

They're at the office now, and Mrs. Baker opens the door and leads the way in. She goes to her desk where she opens a drawer, and draws out a sheaf of paper.

"Like I said, many go on to learn from mistakes. They recognize their flaws, accept them, change, and move on. They become different people. Not everyone can do this, but I think you can, and have made good progress so far."

Stella flushes.

"Thank you, ma'am."

"You're smart. You learn quickly. This is why I want you to write the letter I mentioned before." She sets a sheet of paper in front of Stella and hands her a pencil. "Write it in pencil first so you can erase any mistakes, or reword it if you wish. Then, you can write it in pen."

A little thrill goes through Stella. This is important, she can tell. She wants to do her best.

"Yes, Mrs. Baker."

"There's a small table there you can use to write on. All you have to do is say what you've been doing, how you think it helps you. I've got some work to do. I'll be right here if you have questions. When you're done, I'll look it over."

"Yes, Mrs. Baker."

"You may call me Mrs. Dot when it's just us."

"Yes, ma'am." She speaks in a whisper. "Mrs. Dot."

"I consider you quite special. You're like a little companion, a little pet."

Stella beams. Gosh. Mrs. Baker—no, Mrs. Dot (!)—is so kind. Why would anyone ever think she's mean? Stella eagerly takes the pencil and paper and sits at the small table. She pauses, thinking for a moment, but it doesn't take her long before she begins writing because she knows how she feels in this moment, and what she wants to say.

To whom it may concern,

She stares at the salutation. In the letter-writing part of her English class they studied proper greetings, as well as the structure of a letter, and she likes the organization. It looks right to her, and so she goes on.

My name is Stella Temple. I'm fifteen years old. I came to the Colony two months ago. Being here is really good for me. I get to learn new things that will help me in my future. I know how to sew some already, but maybe I can learn how to make dresses. I get to eat good food regularly. Being here is much better than being at home. My mother and father sent me so I could learn how to do right. I was told I'm redeemable, and that makes me feel good about myself. I feel safe.

Yours truly,
Stella Temple

She puts the pencil down. Mrs. Dot glances up from her own work.

"You've finished that quick?"

"Yes, ma'am, I think so."

"Let's see what you have."

She hands the superintendent the paper with a hint of nerves like she'd felt with teachers at her school. Mrs. Dot reads carefully and after a moment, tips back in her chair, studying Stella in a way Stella can't decipher. She shifts nervously, and Mrs. Dot straightens up, and hands the paper back to her.

"Excellent work. Now, do it in pen."

"Yes, Mrs. Dot. Thank you."

She does as asked and when she has the final copy she takes it to the superintendent, who sets it aside without looking at it again.

"All right, good. Now then . . ."

Stella watches as Mrs. Dot appears to think about what to say next. Since she's no longer working the laundry, what will she have her do? She hopes it's something interesting.

"Remember I said I might have you help Frances Platt? She's close to your own age, although I hesitate because, as you've seen, she can be very challenging."

Stella feels a tiny zip of anxiety bolt through her like lightning. She doesn't want to do this, if given a choice, but she can't tell Mrs. Dot no. How is she supposed to help someone like Frances?

"Ma'am, what would I do?"

"Perhaps try to teach her the alphabet. How to add and subtract. Nothing too complicated. See if you can teach her some basic manners too. She's been quite a challenge for Mrs. Maynard. Frances listens to me because she knows I will not tolerate her foolishness. If she can learn basic skills, she could possibly do some menial work outside the confines of the Colony. Perhaps help her poor mother."

Stella is afraid of Frances with her odd looks and outlandish ways, but she can't refuse, so she gives Mrs. Dot the only acceptable answer.

"Yes, ma'am. I'll try best as I can."

"She has regular chores, so you'll only spend a couple hours a day with her. I'll have you work in the kitchen when you're not with Frances."

Stella perks up at the mention of the kitchen. It makes up for being around the troublesome Frances because she'll get to work with Ruth Foster. This almost has her smiling and she has to catch herself. She shouldn't appear too happy about it or Mrs. Dot might grow suspicious. She might not like that she admires Ruth or knowing she wouldn't mind being like her, even if just a little bit. She seems so brave. And she's pretty.

"I want you to continue to tell me everything you hear and see, is that clear? That part of your reform won't change."

Stella was hoping this would get dropped. She thinks about Melissa along with the other women and what happened to them. They were punished severely because of her—even though she didn't want to admit it, she knows it's true. Her guilt returns, not that it ever left. It's always been there, that not-so-good feeling about her part in it, and she's careful to not convey anything. She lapses into the age-old practice of hiding her true emotions, hiding that she won't do it again.

"Yes, Mrs. Dot."

That night, after she's in bed, she dreams of Cordell arriving at the Colony, her reform ending because she doesn't do what Mrs. Dot wants. She sees him coming up the road, driving fast, his eyes red with liquor and lust, the weight of his hand on her.

Chapter 19

Baker

Baker's irritation grows with every *tick, tick, tick* of the second hand of the clock in her office. The newspaper she peruses daily is shoved off to the side of her desk. She's too annoyed to read. The Foster woman's letter of commendation was not delivered as requested. She despises the blatant disregard of a directive, the nerve of daring to ignore it. Ever since the woman's mother showed up, and Baker was afforded a glimpse of Ruth's true feelings about reform, she's done a slow boil of outrage. She's insulted. The Foster woman is playing a game. She's getting by, doing only what's necessary so she can get out and return to her ways. Baker knows her type. They always end up returning, like that troublemaker Lucy Griffin.

She spins her chair around to face the window. Not all can be as obedient and willing as Stella Temple. Despite what she's been through, she knows what's good for her. Residents like her give Baker the sense of success and accomplishment, unlike Ruth and Lucy and a handful of others who make her feel as if the very energy expended on their behalf is a waste of time. It's about as useless as handing the guideline booklet to one of the mental defectives who can't read. Ruth Foster, for all of her confidence and righteousness, is no different from Lucille Griffin, in that their type typically disappoints. The thought of Ed and his floozy comes from out of nowhere, and Baker grimaces. Ruth Foster is a perfect reminder of the sort he liked: flamboyant, carefree, and lovely to look at. Ed's egregious behavior, his philandering and propensity toward this very type of woman she's trying to conform to society's expectations has always given her an extra sour taste in her mouth.

There's nothing to see outside after the sun sets, and she turns away from the window. She'll go to the chapel and plant herself by the door, and when Ruth appears, she'll confront her. If she hands her a letter with a decent excuse for why it's late, Baker's willing to be generous. If she doesn't? She shoves the chair back and goes into her private bathroom. She stares at her reflection. Her color is high, a sign her blood pressure is up, her anger heating her up so she's damp under her arms. She takes a washrag, runs cool water over it, and holds it to her forehead for a moment. It helps, and she sets her shoulders, ready for what comes.

By the time she arrives, women are beginning to file out. Mrs. Maynard and Mrs. Dillard stand together just outside the door, heads together and deep in conversation. She approaches them and before either speaks, she gets right to the point, directing her comments to Mrs. Maynard.

"I thought I was clear about Miss Foster?"

The housemothers look at one another and Mrs. Dillard speaks first.

"There's a problem."

"Yes," seconds Mrs. Maynard, "a rather urgent one identified only moments ago."

Baker's gaze shifts between them.

"What's the problem? Speak up!"

Mrs. Maynard twiddles with the whistle.

"It's Lucy. She wasn't at the service. It's a big room and I kept thinking I'd spot her . . ."

Baker holds a hand up.

"Please get to the point."

Mrs. Maynard continues her highly irritating habit of dithering with the whistle's cord, and Baker suddenly relates to Frances's reaction of snatching it over the woman's head. Mrs. Maynard finally expresses the concern.

"We don't believe she attended chapel."

Baker's eyes shut briefly, then, as she must do, because they obviously can't think for themselves, at least not Mrs. Maynard, she provides direction.

"Check the dorm to see if she's there. Check if she took anything. Mrs. Dillard, would you go to the quarantine area and make sure she isn't ill?"

Both women hurry away while Baker feels certain she already knows what's going on, but she'll wait for them to confirm her suspicions. She can hear Sheriff Wright when she has to report it, once again highlighting a weak point in managing their charges. The other women continue to slowly file out, some glancing at her as they sidle by. Maybe they know something, maybe they don't. The housemothers return a couple of minutes later, both puffing with effort.

"She's not in the dorm."

"She's not sick either."

Baker's insides deflate with the knowledge that Lucille Griffin has pulled off another escape.

"I'm of a mind to refuse her return here if she's caught. She's a bad influence anyway. Far as I'm concerned, they can take her to jail. Maybe that's what needs to be done."

Mrs. Maynard tsks, and adds her two cents.

"How many times has she done this now? I can't believe it."

Perplexed, Baker ponders the woman. She's the housemother. She's supposed to know where residents of her dorm are at all times. She's about to point this out when her attention is diverted to Ruth coming in the side door. Ruth sees her too. Baker, never fast, manages to close the distance with an uncanny speed. Mrs. Maynard scurries behind, jumping in to berate Ruth as if to make up for the disappearance of Lucy.

"Miss Foster! Weren't you at this evening's service?"

"I don't care for church."

Baker is as surprised by this answer as is Mrs. Maynard, who juts out her jaw and wags finger.

"Now is not the time to be impertinent."

Women like Lucy, like Ruth, with their beauty and confidence, are the sort Baker relishes conquering. Ruth's green eyes, sharp as glass shards, unnerve Baker and she finds she resents her on a personal level, which is unacceptable by her own standards. How on earth can she bear a grudge against a lesser than? Mrs. Maynard opens her mouth to speak and Baker cuts her off.

"And so, where were you, Miss Foster?"

Ruth provides a forthright answer.

"Outside."

"Miss Foster, as you surely know and understand, your cooperation and willing participation determine your success at this facility."

"I've heard."

Baker has never had a resident act so calm, and obstinate.

"You might not want to go to the service, however, it's compulsory, and not a choice. It's part of what we plan for you and we require you participate in what you've been assigned while here."

"I enjoy fresh air after supper, and I lost track of time and because I would've been late, I chose to stay outside. I think there's more of God's presence there than anywhere else—especially outside of these walls."

Mrs. Maynard jerks like she's been shot while Baker has a tinge of admiration for Ruth speaking her mind—but it's very brief.

"While I can appreciate your honesty, trying to slip in the side door and join in with those who did what they were supposed to do is a serious breach, you understand."

By now the others have realized something is going on. The women take their time as they pass, attempting to eavesdrop, and Mrs. Maynard joins Mrs. Dillard in flapping her hands to move them along, and raising her voice.

"This doesn't concern you! Go to your dorms and prepare for lights out, as usual."

Baker and Ruth are like boxers in a ring, facing one another, one cautious, the other imperious.

"What do you know about Lucy Griffin's disappearance?"

"Nothing."

Baker isn't buying it. It's too much of a coincidence. Ruth Foster is lying, even though her expression remains lifeless.

"I take it you don't have the letter prepared either?"

Ruth speaks in a forthright way again, with this devil-may-care attitude.

"No, ma'am, I don't."

"Is there an explanation to accompany your outright disregard of my request?"

If there is, Ruth Foster isn't offering it. Baker turns to Mrs. Maynard.

"See to the nightly schedule. Go to your dorm, Miss Foster, and in the morning be at my office directly after breakfast."

"I'll bring her," Mrs. Maynard says helpfully.

Ruth says, "Yes, ma'am," and joins the other women who cluster around her with alarmed whispers.

Baker interprets their expressions: self-righteous anger, befuddlement, and some even dare to look her way. She's incensed. She can't afford a renegade resident. Someone who holds merit with the rest. Ruth is escorted away like she's an icon, a hero. Baker resents this more than she cares to admit. Where's the thankfulness for what *she's* trying to do? Ruth Foster ought to count herself lucky to be here, as should the rest of them. She's taking advantage of the situation, and abusing her time here instead of putting it to good use. She needs to learn humility and gratitude for what's being done for her. Baker retires to her room, where she spends the night contemplating next steps.

At six a.m. the following morning, in the gray light of dawn, she sits up in bed. After her restless night, her legs are tight and itchy. She rubs her hands down their length. She hates the way they look, how they feel, lumpy and numb in certain areas where skin grafts are unusually thick. She doesn't like looking at them either, but on this morning, she stretches out the scarred limbs and stares while trying not to think of the disgust on Ed's face, which is impossible. It's all she's ever thought about. She'd never admit she envies the women here because for all of their shortcomings, the waywardness of their lives, they've not endured what she has. Despite the shots, what with their hair falling out and loose or lost teeth, they have smooth skin. Oh sure, some have thin scars across their faces, or are pockmarked, but most are free of anything so horribly disfiguring. And most have husbands. Their men might be sorry specimens, but they have them. Baker can't stand when they get someone like Ruth Foster, with her cool beauty and idea of blamelessness. Baker wonders if she were an unruly child, such as herself.

She stops massaging her legs, pulls her nightgown down, and gets up. She knows what she's going to do about Ruth Foster. Thirty minutes later, she's dressed. Breakfast for the institution has started and she has a little bit of time to stop and speak to Nurse Crawford, who's usually in her area early. She heads there, and finds her bent over some files on her desk.

"Nurse Crawford, when is Miss Foster receiving her next round of medication?"

"As per our protocol, she's due for testing, um, let me see, tomorrow as a matter of fact."

"Please do it today. She will be in my office directly after breakfast and I'd like you to be there to take her blood."

"Is there a reason?"

"Yes."

Nurse Crawford purses her lips in that way she has when she wants to say something but doesn't have the nerve.

"Ruth Foster's emboldened behavior of late requires a different approach, is all. I don't want her reform upended by her poor choices."

"I see. No problem, I'll be there."

"Excellent."

In her office, Baker is unable to settle down. She can't stop checking the time until finally, forty-five minutes later, there's a tap on the door. If nothing else, she can appreciate promptness. She opens it and ushers the three women in. The nurse is, as always, serious and businesslike. Ruth apparently hasn't slept either, given smudges beneath her eyes and a pallor that favors her instead of detracting from her looks.

Before Mrs. Maynard can control the conversation as she has a tendency to do, Baker says, "Miss Foster, have you had a chance to think over the issues from yesterday?"

"Yes, ma'am."

"Do you have anything you'd like correct from the last conversation we had?"

Baker isn't surprised when she receives another vacant stare and a cough to accompany it. Baker hates to admit the woman's mother was right: she does look different from the day she arrived. Her black hair is lackluster, and thinner. Those faint circles under her eyes and the puffy skin of her lower lids ages her. This makes Baker happy knowing she looks a little less like that cheating whore who took Ed, and even better, a little less sure of herself this morning.

"We're taking a different route altogether where you're concerned, Miss Foster. Know this, I believe in you. I also believe with a little extra persuasion you'll find yourself on the right path. To that end, I've carefully considered what to do. Your lack of enthusiasm and the opinions you shared with your mother means you've yet to see the benefit of your time here, which, I would remind you, is in a facility of the highest quality with outstanding programs. Since you're unaware of how fortunate you are, I've got to be sure mandatory treatments aren't disrupted and neither is your reform work. Are you following me so far?"

Baker notes the distrust and confusion, as obvious as the bewilderment on Mrs. Maynard's face. Baker is pleased with all this. She's fully in control, as she ought to be, and so she continues.

"Nurse Crawford will take your blood. Once the results come back, we'll see whether or not you'll resume work in the kitchen. You can't be in there if you're a risk for infection. For now, you'll sleep in quarantine and work in seclusion, away from the others."

Mrs. Maynard's mouth drops open, turning the lower half of her face into an enormous cave.

"This isn't how we've operated in the past! What's to be done about the demerits for missing chapel? That's six, maybe more, and worthy of some sort of punishment! Demerits of this nature should result in immediate action!"

"Mrs. Maynard, this *is* immediate action. I've decided what I think is best and that's that."

Mrs. Maynard folds her arms and mutters to herself.

"I'm only saying this is outside of our usual protocol."

Nurse Crawford ignores the drama, and says, "Have a seat, Miss Foster."

The process is very specific, and Nurse Crawford explains what she's doing as she prepares her kit. First, she swabs and cleans the lobe of Ruth's ear. Next, she dries the skin and continues to do so until the area is bright red. Baker stands close and observes so she can show Ruth she reigns over her, from her physical to her mental well-being. She can do as wants with her, and she has no say-so. Nurse Crawford takes a special tube and Baker leans in more, as if highly intrigued, while Mrs. Maynard pouts.

Nurse Crawford, with a rapt audience of one, explains, "This is what's called a Wright tube. It's a very special device."

With practiced skill, she holds the curved end to a droplet of blood she carefully squeezes out, repeating this step until the tiny vial is about half full. She has a Bunsen burner she uses to seal it. She repeats the steps for a second vial, and finally, once both are sealed, she drops them into an envelope.

She turns to Baker, and says, "I'll get these to the Health Department."

Baker nods. "Excellent."

With an inscrutable glance at Ruth, Nurse Crawford leaves, and Baker resumes.

"Now, Miss Foster, here's the most important decision I've made. You're to start over from the beginning. The slate of time you've been at this facility is wiped clean. This means your first two months will not be counted. As of now, I'm implementing my Day One program for you, meaning, it's like you just arrived. Consider this as a positive because it means you can move forward with a sparkling clean record, no history of running off or previous penalties. I'm willing to forget everything and in my reports, I'll provide information as to your progress as if you're a new resident. You begin again, Miss Foster, like a newborn babe."

Baker waits for Ruth's reaction and is intensely satisfied as it appears to have the effect she desires. Ruth looks slightly ill. What remains of the individual who first revealed her stubbornness and unwillingness to conform is nowhere to be found in the individual seated before her. Mrs. Maynard's disposition has turned sour as milk over these proceedings. Baker crosses the room, pulls the door open, and motions for them to leave.

"Mrs. Maynard, please give Miss Foster a task that isolates her and be sure she sleeps in quarantine until we have the results."

"Very well."

Once they're gone, she collapses in her chair. The Foster woman troubles her more than she cares to admit, but, nonetheless, she's managed to brilliantly handle the situation, if she's truthful. Even better, she expects a very different person to emerge, yet another in the long line of success stories she's had over time. The most difficult residents always end up providing a perfect model of reform at its best. They're the ones who make her shine.

Chapter 20

Ruth

Everything she's gone through since coming to the Colony has been for nothing. Once she and Mrs. Maynard are in the hall, the housemother grabs her arm and Ruth jerks it away. Mrs. Maynard, still feeling bested, grabs at her again, digging her nails in.

"I can make it worse for you than it's already going to be."

Impossible, Ruth thinks. As she's escorted down the hall, she's forced to endure a sermon like a recalcitrant schoolgirl being reprimanded by a dissatisfied teacher. The housemother's touch is repulsive and she has to carefully manage her expression.

"It's not the first time this has happened. Matter of fact, your buddy, Lucille Griffin, started over many times, which is probably why she's been here longer than most anyone. You'd do well to remember, there's always atonement for the deliberate abuse of rules. Why the superintendent isn't handling this in the usual way is beyond me."

Mrs. Maynard waits inside the entrance of the dorm while Ruth grabs what she can from her storage box. The housemother goes through her notepad, mumbling about the trouble she causes for everyone. Ruth, while used to her displeased nature, hates being spoken to in this way. It's demeaning. She also hates waiting, which

Mrs. Maynard makes her do in a show of self-importance. Ruth distracts herself by thinking of the evening before when Lucy came searching for her after supper, and told her she was going to "scram."

"Come too," she'd said.

Ruth wasn't brave enough. She could never be so bold again. No one else was willing to try except Frances Platt and her attempts made all of them think it wasn't worth it. Besides, if caught, meditation, group punishment, less food, and the idea of having to spend more time within these walls are serious enough reasons to weigh every decision when it comes to willful disobedience. Ruth thinks about Lucy, imagining her freedom. There was this moment right before she left when she spoke as if she were trying to impart a bit of optimism. Ruth heard the earnestness in her voice and it made her listen carefully.

"Listen. Right 'fore I got brought last time, I got to know this guy. He'd come see me on occasion, you know? He might be able to help. I'm gonna tell him what goes on here, and I guarantee he'll want to come see what I'm talking about. I'm gonna tell him to look for you, so, you tell him everything. Everything, you hear me?"

Ruth experiences the intended swell of hope from the way Lucy speaks of him, like he'd be an ally.

"What does he do?"

Lucy is coy, and won't say.

"Trust me. Someone very smart. I ain't got a clue where he might be, or what's gone on since I got stuck back in here, but if I see him, I'll send him here. I promise."

They exchange a look and it delivered everything worth saying right then. Lucy turned and sashayed off toward the pasture's fencing where she always went to smoke. She didn't appear like she was doing anything wrong, just doing like she'd always done every night about this time, except she kept going, following the line of the fence until she disappeared. That was when Ruth realized chapel services had begun and she'd be late. She stayed right there, watching as evening came with its dark blanket, tucking itself around her as she second-guessed her decision not to follow the prostitute.

Mrs. Maynard brings her attention back to the present by tapping the pad.

"Ah! I've just the thing for you."

She takes off. For someone with her particular infirmity, Mrs. Maynard walks with a briskness that defies the issue. She opens the door of a utility closet that's filled with a myriad of cleaning supplies. Mrs. Maynard retrieves an old tin can of varnish along with a few rags and hands the items to Ruth.

"It will take about a week for your bloodwork to come back. In the meantime, you're to varnish the hallway floors."

"Yes, Mrs. Maynard."

"I want them glowing."

"Yes, ma'am."

The halls are set up like a *T.* At the end of the longest, there are classrooms to the right and to the left are Baker's, Dr. Graham's, and Dr. Greene's offices. The door that leads to the basement is at the far end of the short hall and Mrs. Maynard's closet-size office is on the opposite side. She points at the floors and leaves Ruth to the work. Ruth moves furniture first, sliding a long credenza-style table and two chairs out from the wall. She drops to her knees and begins at the edges. It's not long before the muscles in her arms, back, and knees burn while the fumes give her a headache. She stands to move to a new spot and she's woozy, but it's not an unpleasant sensation. Sounds reach her from the classrooms, women's voices reciting the alphabet along with the voice of someone reading slow and hesitant. For this reason and this reason alone, she can find some bit of good done here. At noon, those in the classrooms traipse by and, at first, Ruth doesn't look up. Her name is hissed. It's Josephine. Josephine mouths something and Ruth can only make out the word "what," before Mrs. Maynard materializes, a special talent of hers.

"Move along, ladies. Miss Foster is on special assignment."

Ruth overhears the comments as they obey Mrs. Maynard.

"Lordy, they got a fancy name for just about everything."

"Yeah, cleaning toilets is 'polishing porcelain.' "

"And fieldwork is . . . what was it? 'Culture and cultivation.' "

There are snorts of disgust and snickers, then a bit of complaining because everyone knows Ruth was the one cooking lately.

"Food's gonna go back to tasting like cardboard."

"Don't you know it."

"Hey, Ruth, when you back in the kitchen?"

Mrs. Maynard yells, "No talking! Move along or no dinner!"

Ruth remains on her knees as their worn shoes scuffle by inches away. She glances up into the strange countenance of Frances Platt, who has her hand held out. Ruth checks to see who's around. Mrs. Maynard is gone, having followed the women into the dining hall. Frances flicks her hand impatiently. Curious, Ruth hands the heavily soaked rag to her. Frances clutches it in both hands and brings it to her nose. She inhales, deep and long, then exhales.

Ruth says, "Don't breathe that stuff. It'll make you sick."

Frances spins around so her back is to her. She does it repeatedly and, alarmed, Ruth stands.

"Hey, stop. You shouldn't do that."

Frances twists her torso so she can look at Ruth and stuns her when she murmurs, "I know," before presenting her back again and covering her face almost entirely with the rag.

Ruth panics. She reaches around Frances's shoulder and snatches the rag away. Frances groans in disappointment, but the varnish is already affecting her. She can't quite figure out how to get the rag back from Ruth because her arms and brain aren't cooperating with one another. She slumps against a wall, hair covering her face. Ruth is wide-eyed and scared. She's about to run and get Mrs. Maynard when Frances pivots, braces herself with her hands to slide along the wall toward the dining hall. Her feet crisscross one over the other. She stops at its door, looks back at Ruth with a crooked grin. Ruth puts a hand to her mouth in horror. Frances's face is stained brown where she shoved it into the rag. Frances touches her forefinger to her thumb, giving the A-okay sign before wobbling out of sight. Ruth braces for the reaction that's sure to come, and it does, seconds later.

"Miss Foster!"

Mrs. Maynard and Mrs. Dillard appear in the hall, supporting Frances between them.

The odd trio come toward her, and Mrs. Maynard mutters, "You. I'll tend to you when I get back!"

Frances bestows an angelic smile on Ruth as they pass by, the saucer-sized brown stain making her light gray eyes stand out. Ruth resumes polishing the wood. She has trouble concentrating as she worries over how to explain Frances's face. Minutes go by. Ruth had been hungry but has now lost her appetite.

"How on earth did Frances Platt come to have that ridiculous stain on her face?"

She jumps. The question comes from behind her, and she gets to her feet and faces the housemother.

"She put her hand out like she was curious, so I gave it to her."

"Why would you do that, considering her obvious lack of intellect?"

Ruth stretches the truth.

"She sniffed at it and handed it back."

"It takes much longer for someone to get into that condition from one quick sniff."

"Believe what you want."

Mrs. Maynard's mouth sags open and she props her hands on her hips, furious.

"You realize I'm keeping up with all this, don't you? Missing chapel services. Not completing Mrs. Baker's request. Jeopardizing the well-being of an individual less capable than you. And now, directly disrespecting a staff member."

Regret for not leaving with Lucy consumes Ruth in the moment. Mrs. Maynard points at a chair.

"Sit. I'll bring your food."

"I'm not hungry."

"Should I include that to the growing list of irresponsible decisions?"

Ruth, exhausted physically and mentally, no longer cares.

"It makes no difference to me."

Mrs. Maynard's quick intake of breath triggers a momentary bit of regret, while the housemother looks almost happy at this point.

"Ah. The real you emerges."

She leaves Ruth and two minutes later she's marching toward her with a loaded tray and a wicked smile. She presents it like a gift. The tray holds more food than usual, an unappetizing pile, enough for two hefty people. A double serving of lumpy rice is covered in anemic-looking gravy nestled against two leathery gray pork chops. There's a big mound of brown beans to go with this, and the coup de grace, two dehydrated-looking biscuits. Ruth blinks. Mrs. Maynard hovers, waiting. Ruth becomes angry and with great deliberation, she picks up the fork.

"I thought since you worked so hard you might want more. See? I can be kind and thoughtful while you, Miss Foster, have much to learn. I'm going to sit and wait right here until you're done so I can be sure you actually eat it all."

Ruth starts to shovel food into her mouth, chews, swallows, and does it again. She never moves her gaze, glaring at Mrs. Maynard mouthful after mouthful. After the allotted thirty minutes, Mrs. Dillard comes from the dining hall returning her group to work, classes, or vocational studies. They walk slowly by the strange scene, Ruth with a defiant look and bulging cheeks, chewing for all she's worth, while Mrs. Maynard grows more hostile by the minute. Ruth scrapes the tray empty and drops her fork with a clatter.

"Here." She shoves the tray into Mrs. Maynard's hands. "I'm going back to work now."

Some distance from the housemother she drops to her knees and begins the endless swiping and polishing. Mrs. Maynard stalks off and Ruth, her stomach tight and extremely uncomfortable, basks in a small win, her first since coming here. Progress is slow, her stomach heavy, but the food propels her through the afternoon. Ruth gets to her feet often to move to a new spot. When she does, her head clears the fumes, and the odor of the Colony building appears more obvious, as if the varnish has enhanced her sense of smell. She misses the kitchen for its homey aroma of cooking. It didn't matter whether the food was good or not, if she closed her eyes, and made an attempt to forget where she was, it brought memories of Sunday dinners at home. In the dorm rooms, and the main area of the Colony, there's a pervasive stuffiness despite regularly opened windows and doors. It's as if the air is as trapped as they are, clinging, stale, and suffocating.

Her labor over the floors goes on for days, while it appears she and Mrs. Maynard have some sort of temporary truce. The housemother leaves her alone, only bringing her tray of food with normal amounts, and leaves them wordlessly. Nurse Crawford greets her with a good morning or a good night, and that is all of the interactions she has. Ruth begins to take pride in the pristine, polished wood floors, a chore that, despite her persistent throbbing body, has her admiring their high shine with satisfaction. The floors are old, but beautiful, and she's not so close-minded as to not notice this, despite her surroundings.

After more than a week, she's worked herself into the section that places her near Baker's office. The superintendent can see her on her hands and knees if she has the door open. This is demoralizing enough, but at one point, she's forced to rise to her feet to allow her to pass. The superintendent glances at her knees, which are as red as apples after days on them.

"Miss Foster," she says, acknowledging Ruth's presence, before she moves on.

Ruth feels like one of those old-fashioned scullery maids. A few days later, while in the hallway where the doctor's offices are, her brain is in a fume fog as she applies a second coat. She's lightly humming to herself, a tuneless noise brought on by the semi-high she's become more or less accustomed to, and has decided is not so bad. Mrs. Maynard approaches and speaks curtly.

"Miss Foster, your results are in."

Ruth, bleary-eyed, sits back on her knees and it takes a moment for her wavy world to right itself. Mrs. Maynard is impatient.

"Well? Get up and come with me!"

Mrs. Maynard is already halfway down the hall when Ruth feels able enough to shuffle along behind her. Mrs. Maynard raps on Baker's door as Ruth arrives.

"Come in."

They enter, and as they do, the bouquet on Baker's desk, a flourish of bright pink color, emits a smell so overpowering to Ruth, she begins to shallow breathe, which makes her dizzier. She can't help but observe the superintendent's overall appearance is in stark contrast to that small burst of color. Baker's clothing is dull, mostly browns and grays, unless she's in a really foul mood and then she wears black, like today. Nurse Crawford is there too. Mrs. Maynard starts the rundown of Ruth's work for the last week and a half, and Baker holds up a finger. She comes from behind her desk and stops in front of Ruth.

"I must admit, I find you to be a most peculiar challenge, Miss Foster."

Mrs. Maynard must have shared the petty infractions she's committed. Ruth surveys those in the room, from Nurse Crawford who's always hard to read, to Mrs. Maynard with her dour expression, and back to Baker holding a piece of paper that must have her results. What has she got to lose in asking the most obvious question?

"In what way?"

Mrs. Maynard says, "Don't ask que—"

Baker interrupts. "Miss Foster, your impertinence, your need to question, to demand, *to refuse*, shows me you've yet to find the proper path toward restoration. You and that troublemaker, Lucille Griffin, have always been unwilling to accept responsibility for why you're here."

"This is how any normal person would react when they're wrongfully accused and confined against their will."

Baker's facial color begins to deepen and her neck thickens. She looks as if she'll combust even as she replies in her usual monotone.

"You make my point. Your results are positive but even if they'd come back negative, I'd keep you here as you've got much more work to do to change your ways. You should feel fortunate to have the chance to correct mistakes past and present. It's no surprise, not really. If I've said it once, I've said it a million times: reform is only possible for the willing. I'll consider next steps once your treatments are done and we test again."

"What if I don't want the shots? What if I refuse? Look what it's doing. Even my mother said I didn't look the same. They're—"

"Nurse Crawford, please explain the consequences of untreated syphilis."

Ruth interrupts, desperate to understand.

"But I had the medication. I thought it was gone, if I even had it."

Mrs. Baker stiffens at Ruth's insinuation.

"You doubt the testing."

Ruth nods, and Mrs. Baker waves at Nurse Crawford, who comes forward, and Ruth is glad as she blocks her view of the superintendent. Almost.

"Most everyone tests negative after the first series, but after six weeks or so, it's possible to have a positive again. This is the reason for constant retesting, to make sure you're actually cured. It's also like a check and balance, with regard to results. The local health official, Dr. Tyndall, said you were 'slightly' diseased. Truthfully, you are either diseased or you're not. This latest test result is questionable, but because it's ambiguous, you must continue treatments until there are consistent negative returns. If not treated, it can have lifelong, if not deadly, consequences in the long run."

A new reality descends, the fear she will never get out. With her arms stiff at her sides, her hands clenched, she has no recourse, no way to argue for herself. Baker and Mrs. Maynard confer in heated whispers and Ruth is left waiting as they discuss her future like she's not there. What's more unnerving is the knowledge they believe they're doing a good job and helping individuals toward what they envision as a new and bright future. They've been doing this so long they can't see beyond what they've been taught or trained themselves. They have their views, adopted and accepted by others of like minds, as to what's suitable and then mandated. A woman living independently, like she was, means she wasn't properly aligned to their idea of what society expects, and immediately categorizes her as depraved, corrupt, or immoral. She's a woman who must be changed, made to behave and live in an acceptable manner in order to earn her freedom. Ruth hopes Lucy finds her friend, whoever he is, and sends him. She hangs on to this possibility because, in truth, it's all she's got.

Chapter 21

Stella

Stella sits in a small room with Frances Platt. They're alone, but Stella isn't saying anything because she's unsure of how to begin. How do you talk with someone like Frances? Meanwhile, Frances sits beside her, her feet together, looking prim and patient. Her shoes are so worn they're falling apart, and the material of her dress is thin in spots. Her hands are busy, though, picking at the edge of the table, unconcerned and not the least bit curious as to why she's there. Stella holds a book in her hands, one she recalls using in first grade with its pictures of apples and cats.

"Start at the most basic level," said Mrs. Maynard.

The housemother handed the book to her that morning and those were the directions, with a discouraging comment.

"No one's been able to get a thing out of her so far, so I don't see the point in this except to keep her occupied and out of trouble."

Forget Frances Platt's ignorance. Stella was even more shocked when she learned quite a few women at the Colony couldn't read or write and learned from books like this. What sets them apart from Frances is at least they talk, coarsely at times, but it's better than trying to communicate with Frances, who, so far as Stella can tell, does so through a variety of noises. She's got to begin somehow because she doesn't want to disappoint Mrs. Dot. She sets the book down and stares into Frances's face, her brows gathered in a line.

"Frances. My name is Stella Temple. How about you say your name?"

Frances decides to pluck her arm hair, her leg jiggling madly.

Stella speaks slow, enunciating the girl's name, like she's a toddler. "Can you say Fr-an-ces? Frances Platt." Stella pauses, then says, "I like your name. It's nice."

This goes nowhere, and results in nothing. Stella caves and retrieves the book.

"Look. I got something to show you. See this book? It's got the alphabet in it, and this is what you should learn first. The alphabet is what we call this collection of letters. There are twenty-six and you know what? Those letters spell every single word that exists in the English language. Did you know there's more than a hundred and seventy thousand words? Learning your letters is the first step to recognizing words and eventually reading. Wouldn't it be fun to read a book, Frances? Here's the letter *A*; it begins the alphabet. Next comes *B*. I can teach you all twenty-six and then how to spell words. I have some flashcards too, so we can look at words that begin with certain letters. Here. I'll show you."

Stella shows the flashcard with a capital *A*, and the little *a* along with a picture of an apple. She bends toward Frances and on the piece of paper she writes Anna, Stella, and Frances Platt, underlining all the *a*'s.

"See?" She uses a pencil to point. "This is a capital *A* for the name Anna. There are two ways to write *A*: big *A*, like this, and little *a*, like this. It matters when you use the big *A*. It's for names that begin with *A*, like Anna, or if a word starts at the beginning of a sentence. You use a little *a* if it's somewhere else in the word. It can get kind of complicated, but eventually you just know it. Then you can learn to read. I love reading. I love school too. I kind of miss it, but if I were able to go, that's means I'd be at home, and boy oh boy, I'd rather be here than there."

Frances stops picking at her arm. She tips her head and scrutinizes

Stella with an unwavering stare from her solitary steady eye. Stella waits, nervous and scared. Did she say something Frances is interested in? She hopes so. Any reaction at all would be good, except she's also seen how wild Frances can get, how out of control, and she doesn't want to set her off. She waits, cautiously meeting the other girl's stare, which is difficult given the physical anomalies. This lasts seconds until Frances yawns, puts her head on her arms, and is about to go to sleep. Stella scoots her chair closer.

"Frances, I'll get into trouble if you don't try to learn. What if Mrs. Maynard walks in and sees you asleep?"

Frances flops her head in the other direction to face the wall and Stella knows she's wasting her breath. Before long, Frances is snoring and she doesn't know how to handle this development. No one told her what to do if Frances didn't do right and Mrs. Maynard only said she'd check in from time to time. Stella sits back with a huff. What's actually going on in Frances's head? At times she acts like she knows stuff, other times she acts out of her mind. What's the word Mrs. Dot uses with her? There are many. Imbecile. That's one. Maybe there's some easy stuff she can show her and it'll make sense, but she has to be awake first.

Stella gets up and walks to the door, opens it and looks out. The hall is empty. There's a *thump* behind her, and she turns around to see Frances is now awake and has picked up the book. She stares at the cover, her mouth contorted in a shape Stella can't decipher. She watches Frances turn a page, then another, before she sets the book down. She scans the room until her attention lands on Stella, who hurries over.

"You want to get started?"

Frances gets up from the chair and walks to the door, her hand on the knob. She pauses to look over her shoulder at Stella as if to say, *You coming?* before leaving the room. Stella shoots up out of her chair and out the door. She scrambles along behind Frances, flustered.

"Hang on, Frances. Hang on, now. We ain't supposed to leave the room."

Frances, her legs almost twice as long as Stella's, speeds up.

"Oooooh! We ain't supposed to go outside, Frances!"

Frances marches across the grounds, leaving the side door wide open. Stella pauses in the doorway, chewing on a hangnail. How's she going to get her back inside? She checks to see who's out there. Off in the distance a small group works in a field, but they're far enough away they can't tell what's going on. Mr. Lumley is directing them in the fine art of driving a tractor. It backfires and Stella jumps. There's laundry hanging on the line and she has a momentary pang, missing the laundry room and maybe even Lucy. At least Stella knew what to do there, because expectations were plain and simple: sort, mend, wash, hang, and fold. Behind her, regular classrooms produce sounds of learning, while those relegated to cleaning the dorms or other parts of the building can be heard calling out to one another.

Frances is now going around the corner of Dorm B. Stella's subdued pleas for her to come back are lost in the wind. She's going to have to do something. She runs across the yard. Of all things, Frances is headed back to the Clap Trap. Stella runs faster. They're in plain view of anyone who wishes to see them. What if Mrs. Maynard or Mrs. Dot happens to look out, and there's Frances loping along and Stella scrambling after her, obviously not handling Frances very well? This reminds her of what happened at school. She wanted to hang out with these kids she thought she'd like and as soon as she sat down among them, they jumped to their feet and ran away from her. She gets annoyed at Frances, then.

When she's close enough where she can speak in a normal voice and not yell, she says, "Frances. Stop. Wait."

She does stop, at the edge of the ditch filled with barbed wire. Stella goes to her side and the two of them stare down at the tangle of rusty wire. Stella can't believe Frances would think about jumping into that again, not after what happened last time. She has to come up with the best way to keep her from doing something dumb, something that could get Stella into trouble too. There's no doubt Frances is no different when it comes to fearing punishment. Anyone who's been around her knows when she's about to get disciplined it sends her into orbit. She knows what can be done to her. Stella licks her lips, and takes the chance Frances will understand her warning.

"If Mrs. Maynard comes to the room like she said she's going to do, to check on us, we'll both be in big trouble if we're not where we're supposed to be. They might whip us."

Frances twitches at the word *whip.* After a few seconds, she faces Stella, as if waiting for her to go on, and Stella does, eyes wide and earnest.

"I don't want that to happen to you, or to me. I don't want to get beat, and I sure don't want to get put into meditation," and she stops herself.

She thinks about this. Mrs. Dot wouldn't allow it, would she? Allow her to be beaten? Get put into meditation? Mrs. Maynard wouldn't hesitate to do either, and would hope for the chance. She's figured out Mrs. Dot and Mrs. Maynard don't agree on many things, and Stella helping Mrs. Dot is definitely one they're at odds over. Frances gets this strange expression. Stella again has trouble knowing how to interpret it, but something is going on in her head. She could swear she's scheming. Unexpectedly, Frances steps away from the edge of the ditch and begins walking back toward the building. Relieved, Stella hurries after her, practically skipping. Frances stops and sticks out a hand as if to touch her. Stella automatically flinches and moves back. She doesn't trust her because, well, she doesn't know what she'll do, but she remembers what happened to Mrs. Maynard that day in the dining hall when her wig was pulled off.

Frances drops her arm and makes an angry sound, like a growl. She rushes into the building and half runs around the corner. Stella doesn't run. It's against the rules. Once she's back in the classroom, there's Frances sitting in the chair, long legs akimbo, waiting. Stella sits too, and her gaze falls on a piece of paper. On it is a short line of *A*'s and below those are little *a*'s. Frances, her expression mostly placid except for what might be a smirk around the edges of her mouth, waits. Stella's confounded. Mrs. Maynard breezes in at that moment. It's almost dinnertime and Stella grabs the sheet of paper and proudly waves it in the air before showing it Mrs. Maynard.

"Look! Look at what Frances did just now."

Mrs. Maynard snatches it from Stella, staring in disbelief at the writing.

"She did this?"

"Yes, ma'am," Stella says, beaming at the housemother, and then at Frances, who chooses the moment to abruptly moo like a cow.

Mrs. Maynard grimaces and says, "Hush up now, Frances!" before spearing Stella with a look. "How odd. She's been here all this time and no one else has been able to get her to do a thing. She doesn't speak and is prone to tantrums. How can this be real? How do I know you're not trying to show off?"

Surprised, Stella shakes her head.

"She *did* write it. I swear."

"You sat right there, and saw her do this?"

"No, ma'am, but it wasn't me. I didn't write that."

"Where were you when this miracle took place?"

"I, uh, I had to use the bathroom."

"You weren't to leave her alone. That's two demerits. I'm sure she's only copying you, *if* she even wrote it, which is highly unlikely. Unless I see this happen for myself, I won't believe it's anything more than a ruse. She's never shown herself to be anything more than uncontrollable, an imbecile, and untrainable."

Stella flinches at the harsh words. How does this make Frances feel? She's right there, hearing it all, and then she notices Frances baring her teeth at Mrs. Maynard, who doesn't seem to be aware, or is intentionally ignoring her. Frances has them fooled. She's actually smarter than they are. Mrs. Maynard sticks the sheet of paper in her pocket, and this worries Stella for reasons she can't explain. What's she going to do with it?

"All right. Enough playing school for the day. Get to the dining hall for your meal and after that, see Opal and Sally. You'll be in the kitchen with them in the afternoons, per Mrs. Baker, helping with supper."

"Is Miss Ruth working in there too?"

"Ruth Foster? No."

"Oh, I thought Mrs. D—I mean, Mrs. Baker said . . ."

Mrs. Maynard's pinched lips and tight expression are a warning. Dejected, Stella does as she's told. She'd anticipated the chance to be around Ruth, and knowing she won't get to work with her is disappointing. She's curious why she's not cooking because everyone knows she's the best. There's not much to look forward to at the Colony, and eating has become a small pleasure, not only for her, but the others too. Maybe Opal or Sally will know. As she walks to the dining hall, she feels a presence beside her. It's Frances. This time as Frances reaches out to touch Stella, tentatively placing a finger on her arm, Stella is prepared and doesn't flinch. Next, she puts her hand on Stella's shoulder and pats it twice. Stella, open-mouthed, waits to see what she might do next. No one pays them any attention. They're hurrying to get into line to get their food, thinking they're going to have a tasty meal cooked by Ruth. Frances gazes at her intently and Stella returns the look.

"What, Frances? What is it?"

Frances comes closer. It takes everything in Stella not to react, afraid she might get clobbered. Frances whispers slowly, using clear, precise words in a mocking, singsong voice.

"Can you say Fr-an-ces? Frances Platt. I like your name too, Stel-la Tem-ple."

Stella sucks in air so quick, she coughs. Frances smacks her back and speaks to her normally.

"Don't you tell nobody. You do and I'm apt to get really mad and bite someone. Maybe you."

Stunned, Stella shakes her head rapidly, an attempt to reassure Frances she won't say a word. Frances moves into the line, and Stella follows and there they stand, side by side. Almost like friends. After getting her tray, Stella sits and, seconds later, Frances drops into the chair opposite her. No one pays them any attention. They're two misfits eating dinner, is all. After they finish, Frances goes wherever she's supposed to go for the afternoon, and Stella goes to the kitchen, still in shock over Frances speaking to her. Sally points to a pile of potatoes and she settles into a chair and begins peeling.

Opal calls out, "I seen you eating with that nut."

Stella peers down the long prep table at Opal.

"She ain't a nut. Nobody understands her, is all."

Opal snorts. "And you do? Good for you." She turns to Sally. "You hear that? She says ole Frances Platt ain't a nut. I say you don't think that unless you're one too."

Both cackle and Stella keeps peeling. Boy. If they knew what she did, they wouldn't be so quick to poke fun. Stella wonders why the other girl acts like she does. It's true she gets a little crazy and flies off the handle, and has some odd ways of behaving in general, but she's nowhere near as dumb as she makes out.

"Do you know why she came here?" she asks the others.

"Nah, we're from over to Dorm B, we don't know nothing about you Dorm A gals 'cept lots of you are prone to running off."

"Nobody in B runs?"

"Shoot, no. We're trying to get outta here. Better get to peeling faster. We got to get them taters boiling pretty soon."

Stella resumes her work, curious to know more about Frances.

Chapter 22

Baker

It's taking much longer than she wanted, but only a few more letters and she'll have enough to prepare a case to go to the board. She needs to figure out the right way to present the material so it makes the best impression. She paces her office floor, her uneven gait soothing to her psyche as she considers options. She's at the point of a possibility when there's a tap on the door. Impatient at the interruption, she crosses the room and yanks it open. Mrs. Maynard gives her a startled look, then holds up a piece of paper.

"I thought you'd want to know about this."

Baker assumes it's another letter. Excellent! They've trickled in and the very idea Mrs. Maynard and Mrs. Dillard had to cajole, then threaten residents to write them left her unsettled. Through this process she's learned some are resentful, which always leads to problems, as she very well knows. It didn't help that, somehow, word got out Ruth Foster refused to write one. The woman has gained influence and is now swaying others. That she's viewed with respect and admiration baffles Baker. Even Stella's influenced. This was exposed by the tiny glint in the girl's eye when told she'd work in the kitchen. She snatches the paper only to see a bunch of *A*'s scrawled across it.

"What's this?"

"Your little favorite wants me to believe Frances Platt wrote it."

Two things startle Baker. First, Mrs. Maynard's use of "favorite," and second, Frances Platt associated with anything remotely intelligent such as writing. Surely there's been a mistake, and if Mrs. Maynard's involved, this is highly likely. The housemother continues.

"I questioned Stella about it, of course. After all, given what we know, it's very doubtful. I think Stella wrote this herself and tried to pass it off as Frances's effort. Quite devious, and exactly the sort of behavior we don't need."

Baker is suspicious too, but she's in a snit over Mrs. Maynard's term for Stella. She shifts the discussion to the snotty remark.

"What do you mean by 'favorite'?"

Mrs. Maynard sniffs.

"Actually, more like favoritism. I can spot it a mile away. It usurps legitimate authority when a child is placed into a position of assisting the adults. We're the professionals in charge, after all."

Baker refrains from snapping at the older woman over her silly insecurities. She doesn't need her to run to the board, so she tempers her reaction.

"It's not favoritism. I see potential and I want to encourage her. Remember, she memorized every rule in the guideline booklet in an extraordinarily short amount of time. She's been useful to me." Mrs. Maynard's mouth turns down and Baker slightly alters the facts to assuage her feelings. "And to you."

"Oh, I don't doubt she's smart, and she knows it. Very dangerous."

Baker scrutinizes the piece of paper again. She can't believe Stella would be so conniving. It could be a sincere breakthrough. Perhaps Frances responded to Stella because they're close in age, as she assumed might happen. If Stella was able to get something out of potato-head Frances, it's more than commendable. Baker grows excited at this possibility. This could be a huge success story. She can see how she might present Stella's story to the board. She would explain she has great potential for a future within reform, perhaps even at the Colony, under the instruction of Baker herself. A scenario such as this would be valuable, a way to persuade the board as to the excellent work done under her guidance. It could be held up as proof that even the most challenging cases like Frances, with a solid foundation, are capable of progress. Baker's dream of the Jennie Award shines brighter than ever before.

"I find this to be fabulous news. Thank you for bringing it to my attention."

Mrs. Maynard is aghast.

"You *believe* her?"

"What reason would she have to lie?"

"I can think of plenty!"

"Enlighten me."

"To please you. To curry favor. To avoid punishment. You and I both know Frances Platt has proven herself incapable of learning time and again."

"This is easy enough to figure out. I have Stella's letter, written in her own hand just days ago."

Baker goes to her desk drawer where she takes out the letter and studies the two pages. What she sees satisfies her.

"Look for yourself."

Mrs. Maynard takes time to read what Stella wrote first. She sniffs as if she's caught the scent of something rotten, then finally begins to compare the two side by side.

"I see the difference, but Stella could've still written these *A*'s by altering her penmanship. Frances has written nothing since she's been here. She occupies a chair in the classroom like a lump of dough, according to the teaching staff. It would be very easy for Stella to pass this off as Frances's work."

Baker puts a hand out for Mrs. Maynard to return the letter, wiggling her fingers impatiently. Mrs. Maynard complies, but remains set in her belief of Stella's dishonesty.

"You're going soft, particularly when it comes to Stella Temple."

"Ridiculous. My experience tells me there needs to be a balance. If we're too harsh, it offers scrutiny, especially if word gets out."

"I know what happened at Samarcand, but this is different. Here, we're dealing with an adult population with the exception of these two. These women need swift, forceful, and corrective action. You can't let them think they have an upper hand. No telling what might happen. You, more than anyone, ought to know this."

"When have I not addressed a disciplinary situation in an expedient and resourceful way? Look at how hard it's been to get the letters. All it takes is one to create problems, and it's not Stella. It's Ruth Foster."

"On that we agree, with regard to Ruth Foster. Personally, I think group punishment was called for, or another stint in meditation, but instead you went with your invented Day One restart. That's less than effective. I could see it working had she been here for six months or longer, but starting over after two months barely addresses those deliberate violations."

"My approach doesn't have to be cookie-cutter. My decision can be made depending on certain situations, and in this case, that made more of an impact. I could see it."

It's a standoff. They stare at one another, neither wanting to give. Mrs. Maynard goes for the last word.

"It implies leniency, and a lack of consistency, but I guess that's my opinion. I prefer to discourage any idea they're getting away with something."

This bickering back and forth wears on Baker. It's tedious and why should she argue with a subordinate? Let her believe what she wants. There are more important things to do, and she's about to change the subject when Mrs. Maynard beats her to it.

"By the way, Hubert and I didn't see you the other night at Mr. Woodall's."

Baker goes behind her desk and drops into her chair. Her head begins to ache as Mrs. Maynard prattles on.

"Everyone came—and I mean *everyone*. Board members and their wives, myself and Hubert, Dr. Graham, Dr. Greene, Nurse Crawford, and even Miss Perkins. There wasn't a spare seat, which I found interesting."

"Why is that?"

"Well, where would you have sat? That's what I thought while there. No. Not one spare seat."

"Maybe I'd have been in Miss Perkins's chair, Ethel. Perhaps she was there because I wasn't."

Mrs. Maynard looks doubtful.

"Either way, speaking of your favored resident, Dr. Graham took care to discuss his cure for Stella, and touted its success. Even more interesting was what Dr. Woodall said. Actually, I'm not sure he intended for some of us to hear."

Baker doesn't like being on the outs, and she likes it even less that Ethel Maynard is privy to this inner circle of information when she isn't. The housemother pauses, her scrutiny of Baker as keen as a hawk waiting on a field mouse to run across the ground. It's Baker's move, but she doesn't take it. Unable to contain herself, Mrs. Maynard shares what she knows.

"The board is accepting applications for a position."

Baker's voice comes out a little high-pitched.

"There's a position?"

Mrs. Maynard moves a hand down her sleeve as if brushing off lint. She avoids Baker's eyes.

"Yes. I thought you would have heard."

"Stop being coy, Ethel. What do you know?"

Mrs. Maynard stops brushing her sleeve and becomes less confident.

"Well, I'm not sure I heard right. It was between him and Dr. Graham, something about a new—or it might've been an additional—superintendent. It was hard to hear, but I certainly understood the word *superintendent* was used in conjunction with the word *application*."

"Why, I wonder where they need someone? I haven't heard of any openings, but accepting new applications isn't uncommon. I don't see why this is so important."

"It's for here. Too much spending in the previous year and not enough results. Or something."

Ethel Maynard mumbles this last part. A curtain of red like the sudden bursting of a blood vessel clouds Baker's vision.

"You must've misheard."

"That's what I thought until I had a chance to confirm with Ellen Crawford. She and I were standing together, you see. She heard it too, and, well, I thought you should know I plan to apply."

The last part is said in a rush and Baker responds just as quickly.

"If that's a threat, Ethel Maynard, be aware, I know of your proclivities. I've heard the whispers. Don't you dare act as if you've got the upper hand here. I know your darkest secret. And it's an ugly one."

Mrs. Maynard's mouth thins, and her voice trembles with anger.

"That's nothing but abhorrent gossip started by that disgusting Lucille Griffin. As if we should believe anything *she* ever said."

"I'm not so sure about that. She's not the only one who's complained, after all."

Mrs. Maynard flushes like she's being throttled and Baker is struck by the blue worm of a vein pulsing on the side of the woman's forehead. She doesn't stop, needing to make it very clear she's the one in charge, the one with power.

"If such a thing were to go beyond these walls, it would certainly place Dr. Woodall in a very difficult and embarrassing position, not to mention your husband. I plan to request a meeting with the board very soon. I hope I won't find it necessary to bring up something so distasteful. With that on your record, I can't begin to imagine the disgrace. It's possible you and your dear Hubert would be forced to leave Kinston altogether."

Mrs. Maynard's brief moment of bravado recedes. The authoritative quality is gone as she insists her intentions are honest and true.

"I only want what's best for those here. Our residents know they can count on me for clear direction and a steady hand. I'm consistent."

"And I'm still the superintendent. I can dismiss who I want, at will."

"You won't. Not when I have the ear of Dr. Woodall, whether I work here or not. I could speak to him tonight, if need be. Let him hear what I think about how things are going."

Their eyes lock, each wanting the other to break, to give way. Baker can't imagine relinquishing her domain to someone like Ethel Maynard. It's insulting, worse in some ways than what happened at Samarcand. With the previous incident, she might concede to a few mistakes, but at the Colony, it's personnel issues, rivalry, and pettiness. She moves to her office door and opens it, her way of communicating the meeting is over.

"If there's any question as to what I'm doing, or how I'm doing it, take it up with the board, and know that I'll be sure to share all I know about you. Now, I have other work to do."

Mrs. Maynard raises her finger like she's going to make another point, and stops herself. She drops her hand, and leaves. After she's gone, the air in Baker's office feels thick and heavy. She flashes back to Samarcand and her heartbeat becomes as awkward as her steps. She breathes deep, placing a hand on her chest. They might be trying to force her out. That friendship between the Maynards and the Woodalls has afforded the housemother an advantage. She's free to drop in at the Woodalls' anytime and make her little derogatory comments here and there. Baker bets she's been doing this all along. She envisions her slowly chipping away at Dr. Woodall's confidence in her abilities. This, after Baker hired Mrs. Maynard because she was recommended by Dr. Woodall. For now, there's another matter to settle. She retrieves the paper with the *A*'s on it, and leaves her office. Stella is kneading dough when Baker motions from doorway.

"Stella, come with me, please."

The wet of Stella's eyes stands out from the flour on her face and her mouth is red, like she's been chewing on her lips.

Baker says to the other two women, "Get back to work, this doesn't concern you."

Stella wipes off her hands while Opal and Sally's distrust of Baker is evident by them moving clear to the other side of the kitchen. Baker shows Stella the paper.

"Did Frances write this?"

Stella responds confidently.

"Yes, Mrs. Dot."

"Mrs. Maynard doesn't believe you."

"No."

"Why not?"

"Because I didn't see Frances do it."

"You didn't see her? Explain, please."

Stella pauses, and Baker can see she's weighing the answer.

"Don't try to think of the right answer, just tell the truth."

"Yes, ma'am."

The flour is no longer what's making Stella's face pale. Fear causes her eyes to dart about and her mouth begins to tremble. She whispers the answer.

"I told Mrs. Maynard I didn't see it because I had to go to the bathroom, but what happened was Frances went outside. I tried to stop her, but she wouldn't listen. I had to go after her. I said we'd get into trouble if we were caught because we were supposed to be in that room. I finally got her to go back in. She's faster'n me with them long legs and all. She wrote that before I got there. I'd been showing her the capital *A*'s and small *a*'s."

Stella's demeanor conveys an earnestness and Baker believes her. She trusts Stella before she trusts Ethel Maynard. Still. What Mrs. Maynard said is possible, that Stella really just wants her approval.

"All right. You may go back to work."

Stella, relieved, says, "Yes, ma'am."

Bakers stands for a moment watching as she walks away, her posture rigid. She hopes the girl isn't too affected by this questioning, but it's necessary to get to the bottom of things. Baker continues through the Colony and out onto the grounds. It's May and though the air is mild with a light earthy scent that comes with turned soil, Baker pays the natural environment no mind. Frances Platt works alongside a few women in one of the many gardens, weeding and planting a few vegetables. She's in the very middle of the cornfield, her bent torso like a camel hump above the others. Mr. Lumley is there too, and gives direction occasionally.

"Them weeds will strangle a good plant, so be sure and get ever' last one. I got buckets over yonder and we're gonna do the watering next."

There's a steady ripping sound as roots are torn out of the ground, and above that, the low hum of conversation. Baker calls out.

"Mr. Lumley, I need to see Frances for a moment."

Mr. Lumley raises a hand in acknowledgment and when he goes by, he gives her black, shiny shoes with the new black shoelaces she bought only a few days ago the once-over. She can never quite get a read on him. His expressions are either comical, stern, or irritated, and they don't ever seem to match what's going on. Like now, he's studying her shoes as if the sight of them is annoying. He approaches Frances.

"Hey now, Frances!"

Frances's head pops up like a gopher, and Mr. Lumley waves at her.

"Come on this a way."

Frances doesn't move. She's a stalwart pine, deeply rooted in place. Mr. Lumley creeps closer and Baker can see his mouth moving, speaking and pointing back at her, but it makes no difference. Frances refuses to budge. The others have stopped working to watch. Frances stares across the field and Baker thinks it's at her, but she can't be sure. Mr. Lumley retreats and comes over to where Baker waits.

"She ain't comin'."

"Mr. Lumley, I can see that."

"You're gonna have to go to her, unless you want me to try to pull her over here to you, but I'm gonna tell you right now, I ain't fancyin' gettin' my noggin knocked sideways."

Baker studies the field with trepidation as Mr. Lumley spits out a steady stream of tobacco juice and studies her shoes again.

"Reckon you're gonna get them clean brogans dusty. For sure."

Useless man, she thinks. Baker carefully circles the field until she comes to the center row where Frances has tracked her progress. She steps onto the soft dirt. It makes her unstable, and her legs tremble.

Heaven forbid she were to fall. She'd be humiliated beyond belief. She picks her way down the row, her fury growing with every step, until she reaches Frances, who at least doesn't bolt. Baker puts the paper under Frances's nose.

"Did you write this?"

Watching the girl's reaction, Baker can truthfully admit that if brains and aptitude were attributed by facial expressions and features, Frances flunks. Her mouth is always unhinged, hanging open like a flytrap. Her eyes, however, are the most troublesome with their wandering ways. Today Frances stands before Baker seeming half asleep, dimwitted as it were, arms and hands limp by her sides. She doesn't pay any attention to the paper in Baker's hands, even as she rattles it under the girl's nose.

"Frances? I'm asking you a question. If you wrote this, then I imagine you can say so. Stella Temple says you did."

Frances begins swaying, left to right to left, making little moaning sounds. The longer Baker watches her, the more she begins to doubt Stella's claim. Frances Platt is a dullard. An imbecile. A *moron*. This makes her feel better about her initial assessment. From the day she came across this one, her write-up was accurate, irrefutable, yet now she's left to wonder about Stella's story.

"All right. All right. Let's not get ourselves worked up. Go on back to your work."

Frances makes some sort of apelike noise before she bends down and claws at the ground in an inhuman manner. Baker turns around and carefully begins her trek back to more stable ground. She is methodical about where she puts her feet, acting as if she's studying the vegetable plants to offset her concerns at turning an ankle. Mr. Lumley was right. Her shoes are going to need a double buffing, and she'll have to soak her shoelaces, but confronting Frances for herself with that piece of paper was worth it. As bad as Baker hates to admit it, Ethel Maynard is right. There's no way the girl has the intelligence to print letters, much less draw a simple straight line. It's a good thing they took care of her too, right after she arrived. She'll never get the chance to populate society with those like her.

On the other hand, Baker is sorely disappointed by this outcome because she has to admit Stella wasn't truthful. Back at her office, she gathers what letters she has and reads them one by one. She pauses, wishing she could make her original presentation the way she'd planned for Stella. That's impossible, now. She must take a new approach. She removes Stella's letter and composes a formal missive requesting the board read through the ones she's able to send. She asks for a meeting as soon as possible to discuss the future of the Colony under her guidance. Let them see for themselves what she has been able to accomplish, almost single-handedly. She has another plan with regard to Ethel Maynard. She can apply for the superintendent job, but that doesn't mean she'll get it, not if Dorothy Baker has anything to do with it.

Chapter 23

Ruth

She enters her fourth month, two if you go by Baker's Day One decree. Ruth's results come back negative and Mrs. Maynard escorts her to the dorm room where, once again, she's among the general population. The room quiets as she goes slowly toward her cot, pulls back the top sheet, and eases down onto the mattress. Her entire body feels as if someone has beaten her with a hammer. Josephine approaches her, concerned.

"Good heavens, look at you. They're bound and determined to keep us down, ain't they?"

Ruth nods weakly. It's close to lights out, but she pulls the rule booklet out from under her pillow. She was given a mandate, and for some reason, she's trying to obey it, trying to play the game. She holds it up, before letting her arm drop back down to her bed.

"I've got to memorize these. I never did."

Josephine shakes her head.

"Shoot. Neither did I, but ain't nobody asked me about it."

"That's because you're not a target."

"I'm sorry. I wish I could help."

"There's nothing that can be done. They do what they want."

Josephine reaches over and squeezes Ruth's hand before going back across the dorm. Ruth props herself up. The other women flit in and out, finishing their nightly preparations, but she ignores what's going on around her. She's staring at the first two rules, "Leaving Building A without permission, three demerits" and "Rudeness to anyone, two to five demerits." She's absorbing this information, the first rule underscoring her thoughts on their restricted movement and the second as a way to further dominate every facet of their emotional state. She can't believe this ridiculous little book. They're grown women, after all. She's growing angry again, even though it's useless.

She goes back to the opening where there's a bit of history. She never paid attention to it, and certainly not to the fact there are other similar institutions. She becomes absorbed by a collection of pictures, women involved in reform work in some way. While studying their photos, she reads the brief explanation of their contributions. Fannie French Morse was the "supreme superintendent" at the New York State Training School for Girls, and created reform methods involving farm work as the ideal method to provide a unique interest. There are others like Kate Burr Johnson, who for decades helped facilitate the idea of reform and spent time at a girls' reform school in Trenton New Jersey. Baker writes of her admiration for their work and what stands out to Ruth is that all of them believe in what they're doing.

A small noise at the foot of her bed takes her attention from the booklet to find Stella watching her with caution. The girl's eyes skim around the dorm quick as sparrows before returning to Ruth. Something about her isn't quite the same as before. There's been a change, and Ruth can't determine what it is.

Stella whispers, "Are you coming back to cook in the kitchen?"

"I don't know."

Stella moves closer.

"I sure do hope you get to work in there again. I was sick a few weeks back and got better because of you. They got me in there helping out. Washing dishes, is all. Mrs. Opal and Miss Sally, they ain't such good cooks. I been hearing 'em"—she gestures at the women milling in and around their own beds—"complaining about how bad everything tastes."

Ruth doesn't respond, waiting to see where this is going. There's a tiny bit of distrust even though no one ever proved it was Stella who got Melissa and the others group punishment. Like most, Ruth believes she had something to do with it.

Stella leans forward a little more, and says, "Can I ask you something?"

Ruth dips her head a little, giving permission. Stella's fingers worry the collar of the nightgown she's wearing and she takes a deep breath.

"Are you a prostitute?"

Ruth is so startled by her directness, and the question itself, she almost laughs.

"No, I'm not."

Stella tilts her head back, eyes narrowing with a knowing look.

"The other, then. Promiscuous."

Ruth does laugh then.

"Nope."

"But you got to have a reason for being here. Mrs. D—Mrs. Baker says everyone's done something wrong."

Ruth isn't laughing now.

"None of us should be here. Not even Lucy, when she was."

Stella's mouth turns down as she continues to pursue the evil Ruth has to have committed.

"Corruption, drinking, depravity?"

Ruth isn't sure where she's headed with her persistent questions, and her dislike shows in the clipped answer she gives.

"No. Why're you so curious about why I'm here? You should be concerned about yourself, and how you ended up here instead of worrying about everyone else."

She instantly regrets that last part when Stella steps back like she's been slapped.

Ruth places a hand to her head, and says, "I'm sorry. The mercuries make me feel pretty bad."

Stella ignores what Ruth says, and mystified, asks, "But if you ain't none'a them things, why're you here?"

Ruth simply stares at her and Stella goes back to fretting with her nightgown.

"They wouldn't do that, would they? Put people in here who ain't done nothing?"

"They would and they have."

Stella crosses her arms and her brow crinkles, as if something is bound to make sense to her in the next minute or two. Ruth would like to be left in peace except Stella's not done talking.

"That doctor said I needed redeeming, but it ain't as easy as I thought. Like today. Mrs. Baker put me to work helping Frances Platt, and things didn't go so good. Mrs. Maynard is fit to be tied."

Ruth offers a small conciliatory, but safe, remark.

"It's hard to please anyone around here."

"Yeah. But, for me, being here is much better than being with Alice and Cordell. A lot better."

This is tantamount to an outburst from a girl who's existed like a shadow since Ruth came. Stella flushes pink, and grows quiet. Ruth reaches over and places her fingertips on her arm. The girl looks as if she's talked herself into a state of wonder at this extraordinary improvement to her previous life. She frowns down at the hand resting on her arm, as if she doesn't understand why Ruth is touching her. Ruth prompts her with a question.

"Who're Alice and Cordell?"

Stella snags a hank of hair, and twirls the strand absentmindedly, her features troubled and dark.

"My mama and daddy. She's sick most of the time. He's . . . sick too."

She stops messing with her hair to cross her arms and hug herself. Ruth waits for her to go on. Stella's mood changes to one that's dark and fearful and she gets the sense Stella's home life must've been miserable. Who else calls their parents by their first names? And to prefer this place, how bad could it have been at the Temples'? Ruth is tired, and wants to go to sleep, but feels like she has to respond.

"I'm sorry about your parents being sick."

"I ain't."

"I'm sure you don't mean that."

Stella shifts on her feet, raises her chin, and her mouth twists, like she might cry and is fighting it. Ruth doesn't understand why Stella is telling her this. She remembers Lucy's warning and picks up the rule book again, hoping to signal the end of the discussion.

"He came in my room at night."

The book falls back to Ruth's lap, and with a hint of dread, she says, "Who came into your room?"

"My nasty, mean daddy."

Ruth is shocked. She waits to see if she'll say more, but Stella doesn't get the chance. Mrs. Maynard's strident command rings out from doorway of the dorm.

"Stella Temple! What're you doing over there? Get to your bed, and get ready for lights out! I think you've stirred up enough trouble today!"

"Yes, ma'am."

She hurries across the room and Ruth watches her duck under the sheet, pulling it over her head and burrowing beneath it. Mrs. Maynard's eyes dart and flit, searching for anyone not where they should be. The light switch goes off. Moonbeams enter through the row of windows so beds and figures in repose are soon visible. Ruth can make out the shape of Stella sitting up, looking across the room in her direction. She turns on her side. She can't blame her for preferring life at the Colony. She escaped something horrible, which means it's another sad story no different from some of the others'. It remains a fact some don't mind being here and for this reason, Ruth's personal feelings are very different. They see it as an opportunity to get away from their humdrum lives, abusive husbands, and critical family members.

Ruth can't sleep. She feels unwell, and lies awake listening to rustling bedsheets, snores, coughs, and breathing. When it's time to get up in the morning, sounds are extra sharp and jangly. She rises from the cot, and the day begins abruptly when the lights come on, and they're expected to snap to it. She's slower getting into the morning routine and Mrs. Maynard is right there, pencil hovering, ready to put marks against her. Ruth escapes into the bathroom, half expecting her to follow. She stares back at herself in the mirror as she washes off her face. The dark circles under her eyes have deepened. She begins to brush her hair and comes away with a brushful of strands. She stares at the bristles and although she expected it to happen, it's upsetting now that it is. She doesn't finish, and leaves the bathroom, not caring it might result in points deducted for presenting herself in an untidy fashion. Back in the dorm, Mrs. Maynard does a double take.

"I'd assign demerits for your appearance Miss Foster, but since you're to work outside, and there's a breeze today, I suppose it doesn't matter. See Mr. Lumley after breakfast and he'll tell you what to do. The rest of you have your assignments. Line up!"

In the dining hall, Ruth sits with Josephine, Natalie, Melissa, and Paula, who all groan with disappointment when she tells them she's been assigned outside work. She eats with some level of enthusiasm, eager to enjoy the outdoors. As she returns her tray, she bends down to peer through the window, waving at Opal and Sally, who both make crying faces at her. She smiles and in seconds, she's got her face to the sun, enjoying the balmy breeze. If she tries hard, she can almost picture herself in her mother's backyard, working in the small garden. Mr. Lumley is near the barn and she approaches him, trying to disregard how weak she feels. He's stuffing a wad of tobacco into his cheeks, his back to her as he watches some of his charges preparing to hoe and weed. One climbs onto a tractor.

"Hey there, Mr. Lumley. I'm Ruth Foster."

He spins around and gives her the once-over.

"Here to work?"

"Yes, sir."

"All right, then. Get you a rake and wheelbarrow from the barn, yonder. You lookin' a bit too peaked to do much more than clean around them flower beds near the tool shed. Dump what you get into the silage pile by the fence. If you get done with that, then maybe you can organize some of the gardening tools in the shed."

"Yes, sir."

When she enters the barn, she's reminded of visits to her aunt and uncle's farm in Pink Hill. Uncle Robert, her father's brother, and his wife, Aunt Suzy, farmed tobacco and corn. Aunt Suzy taught her how to make small potholders out of various scraps of material and apple butter in the fall. Their barn had smelled of sun-beaten wood, stored hay bales, and fertilizer, a unique odor and similar to what she encounters now. To have those happy memories associated in any way with where she is makes her mad. She gets a rake and drops it into the wheelbarrow and pushes it across the grounds. The sun's warmth seeps through the thin cotton dress as she bends to attack the detritus of old leaves, sticks, and flower heads in and around the plants.

She begins to reflect on the women responsible for the plants in the ground, who they were, how they came here, what they thought of as they worked. There's an array of gardenias, roses, Queen Anne's lace, and a variety or two she's not familiar with. An hour later, she's lightheaded from her efforts and takes a pause. As she props herself on the rake handle, her eyes circle the area. She does a double take at the sight of a strange man by the tool shed, partially hidden by an Eastern red cedar. She immediately looks toward the main building. All is quiet. No staff in sight. She looks back at him. Wearing a poorly fitted suit, his hat is tilted back, exposing a strand of blond hair framing friendly features.

He signals her with a small gesture, and in a stage whisper says, "Miss? Can I speak to you?"

Ruth shakes her head, an emphatic no.

"Would you by chance be Miss Ruth Foster?"

Her pulse quickens.

"Who wants to know?"

"Lucy says hey."

Lucy! This is the person she spoke of. Ruth checks around her again. Everyone is preoccupied with work. She signals with a quick movement of her head at the tool shed. If she stands on the backside of it, he can remain where he is, and she'll be close enough to talk. She grabs the handles on the wheelbarrow and walks with confidence toward the structure, her legs shaking with a combination of nerves and excitement. She hurries around to the back and he starts talking quickly.

"My name's Stanley Newell. I'm Lucy's, uh, well, I'm a friend, and a lawyer."

A lawyer. This is better than she could have hoped for.

"Pleased to meet you."

"Likewise. Lucy told me what's going on here, and said I should talk to you, and a few of the others, if I can. Are you willing to talk to me?"

It's the chance she's been waiting for, what they've all been waiting for, someone willing to listen, someone who might be able to help. The audacity of speaking to him is a risk that will come with major consequences if caught. She gives a quick, frantic check, but no one has noticed anything, no one's sounding an alarm. The work of the Colony goes on and so she faces Stanley Newell again.

"I'm more than willing, but I can't be caught. If we're seen, I don't know what might happen."

"It's that bad?"

Ruth's expression is answer enough.

"What's your story? How'd you get here?"

"A local sheriff approached me and said I had to go get tested. He threatened me with civil disobedience if I didn't do as he said."

Mr. Newell writes quickly as she talks.

"What were you doing?"

"Walking to work."

"Walking to work? What is it you do?"

"I work, make that worked, at a diner in La Grange."

"You lost the job?"

"I would think. I've been here about four months."

"Once you got to the doctor, he said you had an infection and made you come here?" He pauses. "Lucy told me some of what she's heard about."

"Yes. The doctor said he had to make sure the public was safe."

Mr. Lumley yells at an inmate and the sound is closer than either of them expected. Mr. Newell holds a finger up, and peers around the cedar, watching the older man.

In a low voice, he says, "Eleven thirty, tomorrow. Right here."

She makes a motion with her shoulders.

"If I can. Things happen where I might not be able to show up. They punish you for all sorts of reasons in different ways and sometimes that means I might disappear for a while."

"Oh. Well, do you think a few others will talk to me?"

"Maybe."

There's a pause, then Mr. Newell says, "I can't make any promises, and this might take a little time."

Ruth says what's she's been wanting to say for some time now.

"If I know anything, I know this: what they're doing is wrong."

Mr. Newell looks at her, and there's something honest, open, and good about him.

He taps his pen on his notepad and says, "That's why I came."

Chapter 24

Stella

Stella enters the kitchen the next morning to find Opal at the stove, apron hanging off slim hips, her reddish-brown hair tidily pulled back in a bun at the nape of her neck. If it weren't for the facial scars, Stella thinks she'd be very pretty, but someone either didn't do a good job stitching them up, or maybe she never went to the doctor. She pursues her investigation of the Colony's purpose, unsettled by Ruth's story. Maybe Ruth Foster is lying, making herself out to be who she isn't. The only way to know is to ask a few others.

"Mrs. Opal, how'd you end up here?"

Opal doesn't answer right away. She pours a measure of grits into the pot of boiling water, adds a handful of salt, sets the lid in place, and lowers the heat. She faces Stella.

"Who wants to know?"

Opal sounds distant, like she's not in the mood to talk, but Stella isn't deterred. She has to know what she did wrong because if Mrs. Dot said women are put here for bad reasons, this must be true.

"Me."

"Why is it your business?"

"I . . . I'm just interested in knowing. We're all here because we done something wrong."

"That's what they claim."

Stella twists her fingers. What would they think of her, if they knew why she was here? The thought sends blood rushing to her head and makes it pound. She can't believe she told Ruth as much as she did. She shares a tiny part of her story, in good faith, as she's heard adults say.

"My parents sent me."

"Oh yeah? Why?"

Opal cocks her head. Stella hesitates, sorting out how to explain her unacceptable life in a way that won't make her sound like Mrs. Dot's favorite description of the inhabitants at the Colony, a miscreant. She falls back on her usual explanation.

"I had a tumor needing to come out."

Opal starts laughing. It escalates to the slapping of her upper thighs in glee, like Stella has just shared a joke. Stella crosses her arms, offended. She tries to keep from showing she's mad, only Opal's outburst escalates and Stella scowls.

"Stop laughing. It ain't funny."

"Oh, honey, don't get mad. Everyone's heard about your 'tumor.' Even us gals over in Dorm B. Just say *abortion*. Don't nobody care some boy knocked you up."

Stella wishes it had been some boy. Opal tilts her head and points to the two scars marring her otherwise flawless complexion.

"This is why I'm here. Courtesy of Jack, my husband." She turns her wrists over where two pink scars run horizontal across the blue veins of her wrists. "So I did this."

Stella cringes. The wounds aren't that old. She's bothered by the puckered red skin, the scars similar to the one across her belly. Opal drops her arms, and shoves her hands into her apron pockets.

"Sometimes marriages start off good until they ain't. There's different reasons for that. Could be money problems. He wants things one way and you want them another." She stares out the window above the sink, then pulls her hands from the apron pockets and studies the scars like she's baffled by their existence. "Now, every time I look at these, I'll think about him and I don't like to. Jack's got a mean streak from here to Sunday, lots of jealousy and what comes with it. I was in the hospital for a bit. Days went by and I never saw him. I ain't heard or seen from him since he dropped me off here."

"You must've done something really bad to make him go on and do that to you."

Opal yanks on her dress in a furious manner.

"You're too young, girl, to know nothing. For my Jack, breathing in the direction of another man makes me a whore. He give me two choices: go where crazy people go, or come here. I chose here 'cause I thought I might learn something about myself, but I ain't learned a damn thing I didn't already know. Plus, those who run this joint ain't got a clue about living in my world."

Opal's chest heaves up and down, her rage like a car's engine revving while stuck in park. Bad memories twist her mouth, and turn her an ugly red. Sally comes into the kitchen and Stella allows herself to breathe again. She didn't mean to start nothing. Sally's carrying a large bucket of lard and sets it down on the floor with a *thump.* Opal points at Stella, commanding Sally to share her story.

"Go on and tell her how you got here. She's going to ask you anyway, I'd warrant."

"What?"

"Tell her how you come here."

"Well, let's see. I got real bad sick and had to stay home a day from the mill. The boss said that made me shiftless and fired me. Plus, I ain't against a drink with the gals, or having me a bit of a good time."

These here women, this is what Mrs. Dot is talking about. Sally's a bonafide ne'er-do-well and a drinker, and Opal was a bad wife, no matter what she says. Opal jabs a finger at Stella.

"Hang on a minute. I heard about you over to Dorm B. Word is you're like a weed in a garden, nobody knows you're around till the damage is done. Ain't that right, Sally?"

Sally grunts in agreement. Her bulky body is an intimidating figure, but it's the scowls and their proximity that dries Stella's mouth. She responds in a shaky voice.

"I . . . I was just curious how others come to be here."

Skeptical glances pass between the women. They don't believe her, and Stella thinks, *Gosh, it was only one time!* Now she wishes Mrs. Dot hadn't asked her because like with those at school, do one wrong thing and no one lets you forget. Sally inches closer, and points in her face.

"Uh-huh. You make sure you ain't flapping that mouth. You do, and we'll know it."

Opal smirks, and adopts a fake accent.

"Oh dear, Sally. I suppose we have those wretched behaviors unbecoming to our fair sex."

Sally's scowl transforms as she plays along.

"My oh my, indeed. What's a girl to do? Mrs. Conway said we were uncouth. And lewd."

"Don't forget bawdy."

"And rude."

"Wait. That was after you pooted! Twice!"

The women shift from suspicion and anger to amused as they giggle at the memory. Meanwhile, Stella persists. Surely they've got it wrong.

"Some ought to be here, though."

They turn to her as one. Opal looks Stella up and down.

"What's that supposed to mean?"

Stella holds her hands out. "I don't mean nothing by it. I'm just trying to understand."

Opal shakes her head.

"Ain't none of us done nothing wrong. I ain't been charged with a crime. You been charged with a crime, Sally?"

"Nope. Unless being a little rough around the edges counts as one. What I know is we're being kept from our homes and our families, such as they are."

Opal bobs her head emphatically.

"What about Linda? All she did was go and see her boyfriend at one'a them army encampments where he was training."

Stella's eyes are round and she looks between the two of them.

"What's wrong with that?"

Sally shakes her head.

"You tell me. Some higher-up saw her and called the law. Her and two others got picked up, told they was trespassing and their behavior was suspicious. Of course they argued, and tried to tell them they knew some of the soldiers there. The officers was rude to 'em, and said, 'Yeah, I bet you do.' Then they made them go to a doctor who declared them infected, to their family's shame. Seems kind'a strange to me that practically every woman brought here is 'diseased.' "

Opal tosses a dish towel over her shoulder and turns back to the pot on the stove.

"One thing's for sure, you better hope they didn't tinker on you more than that abortion. They've been known to fix women but good. Ain't that right, Sally?"

Sally's mood swings in a different direction and her expression turns dark and dangerous.

"I ain't talking about that."

A shiver runs down Stella's spine. What does that mean, *tinker*? *Fix women but good?* They turn their attention to the meal preparation and Stella, bewildered, goes to the large sink to start washing. At dinner, she sits with Frances as they've been doing. Frances gives her a crooked stare before she begins shoveling food into her mouth while humming. Stella looks around the room. What about her? Or that one? And that one? Many sitting in the dining hall are still strangers although she's familiarized herself with their faces and names, but no one reaches out to get to know her better because the Colony's grapevine is efficient. They know about her. Which is why Stella is stuck with Frances, the biggest oddball of all. At least she's better than nobody. She turns to the other girl.

"I thought maybe I could share this book with you."

Frances plows through the chocolate pudding, drops her spoon onto her tray, and it clatters with a sharpness that makes Stella jerk. Frances centers her good eye on her. Stella starts to talk about the book when Frances turns away again, as if she's not interested, or is trying to ignore her. Stella taps on the table.

"Frances, listen. Don't you want to hear about it?" She holds it up. "It's called *The Hobbit*. It's my favorite."

"Stella, if you're through with your meal, would you come with me?"

Stella jumps at the sound of Mrs. Dot so close to her. She had no idea she'd walked up to her.

"Yes, ma'am."

She gets up from her chair while Frances adopts a less than intelligent look, allowing her mouth to hang open as she starts bobbing back and forth while making one of her odd noises. She's pulling what Stella is certain is a con job. It's frustrating Frances behaves like this because how is anyone ever going to believe she's smart and capable of what Stella claims she did if she acts like what Mrs. Dot calls her—a moron. Stella tucks her book under her arm, picks up her tray, and hurries to drop it off before following the superintendent. She isn't upset Mrs. Dot didn't wait for her. She rationalizes she wouldn't want any of the residents to think she's being treated different. Mrs. Dot is smart like that. Stella arrives at her office seconds later.

"Shut the door, please."

"Yes, ma'am."

"We have a serious matter to discuss."

That's when Stella notices Mrs. Maynard is there, lurking in a corner. This discovery is as alarming as coming close to a poisonous snake and Stella freezes just inside the door. Mrs. Dot's features are tight and Stella can't tell if she's angry, or what.

"Yes, Mrs. Dot."

Mrs. Baker reacts like Stella slapped her, whipping her head around to glare at her.

"*Excuse me?*"

Mrs. Dot (Baker!) glances at Mrs. Maynard, edgy and distrustful, and Stella realizes her mistake. She forgot the rule.

"I'm sorry, Mrs. Baker. It just slip . . ."

Mrs. Baker distracts from this by rattling a sheet of paper. Stella can see what it is and the hairs on her neck and arms rise. She knew it. She knew nothing good would come of Mrs. Maynard keeping that work by Frances.

"Were you the one who wrote these?"

Stella feels her face slide into one like Frances's, dopey and dumb. Suddenly, she's ice cold at the realization Mrs. Baker doesn't believe her. Mrs. Maynard has convinced her. Stella's dinner churns in her stomach.

"No, ma'am."

Mrs. Maynard sighs dramatically.

"My dear girl, Frances Platt has been here for some time now, and has proven time and again she's incapable of learning. She's been with many—I emphasize *many*—accomplished teachers at this facility, and none of them were able to get her to even pick up a pencil!"

"I didn't write them!"

Stella hates how her voice rises. She's never been good at defending herself, or arguing. In this case, it's critical, but her ability to keep her voice believable is difficult. Even to her own ears she comes off as too defensive. Maybe even whiny. She clenches her hands to hold them still. Mrs. Baker withdraws a sheet of paper and places it on her desk. She motions for Stella to come forward, and hands her a pencil.

"Write your *A*'s, big and small."

Stella's clammy all over and her mouth fever dry. It's like being in a bad dream, the kind where she can't get away. She does as she's asked and sets the pencil down. Mrs. Baker picks up the paper and Mrs. Maynard comes forward and peers at it as they quietly compare the two. Mrs. Baker hands both papers to Stella, and to Stella's horror, it's impossible to see much difference. Frances has copied her writing so close, even down to the little curve tail on the small *a*—just like Stella—as well as the perfection in the straightness of the large *A*'s.

Her arms straight out, palms up, she pleads with Mrs. Baker.

"I can prove I'm telling the truth. Have someone watch us together without her knowing. Then you'll see she's smarter than you think, but she's . . ."

Stella stops talking at the annoyed and impatient look on Mrs.

Maynard's face, while Mrs. Baker drops the papers onto her desk and turns away. Mrs. Maynard retrieves the one with Frances's writing and holds it up.

"Stella Temple."

"Ma'am?"

"As I've said, Frances has been at this facility for almost a year. We've seen little, if any, change in her, and anyone who's ever observed her has never viewed her as anything more than what she is—that of someone who's dealing with mental incapacities beyond what you would understand." Mrs. Maynard looks at Mrs. Baker. "I don't know about you, but I've heard and seen enough."

"Please. I want to do right, and I ain't gonna lie about it. What good would that do me?"

"That's exactly right, Stella. Go on," encourages Mrs. Baker as she finally turns back to face her.

She looks hopeful and Stella catches the small nod, like she wants her to come up with some obvious explanation. Mrs. Maynard purses her mouth and waits. Stella's consternation grows. She was assigned to work with Frances and she did as asked, but even she can see how her claim might seem like she's proving their knowledge and expertise wrong, and has been wrong all along. The accusation she's not telling the truth rankles, though, because she is, but there's nothing more she can think to say that might help. She'd only be repeating herself.

"Well?" Mrs. Baker prompts. "If you have something to say, and if it will clear up any confusion, please say it."

Stella bites the inside of her mouth, and gives one last final try.

"I didn't write that. Maybe she doesn't know what they mean, but that came from Frances's own hand."

Mrs. Maynard crosses her arms and sighs.

"I must say, this insistence is very troubling."

"Let me speak to Stella."

Mrs. Maynard waves a hand.

"Fine. Do what you must as I'm sure you know my view, but I'll say it anyway. This needs to be handled immediately."

Stella detects a shift in how they're speaking to one another. It's small, but there's something going on between them that's different from before. Mrs. Maynard has an uncommon confidence while Mrs. Dot rubs her forehead like she's no longer as certain. Whatever the rift is, it involves her. Mrs. Maynard keeps standing there, waiting. Finally, she checks her watch, goes to the door, and opens it. Stella's legs are like jelly with relief, but then the housemother adds one final comment.

"I'm sure you'll let me know your decision as to how you plan to manage this."

The door clicks shut and Mrs. Baker collapses into her chair as if she's exhausted. After a moment, she sits up, folds her hands, and sighs.

"This is quite the mess. I thought putting you and Frances together was a wonderful idea and now this . . . this . . . debacle." She waves her hands about. "You know you can tell me the truth. I'd expect it, since I believe you don't want to lie."

"But if I said I did it that *would* be a lie!" Stella is unwavering and she pleads with Mrs. Dot. "Please believe me."

"It's Frances's history, Stella. If there'd been small signs or indications of this being possible, especially after all this time, someone would have seen it before now. Mrs. Maynard won't let this go. Maybe just a small admission? Perhaps that you wanted to believe she could write, so you helped her?"

Mrs. Baker casts a hopeful yet sad look at her, as if wanting her to break down and spit out a confession that suits their way of thinking. Stella is beginning to understand it doesn't matter what she says. Something's going to happen, and the woman she thought of as her rescuer will be the one to decide.

Chapter 25
Baker

Disappointed though she may be at the moment, deep down Baker is certain there's never been a resident quite as promising as Stella Temple, despite her troublesome history. Stella is like a baby bird, shoved from the nest due to unwanted flaws of nature, but in a different environment, she thrives. She sent Stella out of her office so she could think more clearly about how to handle the Frances Platt problem without those nervous, sad eyes watching her every move. Once she was out of sight, Baker began plodding around the office. It's not a small thing, what's going on with Stella saying one thing, and Mrs. Maynard another. The facts are on the institution's side, unfortunately. It's a regrettable situation and requires delicate handling, like being polite to bad company who refuse to leave.

The biggest hurdle has been the girl's refusal to admit her error, which pits Baker directly against Mrs. Maynard. Baker stops pacing and grimaces at the idea of caving in to the housemother's wishes, yet sees a unique opportunity borne of this dilemma. If Stella has to endure disciplinary measures, at least it's a chance to prove what's been said about Ethel Maynard isn't something out of the Colony's rumor mill. While she has no way of knowing what this will do to the girl, allowing Mrs. Maynard her way could reveal her vile and strange depravity. Baker crosses the room and opens the door to find Stella sitting on the bench across the hall, like a criminal waiting for a jury to come back with a decision.

"You may come back in, Stella."

"Yes, ma'am."

The girl gets up and approaches the door, limp hair partially covering a pale cheek. Baker stares. Look how small she is. She's gained no weight since she's been here, and still has the appearance of a twelve-year-old. She averts her gaze. She must stay firm in her decision. Once they're back in the office, she gets right to the point.

"There must be punishment for the issue concerning Frances Platt."

There's a quick intake of the girl's breath, and afterward, any other reaction is kept hidden behind wary brown eyes. Baker is firm, conveying the decision is made. She won't allow any pleading, if it comes.

"It will be quick, and then it will be done. Come along with me."

They leave the office and walk down the long hall toward the front of the building. Various Colony activities can be heard, from the murmur of voices to the whir of sewing machines from a vocational class directly across from the kitchen. Mr. Lumley yells at a group outside, instructing them to "put your backs into it!" The silence coming from Stella is unreadable, troubling. She's always been rather forthright, and honest, and this quietness worries Baker, but her focus is to coordinate this so she catches Mrs. Maynard displaying her unseemly behavior. If Stella takes on a resentful attitude and proves to be a disappointment after all, better to know now before she expends more effort and time on an irredeemable individual.

When they reach the end of the hall, she can hear voices through the closed doors. Baker listens as they pass, and gets that surge of pride and well-being that always comes with knowing residents are deeply engaged in important work. Stella is a step behind, dragging a little, and Baker can't think of a thing to say. She can't assuage the girl's fear or downplay what's about to happen; it would be a disservice, not only as to the reason behind it, but with regard to instruction on personal behaviors and consequences. Every mother, teacher, and reformer, anyone who's associated with the disciplining of troubled individuals understands fear is a very persuasive tool. Baker imagines this will have to happen only once, and Stella will understand it was an essential part of her growth and development. This is what Baker will talk to her about when it's over.

The last door at the end of the hall is Mrs. Maynard's office and is so small it barely holds the desk and chair, plus one more for visitors. The door is open and Mrs. Maynard can be seen at her desk writing furiously. She looks up as they approach, and quickly shoves the paperwork off to the side, and shuffles a few things to cover whatever she was working on. Once she stops rearranging the desktop, she sits back, folds her hands, and adopts the attitude of a subordinate. Baker knows all too well it's nothing but a show. She states her decision.

"Group punishment is to be administered, the sooner, the better."

Mrs. Maynard's mouth pinches into a tiny, wrinkled orb and a bizarre sound comes out of Stella, a sharp, high-pitched squeak of alarm. She flaps her hands, Frances Platt–like in her distress, which becomes more obvious as she speaks in a frantic voice.

"Okay! Okay! I wrote it! I wrote it!"

"Ah! Now. See?" Mrs. Maynard stands and her spine produces a dry crack in protest. "There we have it. The truth. Finally."

Baker gapes at Stella. Why didn't she say this when they were alone in her office, and not in front of Ethel Maynard? The housemother raises her chin, triumphant, as if praise has been heaped on her by the pope himself. Stella, unaware of what the punishment was until now, is panicking. Smug and self-assured, Mrs. Maynard gloats.

"I knew it all along. It's always best not to favor any one individual, but to see them objectively so when they come to their senses, no one is caught off guard."

Baker would like give Mrs. Maynard a reminder about hierarchy but can't afford to demean herself by arguing. She wouldn't put it past her to use this very moment against her when interviewing for *her* job. Baker turns to Stella. The girl looks absolutely broken, destroyed, and it makes her question not only her judgment, but this decision, yet she can't change her mind, not now. She's highly experienced with reactions and outcomes. Time and again, it's shown that in the end, while not easy, what was gained was a crucial lesson and through that very process, most often than not, improvements are seen. If, from that point on, the path forward is followed on the straight and narrow, all will be well.

"Mrs. Maynard, we don't need to discuss the nuances of what's going on here. Please select those who should be involved as well as the ones who need a reminder, and will benefit from attending."

"Well, let's see." She tips her head up to stare at the ceiling as she starts to tick off names. "Frances and—"

"Just a moment. Frances?"

"She went outside of the building without permission while this supposed lesson was going on. Stella can confirm this. Isn't that right?"

Mrs. Maynard turns to Stella, who's clutching her elbows, shaking and on the verge of crying. Baker's sense of justice skews in favor of Stella as she tries to rationalize why she confessed at the eleventh hour. More than likely, she admitted she wrote it in a desperate attempt to appease and to try and avoid what was going to happen anyway. Baker closes her eyes. She has to see this through, has to be the sort of superintendent she's always been. Practical. Measured. But most important of all, unemotional. She turns away from the white-faced girl, and makes herself disengage.

"Fine. Who else?"

"Eileen Glover, Tracy Adams, and Ruth Foster."

"This is about Eileen smoking in the dorm, and Tracy refusing to scrub the toilets?"

There's an affirmative nod.

"And Ruth Foster? What's she done?"

"She's slacking off. It started with her appearance, but more worrisome is this air of secrecy about her. Several times now I've caught her whispering to others, and as soon as I'm anywhere nearby, she stops. Something's going on. She's never seen group punishment, and quite honestly, I think if everyone witnesses it once, it will do wonders for adjusting their dispositions."

A thought materializes, and Baker seizes on another potential advantage.

"Okay, fine. Let's have all of them observe."

Mrs. Maynard echoes her words, and sounds flummoxed.

"All of them?"

"Precisely what I said. Everyone is to meet in the central hall. I'll announce it."

Baker continues to avoid Stella's gaze. It doesn't help she begins to sound similar to Frances when she gets herself worked into a state. Baker is certain if she allows herself a glance, she'll make the foolish mistake of giving in and that would be unconscionable. She must remain committed, otherwise she'll appear weak, and the accusation of favoritism by Mrs. Maynard would be proven. As impossible as it seems, it's as if the girl senses something within her, a weakness, a tiny crack in her determination. Maybe from her barely perceptible hesitation because she begins to beg.

"Please. I'll do meditation. Put me there. I'd rather do that. Can't I do that? Please? Please?"

Pleading isn't new. It's not the first time a resident has tried to alter their outcome by attempting to play on the heartstrings of herself or the staff. Not that anyone ever thought she had a heart.

Before Baker can respond, Mrs. Maynard says, "The decision is made, and it's final. Furthermore—"

Annoyed at the housemother for assuming control again, Baker cuts her off and addresses Stella.

"Accepting responsibility for mistakes and actions is one of the first and most important steps in reform. After accepting responsibility, you then accept the punishment with a clear understanding there are consequences for incorrect behaviors. Everyone is handled accordingly"—she makes certain to glare at Mrs. Maynard—"and must endure the penalties. That's all there is to it."

Stella's response, to Baker's dismay, is to shake her head and she doesn't stop. Her hair swings wildly and Baker is reminded of a young girl at Samarcand who never recovered after group punishment. She took to rocking in place, and the only time she wasn't engaged in that most unbecoming and witless routine was when she was asleep. Ultimately, they ended up sedating her, and sending her off to Dorothea Dix Hospital in Raleigh with the suggestion of imbecility. It was later said she suffered some sort of mental break, and Baker felt vindicated in her decision to place her there. She hopes this won't happen to Stella, but who can tell?

"Stella Temple. There is no need to digress further in your behavior!"

She speaks sharp and with authority and this appears to snap her out of it.

"No, ma'am."

The usual soft lilt in her voice has gone flat.

"Mrs. Maynard, go on and take Stella. I'll see to the others."

"Come, Stella!"

Mrs. Maynard's fingers latch onto Stella's upper arm as if the girl might bolt, and Baker retreats to her office. In thirty minutes or less this will be done. At her desk, she accesses the intercom.

"Attention, attention, please. All staff and all residents report to the central hall of Dorm A, first floor, immediately."

She waits a few seconds and repeats the message, then listens to the sound of forty-two pairs of shoes clomp and shuffle from their various points around the facility into the hallway outside her office. She waits until it's relatively quiet, opens the door, and walks to a central point in the hall. She can sense them watching her. They are lined up in four rows, and they're filled with nervousness and curiosity. Some smooth their hair while others stare straight ahead. Mr. Lumley is with a small cluster of educators off to the side where every head is bent toward someone and mouths are moving. Neither Dr. Greene nor Dr. Graham is on site today, and for that she's grateful. Nurse Crawford looks around in a worried manner. She can take her aside later, and explain.

Stella is next to Mrs. Maynard and the housemother twitches the infamous hickory switch against her leg. The hem of Stella's dress quivers, a small, singular earthquake of emotion. It's so quiet, it's as if the women are mannequins before her, and if it weren't for their wide, blinking eyes, Baker would question if they're alive. Good. They know this is serious and she must use these next few moments to her advantage, to have punishment meted out as an example in which there can be no question as to the reasoning behind it. She draws their attention when she raises her hand.

"Ladies. Punishment is never the first step. You have choices to make each day. You're given ample time and multiple chances before action is ever taken. I believe most of you want to do what's required of you. These chances—we'll call them opportunities—are in the form of demerits. Every now and then one of you makes a choice, or a decision such that demerits alone aren't adequate. It's the sort of violation that draws immediate and swift action, one intended to teach."

Everyone glances toward the group of women clustered around Mrs. Maynard while Stella has gone a deathly shade of white. Baker forges ahead.

"You've all heard of group punishment, but most of you have never seen it carried out. Let these next few minutes be the deterrent you need when you're thinking of violating rules. Let it be the humiliation you want to avoid, at all costs. Here we have Stella Temple, who was asked to help Frances Platt. She later fabricated a story to curry favor, and then lied about it. For that regrettable decision, group punishment will address the issue. Eileen Glover, Tracy Adams, Ruth Foster, and Frances Platt, please step forward."

Eileen and Tracy immediately do as asked, but Ruth and Frances don't. Ruth actually takes a step back and begins to argue.

"I won't be a part of this."

Baker can't believe her audacity and didn't account for it.

"You will, or you'll get the same thing."

"I will not!"

Sweat forms on Baker's upper lip. She can't afford to have a word war with Ruth Foster in front of the residents.

"Miss Foster, listen carefully. You *will* face the same consequences."

"I'm a grown woman. You can't be serious."

Baker squares her shoulders. She must win this moment. It doesn't help when Frances starts behaving in a way that makes Baker want to send her straight off to Dix. She's growling in Baker's direction and baring her teeth while Ruth still refuses to budge.

"Frances!"

Frances's features smooth out and her wonky eye rolls in a disconcerting manner.

"Go. Stand. With. Them." Baker points to Eileen and Tracy. "Now."

Still growling, Frances scuttles over to the women, who move away as she begins crowing like a rooster. Baker smacks her hands together.

"Frances Platt! If you don't stop this minute, you'll get group punishment too!"

Frances's crowing subsides with a croak. Baker turns back to Ruth.

"If you refuse, it's meditation, and you can expect an extended stay."

Ruth says, "I'd rather have that than have her touch me."

Baker almost smiles while Mrs. Maynard stiffens and a deep flush crawls up her neck and face.

"One more, Mrs. Maynard!"

The housemother takes out her notebook and runs her pencil tip down the demerit list.

"Maude Turner. Smoking in the bathroom, late to class, and general sloppiness."

Maude emits a sound much like Frances, a growl of sorts. She goes and stands beside Eileen, Tracy, and Frances. Baker scans the women once more. Many remained motionless for most of this, while those participating look as if they want to throw up. Frances has gone stonelike. Baker nods at Mrs. Maynard.

"Please carry on as you have in the past. Report to me when this is done."

Baker proceeds down the hall. Behind her, she hears Mrs. Maynard instructing Stella to lie down and for the others to hold an arm or leg. Baker rounds the corner, and enters a door to one of the classrooms. The rooms run the length of the central hall, and are all joined by internal doors one leading into the other. She hobbles quickly through each classroom, five total, and comes to the last, which gives her a perfect view of the hall she just left. She eases the door open a crack. They're right where she can see.

Stella's arms have been stretched above her head. She's quiet, while sobbing comes from a few residents even though nothing has happened yet. Mrs. Maynard taps the switch in her palm and in looking at her, Baker is filled with revulsion. She can see what's right there. Eagerness. There's really no need for anyone to hold Stella; she lays there as if dead. Frances is the only one who isn't holding an arm or a leg. Instead, she squats by her head, glaring at Mrs. Maynard. Every now and again, she pats Stella's arm. Mrs. Maynard raises her arm. The first strike comes whistling through the air to land on Stella's backside. Everyone flinches, even Baker from her secret spot, and Frances falls back onto her rear. She stays there, bug-eyed. Again, Mrs. Maynard's arm rises and descends. When it lands again, Stella makes a whistling sound of pain. Mrs. Maynard increases speed, consumed by a burst of energy.

Baker doesn't know where the housemother's ability comes from, given her condition, but there's an uncanny zeal to her movements that defy her physical disability. Baker's gaze roves, assessing reactions. Eileen, Tracy, and Maude have averted their faces, even as they hold Stella's limbs in place. So has Ruth Foster, and Baker sees tears on her cheeks. Frances . . . Baker is startled. She's staring at Baker. The shock of discovery is so unexpected, Baker is locked in place, transfixed by the inferno of rage in Frances Platt's eyes. Her lips are pressed thin while her chest heaves up and down. Despite the bizarre imbalance of her gaze, there's an uncanny intelligence there Baker can't deny, and she begins to doubt herself, and believe Stella. Several things happen over the next few seconds. Mrs. Maynard descends into that unnatural way of hers, smacking her lips and growing more fervent with each strike. She's no longer with them. She's some other place, and to Baker's disbelief, groans accompany the hits.

"Yes. Yes. Yes."

"That's enough!" cries Ruth. "Stop it!"

As soon as Ruth yells, it's an emotional dam breaking. Some of the staff rush forward to keep Mrs. Maynard from hitting Stella again while Ruth tries to grab the switch. With unbelievable grace, the housemother whips around and flails at her, landing a strike or two before she can duck. Ruth retreats with a little scream. The scene descends into chaos, with inmates and staff clamoring in loud voices, protesting the punishment. They bunch together as one with hands over their mouths, or wringing them in distress. There's crying and shouting at Mrs. Maynard as Baker launches herself from the classroom and manages to snatch the switch away. She stands with it in her hands, rigid, and with a very strong compulsion to descend on the woman and give her a taste of what she delivered.

This has become a calamity, a disaster of outlandish proportions. This is ten times worse than she expected. She wasn't prepared for this, this level of madness. Stella breaks her silence and her high-pitched wails echo through the big hall. Every eye is on Baker and she can sense the residents' resentment—no, their hate. The staff look confounded, and upset. She got what she needed, but at what cost? This has created an atmosphere of distrust and suspicion. The housemother puts a hand to her lower back, and the other to her chest, which heaves up and down. She adjusts her glasses and tucks in a strand of hair that has worked its way loose from beneath her wig.

"Now, then," is what she says, her breath coming out in puffs like she's run around the grounds.

Baker's intuition ramps up. Judgments are forming. Opinions

churn and fester. Respect is diminishing and if anything is to remain of it, she has to bring control and a sense of order back. She must somehow salvage what has been done. They can't see her rattled, and even though she is, she must act with proficiency and restore calm. She needs to command their attention and make it clear she doesn't approve. Baker gives the women of the Colony a once-over, reading the room. Ruth Foster is disgusted, and Baker sees this same expression on many other faces, while others are exhibiting shock. Meanwhile, Frances is sending out looks of pure and uninhibited hate, directed at her. Baker lifts her hand.

"Stella. Your punishment is concluded and your demerit record is fully expunged."

Frances begins patting Stella on the arm again, and Baker believes it's more soothing to her than Stella. The residents are a sorrowful-looking lot, while the staff begin to whisper behind their hands. Baker thinks quickly and attempts to repair what's happened.

"Stella, you will resume the important work of reform with a clean record. You should be commended for bearing what was an abhorrent overreaction on the part of Mrs. Maynard. Rest assured, she will be reprimanded for her behavior, which was completely out of line."

Several residents murmur and nod their heads. Stella, her head hanging with shame, doesn't acknowledge Baker's attempts to rectify the housemother's transgression. Mrs. Maynard gasps and, with incredulity, waves her hands about wildly.

"I only did as I was told!"

"Mrs. Maynard, don't disgrace yourself further. Please return to your office, and assume desk duties until I say otherwise. Nurse Crawford, if you could please see to Stella?"

Baker then addresses Ruth.

"Miss Foster, as you know by now I will always respect a resident's choice, and you made one when you refused to follow a directive, fully understanding the consequences as they were immediately explained to you. Come with me. The rest of you, go back to your assignments. We are done here."

Baker doesn't wait to see what any of them do. Mrs. Maynard, mouth still agape, huffs with indignation but turns and walks in the opposite direction to her office. Baker knows from past experience if she presumes an individual will do as told, more likely than not they will. Sure enough, she hears the group disperse and behind her come light footsteps. She rounds the corner of the hall, and her peripheral vision relays Ruth Foster trailing her down the hall toward the basement.

Chapter 26

Ruth

Still vivid in her mind is the meditation room with its unique smell, damp chilliness, and endless days and nights of monotony, and yet Ruth is still glad she refused to participate in the group punishment. Watching as Baker hobbles along just ahead of her, Ruth imagines running, but that thought is as fleeting as a second in time. She can't make things worse for herself, although she can't imagine it getting any more difficult, except Lucy said it would. She'd said that's how they did things with the troublemakers, that they have it worse than the rest.

Then there's Stanley Newell. He'll come, and she won't be out there to meet him. He'll think she's changed her mind. This thought slows Ruth's steps and Baker, ever vigilant, misinterprets her pause.

"Second thoughts and regret will get you nowhere," she warns over her shoulder.

Ruth ignores her. At least before Newell left she told him that if she went missing, it would mean something happened to her; if he wants to know what really goes on here, let him see her after she's released from Room Two. They arrive at that all-too-familiar door and Ruth's eyes dart to Baker. The superintendent's color is high as she yanks out the key ring and furiously sorts. Ruth figures she has nothing to lose.

"How long will I be in here?"

Baker doesn't reply right away. She finds the key, shoves it in the lock, and pushes the door open. She gestures at Ruth with a wave and Ruth steps inside and turns to face Baker. Baker's face is still as a mask. Her flush has subsided a little, and she's become the superintendent Ruth is most familiar with—aloof, calculating, with a hint of cynicism overlapping anything else.

"That's up to you, Miss Foster. It's always up to you."

"One of these days someone's going to find out what goes on here."

"Mind yourself, Miss Foster. Those sorts of threats do nothing but get you into more trouble. Women like you require exactly what this institution provides. Promiscuity and other corrupt lifestyles are a certain stain on society. I can't understand why this is so hard to comprehend. Don't you want to be respected and thought well of?"

"I was, but now, after being here, I imagine my reputation will be ruined. You're not doing me any good, Mrs. Baker. You're not doing anyone any good."

She turns away as the superintendent's flush returns. Baker shuts the door and locks it. Ruth feels her way over to the stinking little cot and sits. She's almost immediately nauseous from the odors wafting around from the familiar mildewy dampness, to the disgusting bucket. She doesn't move for a long time. The meals, if you can call them that, come as before. The door opens, a tray is shoved in, and the door shuts. She's given less than the first time, nothing more than a bowl of watery oatmeal for breakfast, black coffee. Lunch and dinner don't change much: a few potatoes mixed with corn, or sometimes plain beans with a slice of bread or, to change it up (she thinks this in amusement), rice with three or four pole beans (she counted) and again, black coffee. Enough to keep her alive. Everything is the same, and somehow worse. Aside from her own breathing and the growling in her stomach, the only sound is the same slow drip from the faucet over the wall sink.

She waits, hunger crawling through her middle like a wild animal. She fidgets, plucks at a blanket thread, daydreams of the warm sun, and tries not to think of the days in the kitchen and the food she prepared. If there were any good moments at the Colony, it was then. She pulls out strands of hair. Nudges teeth with her tongue, dismayed to find one loose at the back. Taps her fingers in time to the faucet's drip. She sleeps, somehow, most of the time, only getting up when the breakfast tray arrives, and the same routine begins again. Time passes. One day, Baker comes and ask questions.

"What do you think about your decisions? Have you considered your mistakes? Are you willing to allow us the chance to help you?"

Ruth has had time. Plenty of it. The sooner she gets out of this room, the sooner she can speak to Mr. Newell, and the sooner he can help. She's willing to say whatever is necessary if it means her release.

"Yes, Mrs. Baker. I've thought everything through carefully. I should've done as you requested and written the letter for one, and I should've helped with group punishment."

Baker's remark is filled with skepticism.

"Is that so?"

"Yes, ma'am."

"Good. Let's see if you mean it."

The superintendent opens the door and motions for Ruth to follow her. They walk down the narrow hall and Ruth gulps in breaths of fresh air. Baker leads her into another room. It's empty but what draws her attention are the chains hanging from two hooks in the ceiling. On the cement floor directly below are two lighter-colored spots. Ruth sees them for what they are, worn areas, and an image comes to her of a person standing there unable to move. Her teeth begin to chatter and she hugs herself.

Baker says, "Wait here."

Ruth is left there, her mouth dry as a desert, her chest retracting and expanding quickly, an accordion of anxiety. Her thoughts act like snow flurries in wind. She isn't sure what's going to happen, but prepares for the worst. Baker comes back with the housemother from Dorm B, Mrs. Dillard, and she's accompanied by three women Ruth hasn't met as well as Frances Platt. Frances grimaces at her and begins to sway back and forth, clearly anxious. Baker motions at the odd girl.

"Frances Platt was caught stealing food in the middle of the night and is to receive punishment."

It was a trap.

Before she can think about what she just claimed, she says, "I won't do it."

The other women don't move as she and Baker square off.

"Do you think you can say what you think I want to hear and that's the end of it? You must prove yourself, Miss Foster, otherwise it's deceitful and that, in and of itself, is a sign of poor character. There must be sincerity in your actions and words. It's the only way you'll ever reap the rewards of a true reform."

Baker is blank-eyed and calm while Ruth gets mad at herself. She should've known better. Mrs. Dillard and the three women look on while Frances Platt begins picking at her eyebrows.

"No matter what you say, I won't do it."

Baker's face burns, a fire ignited within, while Ruth emphasizes her decision by crossing her arms and looking away. Frances starts snarling in the background.

"Frances."

Baker says the girl's name so quietly it's barely heard, but Frances stops. The others who've been watching the scene before them with round, troubled eyes grow more uneasy, and Baker shifts her attention to them.

"You've been told what your role is. This is a warning to you not to start off on the wrong foot." She addresses Ruth once more. "You can set an example, or not. Take control of your future, or not. It's your choice. I've said this all along."

There's no need for any more conversation. Ruth understands that it's not in her to hurt another individual, even though defying the superintendent once again will put her back where she just came from. She doesn't speak. Baker points at the other women. Two grab Frances, who shrieks. They drag her kicking and twisting into the center of the room and she's held so the chains can be attached around her wrists. This is done by the third woman and Mrs. Dillard. There's a click and they're in place. Ruth clenches her hands into fists as fury washes away caution.

"You don't care anything about the women here. You're just like Mrs. Maynard, you enjoy this."

Baker frowns and Ruth enjoys a brief moment of triumph as the superintendent appears disturbed by the accusation. Baker looks at poor Frances, whose arms are stretched over her head so that the toes of her shoes barely touch the floor. Now Ruth understands how the spots were made and can't imagine how many have been through this. The three residents and Mrs. Dillard get out of the way as Frances uses her body strength to lift herself and thrust her legs out in an attempt to kick them. Frances continues to react wildly and her uncontrollable behavior gives her a very demented appearance. Like a livewire carried by frequent currents of eruptive, emotional electricity, she continues to whirl and kick.

"This could be you next, Miss Foster."

Ruth can't stand to see what is happening to Frances Platt and is close to tears.

"Then let her go. Put me there instead."

Frances screeches and Baker points with authority at the girl.

"Control yourself, Frances Platt! Or else!"

Or else? What more could they do? Nausea laps at Ruth's insides like waves of the ocean washing up on shore. Frances goes limp, head back, face aimed at the ceiling. Her chest heaves from her exertion and her eyes glisten. Ruth is certain she's crying. The three new inmates huddle together with their hands over their mouths, big eyed and staring. Mrs. Dillard has a hand on her chest, as if she's trying to keep her heart from leaping out of it. Ruth feels sorry for the new women and wishes she could offer advice like Lucy did for her months ago, but there's no need, not after what's just happened.

They can see what kind of place this is and no matter what they're told, this moment will be what they remember. Baker smooths her hair, which isn't out of place.

"This is why rules ought to be followed. It doesn't take much for a situation to turn into pandemonium. Let this be a lesson. You three"—she points authoritatively at the residents—"go back to your assigned duties. Miss Foster, you'll return to meditation until I can deal with you. Mrs. Dillard, please escort Miss Foster and thank you for your assistance during Mrs. Maynard's absence."

The three women hurry from the room, followed by Ruth and Mrs. Dillard. Ruth gives one final look at Frances. Her hands have turned bluish in color and she's muttering under her breath. Mrs. Dillard's demeanor is stiff and off-putting. As soon as Ruth enters the meditation room, the door is shut and she lowers herself onto the cot. She didn't think she could grow any more disheartened, but this particular incident has left her questioning the sanity of those here. She gets up, paces the room. Eight steps to the far wall, eight steps back.

She loses track of time, not that it matters. She keeps moving, the size of her world constricted by not only the space, but her emotional state. Unwittingly, she's more or less on a hunger strike because when food is delivered, she doesn't eat. She can't. It's as appealing as the dirt and grime covering the floor, and she can't get past that other room, and witnessing what went on with Frances. This goes on for six consecutive meals. When she reaches a state where she's certain she's about to collapse, she lies on her back, an arm across her forehead. She sleeps.

She has no idea how much time has passed when she's awakened by a sensation. The room is dark, but what startles her is the hand on her arm. She scrambles to get off the bed except that same hand presses down on her to keep her where she is, and a voice whispers.

"It's me, Nurse Crawford. I'm here to tell you, you must eat."

Ruth relaxes, and replies in a lifeless voice.

"What for?"

"Listen to me. I've been told your trays are coming back to the kitchen untouched and that if you don't eat, it will be handled. Trust me. You don't want it handled. They'll do to you like they did to Stella."

The tension in the nurse's voice gets Ruth's attention. Even though it's dark, the room spins and she clutches the edge of the cot for balance.

"How did you get in here?"

"I have a master key—for emergencies. At this point, you're an emergency, in my opinion. I brought something for you."

Ruth catches a whiff of food.

"If it's potatoes and corn, or beans, no thank you."

The nurse holds a bowl out to her like a gift. Ruth sniffs the air. It's enticing. She takes a sip and instantly recognizes it's vegetable beef soup. She reaches her hand out and Nurse Crawford gives her a spoon. Ruth dips it in the bowl and once she begins, she can't stop as the basic human desire to survive takes over, plus it's really, really good.

The nurse murmurs, "There you go. Finish it. I brought it from home. It might not be as good as what you'd make, but I tried."

Ruth slurps and says, "It's pretty darn good."

She hands the empty bowl back. Nurse Crawford doesn't get up to leave, but instead speaks softly.

"I don't know why they do this."

This is unexpected. Ruth stares at the outline of the nurse, and snorts.

"Because they can. No one says anything to stop it, not even you."

Nurse Crawford draws back at her directness, and for a few seconds doesn't move. Eventually, with a voice that's soft and thoughtful, she begins to talk.

"I tend to the nursing side of things, and the staff, well, they handle the rest. I worked too hard to get this job to take a chance in losing it."

"But don't you think this is wrong, keeping us against our will? None of us was charged with any sort of crime. We're given shots that make us sick. I felt fine before I came here. What if it were you?"

Ruth thinks Nurse Crawford won't say anything else, but she does, and it's not what Ruth expected.

"It *was* me several years ago."

"What? You were an inmate? Here?"

"Not here, but another facility. There's more than this one, you know. They have them across the United States. I received behavioral training for about a year."

"Across the United States?" she repeats. Ruth's shoulders sag with the enormity of this "plan." Thousands like her could very well be experiencing similar circumstances. Nurse Crawford turns to Ruth.

"My family were poor, but we could feed ourselves, that is until my father lost his job. Then we lost everything, our home and all, because we couldn't keep up with bills. After that, my father, mother, two sisters, a brother, and myself lived where we could, sometimes in barns, sometimes in the woods. We were sickly. It was hard to find work. My younger brother and sisters had hookworms and my father developed tuberculosis. Right after he got a job at a local mill, and just when we thought things might get better, his illness took him. I was sad, but more than anything, I was angry because he was gone and it didn't seem like our life was going to get better. As the oldest, it was up to me to help. Mama got work at the same mill, and at first I stayed home taking care of my siblings until I got other ideas on how to help my family. I was the same age as Stella when I got into the kind of trouble that puts wayward girls in places like this. Petty theft of food, mostly. But sometimes I was the one doing the giving instead of taking, if the money was right."

Nurse Crawford is off in her own world, reminiscing, unaware Ruth is staring at her in astonishment.

"We ate, though, until I got caught, and Mama couldn't say a word to me, couldn't even look at me. I was so ashamed. I promised myself I would make her proud again. I was sent for reform, and it was there I learned of the New Deal program that provided training to become a public health nurse. I saw it as a way to do something to better myself, but mostly to give Mama a reason to look at me like I wasn't a disappointment. I got out on parole and one of the housemothers stayed in touch and helped me understand the program. I stayed out of trouble, graduated from high school, and then I applied, and here I am today."

"But do you agree with what they do here?"

"What I know is most every farm colony, detention hospital, or reformatory practices some form of corporal punishment. Some are harsher than others. Those in charge here aren't the worst, if you can imagine. I tried to get them to consider other ways, but they're the ones with experience, is what I'm told. On the other hand, you could say I'm a good example of how it can work if the individual allows it."

"That sounds like you're on their side."

"I'm saying, don't fight it. Do what you need to do to get out, then try to forget about it."

Ruth is certain she'll never forget about this place, or what's been done.

"What about Frances? Do you know what they did to her?"

"Yes. She was out after a couple of hours. I had to wrap her wrists, but she's okay—as okay as someone like Frances can be. She's been sent away, though."

"Where?"

"Probably to Dix. That's the mental hospital in Raleigh." She stands. "I've stayed longer than I should have. I'm glad you liked the soup."

Without a backward glance, the nurse slips out, leaving Ruth conflicted about her experiences and her advice. Another day passes and her pacing continues nonstop. After Nurse Crawford's small gift, the meals return to the previous unappetizing and restrictive amounts, and she just can't stomach them. The benefits from the soup last only a short while and soon her weakness returns. It's midmorning when her neighbor, whoever it is, begins crying, her wails loud and coming through the wall. Ruth can make out muffled voices. She shuts her eyes as the sounds in the neighboring room escalate. It's impossible not to react and Ruth's mind switches between fear and trying to guess what's happening. *They're suffocating her. They're choking her. They're killing her.* She can see it in her head, like a movie.

Her body breaks into a sweat even though she's freezing. The other door squeals opens and slams shut. The jangle of keys is outside Ruth's room. This drives her to a corner, where her brain begins to sound the alarm, *I'm next, I'm next, I'm next,* and she feels the urge to shove past whoever's on the other side and run for her life. There's the mechanical twist of the lock, and three people quickly fill the tiny room. Baker is in the lead, leading Dr. Graham and Nurse Crawford, who flank her. Baker speaks softly as she always does, in the voice Ruth has come to dread. The softness is a ploy because in reality the woman is as hard and rigid as granite.

"I'm left with few choices. Remember, this is no one's fault but yours, and these are the consequences of your actions. Your refusal to comply is justification for a lesson to encourage your absolute cooperation as you strive to improve. It's unacceptable to refuse a direct request. Once is bad, but three times? I've been lenient. I need you to agree with what I'm telling you. Do you agree with what I'm saying? If so, repeat after me, *Mrs. Baker, I am ready to accept your guidance, continue with my reform, and work to become a proper resident at the Colony.* If you don't comply, I'm forced to proceed differently."

Ruth hears everything, but her focus is on the last part of what Baker says. *Proceed differently.* A moment of soaring fright steals her breath and words. She's never experienced this level of panic. She focuses on her issued brown shoes and shivers in the thin, light-brown dress sewn by previous inmates. Had they lived this same hell? Her dark hair hangs damp with sweat even as she grips the threadbare blanket around her shoulders. The delay in responding is her folly. Baker waves her hand in a commanding manner and Nurse Crawford comes forward and softly takes hold of Ruth's thin arm.

"Wait," says Ruth.

Mrs. Baker's expression is impassive.

"Yes?"

Ruth doesn't know why she said that. She stares at the nurse with confusion and despair. Dr. Graham observes her as if she's a lab rat, and scribbles with decisive strokes on a thick notepad. Nurse Crawford's mouth trembles, and her eyes are troubled. Baker speaks firmly.

"Nurse Crawford."

It startles the nurse, and she takes the prepared syringe Ruth hadn't noticed, jabs it into her arm, pushes the plunger, then steps away immediately. Ruth doesn't move. She stares at the spot where the needle went in. Baker, with a quick nod of approval, goes to the door, and offers one last parting comment.

"We'll see how you're thinking when we return."

The room empties, and the door shuts. The lock clicks. The back of Ruth's knees are against the cot and she sinks down onto it. Within minutes her gut cramps and becomes extremely uncomfortable. Nausea overtakes her midsection. She grits her teeth against it, which is useless. She's had nothing to eat, but whatever's in her stomach burbles. She makes a lunge for the sink because even in her state of misery, she's aware the bucket would only make this worse. The next few hours unfold in waves of purging that eventually result in the dry heaves. When the drug wears off, she lays exhausted on the cot, her head throbbing, dehydrated and weak. She dreams of her mother's cool hand on her forehead. As quick as the nausea came, it's gone and right on schedule, a tray is brought. There's a bit more food and she manages to eat, somehow knowing it will help her still sensitive stomach. Even so, the less than adequate portions make things worse.

On what she believes is the end of her third week, Ruth is in a state of failure. She's unsteady on her feet, her head is a constant ache, and she can't stop shaking. She shuffles around the room senselessly and when the door opens, she doesn't seem aware. Baker, Dr. Graham, and Nurse Crawford are in the doorway, peering in at her. Baker speaks first.

"You're in luck, Miss Foster. No one requires group punishment, or a visit to our special room."

Ruth stops her endless circle, braces herself against a wall, and squints at them. She puts a hand to her hair, and her fingers get caught in the knots. She's filthy, beaten, and has decided no matter what, she'll do or say whatever is needed to get out of here. Nurse Crawford rushes forward, grabs her wrist, and takes her pulse.

"Her pulse is racing. She's dehydrated."

Mrs. Baker moves closer.

"Miss Foster, did you hear me?"

Ruth stares at the superintendent while Nurse Crawford's heightened concern is apparent.

"She may have had too much."

Dr. Graham harrumphs.

"I told you the dose, so unless you changed it, it was accurate."

"Not that. This . . . this room. Meditation."

Ruth answers Baker.

"Yes, ma'am. I heard you. I'm ready."

Baker gives her an odd look, and speaks to Nurse Crawford.

"Take her back to quarantine. See to her so we can get her back with the others."

Ruth steps across the threshold of Room Two. Her voice cracks as she scuffles down the hall alongside Nurse Crawford.

"Thank God."

Nurse Crawford bends down and whispers in her ear.

"It's over now."

"Nurse Crawford!"

Ruth goes rigid, her heart flailing inside her chest as Nurse Crawford pauses to acknowledge the superintendent.

"Yes, Mrs. Baker?"

"No mollycoddling residents!"

"Yes, Mrs. Baker."

Moments later, Ruth gratefully enters the quarantine room. She could sob from relief but she's too weak. Nurse Crawford is solicitous, first weighing her and tsking over the dramatic drop of pounds.

"I've got to fatten you up."

After Nurse Crawford takes her temperature, Ruth gets to bathe, and wash her hair. It takes every bit of her energy to do this. The nurse makes her undergo another test, and brings her food, but what Ruth wants is sleep. After only a few bites, she's helped into the bed and slips between clean, crisp sheets. She descends quickly into a dark void of nothingness. The next morning, she opens her eyes and looks outside where the sun shines bright.

Chapter 27

Stella

In the days following group punishment, Stella's movements are slow and pained. The backs of her legs and buttocks are sore, the skin tight and swollen. It's hard to bend down, much less walk. She's spent these last few months filled with the hope she could become something, someone who could change, someone who could fit in, and now she's lost her motivation. She feels listless. What's she supposed to do now, an outcast among the outcasts? She should've known it was too good to be true. People tend to look for faultiness in places like this. She'd been determined to alter herself, but now she might as well accept her path to restoration is ruined. Accept she's unworthy, a letdown. She'll never be the individual Mrs. Dot—*not Mrs. Dot, Mrs. Baker*—expected. She's not worth the effort.

The one good thing about kitchen work is it's done while standing. Opal and Sally cast a glance or two her way, but in general leave her alone except to accommodate her slowness and poor effort.

They says things like "You do the dishes; we'll serve so you ain't got to move around too much," or "Here, let me carry that outside and dump it; you stay put."

Stella acknowledges these considerations with a little smile or a nod. She might as well remain in the background since she doesn't feel like facing anyone after her humiliation. Strangely, the one person she wouldn't mind having around is Frances, except Frances is gone, whisked away, perhaps never to return. Stella doesn't know where she went, but the thing with Frances is she never expected Stella to be a certain way. She was simply there, giving little pats on Stella's arm every now and again, more of a reassurance to herself is what Stella thinks, but no matter. Why couldn't Frances be here now, when she truly needs her? Improbable friends, unlikely to ever be viewed as anything but strange, but friends they were. She'd be a comfort because Stella's mental state is as tender as her backside.

Later, when she's back in the dorm, those who witnessed her punishment attempt to rally around her. Josephine, Natalie, Paula, and even Melissa try their best to get her to react to their silly jokes and words of comfort, as if she belongs. She resents it. *Now* they're nice to her. Why couldn't they be like this before? Why did it take something like what happened to make them see her differently, perhaps as one of them? It won't last, she concludes, and sure enough, her intuition holds more weight than their words. After a while, their concern fades, or maybe it's because she refuses to speak or acknowledge them. Or maybe it's because they weren't sincere to begin with.

As if this weren't enough, her guilt over how long Ruth Foster is being kept in meditation eats at her, especially at night when the dorm buzzes with speculation as to how long she'll stay this time. From her bed, she glances about with suspicion, certain they're talking about her, blaming her. Ruth probably does too. Stella would. If she can excel at any one thing, it's guilt. It's a way of life for her. Look at the reasons she came in the first place, bearing the responsibility for Cordell's behavior. Loneliness wallops her while tears puddle behind her lids and want to spill over and down her cheeks. She won't cry. If she starts, she won't stop.

In spite of Stella's internal angst, she's not so shut down she's not paying attention to the absence of Mrs. Maynard. She counts her blessings. There's gossip among the women over the housemother's lurid behavior, and even more about how Mrs. Baker abruptly appeared from out of a classroom. Stella didn't see any of this. She was too traumatized, hurting too much, wanting her shame to end, maybe forever. Who would miss her, after all?

A few nights later while getting ready for bed, she approaches Josephine and frames her words carefully.

"Maybe Mrs. Maynard will be kept away from us for good."

Josephine stops fluffing her pillow, throws it on the bed, and sits. Stella shifts from foot to foot, still preferring to stand because sitting remains out of the question. Josephine stares down at her ankles and turns them in circles like she's exercising them. They're swollen, and the blue veins pave her skin like a roadmap.

Josephine says, "She's not doing nothing but sitting in her office from what I seen. Staring off into space." She glances at Stella, then back across the room, keeping watch. "She ought not be here. She ought to be fired."

Stella wishes that would happen. If she never had to face her again, she'd feel so much better. The woman gives her the same disgusting, unpleasant feeling she got with Cordell. She can still hear the way she sounded. Some could've said it was exertion, but what Stella heard were the same sounds her father used to make. She gets queasy thinking about it. Josephine gestures at the clock.

"Better be done with your bedtime stuff before Mrs. Dillard comes."

The thought of breaking rules doesn't bother Stella, not like it once did. She moves to do what she's supposed to, but takes her time. A few seconds later Mrs. Dillard is there. She looks around, and then scowls at her pointedly, as if to let her know she saw her lollygagging. The lights go out and the room is dark. Stella eases onto her cot and lies facing Frances's empty bed. The night Frances disappeared, Stella had seen her leave her bed, but she'd quickly shut her eyes, not wanting to know what she was up to. She couldn't get into more trouble by following her, not now, not when she understood even Mrs. Baker can't protect her. She'd waited for her to come back, but eventually fell asleep. The next morning Frances's bed was as she left it, covers barely moved, almost like she'd slid out from under them while they were tucked under her chin. Stella wasn't concerned because Frances often got up before she did. That morning she'd wobbled awkwardly, painfully, down the hall where the bathroom was already filled with women hogging sinks and toilets. While she'd waited for one or the other to be available, she'd expected her friend to barge in any minute. In the time it took her to wash her face, brush her teeth and hair, she still hadn't shown up. Stella crept back to the dorm and, as is often the way of news circulating, hushed voices had made the room sound like a hive. Stella heard then, and was almost sick.

"She got caught stealing food."

"Oh no."

"She's in for it now."

Stella's memory of that moment was of panic zinging through her like electricity. She'd put a hand to her head, knowing she couldn't handle seeing another punishment, not so soon after her own. Heads were bent toward one another, discussing the crime of stealing within a place like the Colony. A serious offense, maybe the worst of all. A new tension developed among the residents as they debated repercussions. The talk continued sporadically for the rest of that morning and into the evening. Finally, after several days, there was no reappearance of Frances, and no more talk of her either. She'd vanished, just like that, while Mrs. Dillard and Colony teachers moved through the usual schedules as if nothing happened. They urged everyone to complete their work and go to classes with the usual energy and enthusiasm. After all, reform must go on. How many days ago was that? Stella isn't sure. She tosses to her other side. Frances's empty bed gives her the feeling she died. Somehow, her body's needs overtake her thoughts, and her eyes close. When she wakes up the next morning, she doesn't look at Frances's cot. She doesn't allow herself to even think of Frances Platt. She stops looking for her.

Not long after Frances's disappearance, everyone is in the dorm and waiting for lights out when several gasp and begin to call out greetings. Stella turns, hoping it's Frances and instead it's Ruth Foster. Her recent ordeal is disturbingly obvious and Stella's guilt blooms as big and broad as the pain inflicted by Mrs. Maynard. She stares at Ruth because it's hard not to gape at the difference between the beautiful young woman she'd first seen to the one she sees now. Never robust to begin with, Ruth's on the verge of skeletal with sunken cheekbones, emphasizing her eyes and making them enormous. Her hair is thinner, and has lost its gloss. Her once pink cheeks are ashen.

Josephine says, "Thank God, child. You made it out."

Ruth doesn't seem to hear this. They watch her lower herself to her cot with a mixture of shock and sorrow. She turns on her side so her back is to everyone. Stella creeps over to Josephine, disturbed and unsettled.

"I wish she'd just gone on and done what she was supposed to do."

"Hold you down?"

"Yeah."

Josephine is quiet for a moment, then shakes her head.

"She wouldn't think of it. Good people in moments like that are braver than most."

This makes Stella feel even worse. She slinks back to her side of the room and the dorm is as quiet as she's ever heard it. A few seconds later, that quiet is broken by a weak voice.

"There's this other room."

It's Ruth. She's sitting up, the light from overhead hitting her at an angle that emphasizes the shadows under her eyes. Stella sits up too, ignoring her discomfort. Melissa, Natalie, Paula, and others break the rules, daring to be out of place so close to lights out. They gather around Ruth, wanting to hear what she has to say because knowing helps them prepare for what could happen to them. She begins softly, as if the words are so heavy, she can barely lift them up and out of her mouth.

"While I was in Room Two, Baker came. I was ready to say anything to get out of there, and said I was ready to do what she wanted. She tricked me. She took me to this other room and a couple minutes later, Frances was brought in with three other women I didn't know from Dorm B. Mrs. Dillard was there too. Baker said I had to prove I was ready, and the only way was to be part of Frances's punishment. Like before."

Ruth scans the faces circling huddled near her and stops on Stella's. She pulls at the neckline of her gown in a restless manner. She begins again and Stella wants to put her hands over her ears, fearing what happened to Frances. She makes herself listen. She has to know.

"I refused. Again. There are chains in that room that hang from a grate in the ceiling. The other women were made to secure Frances's wrists. Her toes barely reached the floor. We all know how Frances can be, but she's never intentionally hurt no one. After she was suspended like that, she went berserk, trying to kick whoever she could. Those other women didn't want to be a part of it any more than I did. I got a glimpse of her before I was taken back to meditation. I'm sure she was crying."

Many signal disapproval with grumblings of resentment and defensive posturing. Stella's hands press hard on her cheeks as a layer of unshed tears turns the women in their white nightgowns into shimmering angel-like figures.

"Where is she now?"

This from Natalie.

"Nurse Crawford told me she's been sent somewhere for some other kind of treatment."

There's a sound in the doorway. Mrs. Baker fills the space with Mrs. Dillard just behind her. No one knows how long they've been there and everyone dashes to their beds. Stella cowers and doesn't want to look at the superintendent, doesn't want to catch her attention. She concentrates on a spot on the wall, near the doorway.

Mrs. Baker says, "Let's put the rumors to rest. A few days ago, Frances Platt was caught stealing food out of the kitchen. She was punished for it and is receiving the best of care now at a specialty hospital. As we all know, she's challenged in more ways than one.

That's all there is to it. There's no need to concern yourselves beyond what you ought to be doing. So, look after yourselves, do as you should, and you'll have nothing to worry about."

Everyone, including Stella, notices as Mrs. Baker says this, her attention is riveted on Ruth Foster. The lights go out. Mrs. Dillard leaves but Mrs. Baker remains in the doorway, silhouetted by the hall light behind her. She continues to stare in Ruth Foster's direction. Stella's grateful for the camouflage of dark as a chill runs through her. She shuts her eyes, willing the superintendent to leave. When she opens them, the doorway is empty, and the hallway is dark. Her muscles loosen and her heart rate calms. She has trouble getting to sleep after this, and so do several others who rustle and flap their sheets throughout the night. The few who are somehow unperturbed by events at the Colony snore.

The next morning, Stella is up before the morning call and gets to the bathroom first. She is going to become invisible, stay to herself and out of everyone's way. The morning goes as it should with the usual escort to the dining hall, and Stella enters the kitchen to help serve. Opal and Sally are there, the food cooked and ready, and Stella begins sliding empty trays their way for them to fill. After the residents are served, the kitchen workers eat, but this morning Stella struggles to swallow the rubbery, overcooked eggs and a biscuit so flat, she can't split it. Opal and Sally eat what she doesn't and Stella would like to think this is because they like her and don't want her to get in trouble, but it's about always being hungry, especially Opal.

Stella fills the big industrial sink, and begins the mindless task of washing forty-something trays that will, of course, be without a scrap. She listens to the other two giggle over who knows what until they abruptly stop, and it's like a warning shot. Stella turns around to find Mrs. Baker is in the kitchen. The superintendent yields the same expression of disinterest as she surveys worktables, the stove, the pantry area, until her gaze lands on Stella. The tray Stella holds slips from her fingers. Luckily there's only a bit of a splash, imperceptible to anyone but her. She ducks her head and resumes washing. When Opal squeals with laughter at something Sally says, Stella's shoulders relax, but just to be sure, she checks. The room is empty but for them.

The visits from the superintendent continue, right after breakfast each day. After a few mornings, Stella finally manages to meet Mrs. Baker's eyes. It's not for long because Mrs. Baker's features are passive, unrevealing. Stella fixates on this, and can't understand why she wishes for Mrs. Baker's approval again, but she does. She wants the superintendent to return to the idea she holds promise, to discuss plans for her future like she did before. After spending more time than she cares to admit dwelling on it, she has to accept Mrs. Baker no longer sees her as any different from the others, even if she did wipe her record clean. She's now one of the immoral, her ability to change questionable. Filled with dismay her chances to become a good person are ruined, she ignores the superintendent as best as she can.

Eventually, Mrs. Baker stops coming to the kitchen, and Stella only sees her at a distance coming out of her office or walking down a hallway. Her fear of being sent home is revived. If she were asked right then which was worse, the Colony or home, there's no way she'd want to go home and doubts she'd stay if she were sent back. Weeks pass and Mrs. Baker comes nowhere near her. Stella begins to obsess there's a decision coming, and that the next time she acknowledges her, it will be to say that's what's happening.

It's late June and Opal and Sally sit just outside the door at the back of the building, peeling potatoes, when the superintendent returns once again. Stella is caught alone in the kitchen where she's filling up pitchers with freshly made sweet tea.

Mrs. Baker says, "Hello, Stella."

Caught off guard, Stella stops her work and respectfully replies.

"Hey, Mrs. Baker."

"Have you had a chance to think over what happened?"

"Yes, ma'am."

"And?"

Stella squirms internally. She'd told the truth, then lied hoping Mrs. Baker wouldn't punish her, but that backfired in the worst way.

She wrestles with what she sees as a betrayal. She was told she was different from the rest. There are things she'd like to say, the words as dangerous as the knife Opal used to cut her wrists. Dangerous for no one but herself. She has to say something.

"Ma'am, I wish none of it happened."

It's the best she can do.

Mrs. Baker tilts her head as if considering her words. The superintendent takes a hand and brushes it across the worktable.

"Put whatever negative thoughts you're having behind you. The best way is forward, not backward. You know this, I'm sure."

Stella wants it to be like before, to believe she can be special, not the old, broken Stella Temple. She doesn't think it's possible, but again, she responds in the manner expected.

"Yes, ma'am."

Mrs. Baker seems satisfied with this exchange. She turns to leave, but her right leg doesn't follow her body's wish. There's a moment where Stella is sure she's about to fall, and she thrusts her hand out. Mrs. Baker, ever vigilant about preventing such a thing, grabs hold of the doorframe, steadies herself, then lets it go. The superintendent's face washes pink, a moment of embarrassment and vulnerability, and the small, dead spot in Stella Temple's heart that formed like a callus toward Dorothy Baker softens ever so slightly.

Chapter 28

Baker

Mrs. Maynard's degenerate behavior on full display for the entire population of the Colony to see, while unfortunate, gives Baker what she needs and yet she finds herself strung out over calling Dr. Woodall. She stalls, contemplating and imagining the conversation in her head. This doesn't help and only gets her more worked up. She begins to realize if she doesn't go ahead, her case against the housemother won't seem urgent, or even critical. On a Monday morning, first thing, she calls. While she waits for him to come to the phone, her hands sweat, and she can feel moisture beading on her upper lip.

"Hello!"

He sounds impatient, which doesn't help. She gives a short description of the group punishment disaster while holding back on the more sensitive part of Mrs. Maynard's actions.

"There's more to this, but I can't discuss it any further over the phone, not something of this nature. A situation was brought to my attention and I wasn't sure if there was any validity to it. I can assure you, it's imperative you hear about this."

Dr. Woodall pauses, and while she waits for him to speak, Baker could swear she hears the operator breathing into the line.

After a moment he says, "And this concerns Mrs. Maynard specifically?"

"Yes, and I'd rather not say any more on *this open line*."

There's a faint gasp, a click, and Baker snorts to herself. Every time she makes a call from the Colony, she's positive the local operator listens in. She's most likely bored and hoping to hear something salacious. It would be a huge scandal if word got out about this unsavory behavior, particularly involving a staff member. Baker hears paper rustling, then Dr. Woodall speaks.

"I can't meet for some time. My calendar is full for several weeks."

"There's no adjustment you can make, an exception?"

"I'm afraid not."

"What's the earliest day and time you have?"

"It will be a couple of weeks, at least. I can meet mid-July."

Baker has no choice. They finalize the details and she's careful to mark it on her desk calendar in red pen. She spends the following days as usual. Typical Colony issues come from a few residents who challenge Mrs. Dillard and the teachers in small ways. She updates Frances Platt's records and holds out hope Dix Hospital will keep her, even if it means losing the generous donation from her parents for keeping her housed at the Colony. Mrs. Maynard's presence is scant given her restricted duties. Keeping her out of sight has proven smart to prevent the residents' hostility from growing. She continues to review what she's done for their good and keeps record of it, especially the turnaround in Ruth Foster after the last isolation.

The big day finally arrives and Baker has her hair done. She brushes her best suit, tightens a button, and polishes her shoes. As she dresses, she puts on a new pair of black stockings. Five minutes before two, she gets out of a taxi in front of a large three-story building in downtown Kinston, and is escorted into Dr. Woodall's empty office by his secretary, who leaves her there alone. She takes a moment to look about. There aren't any windows in Dr. Woodall's office. This wouldn't do for her. There's pinewood paneling on the walls, and a large oil painting of some bucolic landscape hung behind the desk—which she happens to note is smaller than hers. Interesting.

On the credenza behind the desk is a picture of two children, a boy and a girl, elementary school age. How cute. His grandchildren. Aside from two matching upholstered chairs of a blue-and-white toile—quite ugly, in her opinion—angled toward one another in a friendly fashion in front of the desk, there's not much else to see.

She sits in one of the hideous chairs. She breathes deeply, steadying her nerves. She believes what she has to say will get Ethel Maynard immediately replaced. A few minutes pass and Ralph Woodall breezes in, bringing with him the scent of hair tonic and cigarette smoke. He slaps a stack of papers down on his desk, drops into his chair, and greets her all at once. He isn't anything like Baker expected. They might be close in age; actually, she's almost certain he's younger. She can't say why this is disconcerting, but it is. His hair is only beginning to show a few gray threads, and his eyes are dark. Above them sit thick eyebrows prone to become bushy, but for now, they're well behaved, and give him a brooding look that he directs at her.

"Something to drink, Mrs. Baker? Coffee? Water?"

"Coffee would be nice."

He presses a button. "Barbara, coffee please." He releases it, and places the tips of his fingers together, staring across the expanse of his desk at her.

"Let's get right to it, then. Is this about the letters you sent, or perhaps about the new position?"

She needs to say something, but he's caught her off guard.

"Well, no. I'm actually here for the reason I mentioned on the phone, although I'd love the opportunity to discuss those matters as well."

Baker is happy with how she sounds—calm, collected, and professional.

"Right, right. Your initial request for this meeting has something to do with Ethel Maynard, specifically? Your phone call was quite timely. I planned to have you come in, because of course I think it's only fair I hear your side as well, given your position there."

Only fair I hear your side as well. Baker is thrown again. Damn her.

Mrs. Maynard saw an opportunity to influence Dr. Woodall's viewpoint in advance, she's certain of it. She doesn't like that she's been discussed preemptively and it rattles her. She shifts on the chair, and crosses her ankles. She's not about to let them think they have some sort of advantage. Might as well get it out in the open.

"I highly doubt Mrs. Maynard shared the specific reason I'm here, seeing as how it's a delicate topic."

"I see."

Her legs get that itchy feeling she hates, like ants crawling, and she wants to reach down to rub them, but she can't. Dr. Woodall uses the intercom again. What he says is so unexpected, she reacts with a small jerk, and covers by reaching up to pat her hair.

"Barbara, also, please send in Mrs. Maynard."

Seconds later, Ethel Maynard enters as if she was waiting right outside. Baker's certain it's a setup, and entertains the idea of submitting her resignation then and there. The fact this enters her mind stuns her, but this is how she's always been. It's what she calls *jumping off the cliff,* which is her reaction to the unexpected, to feeling trapped or misunderstood. It's her way to regain control. Such dramatic decisions can fail, though, and she's learned to rein in these overreactions. She can't let them gang up on her, not when she's doing the good work, the necessary work. The Colony's operation has been exemplary. Where's the gratefulness? Dr. Woodall smiles warmly at Mrs. Maynard before he turns to Baker, and maybe it's her imagination but that smile slips away faster than an anchor dropped into a black, black sea. He clears his throat, and folds his hands on his desktop.

"I thought it important for those involved to have frank, open discussions, but Dr. Graham is seeing his regular patients at the clinic this morning, and Dr. Greene is attending a conference. Both offered some input, which I'll share. Ethel—that is, Mrs. Maynard—was available to come today, given her current assignment has her more or less restricted from doing the job she was hired for, if I'm understanding this correctly. Is that right, Mrs. Maynard?"

"Indeed, it is."

They nod amiably at one another and Dr. Woodall returns his gaze to Baker.

"It's a good practice to fully understand one another, wouldn't you agree?"

Baker's internal response erupts, a volcanic hot flash followed by her hoarse reply.

"Of course."

Her hands knot together. Meanwhile, Dr. Woodall isn't giving anything away. He glances from one to the other. No one ventures to say another word and there they sit. It grows awkward, and then Barbara comes in again with coffee, three cups, and that breaks the moment. Baker studies how Dr. Woodall and Mrs. Maynard feign deference to one another over the coffee tray.

"You first, please."

"Oh no, please. You're the guest."

Baker's stomach tightens and she feels a headache coming on. The phoniness is almost more than she can bear. This simpering version of Ethel Maynard is nothing more than a show. They turn to her as one after they've fixed their coffees. Mrs. Maynard picks up the coffeepot and raises it, offering to pour Baker a cup. It will seem petty to refuse, but that's what she wants to do given the apparent triumph barely keeping the housemother from grinning at her as if she's already won.

In a voice as gracious as she can muster, she says, "If you don't mind."

"Not at all."

Baker resigns herself to the moment. Mrs. Maynard hands the saucer and cup to her and coffee sloshes over the side. Baker sets it down on the side table between the chairs. She can't drink it now. Etiquette requires her to use the saucer provided and it's almost full. She doesn't trust herself not to spill it. She can't determine if this was intentional, or if Mrs. Maynard is feeling the effects of this meeting as well, despite the obvious comradery with Dr. Woodall. They sip together in companionable silence while Baker twitches and fidgets, her legs buzzing under her stockings.

Dr. Woodall sets his cup down, and says, “I’d like to hear what you have to say, Mrs. Baker.”

She contemplates how to begin. She wasn’t expecting to have to do this with the housemother sitting beside her. She can’t help but sift through what annoys her about the woman, but that’s personal and counts for nothing. She can’t nitpick over personality traits, or find fault with her being unable to straighten her back any more than she can blame herself for walking with a limp. She needs to say what she came to say, stick to what happened, and if possible share a few other instances where Mrs. Maynard’s decisions sowed disorder. She begins with the most egregious, one she’s assigned a formal name, the Stella Temple beating.

“Mrs. Maynard and I had a disagreement with regard to a resident, Stella Temple.”

“Over what?”

“Her claims that Frances Platt wrote the letter *A*.”

Dr. Woodall frowns.

“Frances Platt, the imbecile?”

“Yes. Stella is highly intelligent. As part of her reform, I asked her to work with Frances on a simple lesson. Teaching her the alphabet.”

Mrs. Maynard interrupts.

“We’ve had skilled teachers try to teach Frances, and they failed.”

“That’s an aside and not the focus here.” Baker faces Dr. Woodall. “Mrs. Maynard believes Stella lied, while I’m not so sure she did.”

Mrs. Maynard goes to interrupt again, and Dr. Woodall holds up a hand, and motions for Baker to continue.

“There’s a rumor concerning punishment, specifically group punishment. I didn’t believe what I heard at first. It’s not uncommon for residents to sometimes exaggerate these moments, usually because they’re angry for being disciplined. I believed this to be the case mainly because the individual who continued to perpetuate this story wasn’t trustworthy given her background.”

Dr. Woodall is taking notes, and pauses. "Who's the individual?"

"Lucille Griffin, a prosti—"

"Yes, I know about Miss Griffin's background. Of course I agree, rumors in such an environment tend to behave like . . . fire."

Baker's chest squeezes. Is it coincidental, the word he uses or intentional? She detects nothing in the way he's watching her, except there was an almost imperceptible pause before he said *that word*. When Mr. Thaddeus Gray hired her five years ago, what he cared about was her credentials, her experience, not her downfall, which to his mind was a bad rap perpetuated by the Samarcand girls, the parents, the local police, and the newspapers. Dr. Woodall, and maybe even Mrs. Maynard, might've checked her old records. Samarcand and her disgraceful exit would be in there. Baker shifts on her chair, her own pause no longer than a breath.

"It would have remained a rumor had I not seen with my own eyes the abhorrent behavior exhibited by Mrs. Maynard during Stella Temple's discipline. It wasn't a correction done for the benefit of teaching. No, sir. It was a beating accompanied by very disagreeable behavior."

"And what was that?"

"Enjoyment."

"Enjoyment?"

"Yes."

Mrs. Maynard flings her hands about, a mini tantrum of emotion.

"Absolutely absurd and disgusting! I did as I was told, nothing more!"

Baker directs her comments to Dr. Woodall with assurance.

"She administered the punishment, and the force she used was excessive. She lost control. The residents became very upset. The goal of group punishment—"

Dr. Woodall interrupts.

"How could you tell it was enjoyable? Did she speak? Did she do something?"

"I could tell. It was obvious."

"Do you know how many times the individual was struck?"

Baker hadn't counted. She had no specific answer, so she says what comes to mind.

"Too many."

"Did you provide the specific number this resident was to receive?"

"I trust the staff to know what's appropriate."

"There's no limit, then."

"Of course there's a limit."

"Well, what is it?"

He's arguing with her and Baker decides he's a sanctimonious ass.

Her voice tight and low, she says, "The limit is before a resident sustains the sort of injury inflicted on Stella Temple. Usually three."

"Except one is too many for your *pet*."

Baker cringes at the use of the word. She retaliates with more clarity, with what she saw that she can't get out of her head.

"She kept licking her lips, and . . . and made some untoward sounds as she hit Stella."

"'Untoward'? What do you mean?"

"Moaning."

Baker is satisfied to see Mrs. Maynard's and Dr. Woodall's faces flush, hers bright pink and his deep red. He drops his eyes to his desktop, and he's either speechless or dumbfounded. Mrs. Maynard grows hostile and indignant. She throws an arm out, pointing at Baker as she addresses Dr. Woodall.

"That's not true. Does that sound like me? I'm an upstanding member of this community. I'm insulted by this accusation, which is highly offensive."

Baker makes a derisive sound.

"We can agree on that. I intentionally watched everything from Classroom A so I could see if what was rumored was actually true. It is. The person you are inside the Colony isn't the same one Dr. Woodall sees before him now."

Baker relaxes against the back of the chair, confident Dr. Woodall understands. After all, anyone with intelligence knows human behavior is like being on stage when in public. Mrs. Maynard points at her.

"And the same could be said about you."

Dr. Woodall shifts in his chair and taps his pen on the desk. Baker wishes none of this were happening, that she was back in her office looking out over the fields as those in her care labored toward their better selves. He stands abruptly and addresses them.

"I can't have the two of you at odds. It's an absolute must for staff to work together to ensure the best environment for all involved. I'll have to take this sensitive matter before the board, given the nature of it."

The restraint Baker's kept during the meeting disintegrates even as she knows anything she says in this moment might impact a future, important decision. She can't help it. She's spent the last five years proving herself worthy all over again, while Mrs. Maynard is hell-bent on undermining her authority and trying to take her job.

"For what it's worth, Dr. Woodall, I can assure you, Ethel Maynard is not up for the job of superintendent. What about the letters I submitted for review? They're outstanding samples from the residents themselves of the good work under my supervision. That should count for something, particularly considering this is the first and only complaint brought to your attention about the Colony, and it's not relevant to *me*. It's about Mrs. Maynard, and I'm the one bringing it to light."

"It's not the only complaint. There've been several. Dr. Graham and Dr. Greene have brought up a few instances, actually, regarding you and so have some residents. What was the word Dr. Graham used? Give me one moment." He rifles through a few papers. "Ah, here it is: 'barbaric.'"

That son of a gun. He's using her own words against her. She keeps herself still, and hopes to appear unperturbed as she contemplates these new developments. She's clearly at a disadvantage, but that's not all. Dr. Woodall drones on.

"Dr. Graham believes your methods are, at times, questionable. Dr. Greene thinks you're in it for yourself, for the recognition instead of the good of the women. As superintendent of the facility, you should be setting an example for staff and any sort of disciplinary measures you mandate should be bound by the same restraints you expect."

Baker has recovered enough to defend herself.

"Well, of course. After all, I wrote the handbook that's in use throughout the state and beyond. I find it amusing you'd think I don't follow my own rules. Dr. Graham and Dr. Greene aren't without their own faults, if you'd care to hear them? They relate to proper protocol within the staff hierarchy as well as decisions concerning certain procedures."

Dr. Woodall rubs his face and resumes tapping his pen. After a moment, he checks the clock on the wall.

"I'm afraid we've run out of time. If you wish, submit it to me in writing. Otherwise, I need to think on what's been discussed today and, as mentioned, take it to members of the board. Please reinstate Mrs. Maynard to her usual duties. It's not safe to operate understaffed. You should know this, Mrs. Baker. Making decisions with this in mind is paramount. You'll be notified of the board meeting and its results as soon as possible. If you wish to have your grievances addressed regarding Dr. Graham and Dr. Greene, you need to get them to me quickly."

She doesn't know how to respond, and it doesn't matter because Dr. Woodall concludes the meeting by walking to the door. Mrs. Maynard's expression is smug and victorious. Baker sits unmoving, and a few seconds pass before she grabs the arms of the chair and forces herself up. She maintains her dignity by extending her hand toward Dr. Woodall. He barely grips the ends of her fingers, the handshake appropriate and polite, but she hates it because it signifies something less than an agreement between equals. Her earlier evaluation of him congeals a bit more and she adds another adjective, sanctimonious, *arrogant* ass. She ignores Mrs. Maynard as she exits the office.

The secretary who's busy typing looks up, surprised as she passes her, and says, "Oh, the meeting is over?"

Baker is already halfway down the hall, departing the building as fast as she can. She requested the cab to wait, and when the driver sees her, he gets out and hurries around to open the door.

"That didn't take too long. I hope it went well for you."

Baker isn't in the mood for chitchat.

"Let's go."

On the return trip, she lowers the back window. She doesn't care she just had her hair done or that it's growing hot. She lets the stifling air blow against her face, like the blast of a furnace, and her mind abruptly rekindles a very old memory. The initial strike of a match, that certain scent, cradling the baby flame . . . she bites the skin of her inner cheek, breathes deep, diverts her attention to the scent of pastures, and the view of a hog farm. It's been a very long time since she permitted any unrestricted liberty of thought in that direction. It's forbidden territory, only the desire is easy to revive because it's never left, not really.

The taxi driver pulls up to the entrance and she sits staring up at the two-story Colonial-style brick building. Right here, within this very building, she's done her job. She's taken in the broken women society demands she restore. This is what her work is about, and always has been. To have it questioned is on par with Mrs. Maynard's depravity as far as she's concerned, and it's more than disheartening. She can't think about it.

"This where you meant, right?"

She turns her attention to the driver.

"I'm sorry. Yes."

She reaches into her purse, pays him and adds a tip.

"Why, thank you, ma'am! Call anytime. Ask for Amos."

Once inside the building all that is familiar and comforting surrounds her, from what some might call musty and others might think of as institutional, but for Baker, it's like coming home. She can hear the common sounds of classroom work, and the rattle of pans from the kitchen as she goes to her office. Her steps drag more than usual. She's tired, and needs a moment to sit and think about what took place, and what it might mean. In the five years she's been at the helm, her authority has ruled, but now it feels as shaky as her legs. On her desk is an envelope from Dorothea Dix Hospital and that can mean only one thing. *Please let them keep her.* She rips it open and as the paper within unfolds, she reads the following:

> *Concerning Frances Platt: Arrangements for transport of individual to return to the State Industrial Farm Colony in Kinston is set for July 16th, to arrive early morning.*

That's tomorrow. Baker closes her eyes. She's conflicted about Frances. She can't shake the memory of the way she looked at her the day Stella was whipped, but even more worrisome is the undeniable sense the girl has somehow played them all for fools.

Chapter 29

Ruth

Ruth ignores how weak she feels as she gets up and walks carefully to the bathroom, her hand sliding along the wall to keep her balance. There are several women splashing water on their faces, brushing their teeth or hair and taking one last quick glance in the mirror. They murmur "Good morning," as they hurry out the door. Ruth stands in front of an empty sink. She doesn't lift her head. She doesn't want to face the mirror, afraid to see what might be reflected there. How she looks certainly has to match how she feels.

Josephine, Melissa, Natalie, and Paula are there and no different from her, with rashes, hair falling out, nausea, and general fatigue. To think when they arrived they had none of these afflictions. Maybe some had a few medical issues, normal things like needing to see a dentist for a cavity, trouble with asthma, heart conditions, perhaps anemia. The fact is, before the Colony, none were as they are now. They turn to her, voices raised in a clamor.

"What're you going to do?"

"You can't get put back in that room again."

"My goodness, you're white as a sheet and much too thin."

Stella lurks in a corner like a small mouse trying to escape notice, as if she'd like to disappear into the wall. The brutality of what she's been through obviously left more than physical marks. Ruth speaks to her gently.

"Stella, you doing any better?"

Stella doesn't answer and Ruth bends down to splash her face. She straightens and while reaching for a hand towel, Stella makes her wishes clear, her voice low, but certain.

"I appreciate what you done, but don't do me no more favors. I don't need nobody's help."

Ruth spins around to stare at her. Stella's expression is cynical and the quick glance she sends to the others is just as suspicious. Josephine gestures with mild irritation, flapping her hand dismissively.

"Best to just leave her alone, Ruth."

Ruth doesn't want to give up, and turns back to Stella, attempting to reassure her.

"Stella, I'd have done the same for anyone."

"Yeah. It sure wasn't because it was me."

Stella rushes from the bathroom like a small furious tornado, and Josephine shakes her head.

"That one ain't been right since that whupping."

Ruth folds the towel.

"I guess I wouldn't be either."

Josephine nods her agreement as she and the others hurry back to the dorm. Ruth takes extra care as she combs her hair, but the strands fall no matter what. Back in the dorm room, Josephine is pulling on her socks and Ruth shares the other news with her.

"Lucy sent a friend."

Josephine stops yanking her socks on over her swollen feet.

"A friend? What do you mean?"

Ruth quickly fills her in about the lawyer, how he came, what he said, and what they arranged.

"He might've given up on me. I think Lucy would tell him to keep trying if I suddenly disappeared. She'd know it was because something like meditation happened."

Josephine clasps her hands, prayerlike.

"Oh, this is good news, I think?"

A familiar voice gets their attention, and both women turn as one, dismayed to see Mrs. Maynard in the doorway.

"Let's get on with it! You have one minute to be ready for breakfast."

Ruth grimaces.

"Heaven help us. She's back."

She quickly smooths her bed covers before pulling on her own socks and shoes while Josephine crawls about on her hands and knees, frantically searching under her own cot.

"Where's my doggone shoes?"

She scurries to the end of the bed and checks the storage box, then returns to looking under her cot again. All the while, Mrs. Maynard watches like a grim sentry. Ruth helps her as Mrs. Maynard tracks time on her watch.

"All right, everyone! Josephine Littles! What's going on here?"

Ruth whispers to Josephine.

"Take the demerits. We can look later."

"I can't work without no shoes."

Josephine and Ruth hurry to stand at the foot of their beds as Mrs. Maynard walks down the center of the room. One by one Mrs. Maynard passes by the women, eyeing them up and down, looking for faults. She stops in front of Josephine.

"Where are your shoes?"

"Ma'am, I can't find them."

"How can you lose a pair of shoes from one day to the next?"

"I can't say as I know how that could happen, ma'am."

"You realize that's three demerits for not being dressed properly; loss of property, five demerits; and late for lineup, two demerits. That's ten."

"Yes, ma'am, that I do know."

"You're at the limit. One more and it's trouble for you."

"It sure is, ma'am."

Mrs. Maynard doesn't move on. Ruth is a knot of tension as the housemother decides whether Josephine is being smart with her or not. *Be careful, Josephine.* Mrs. Maynard moves on, speaking as she goes.

"There's going to be some changes around here, and they'll come soon enough. For now, Miss Littles, you'll go without until you either find the ones you were issued, or do extra work to earn a new pair. I expect you to make an effort to keep up with what you're so graciously given upon your arrival."

Josephine bends down and removes her socks.

"Yes, ma'am."

"All right. Let's get on with work assignments. Ruth Foster, you're back in the kitchen with Opal and Sally."

There's a small cheer that is quickly squashed by Mrs. Maynard blowing on her whistle.

"Stella Temple. Stella Temple. Hm, let's see. What should I have you do? I know. Bathroom duty. The rest of you continue with your schedules as they are. Now, let's proceed in a ladylike manner to the dining hall. Be mindful of your table manners. This is an area that needs drastic improvement from what I've seen lately, and we begin work on it today. Now, march!"

They move, two single lines parallel to one another, out the door of the dorm and on to the dining hall. Josephine is in front of Ruth. Her friend's bare feet grab at Ruth's heart. It makes the older woman appear vulnerable, out of place, a target. The missing shoes don't make sense. It's like some cruel prank, but everyone at the Colony likes Josephine. At least it's warm outside if she has to work without them. Once seated, Ruth eats with her thoughts on the hope of seeing Mr. Newell. Even if he doesn't come today, he might tomorrow, and because of that, she'll be in that spot each and every day. The clatter of utensils is steady as is the drone of conversation. She glances at her tray. Her stomach is getting used to having more and she's already full, yet she still has half of what was given to her.

She scoops more grits into her mouth when someone at the table behind her says, "I'll be doggone if it ain't ole Frances Platt."

Ruth twists in her chair to see Frances with Baker, who's holding her upper arm and leading her to the serving window. It's a curious scene. Mrs. Maynard stands only a few feet away and when they pass within a few feet of her, Ruth expects Frances to react in some way toward the housemother. She does nothing. She doesn't act like she even sees her. Baker smiles. Actually smiles. Ruth can't recall having ever seen the woman's teeth. Baker releases her arm so Frances can retrieve a tray. Ruth squints. Frances's eyelids droop and she's a bit unsteady.

Ruth leans toward Josephine, and says, "She looks half asleep. Do you think she's on some sort of medication?"

"Ain't no telling what they done to her."

They watch with heightened interest as Frances navigates the dining hall with Baker a step behind. Frances heads straight for Stella until Baker puts a hand on her shoulder and guides her to a different table. Before, something like this would send Frances into a fit, but today's Frances is docile and accepts Baker's redirection. She plops down heavily onto the chair. She doesn't pick up a fork to begin eating. She doesn't seem to know exactly where she is, or what she's supposed to do. Her one moment of alertness at the sight of Stella disintegrates as quickly as it came. Baker bends over to speak to her, nudges her, and points at the fork. Frances stares at it for a second, picks it up, and begins to eat, robotic and stiff. The others resume their meal and before long the dining hall is once again filled with normal sounds that come with a large group of people consuming a meal. Soon after Frances's reappearance, chairs are shoved back and trays are taken to the drop-off window. Ruth gets up, her tray somehow empty. She goes by the table and notices Stella's tray is full. The girl can't seem to take her eyes off Frances. Ruth stoops to the curve of her ear.

"You helped me when you told me I had to clean my tray, so now I'm telling you the same. You got to eat so you don't get in trouble."

Ruth straightens, and waits. Stella is a statue, her brand-new apathy completely out of character. Out of all of them, she was the one who thrived under the rules of the Colony. How different she's become since her beating. Ruth isn't surprised; this place changes them all, especially the naïve. She walks away, and into the kitchen to cries of welcome from Opal and Sally.

"Thank the heavens, you're back!"

"I sure wish you'd made notes."

"You should'a heard the complaints."

"We been holding on best we can. Nurse Crawford told Baker some done lost whatever weight they'd gained. I don't know how when they got to eat everything. My cooking ain't great, but to be sure it ain't *that* bad."

Ruth doesn't want to hurt their feelings, but she found breakfast this morning particularly dull, even after she added salt and pepper. It was plain, emphasis on plain.

She says, "I'll show you. What're you thinking about noon dinner?"

Opal grins.

"Nothing. Not with you here."

Sally says, "We got some hamburger meat in the other day. We got to cook it 'fore it goes bad."

"What've you got from the garden?"

They give her a list of what's been stored in the pantry. She drags up a chair to the worktable.

"I'll need to sit. I can't stand for too long."

"It's okay. We'll help. We got to learn what you're doing anyway."

Before long, the kitchen is filled with the aroma of a hamburger casserole with Opal and Sally tending the pots and pans as Ruth preps vegetables and guides them. Soon, the clock says eleven thirty, and they declare she's a magician. They're extra happy because they get to have a free period for once.

"We was always running behind 'cause I guess we ain't as organized."

They walk out onto the sunlit grounds to stand in the shade of an old elm. They pull out packs of Chesterfields from stained and grease-spattered apron pockets and quickly light up. Ruth is anxious to see if Mr. Newell is waiting; however, she stays for a bit of small talk to prevent the questions sure to come if she rushes off too quickly. Opal taps her cigarette, the ash falling and catching a breeze. She lets out a plume of smoke, attempts a smoke ring, then sighs.

"Law, I must've burned countless pans of biscuits. I served 'em anyway. Waste not, want not."

Ruth props against the trunk, nudging a clump of dandelion weed with the toe of her shoe.

"I missed cooking. It's something I enjoy doing."

Opal says, "You got a knack for it. You should open up a place one of these days. You know, after here."

Sally gets another cigarette and lights it with the end of the other.

"I can't picture that day."

Opal shakes her head and says, "Me neither. It don't seem possible."

Ruth lifts her face to the sun and breathes deeply. The memory of Room Two and its dank odor is never far from her thoughts, especially on a day like today. She motions at Opal's wrist.

"How much time is left?"

"We got twenty minutes, plenty of time."

"I've got a bit of a headache. I'm going to Nurse Crawford for some aspirin. I'll be right back."

"It's them shots."

"Yeah, I know. This one's really bad."

Ruth goes back inside the building and out one of the doors on the opposite side where she faces the expanse of the Colony's rear walls and the fields that are midstage in their growth cycle. Straw hats bob between rows. She saunters along so it won't appear as if she's moving with any sort of purpose that might catch the eye of one of the staff. Her heart pounds with nervousness as she reaches the meeting spot and gives a quick look around. Nothing. She bends to sniff at some honeysuckle attempting to overtake a wax myrtle. After several minutes of dawdling, she's overwhelmed with disappointment. Although she prepared herself for the possibility of this happening, it's still hard. With no way of knowing what sort of person Stanley Newell is, whether he's honest and decent, or not, she has to go with her gut, which tells her he'll come back. One of these days. She sits on an overturned bucket, and enjoys the peace and quiet before she goes back to help serve.

She goes again at six thirty, and the next day, and the next. She tells herself to keep on, but after a week she's beginning to think he won't be back. He's given up on her. Ten days pass, and she goes to her bucket and sits, expecting to do as she has all along, soak in the sun and peacefulness. She's only been there a minute when she hears a low, short whistle. Her heart skips. She looks toward the cedar tree and there he is. Mr. Newell leans forward a bit, staring in a way that's embarrassing.

"What on earth happened to you?"

She mistakes his meaning.

"I couldn't help it. I was placed in meditation."

"Meditation? Uh, okay, I probably need to know what that is, but what I mean is, and no offense, you look like hell."

She shakes her head.

"I look better than I did a week ago."

Mr. Newell takes out his notepad.

"Tell me."

Chapter 30

Stella

Stella's appetite all but disappears when Mrs. Maynard returns, but when she's assigned to work in that dank bathroom with its mildewy smell and ugly puke-green walls, she's of a mind to pull a Lucy and run. A single bulb beyond the door dangles from a long cord and she reaches up without looking to pull the chain. The light is temperamental and flickers, then burns steadily, illuminating everything she'd care not to see. She moves farther into the room and pulls the chain on a secondary light. She needs light because the window is nothing more than a narrow strip, six inches by eighteen. This is so no one can use it to escape. She sets the bucket of disinfectant on the floor and begins to scrub out the first toilet.

Mrs. Maynard gave her this job for a reason. Everyone knows cleaning the bathroom puts a person in their place. Shows them their worth. It's the most hated assignment out of all they're required to do and the one you get if you need a reminder of where you fit in the Colony's hierarchy. The kitchen or even the laundry room is where Stella wishes she was right now. Lucy, known instigator and troublemaker, somehow made the laundry room her own, in her curious way. Stella could make it her own too, hidden away with only the fresh scent of Oxydol detergent and the chugging sound of the washing machine for company. She'd prefer being tucked away and out of sight of prying eyes. The Colony no longer feels the same. Her haven is spoiled, her well-being disrupted, and this place has become as precarious as home.

She's interrupted several times. Once when Josephine comes in, then Natalie, and both speak, but Stella barely acknowledges them and keeps working. She moves on to cleaning the sinks, then the floor, robotically dragging the mop across it in wide sweeping strokes when Patsy comes rushing in.

"Have mercy, I'm sorry, hon, but it's a doozy this time!"

"What?"

"I always get it bad, but this time beats all."

Stella stares at her stupidly, but Patsy keeps talking as if Stella knows what she's going on about.

"I didn't think I was going to make it since I was way over yonder in the back field. Looks like Mrs. Maynard is giving you another lesson."

Patsy snickers as she sits on the toilet. Stella raises her shoulders to reflect she doesn't care, and keeps her eyes averted, mortified that Patsy would just plonk herself right down without a pardon me, or any other warning.

"I'll go out and wait till you're done."

Patsy shakes her head. "Don't worry about it. Ain't a lick'a privacy in this joint no how. You just keep cleaning. I'll try not to be long."

Stella picks up the bucket and moves to the farthest part of the bathroom as Patsy begins to address her issue, which is when Stella finally understands what she meant.

"Gawd. I got the worst cramps. Feels like a knife going through my belly."

Stella stops mopping as she recalls she hasn't had a monthly in a long time. Alice treated it as a shameful part of life, so much so that Stella did likewise. She told no one when she first got it, learned to take care of herself, and struggled through it each month. It stopped after Cordell caused her predicament. Patsy keeps talking, but Stella isn't paying attention, she's busy calculating the time that's gone by. It's late July, about five months since she arrived and she hasn't had even the tiniest of signs. There must be something wrong with her. She needs to talk to Nurse Crawford. She'll know. Patsy raises her voice.

"Hey, did you hear me? I asked you to get me some toilet paper."

"Sorry. I'll be right back."

Stella hurries out and heads down the hall, not running, but close. She can hear Patsy yelling after her, but she doesn't stop. She zips around a corner and almost runs into Mrs. Baker. She stumbles to a stop, and backs up a step or two, unable to hide her distress.

"Stella?"

Stella is confused about Mrs. Baker, and is out of sorts around her. She wants to continue on her way; she needs Nurse Crawford to tell her she's not been "fixed but good." Mrs. Baker waits for Stella to say something.

"Hey, Mrs. Baker."

"Is everything all right?"

"Yes, ma'am. Everything's fine."

This is the difference now. Before, she might have told Mrs. Baker that she was going to go see Nurse Crawford because something was off with her insides. After all, it was Mrs. Baker who made sure she got better when she was sick after her operation.

"For a moment, I thought you looked scared. Are you scared?"

"No, ma'am."

"All right, then. That's good. I was actually on my way to find you. There's something I wanted to tell you."

"Yes, ma'am."

"I believe you."

It takes Stella a moment. She thinks she knows what Mrs. Baker means, but she isn't sure, so she offers the usual response, then waits.

"Yes, ma'am."

Mrs. Baker frowns.

"To be specific, I mean about Frances and her writing. If there's anything more to be said about this unfortunate incident, it's that mistakes can be made when there are individuals who want to cause trouble."

Stella's eyes widen in wonder and the tiny spot in her heart that softened ever so slightly when Mrs. Baker's leg failed her expands a little more.

"Oh. Thank you, ma'am."

"I wanted you to know."

Even with this admission, Stella can't forget what happened. The group punishment's humiliating moments play over and over in her mind all the time. She can't escape them any more than she could escape Cordell. She'd been helpless, unable to save herself, trapped and forced to endure. She doesn't like feeling that way. She wants to be stronger, speak without fear, stand up for herself. She wants to be brave, and independent. Like Ruth Foster. She says none of this and Mrs. Baker doesn't seem to want or expect anything more. The superintendent gestures with her hand for Stella to follow her. Stella looks toward Nurse Crawford's office. Her dilemma about her personal problem will have to wait. Mrs. Baker enters her office and stands at the window. With her back to Stella, she begins to talk, softly at first, then with more emphasis.

"I found out Mrs. Maynard assigned you to clean bathrooms and I'm sure she did it out of spite. That's how she is. That isn't the sort of work you should be doing. I will have someone else assigned. You're going to start helping Miss Perkins in the budget office. You'll learn about the financial side of this institution. I want what's best for everyone, but I'm sure you know this. Stella, I think you'd be a perfect candidate for a special program I want to implement. 'Reformed to Reformer,' is what I call it. My instincts are excellent when it comes to choosing those who will excel, those with a future. You're young, malleable, and smart. I don't want you to worry because I still have high expectations for you. And if you don't think it can happen, speak to Nurse Crawford. She'll tell you."

She faces Stella, smiling in that way she did back when they first met. It's a wonderful smile, natural, filled with confidence and knowledge, and is as comforting as a blanket. Stella is caught by it and awash with gratitude. She wants to change and she wants to do it the right way, as she should.

"Thank you, ma'am, but I don't mind doing that work if I'm supposed to start over again."

"It's not necessary. It's for those who're troublesome, and it's exactly because of that attitude you shouldn't be doing it."

"Yes, ma'am."

"First thing tomorrow after breakfast, report to Miss Perkins. She'll be expecting you."

"Yes, ma'am."

"Last thing, Stella. Frances is doing better at the moment. She's on medications to help her. All the same, she's liable to be unpredictable. Keep your distance for now. This is in your best interest. If she continues to behave with restraint, and doesn't cause issues, I'll set something up for you to work with her again. If this happens, it will become part of your training again. We'll see. I can't make any promises."

It's like she's in a dream.

"Yes, ma'am. I'm very grateful."

"Excellent."

Mrs. Baker shares the special smile again, and motions that Stella can leave when she realizes Mrs. Baker might want to know she was actually on her way to speak to Nurse Crawford, only about something different.

"Mrs. Baker? Ma'am?"

Mrs. Baker is about to settle in behind her desk. She hesitates, staring at Stella curiously. This makes her unexpectedly afraid again. Surely Mrs. Baker would want to know she needs to see the nurse. She could be very sick.

"I'm sorry, but I believe you should know about this, in case there's something wrong with me."

Mrs. Baker's response is abrupt, cautious.

"Wrong with you? Whatever do you mean?"

"I ain't well, it's, um, it's kind of hard, you see, I . . ."

"No. No. No. That will never do."

Stella freezes, her words locked inside her throat like a big chunk of meat she's swallowed without chewing. Baker wags a finger at her.

"You need to learn to speak firmly, with confidence. Don't hem and haw around. Now. Begin again."

Stella shifts on her feet, and starts over.

"Ma'am, I need to see Nurse Crawford because I ain't had no monthly cycle in a while. First, it was because, well, you know, my situation when I come here, but I still ain't had one. I must be sick; something's got to be wrong."

Mrs. Baker drops into her chair and it takes her several seconds to respond.

"I see."

Stella isn't sure if she should keep talking or not. She explains a little more.

"Yes, ma'am. I mean, I had that operation for um, my situation and soon after I got that infection. Maybe that's why. I want to ask her if that's it. I don't want to ask Dr. Graham. I don't like him."

"That makes two of us."

Mrs. Baker swivels her seat so Stella is looking at the back of a perfectly coifed hairstyle. She pictures what Mrs. Baker sees as she stares out the window—the grounds, the sky, a few birds, perhaps. She scratches a bug bite on her arm, and begins to regret bringing her problem up. She can hear the ticking of one of the Colony's clocks. Finally, Mrs. Baker turns the chair back around.

"Actually, this isn't a topic for Nurse Crawford. It's something you and I should discuss. I knew this would come up one day because, like I've said, you're a smart girl. Now is as good a time as any to explain, given my plans for your future."

"Yes, ma'am."

Mrs. Baker is speaking to her in a way she hasn't before—with caution. There must be something really wrong with her. What is it? Is she going to die? Did Dr. Graham find something else inside her when he operated?

"Society requires young women such as yourself to be helped

so the mistake that brought you here to begin with isn't repeated. It's hard for the general public, those who lead proper lives, to understand this sort of trouble. While training can take place, it's also believed there's always the chance improper behavior might happen again. To avoid unwanted pregnancies, sometimes extra measures might be advised to prevent this from happening over and over. We've seen it, time and again. The local doctor your parents took you to made such a recommendation and it was carried out. This is why your body isn't functioning as before. It's changed. You'll have a new life now."

If she's to believe what she's hearing, she will never be the same again. It's slow to sink in despite the heaviness of the truth, as heavy as Cordell's unwanted weight on her, as heavy as the bulk of her mama, as heavy as the thought of Dr. Graham leaning over her, snipping away, willy-nilly at her insides. Stella's eyes are wet. It's true. She's been "fixed but good." Mrs. Baker keeps talking and she tries to listen.

"There's nothing to be done about it except move forward. Think of it this way, Stella, you've got your whole life in front of you, filled with all sorts of possibilities. The only person you have to worry about now is you. You, *your* happiness."

Stella's entire body grows hot, like it did when she was sick and had that fever. She feels sick again, but in a different way. Her chest hurts and her fingers curl as an uncommon rage takes hold of her.

"I've been fixed but good. That's what you mean."

That voice isn't hers. It sounds different somehow. Stella presses her palms into her eye sockets. What if she had wanted that? A house full of kids to love on? Her make-believe family, one that was different from what she'd been given with Alice and Cordell, disintegrates like a dream after waking up. It can never happen, not now. She turns away from Mrs. Baker. Another betrayal from someone she trusted. She moves toward the door, only what Mrs. Baker says next makes her legs go weak and she stops with her hand reaching for the doorknob. She can't move.

"Could you have stopped him, your father?"

Stella doesn't want to return to this memory except she has no power to keep it away. It's in her head the same way her heart is in her chest. She recalls how she tried. How she fought, bit, scratched, and sometimes begged even as he violated her. Mrs. Baker continues, building on her doubts, fears, and worst of all, her unsavory history.

"The truth is, at some point, you would go home, then what? What if the surgery hadn't been done? What then, Stella?"

Stella's brief moment of rage falters, as brief and impossible as any moment of triumph she's ever had. For once, Mrs. Baker doesn't demand a response. Instead, she lays out Stella's real future, not the imaginary one, the one she can never have. She tells her the one she was destined to have, had it not been for her and the Colony.

"Your father wouldn't have let you be. You know it and I know it. You'd have become pregnant again. You'd have had a bastard, incestuous child, or you'd have returned here and finally had the surgery that's given you a new beginning, a different future. I know, because I've seen it happen. Be glad you were spared that. Be glad and be grateful. You're one of the few who can still be salvaged, Stella."

It's true. What Mrs. Baker says is true. She should thank her lucky stars.

A quavering "Yes, ma'am," is all she can manage.

"Remember how I said we're alike? I have my own story too. Different from yours but no less horrible. I was seven years old. I almost died because of what I did, and my parents were never the same around me afterward. Even into adulthood, they never forgave me."

This draws Stella's attention.

"What did you do?"

"I'll tell you one day. The main thing for you to know is, I enjoy my way of life, doing this very important work. You can have something similar. As a matter of fact, I have no doubt you can. Despite my own life's sorrows, look at what I've done. I'm successful, well respected, and I can help you lead a decent life."

She studies Mrs. Baker, zoning in on her eyes. The one place anyone can see the truth about a person.

"Mrs. Baker, can I ever be happy?"

Mrs. Baker appears taken aback by this question, as if she didn't expect it. Stella continues to study the superintendent closely. She needs to know if Mrs. Baker is doing this for Stella's own good, or for herself. She already knows how it is when someone's doing it only for themselves. The superintendent, after a rather lengthy bit of time, answers.

"My mission, *our* mission, is going to make others' lives better. And with that, I suppose comes a reputable future, one in which you could be content. That's as good as happy in my book."

The answer isn't exactly what she wants and the depths of the superintendent's gaze tells her very little. Stella looks away. Has she ever been happy or maybe, as Mrs. Baker puts it, content? Yes. She can truthfully say she has, right here, at the Colony. It made her happy when Mrs. Baker gave her a special assignment. When she bragged over her abilities. Told her she was smart. Making her go through group punishment ruined that, but she's admitted she believes her now, and Stella discerned a tiny bit of guilt in Mrs. Baker's voice for not doing so to begin with. A tiny bit of an apology, even. Besides, what would she do if she wasn't at the Colony with Mrs. Baker? She'd have to return home, and she definitely wouldn't be happy there. She doesn't want to think about that happening. She'd certainly pull a Lucy if Cordell came after her. Does she love her parents? Maybe Alice, despite all. Never Cordell. Not anymore. Not after he destroyed her trust. She hasn't missed them or her old life.

It's interesting to think of it this way. *My old life.* Can she be content here with Mrs. Baker teaching her, helping her to learn to be better? Stella knows the answer as she looks at the woman she now sees as her unlikely savior. She bestows a timid, trusting smile on the superintendent, and lets go of her past.

Chapter 31

Baker

Baker is confident Stella is going to be fine, while her own future hangs as precarious as that of the women she's trying to help. The length of time it's taking Dr. Woodall to make a decision is testing her resolve, so much so her bouts with heartburn are constant. She tries to view the delay as a good sign and assumes they're taking their time because they care not only about the future of the Colony, but about her. It's been a peaceful weekend at the cottage where she's gone through her notes from the first five years at the facility. She's found useful information that might prove valuable if they ask questions about the challenges she's overcome as a superintendent, and about the difficult individuals who turned out well after all. Some of the cases bring back bad memories. She knocks back a healthy swig of milk of magnesia, then tugs on the velour belt encircling her waist.

She's still sitting at her kitchen table in a housecoat and nightgown on a Monday and it's already midmorning. She should've been in her office hours ago. She would admit to no one she's feeling out of sorts. Lowly. The quiet over the weekend has done nothing to calm her sense of impending doom, so she might as well start to think about what's before her. She ticks off the list in her head, which makes her feel efficient. Normal. It's imperative, for one thing, to call Frances

Platt's parents and provide them with an update on their daughter's progress. She can do this later on today. Frances's parents will more than likely agree to keep her here for another three months once they hear how well she's doing, and Baker will be reassured of the funds that come with that.

She considers this a real success story. Frances's behaviors are finally managed, thanks to paraldehyde, a sedative used to calm patients, but with no thanks to her own supposed medical staff. After her release from Dix, Frances was sent back with a prescription for it, something Dr. Graham never suggested. She didn't ask why because questioning Dr. Graham's decisions never produce anything but his annoyance. The new prescription is more secret ammunition for her own defense. After learning of the complaints made against her in Dr. Woodall's office, she understands one thing: her suspicions were right. They're working against her, in cahoots with Ethel Maynard, who needs to be reined in. She's flitting about like she's in charge, making decisions that should be brought to Baker.

She's startled out of these dark musings by the invasive buzzing of the cottage intercom. Someone's finger presses it over and over. She knows only one person who'd have the nerve and her irritation grows. She rises from the kitchen chair and mashes the button near the front door so hard it feels like her fingertip might push through the back of it.

"What is it?"

Mrs. Maynard's annoying, reedy voice crackles through the speaker. "We have visitors. Important visitors."

Baker isn't in the mood for vagueness.

"Mrs. Maynard, *who* is here?"

Mrs. Maynard is equally ill-tempered.

"Important ought to tell you. Dr. Woodall and some of the board just arrived. They're getting out of their vehicles as we speak. I suggest you come quickly. You should've been here anyway."

Baker's stomach churns as she closes her eyes. Dear God, and sweet Jesus. What happened to the common courtesy of a phone call? A note to say a visit is planned? Some kind of warning?

"Please tell them I'll be there momentarily."

There's nothing from the other side. Baker pushes the button repeatedly. "Hello? Mrs. Maynard, did you hear me? Inform them I'll be there momentarily."

Dead air. Heat builds inside her like a furnace cranked on high. She moves as fast as she can to the small bedroom. On the bed, a suitable twin, is her mother's yellow rose quilt. It's the only homey touch in the otherwise utilitarian room that holds a dresser, a nightstand, and a chair. Stacked in a corner are the guideline booklets for the Colony. She goes to the small closet where there are exactly five dresses: one brown, two navy, and two black. Her shoes, a brown pair and a black pair, sit side by side, polished and ready. She pulls out the black dress and her black shoes. She retrieves a clean pair of black stockings hanging over a hook off the bathroom door. Black, black, black, in case the news is horrible. Of all days for her to dawdle. She hates Mrs. Maynard is right. She should've been there. The housemother is probably telling them this very minute she's late instead of covering for her. The old bat will hint and suggest she's turned lazy, ill-suited for the ever-present demands of the institution.

Baker hates rushing. Her fingers grow clumsy, and she accidentally shoves one through a stocking. She grabs another out of her drawer, begins again, and by the time she's hooked the band of each to the top of her girdle, she's sweating. She takes a second to face an open window. The breeze doesn't help because it's turned warm and humid. She pulls the dress on and shoves her feet into her shoes. She leaves the room and detours for only a moment into the bathroom. Her hair is holding up, and she gives it a quick little pat before she's in the entryway grabbing her keys, notepad, and purse off the small table. She shuts the door behind her. She has no idea how much time has passed. It feels like hours.

She picks her way carefully along a natural path that runs between the Colony and the superintendent's cottage. The path was cleared of treacherous roots by Mr. Lumley at her request and it's a walk she usually enjoys, despite her affliction. Today she's too preoccupied by Mrs. Maynard's curt manner. Maybe she knows something. Maybe because of the friendship with Dr. Woodall he's already told her what they decided. The last few feet challenge Baker and she has to slow down. She's sweating and out of breath, but she can't dilly-dally.

She enters through the front door and sees four visitors, plus Dr. Woodall, gathered in the foyer. Mrs. Maynard is using her cane to point to the long line of portraits commemorating those who came before them right after the building was constructed in the late twenties. Baker can't understand why didn't she show them into her office and offer them something to drink. At the sound of her arrival, they turn. She goes toward the group as confidently as she's able. She doesn't smile because none of them are.

"What a nice surprise."

"Mrs. Baker."

"Dr. Woodall."

She offers her hand and gets the same tepid handshake as before. She turns to the others and goes through the same ritual, although Mrs. Younce at least grips her hand more firmly, even if she doesn't look at her. Baker can't read their expressions. Each of these individuals—Mr. Allen, Mr. Doyle, Mr. Bullard, and Mrs. Younce—have earned their way onto the board through a variety of occupations including the State Board of Health, Public Welfare, penal or corrections facilities, Public Works, and so on. They're formal, reserved, and even though she knows them and has communicated with them on more than one occasion, they act as if they've never met her. The atmosphere is thick with tension, while Mrs. Maynard appears at ease, almost . . . giddy.

"Please, let's go into my office. I can offer you refreshments."

Dr. Woodall turns to the others as if to seek agreement before he makes a flourish with his hand for her to lead the way. Once they're in the office and before she has a chance to request any beverages, Dr. Woodall takes control of the meeting. The fact that none of them sits makes her uneasy.

"Mrs. Baker, let's start with this. Mr. Gray spoke highly of you when you arrived and things went along fine for a while. It's unfortunate you didn't choose to make Ethel Maynard your advocate;

rather, over time, you've made her your adversary by treating her with ever increasing disrespect. That goes for Dr. Graham, and Dr. Greene, highly reputable individuals with many credentials to their names. Nurse Crawford, as a close observer, believes some of your methods are questionable, particularly when it comes to the time residents spend in meditation. No one should spend more than three days in isolation or it becomes detrimental to their health, physically and mentally. This is a standard you've broken on numerous occasions lately."

Baker is lightheaded, weak. She would like to sit but remains standing. She's in front of a firing squad. This thought, the pun in it, makes her want to laugh, except this is no laughing matter. They're going to let her go. It's the end for her and her time at the Colony. Dr. Woodall looks about at his colleagues, who make motions of approval. He continues.

"We thought it appropriate to come here and give you our decision in person. While we're here, we'd like a tour of the facility and the grounds. We want to see the residents in their environment. Mrs. Maynard has graciously agreed to show us the facility and you should be part of that as well. Now, to the matter at hand, which is what I'm sure you're anxious to hear. Mrs. Baker, we've come to inform you that as the superintendent of this facility, you'll continue on in that position."

There's a gasp from Ethel Maynard. Baker is stunned and her body experiences a whoosh of heat and what follows is a rush of renewal and confidence, a sense they understand. They believe in her and her hard work, and it's a vindication, a . . . Then Dr. Woodall says one more thing.

"However, you're on probation, effective immediately."

Probation. Like a common lawbreaker. The moment of exoneration is extinguished, like a bucket of water thrown onto a spark.

"We've decided this will be for a three-month period, and I'm going to warn you right now, if there's one complaint—one—your time here will come to a swift and conclusive end. That is our decision with regard to your particular situation."

Baker's hand goes to her throat. Her heart pounds with enough force she can feel it all the way down to the destroyed tissues of her legs. She goes to the chair behind her desk to gather herself. It's not ideal, it's not what she'd hoped, and the chastising tone is mortifying. As if she's ignorant, a fool who doesn't know better. She attempts to pay attention, then is further dismayed at the next decision.

"Mrs. Maynard is to be promoted to assistant superintendent on a trial basis, also for three months. She's to be commended for enduring what appears to have been a complicated and difficult environment, which after today, I expect to improve. She will be responsible for hiring a new housemother to oversee Dorm A immediately." Dr. Woodall pauses for a moment, as if to allow Mrs. Maynard the time to smile and nod at the others, clearly gloating. "There are many factors which have contributed to our decision, but suffice it to say, and while difficult to make, we believe this is the right one. Consider, perhaps, the excessive reprimands you reported regarding Mrs. Maynard may have come from her having too much to do. At any rate, I have met with Dr. Greene, Dr. Graham, the teachers, Nurse Crawford, and of course Mrs. Dillard, of Dorm B. There is the consensus, Mrs. Baker, you're difficult to work with. Running a facility like this is built on the trust of those who work in partnership with you and support you, and the same should apply in reverse. I'm afraid that's the element that appears to be missing here. We're giving you the time to fix the issue. If in the allotted time we don't see tremendous improvement in these relationships, you know what to expect."

Baker rises from her chair, her face as roasting hot as if she'd stuck her head into an oven.

"You have my word; I'll always do my best."

It's all she can manage.

"We'll hold you to that. All right, shall we tour the facility?"

Without waiting for her to take her rightful place as *the* superintendent, Dr. Woodall, Mr. Allen, Mr. Doyle, Mr. Bullard, and Mrs. Younce move toward the door led by Mrs. Maynard. They file out, and Baker remains behind. What they've done is made it impossible for her. They're placating Ethel Maynard, who will interfere and cause issues to make her look bad. Dr. Woodall said one complaint, and that's it. They might as well send her packing right now, for all the chance she has of preventing that. Baker forces herself to her feet. She's got to follow them. She has to play the part of interested and enthused party, act like she's perfectly fine.

Once she's in the hallway, she sees them heading for the classrooms. Mrs. Maynard's mouth moves nonstop and she has a moment of satisfaction when Mr. Doyle stifles a yawn and Mr. Allen checks his watch. She'd rather not be a part of the charade, but in an effort to exhibit goodwill she joins them. After the classroom visits, where work is going as well as can be expected for those who can't read or do practical math, a tantalizing smells draw them to the kitchen next. They step into the space where Opal and Sally are busy preparing the noon dinner. Baker is instantly on high alert. Where is Ruth Foster? Mrs. Younce asks a question.

"Is your meal preparation based on any particular recommendation?"

Opal looks at a loss, while Sally says, "Ain't nothing but good ole plain cookin'. Like your mama done, maybe."

Both are rather unkempt, with flour-dusted faces and grease-spattered aprons. Mrs. Maynard, preening as if she's been handed a blue ribbon at a county fair for the best pig in the show, takes credit for the menu, one that Baker knows is specifically written up by Nurse Crawford. She doesn't bother to correct the record. Who cares? Not her.

Dr. Woodall says, "I'd like to talk to these ladies for a moment."

That's a generous nomenclature toward these disreputable specimens of womanhood, Baker thinks. He heads straight for Opal. Soon after he begins speaking to her, Opal shakes her head. He says more and she nods, briefly touching her hair. He appears to be waiting for her to respond further, but she doesn't. He turns to Sally. She's got her hands stuffed in her apron pockets, and has a less than friendly expression. He apparently makes a joke. Miracles will never cease because Opal grins while Sally bats her eyes like a smitten schoolgirl. After a minute and one last glance around the kitchen, he returns to those waiting.

"All right, what's next?"

By Baker's assessment, the interaction with the kitchen staff went better than expected. Perhaps Ruth Foster not being around was a blessing. It doesn't discount she's not where she's supposed to be, but Baker could see her pulling a stunt like Lucy Griffin, yammering on about unfairness and punishments instead of seeing it as a privilege she's been given. They walk outside with Baker trailing behind like an afterthought. The sky is a deep blue and the sun is straight overhead. Residents are scattered about the full and colorful fields, the view reminiscent of a Norman Rockwell painting. Baker is overcome with that familiar sentiment she often gets while at the window in her office, meaning what she sees pleases her. The organized rows, the efficiency of the work, the rosy faces and windblown hair. A picture-perfect scene of trained domesticity. Surely her visitors can see this too?

The residents take notice of the visitors near the fence. They glance over every now and again curiously, but keep working. Baker carefully scans the group to see if there are any potential troublemakers. Among the field-workers are Josephine, Frances, Melissa, Pauline, and a few from Dorm B. Everyone is pulling weeds, moving forward inch by inch, working in tandem and with a low hum of friendly conversation. There's no sign of bawdy behaviors, uncouth manners, or laziness.

Dr. Woodall points at an individual and turns to Mrs. Maynard.

"Why is that woman working without shoes?"

Mrs. Maynard has no need to look where he's pointing.

"That's Josephine Littles. Somehow she lost the pair issued to her. How, I have no idea. I told her she had to find them or she'd have to work without until she earned another pair."

Dr. Woodall is already shaking his head.

"No. No. No. Please see she gets a pair immediately. That's unacceptable. She shouldn't be out there working barefoot. She could get hookworm. We're to care for the health of our residents in all ways, Mrs. Maynard, not just venereal diseases."

Baker hides her grin. At that moment Mr. Lumley comes out

of the tool shed pushing a wheelbarrow, his straw hat sitting back so it shows off his white forehead in stark contrast to the rest of his sunburned face. If it weren't for him, she never would've noticed Ruth Foster scurrying toward the back entrance of the Colony. To her further shock, a man in a brown suit watches until she disappears inside, and then he leaves, going in the opposite direction. No one else sees this, but from that point on, Baker has a hard time paying attention. After a few minutes of Dr. Woodall questioning Mr. Lumley about the crops, he signals it's time for the group to go. They meander toward the front entrance and once there, Dr. Woodall, his manner matter-of-fact, drops yet another alarming decision.

"One more thing, Mrs. Baker. All new funding requests for this facility are on hold until further notice."

"Yes, Dr. Woodall."

Glumly, she stands side by side with Mrs. Maynard as the car goes down the drive only because she must. Mrs. Maynard waves gaily as if she's seeing off family members. Baker, if she weren't a lady and could make a certain gesture at the departing car, would do so. She's seething, highly upset. Once they're out of sight, she turns to the housemother.

"Do not underestimate me, Ethel Maynard."

Mrs. Maynard has the good sense to not respond, and Baker retreats to her office. She needs time to think. She's got a sour feeling in her gut about many, many things. Her probation, Mrs. Maynard's promotion, and the final blow, her request for funds on an indeterminate hold, which means the Colony's future is stagnant, and so is her career. The least of her concerns is Ruth Foster dilly-dallying with some man. The old Baker would've confronted that and these other issues head-on. Truth is, in this moment, she's not feeling up to it. She positions herself in her favorite spot and takes herself back to the lovely view of the grounds, the fields, and the work being done. It only serves to remind her of what she might very well lose. Her domain. Her world. A way of life. She can't let this happen. Not again.

Chapter 32
Ruth

When Mr. Newell shows up at their next meeting, he tells Ruth he spent some time with her mother and explained he was meeting with her.

"She told me she came here looking for you a while back."

"She did, but of course Baker has a way of turning explanations around so it was like I'd done something wrong. Even if any of us were, to use her words, loose, immoral, degenerate, or harboring some disease, is there a law that's been broken?"

Mr. Newell looks down the road and then at his feet. Ruth grows anxious. He reaches for a cigarette in his shirt pocket, offers her one, and she refuses. After it's lit, his answer is indirect.

"What's going on here has been going on a while. This facility opened in 1929 as a penal colony for white women, but some are older than this one."

"How old?"

"Since before World War One, maybe longer. You're not going to like what I've found out."

They stand together for a moment, and then Ruth shrugs.

"Might as well tell me. I need to know, one way or the other."

"Given the current situation overseas, the government added more men to the armed forces. This allowed a group called the American Social Hygiene Association to join with other government agencies, and they can request physicians to report cases of disease in their communities. They're allowed to hire private investigators who can round up individuals for confinement and treatment. Like what was done with you. Basically, if a person's behaviors are questionable, or if they appear suspicious, they're considered a national security threat."

"How ridiculous. A national security threat?"

"It's because of what happened in WW One. Hundreds of thousands of men were infected with syphilis and gonorrhea and couldn't go into battle. The government fears the same thing happening and wants to nip it in the bud. They take it seriously, as you know."

Ruth slumps against the tool shed, despondent. The government believes this institution is exactly where she needs to be, no matter her story. Mr. Newell stubs out his cigarette.

"Don't lose hope. I don't yet know everything about this situation, and plan to keep searching. There's got to be something, somewhere, a court case or cases, where a precedent has been set."

Ruth isn't encouraged, but if nothing else, she can appreciate his honesty. She's not willing to make him feel guilty or bad, simply because he's not telling her what she wants to hear.

"Thank you for letting me know how this works." She glances over her shoulder. "I've got to go. Last time you were here, Baker was outside and saw me as I was going back into the building."

His brows come together, and his mouth gets thinner. She's seen this expression before after describing everything that happened to her.

"Did she say anything about it?"

"No, but, that's how she is. Just so you know, if I go missing like last time, she's got me locked away somewhere. I've hardly seen her, though. Mrs. Maynard is in charge, or at least she acts like it."

"If that happens, I'll show up at those front doors, and tell her I represent you, and I've been unable to get in touch with you. Who cares if she finds out at that point?"

Ruth almost giggles as she imagines the scene.

"That almost makes me wish she *would* do something. Anyway, thank you. For everything."

"No need to thank me, not yet." He tucks his pen into his pocket. "It's going to take some time. By the way, if I'm able to put a case together, Lucy said she's willing to go to court. Are you?"

Ruth hadn't thought this far ahead.

"What are our chances?"

He sounds hesitant.

"I don't know, but you can bet I'll do my best."

"I'll go to court. You bet I will."

"Good. Do you have any idea about the timing of your parole?"

"No. What I'm told is, 'It's up to you, Miss Foster.'"

He looks disgusted, then glances at his watch.

"Let's meet here again in two weeks at this same time, and I'll give you an update."

"All right."

"Hang in there, and be careful."

She knows he means for her to keep her head down, don't draw attention, and get by. As soon as he's gone, she begins her walk back to the building, thinking how those two weeks stretch before her like an endless highway. She's close to the building when she spies Stella peering out from a first-floor window, and when their eyes meet, Stella lets the curtain fall back into place. Is she back to spying again? Ruth pushes the door open and checks the large clock on the wall. There's still a minute left and she lets out her breath in relief. The hallway is empty and she can hear Opal and Sally laughing over something as she hurries toward the kitchen.

"Hey, Miss Ruth."

She stops and spins around to face Stella, her hand to her chest.

"You scared the daylights out of me. I've only got a minute to get to the kitchen. Do you need something?"

Stella tucks her hair behind an ear. There's something different about her. She's less anxious, almost tranquil, not like she was when Ruth first came, insecure and unsure of herself. At this moment, she almost looks like someone who's received good news after a long wait.

"What're you going to do when you leave from here?"

Ruth doesn't have time for chatting, but keeps her voice calm, and uncaring.

"I suppose I'll go back to work at the diner. Or maybe I'll do something different."

"You ever think about getting married, having babies?"

What a strange question, right out of the blue. Ruth checks the clock again.

"I don't know. Maybe. If the right person comes along."

"I can't have no babies. Not now. Not after that operation."

Ruth draws back a little, unsure of what to say. Stella behaves as if there's nothing wrong with what she just shared.

"What're you talking about? You had an abortion."

"For someone like me, in bad trouble like I was, I can't be allowed to make them same mistakes again. Now, I ain't got to worry about it. It don't mean I ain't got no future, though. I can be like Mrs. Baker. She said so. Like, helping people and all. I can do good things."

Ruth is speechless while Stella peers at her as if searching for approval. She opens her mouth to ask another question when a young woman Ruth has seen only once or twice before, and always impeccably dressed, comes around the corner. As soon as she sees Stella, there's immediate relief on her face and she hurries toward them.

"There you are. When I came back you were gone."

"I had to go to the bathroom and then I saw Miss Ruth, so I was saying hello."

"Well, come along now, we have a lot to do."

"Yes, Miss Perkins."

Can't have no babies. Not now. Not after that operation. This is what Ruth hears in her head as Stella follows Miss Perkins. The clock strikes the hour. Now she is late, again. She dashes down the hall, praying she won't have an encounter with Mrs. Maynard, or Baker. She makes it to the kitchen without incident where it's hot as an oven, even with the back door open. Opal and Sally are prepping the sides, their faces beet red as they work like fiends. Ruth jumps in to help them, apologizing for being late.

"Stella stopped me and said something strange."

Sally makes a noise.

"Pfft. Strange here means normal. What did she say?"

Ruth bends down to look out the serving window and sees a line of women waiting.

"I'll tell you when we're done."

They quickly begin filling trays and sliding them out the window into waiting hands. Exclamations are made over what's being served. This produces a small smile from Ruth. Today she's fixed chicken pastry, green beans, cornbread, and her deluxe peach cobbler for dessert. After they've served the inmates, they fill their own trays and move into the dining hall where Opal and Sally join Ruth at her table with Josephine, Melissa, Natalie, and Paula.

"Ruth's got something to tell us."

Ruth picks at the food, her appetite yet to return. She finally sets her fork down and turns to those at her table.

"Stella came for an abortion, and said she can't have children now."

Opal nods, her mouth full of chicken pastry.

"I knew it, I *knew* it. I figured when she showed up here pregnant that was going to happen."

Ruth puts a hand up, her head starting to hurt again.

"That's sterilization, isn't it? They sterilized her?"

Opal nods.

"That's exactly what it is."

Sally's face hardens.

"They done it to me. *Me.* Twenty-eight years old. It didn't matter I might've wanted me a couple young'uns one day. I worked tobacco since I was old enough to get into the field beside my mama. Barely had a chance to do no learnin'. Can't hardly read. I can write my name, but that's about it. How's that my fault? What was important was my baby brothers and sisters got to eat. Them doctors talked me into it, made it sound like it was my only choice. They said if I'd do it, my time would be reduced. I'm supposed to get out of here shortly. That was the deal."

Ruth is paralyzed by Sally's story. A memory of something very different from what the outraged woman next to her experienced nags at her. She'd gone to a county fair with her friends when she was in high school. She'd seen a tent set up to teach about sterilizations and a sign that said SOME PEOPLE ARE BORN TO BE A BURDEN ON THE REST, with flashing lights to explain how funds were spent for addressing certain social issues. It got her attention, and when she was back home she brought it up to her mother.

"Oh, honey, the government's been involved in efforts to improve humanity for years. Your father and I went to a few educational sessions. The argument was about desirable and undesirable traits, and if animals and plants are bred selectively, why not humans?"

Her mother went in search of an old newspaper and put it in front of Ruth, pointing at a picture of a baby. Ruth glanced up at her mother.

"Who's this?"

"That's you! I entered you into one of those Better Baby contests and you won. See? You have a ribbon. I keep it in your baby book."

Ruth didn't dwell on this at the time. She was young, carefree, and she wasn't worried about what the government did or didn't do; she was having fun. Stella's and Sally's stories mean this could happen to any of them. It could happen to her. Sally begins to eat again, talking between mouthfuls.

"Ain't nothing any of us can do. It's out of our hands because people with a lot more clout are the ones in charge. It don't matter what we think or say."

Ruth leans back in her chair, her arms folded. It's true. After all, look at them. Here they sit, doing as they're told, when they're told, and without any choice in the matter. With this realization comes the certainty Stanley Newell can't do a thing either. It's very possible he's wasting his time.

Chapter 33

Stella

Stella's latest habit since Mrs. Baker (now Mrs. Dot again!) said she believed her is to leave her bed early and get ready even before the new and recently hired housemother, Mrs. Rutherford, rouses the dorm. Stella's newfound confidence and restored eagerness to please are curious to her dorm mates. They don't get it.

They say, "You act like you like it here," or "What have you got to be so happy about?"

She can't tell them, so they eye her with either suspicion and bewilderment, or both. On a Monday morning, in early August, she's up and rambling in her storage box at the foot of her cot for her clothing and shoes. Those close by prop up on their elbows and watch in irritation as she gets her things. Frances is laid out on her cot, belly down, arm hanging off, hair in her face. Stella bends over close to her ear.

"Hey. Frances."

Nothing. Josephine waves in the direction of the clock on the wall that's barely visible in the predawn light.

"What in the world? Why're you up so early again? Go back to bed!"

Mumbles from the others chime in.

"Yeah. Keep it down. We got ten more minutes."

Stella ignores them and creeps out of the room. She hurries down the hall and makes use of the empty bathroom. The girl staring back at her in the mirror looks like the same old Stella, but that's not true. Inside, she's different, very different. She's definitely not the same old Stella. She's heading full speed toward the new and improved Stella, whoever that person will be. Soon, she's dressed, her face washed, hair and teeth brushed, and she's back in the dorm. As soon as she sits on her bed, *bang!* The door is thrown open, not by Mrs. Rutherford, but by Mrs. Maynard, and the light is flipped on.

"Up, up, up!" is followed by a long, shrill whistle.

Mrs. Maynard spots Stella already dressed and ready.

"What's going on here?"

"I couldn't sleep."

"Were you told to get ready early? None of you"—and she sweeps a hand around the dorm while the women stare at her in a dazed, half-asleep fashion—"is to take it upon yourself to disrupt the set schedule! That's two demerits for you, Miss Temple, for breaking the rules! What do the rules say, Miss Temple?"

Stella's newly found confidence vanishes, not only at the sight of Mrs. Maynard, but because, once again, she's somehow managed to do the wrong thing. The old Stella nudges, tries to inhabit her skin and take up residence. She's got to answer Mrs. Maynard, whether she likes it or not. She summons her voice from the locked place inside her and does her best to keep it from shaking.

"On page four of the handbook, paragraph two, it says we're to rise at six o'clock a.m., but it also doesn't say we can't get up before then."

Mrs. Maynard narrows her eyes. The other women freeze, waiting to see what's coming next. Stella can't believe that came out of her very own mouth. Mrs. Maynard will definitely have it in for her now, even though she's telling the truth. Stella knows this as sure as she knows her father would still be messing with her if she were at home.

From the back of the dorm, Ruth says, "We're going to be late. Whose fault is it going to be if we're late?" In a low voice that's barely heard except for those closest to her, which includes Stella, comes the answer. "Not Stella's."

At that moment Mrs. Rutherford appears, looks at her wristwatch and at the clock on the wall.

"Is everything all right, Mrs. Maynard? It's just now six o'clock."

Confusion crosses Mrs. Maynard's face as she turns to the new housemother.

"It is? I saw her coming out of the bathroom, and was afraid my watch was off. Well, a bit of an early start never hurt anyone, did it?"

A snort comes from behind Stella. Frances is sitting up and awake. Mrs. Maynard leaves as quickly as she appeared and Stella slumps, the backs of her legs sweaty and her hands shaky. Frances skips by Stella and for the first time since she's been back, reaches out and gives Stella a tap on the arm as she goes to the bathroom. After that, everyone hurries while Stella relaxes. She likes not feeling rushed. The rest of the morning is even better. She eats with enthusiasm, and impresses Miss Perkins with her ability to remember numbers. Right before her free period, she's summoned over the intercom by Mrs. Dot, and she can't help it when her stomach flip-flops. She's not so at ease that a request like this doesn't affect her, make her worry something has gone wrong once again.

"Miss Perkins. Please send Stella to the superintendent's cottage. She's to help clean it."

Miss Perkins turns to her and tips her head toward the door.

"Better go on."

Stella's mood backslides. Maybe what happened this morning has been reported as being sassy, and she's back in trouble again. She's back to household chores, but at least it's not the bathroom. Outside, Mr. Lumley points her down the obscure path to the cottage, which she's never seen, but knows about. Mrs. Dot opens the door.

"Come in, Stella."

Stella would like to admire the inside, but she waits for Mrs. Dot to get onto her. *So soon, and here I thought you were back on track.* Mrs. Dot reaches over to an item draped over the back of a chair. It's a dress, with tags still on it.

"This is for you." And she gives Stella a big smile. "You and I are going on an errand to Kinston. I know you thought you were coming to help clean. This will be our little secret."

This is so different from what she expected, her reaction is spontaneous.

"Oh! Yes, ma'am! Gosh, I thought I was in trouble because of this morning."

"This morning? What happened this morning?"

Stella wishes she'd not said anything, but she explains, her voice low, and Mrs. Dot has to tell her to speak up.

Stella repeats what happened, and adds, "I didn't think it was wrong. The handbook doesn't say we can't get up earlier."

"That is nothing to worry over. Go on and change. I hope it fits. You're not very big, and I had to do my best as to your size. The taxi will be here any minute. We'll talk more on the way to Kinston."

It's like Christmas, although for Stella's family, it was never celebrated. She imagines this must be a little bit of how it feels. She loves the dress. It's a dark green with a white sailor collar. After she's ready, she comes out of the bathroom and Mrs. Dot gives her an approving nod. In the back seat of the taxi, Stella talks with enthusiasm about her work with Miss Perkins.

"She's showing me how to keep track of expenditures in the accounting log. We're going to go through all of the receipts for this month and she's letting me do a lot of it by myself. I like it. It's like math!"

That pleasant smile spreads over the superintendent's face. The taxi lets them off in the downtown area, and parks under a shade tree to wait as instructed. Stella walks proudly, side by side with Mrs. Dot. Their reflections in the store windows is what she particularly likes because they look like the others who stroll by in the opposite direction, like they're out and about on the town for a lunch break.

Mrs. Dot leads her into a store to get some stationery and two new pens, and after that, they go to the drugstore soda fountain.

Mrs. Dot says, "Let's have an orangeade. How does that sound?"

"Yes, please."

She orders from the druggist.

"One for me, and one for my niece."

Stella's heart jumps. Niece? She's learned to expect the unexpected from Mrs. Dot, like this trip. Mrs. Dot explains in a low voice it's easier to introduce her this way.

"Rather than resident of the Colony, you see."

Stella doesn't mind being a pretend niece. She's never thought much about her identity, except when she was back home and where she was part of a family with a reputation of being delinquent on payments despite Cordell's decent job, and a mother who was half crazy. She likes being someone else. Together they watch as the druggist squeezes juice from fresh oranges into two paper cups, adds crushed ice, tops it off with sugar water and a vigorous shake to mix it up. They sit across from each other in a booth—because Mrs. Dot can't manage the stools at the counter—and enjoy their drinks. In doing this, Stella sees a whole other side of Mrs. Dot, one that's more relaxed, and the bands of anxiousness loosen within her own chest. Stella surreptitiously studies the superintendent and decides she *could* be her aunt, or a kind neighbor, like Mrs. Beale.

Once they finish the orangeades, they trace their steps back to the waiting taxi and enjoy a peaceful ride back to the cottage, at ease and, Stella decides, happy. Not content. Happy. After they're dropped off, they go inside, and she changes back into the ugly brown state-issued dress. She hangs the green one on the special satin hanger, running a hand down the material that feels rich and expensive. Does Mrs. Dot look at her with pity? She hopes not, but why did she do this? Is she still trying to make up for what Mrs. Maynard did? She won't think about it. Mrs. Dot has her best interest in mind, is all. She comes out of the bathroom with the dress and Mrs. Dot puts it away in the hall closet, then turns to her.

"Let me show you something."

Stella follows her into the living room and the superintendent pulls a scrapbook off a shelf.

"These photos are from when I worked as superintendent at a different place ten years ago. There were plenty of girls, just like you with their own troubled pasts. Many of them went on to lead good, productive lives. Not all, but enough. Like this girl here. Her name was Nancy Strickland, and here, in this newspaper article, it says she went to work in Child Welfare. As you can see, it's possible to do many good things, and I know because it's happened before. That's what you need to remember."

Stella is fascinated by this information, but it's the photographs that really captivate her. The girls are not only her age, but some are much younger, and the name Samarcand sounds so different, almost magical. She studies their faces closely. She sees them working outside, dressed in overalls, having their pictures taken with big smiles. Some are sitting in chairs underneath pine trees, and there's even a friendly-looking dog between two smiling girls in one of the pictures. She turns pages and points out the buildings.

"It looks nice. I bet they liked being there and getting help from you. I would've liked being there."

"You're different because you understand what it's all about. There were those who didn't like being told what to do and liked to cause trouble."

"Mrs. Dot, what made you leave and come here?"

There's no immediate answer and Stella glances up to find the superintendent no longer looking at the scrapbook. Instead, she's turned her head to the window. *She's not here*, Stella thinks. *She's gone back there, or somewhere.* Stella resumes studying the photos, wondering about the superintendent's past that seems to trouble her at this moment. Mrs. Dot finally speaks, but the story she tells isn't what Stella would've expected.

"Some of the girls, known troublemakers, burned two buildings down. If it hadn't been for Mrs. Libby, the housemother who worked with me, I might've perished. Fire"—and she gestures quickly at her legs, then at the scrapbook—"has always, in some odd way, directed my life. I was forced out. Just like they want to do to me here."

Stella experiences a pulse of anger on behalf of Mrs. Dot for the unfairness of it. The superintendent holds out her hand for the scrapbook.

"You better get back to Miss Perkins."

Stella gives her the scrapbook and goes to the door. Now that she's been inside the cottage, which has a homey feel, she hates the idea of returning to the Colony with its sterile, functional interior and noise from the others.

"Thank you, Mrs. Dot, for taking me into town. I had a really good time."

There isn't any reaction, and Stella can tell the superintendent is back to Colony mode. As she turns to leave, Mrs. Dot cautions her.

"Don't talk about this. People tend to get jealous and I can't have Mrs. Maynard finding out. She's trying to cause trouble for me, and trouble for me means trouble for you. If I end up leaving, they'd most likely send you back home. I will make sure the paperwork is completed so that you can stay here, if that's what you'd want."

Stella's eyes grow huge, and the old panic returns, even as she tries not to overreact. She can't go back home. If that's where she gets sent, she won't stay. She'll do a Lucy. She swears this to herself.

"I wouldn't want to go back home, but I wouldn't want to stay here either, not unless you're here."

Mrs. Dot doesn't look at her and her answer does little to help.

"Try not to worry. Everything will be fine."

"Yes, ma'am."

Those bands of anxiety that relinquished their hold earlier clamp tight around her insides as she considers uncertainty is already back in her future. That afternoon as she works with Miss Perkins, she occasionally presses her hand against her stomach.

Miss Perkins says, "Did you have anything to eat after you cleaned the cottage?"

Stella uses that as the excuse.

"No, ma'am, but it's all right. It's almost time for supper."

Days pass and Stella is consumed by worry Mrs. Dot will lose her job. Her animosity toward Mrs. Maynard grows and she can't sleep. She tosses and turns at night, dwelling on the awful sounds Mrs. Maynard made as she stood over her. She's never thought like this before, but she wants revenge. She wants revenge for herself and for Mrs. Dot. She'd never dream of telling anyone—well, Frances, maybe. Now that Frances is under medicinal control, they're allowed to eat dinner and supper together. Stella's happy about that, except her companionship isn't quite what it was before. Stella talks to her, but most of the time Frances sits slouched like a rag doll. This is how Stella pours her heart out and doesn't worry she's disobeying because talking to Frances in her new state of mind is like talking to herself, or to nobody.

"Frances, Mrs. Dot could lose her job because of Mrs. Maynard. It makes me so mad." She sucks on an orange slice, then leans into her friend. "What if Mrs. Maynard ends up in charge?"

Frances's back is rounded and her head is tucked into her neck, giving her the look of a turtle. She starts rocking back and forth, and Stella continues.

"Mrs. Dot is strict at times, but deep down, she only wants to help us. She used to be at this other school, and that place was different because it was mostly girls, like you and me, some even younger. She told me some of them set fire to their dormitories and because of that, she got to come here. But she could lose her job again. Mrs. Maynard is the one who's mean and hateful. I don't like her. At all."

Frances sits up straight now, woozy and a little drunk seeming, her body weaving slightly. Not all here, Stella believes, until the other girl speaks, her voice low and gravely.

"I don't like either of them. At all."

Stunned, Stella whispers to Frances.

"You're playing a game, aren't you, Frances."

It isn't a question. It's a statement. Through a drug-induced haze, Frances's eyes gleam and she reaches over, but instead of patting Stella's arm, she leans into her for a brief second, then stands. Stella smiles up at her. Frances doesn't smile back, but that doesn't surprise

Stella because Frances never smiles. Frances picks up her tray, takes it to the window, and drops it off. As Stella watches her leave the cafeteria, she thinks about what she said, and has only a brief moment of worry. But since she didn't say anything about the cottage, or the outing, and that's what Mrs. Dot told her not to talk about, telling Frances about the other stuff won't matter.

Two nights later, everyone is in bed and the whispers of conversation have been replaced by snores and the soft breathing that comes with sleep. Stella is awake and because she's awake, she sees Frances getting up again. She reaches out as she passes by and Frances stops. Stella can't make out her face. She sits up.

"Frances, what're you doing?"

Frances places a finger to her lips and with exaggerated stealthy steps she sneaks out of the room. Stella swings her legs over the side of the bed and sits for a moment. After what happened last time, Frances might be sent away for good if she's caught stealing food again. Stella contemplates what to do. If she follows, she risks being found with her, and the very thought makes her sick to her stomach. She observes the sleeping forms as she waits, sweaty and disturbed. She's about to risk it when the girl creeps back into the room. She slips by Stella, who watches as she gets in the bed, turns on her side, and is asleep in minutes. Where did she go? What did she do? Stella lies back down, relieved. Soon after, she finally falls asleep too.

The next morning, she awakes to find Frances watching her. The girl gives her a wily look before donning her usual ignorant guise. There's no alarm sounded about food missing, and the morning goes as it should. Stella forgets about Frances's little escapade as she helps Miss Perkins, their heads together as they carefully allot certain amounts of money to various categories. It's midmorning when they hear a commotion outside the office. They both raise their heads, listen more closely, and what they hear is Mr. Lumley yelling. At first, they're confused, but the confusion turns to alarmed panic once they can make out his words.

"Fire! Fire! Dorm A!"

Stella spins around and, through the window, she sees an angry orange flame shooting out of the building. Smoke begins to swirl from the doors at each end of the structure.

Miss Perkins grabs hold of Stella's hand and they run out of the office to hear Mrs. Maynard shouting into the intercom, screeching with intensity.

"Code F! Code F! Everyone! Outside! Outside! Get away from the dormitory! Gather at the Administration Building, at the front! I repeat, Code F! Code F!"

Miss Perkins and Stella are in that spot in seconds as women flow in from all directions. Josephine, Melissa, Paula, Natalie, Ruth, Opal, Sally, Maude, and Patsy, along with dozens of others, run from the kitchen and classrooms, and those in the fields come too. Everyone must be accounted for and Mrs. Maynard begins roll call. Two minutes later, everyone is present except the superintendent and Frances Platt.

"Frances Platt! Dorothy Baker!"

Mrs. Maynard yells and blows on her whistle uselessly. Heads turn, searching the area and amongst themselves. Stella's mind becomes this dark little knot, not wanting to accept the thoughts trying to come. Like, did this have to do with Frances getting up the night before? Her gut tells her it does.

"Frances Platt! Mrs. Baker!" everyone cries out.

The cluster of white-faced women turn to face the fiery building with the realization Frances Platt and Dorothy Baker aren't among them.

Chapter 34

Baker

Baker, ensconced at the superintendent's cottage, reviews the history of Nurse Crawford's medical records with great alarm. The housemother was out of control many times and perhaps worse is the realization she, Baker, did nothing to address it. There isn't any follow-up, or details. No reprimand. No additional training. Nothing at all. How can she present any sort of case to the board to oust Mrs. Maynard if she appears to have had no issue with how she handled residents? She stands abruptly, stacks the papers together, stuffs them into a leather satchel, and places it for safekeeping in her closet. She glances at the time. She needs to get to the Colony before Mrs. Maynard notices she's running late once again.

Baker goes into the kitchen to shut the back door and is met by a faint, yet highly perceptible and all too familiar odor. *Something is burning.* She peers through the screen searching for the source. Above the tree line and in the direction of the Colony, the sky is dark as if a storm cloud has moved in, only this is thick dense smoke. It rises in a huge plume above the hardwood and pine trees, growing darker and thicker by the minute. Transfixed, she tries to make out what's on fire and can't. If it's Mr. Lumley again, she's going to release him on the spot. She reenters the cottage, makes her way to the front door, and starts down the path and is met with the sight of bright amber spirals like curly ribbons wrapping in and around the trees, expanding, shifting shape. This unfortunate, yet spectacular, sight is accompanied by a distinct crackling sound. She can hardly believe her eyes. She veers left and her mouth fills as it always does at the sight. Her legs tingle and itch.

She shouldn't stop, but she can't help herself. She falters, comes to a standstill, and watches the flames eat until full and move on, always hungry, always wanting more, more, more. She understands this about it, how it searches out what it wants, because as a child, she became well acquainted with its behavior. Just like that she's seven years old again, and the past she's kept hidden from everyone she's ever known, an untold story best kept secret, sneaks its way back into her present.

They said time and again, "Leave the matches alone!"

Seven-year-old Dottie Baker wants to obey, but she can't help herself. She adores the acrid scent right after the strike, the moment her mouth waters and her leg muscles turn to jelly from the thrill of it. This simple desire she has, scraping a sulfur tip across the sandpaper-like strip, grips her in a way she can't understand. The tiny twirling flame on top of the wooden end entrances her and she lets it last until she's forced to shake it out, only to do it again and again. Even if she can't understand the urge, she knows disobeying adds to her excitement.

Papa has whipped her many times, all the while yelling, "Why? Why do you do this?"

He even grabbed her hand once and held it close to a lit match so she'd understand it could hurt her. She knows, but nothing bad will happen because she's very, very careful. Part of the thrill is sneaking the matches off the shelf. She gets this funny feeling when she knows she's going to play with them and her heart booms in her chest as she creeps about searching for the best hiding place. She chooses meticulously, always picking a different spot.

On the day she learns she's not in control like she believes, she's safe and secure behind the curtains of the window in the sitting room. She strikes one of many already, moving her arm to make the flame dance and flutter. She raises up a bit, peeks through the window, and sees her older brother, Tommy, throwing a ball into the air and catching it. Her younger sister, Suzanne, is with Mama on the front porch swing helping snap beans for supper. Helping like Dottie should be doing. Mama gazes down at Suzanne and smiles at her. This distracts Dottie. Her eyes narrow, coveting the look bestowed on her little sister. Most of the match is consumed as Dottie scrutinizes their interaction. The flame reaches her fingertip. She drops the match and sticks her finger in her mouth.

It lands on the edge of the lacy curtain and the material acts like thirsty ground in a drought. It soaks up the ember and swiftly doubles in size, then it's bigger, and when Dottie notices, it's twice the size of her hand, and seconds later, even bigger. Dottie, alarmed, smacks at it, but that makes things worse, sending sparks in different directions that also catch. The flames run, stretch, and reach, like a chained dog suddenly set free. Mama keeps a pail of water by the wood stove in the kitchen and Dottie jumps up to go get it. A finger of flame touches the stocking on her leg and latches on. It crawls about like a small animal, feeding off the material of the drapes, then both her stockings. She bends down to slap at her calves.

Meanwhile, the blaze busily climbs the curtains. She can't know that by bending over the hem of her dress touches part of the burning curtain, nor that the fire is not only gobbling her stockings, but has begun to eat its way around to the front. The hem of her dress ignites as her hungry, fiery friend consumes the remainder of the curtains. At the sight of her lower half turning orange, red, and yellow, she panics. There's a hall mirror and she catches sight of herself as she races by. The fire hugs her back and she can feel it and it sends her into the yard. She doesn't cry out. She's a silent, tiny torch streaking about like a comet. It's Mama who screams. Within the house, half of the sitting room is engulfed and the fire is now in the hallway. Mama catches her, covers her with her own body while screaming for help.

Dottie's next memory is the hospital. The medications. The therapies. Mostly, the pain. After a long time, she's able to walk again, but due to scarring on her right leg, it will remain slightly bent for the rest of her life. Her parents never speak of this mishap. Not when they have to go live with her grandparents for a year while the house is repaired, not when they move back in. On the first day she enters the house, Dottie swears she can still smell burnt wood, but she never mentions this. No one calls it an accident. No one reassures her in any way she's forgiven. Dottie wishes they would punish her, wishes Papa would take his belt and beat her scarred body black and blue. Her mother's only response is to make sure she keeps her disfigured legs covered at all times, even in the summer. Their sadness and disappointment are palpable and Dottie understands they no longer look at her as they once did.

Baker is conflicted by the sight of her old friend. It scampers toward Dorm B because, as she can clearly see, Dorm A is all but gone. She puts a trembling hand to her mouth. It's Samarcand all over again. As flames climb the side of the second building, she attempts to reassure herself telling Stella about the fire doesn't mean anything. To be sure Stella couldn't have done this, but how else did it start? She gets her answer when she notices the lone figure in a tattered, telltale brown dress about a hundred feet away. Her head is tipped upward, watching the flames reach the roof.

Frances Platt holds a red can with the word *gasoline* painted in white on its side. She turns and their eyes meet and Baker understands she absolutely underestimated this girl; they all have. A piece of burning material lands near Frances. It doesn't faze her even as the force of it hitting the ground makes her hair fly up as if caught in a sudden breeze. Baker takes careful steps, her hand extended to the girl, motioning, *come, come*. She's close to the raging heat, too close. It must be different this time. This time Baker must win because she's already lost enough.

To her right, the last vestiges of Dorm A still portray a stunning display of hot fury. Baker wobbles across the uneven ground, moving faster than she can manage. She loses her balance as her bent leg, always unreliable, betrays her and she lands with a solid *thump*. She's unhurt, but jarred. She eases over onto her back and the black, billowy cloud overhead is like a harbinger of doom. Suddenly, Frances's face blocks her view. She gazes down at Baker, then shifts her attention to the buildings.

"Frances," Baker croaks, "you did this. Why?"

She smells gas, sees tiny smudges of soot and ash covering Frances's face and clothes. Frances returns her gaze to Baker and whispers:

"Tell Stella her wish came true."

A winter cold engulfs Baker as she grapples with two things: Frances speaking intelligently and the mention of Stella. She struggles to sit up, and Frances presses her back down.

"Not yet."

Frances lopes away, swinging the gas can in a casual manner. Baker is overcome by a coughing fit as the smoke starts to thicken around her. Gasping, she rolls onto her belly and pushes herself to her knees. By the time she's on her feet, Frances has disappeared.

"Frances!"

Undulating glasslike waves of heat blow around her. Sweat trickles down her face as she scans the woods and the area where she last saw Frances. It's as if she was never here.

"Frances!" Baker yells again.

A wail of sirens overtakes the sizzling sounds of the structure. Toward the Administration Building, several women turn when they hear her yelling and run toward her. Baker moves as if in a dream toward the remains of Dorm A. She's close, so close she could almost reach out and touch the edges of a blackened doorframe where red embers still pulse with life and could reignite at any moment if given the fuel. A few residents scream at her.

"Get back! Get back!"

It's Stella who grabs her by the elbow and pulls her away. Everyone crowds around, asking questions as they return to a safer distance. Fire trucks, the sheriff's department, and an ambulance pull up. The two fire trucks drive over the grass to get closer to the dormitories. Mr. Lumley hands her a damp handkerchief and she wipes the soot and ash off her face, breathing heavily, like she's been running. She points where the fire trucks now block her view of where she fell. She whispers one word:

"Frances."

Mrs. Maynard doesn't appear to hear her she's so rattled by what's happening. She whacks her cane on the ground for emphasis.

"Are you crazy? Why would you get so close? What were you doing? Have you seen Frances?"

Baker gestures weakly.

"There. With Mr. Lumley's gas can. I don't know where she went."

"Frances?"

This is from Stella, whose eyes are red and streaming, either from smoke or emotion. Baker pants out one word:

"Yes."

Nurse Crawford is at her other side.

"Let me make sure you're all right."

"I'm fine. We need to find her. Maybe she's hiding in the woods. Maybe she didn't mean for it to get out of hand. Maybe she thought . . ."

They're watching her. Listening to how she sounds. It's apparent by their expressions they don't know what to make of her reaction. The roof collapses in on Dorm A, sending sparks whirling into the air, and the women turn their attention back to the mesmerizing sight. All around them, the firemen scramble to drag the hoses close enough to fight the blaze.

One yells, "Get water on it, hurry! Don't let it get to the woods."

Mrs. Maynard, her voice elevated to emphasize urgency, says, "We have nowhere for them to sleep! What're we to do?"

Everyone turns to Baker, waiting for her to fix it. This is what she does best. She gets ahold of herself, and takes charge. She sends Ruth, Opal, and Sally to the kitchen to prepare a meal for everyone, including the firefighters. Stella and several women are sent down to the laundry to gather sheets, blankets, and whatever they can find to temporarily convert the classrooms into sleeping quarters. She goes to her office, and without allowing herself to think ahead as to what this next step will mean, she places an urgent call to Dr. Woodall.

"The dormitories were set on fire and are a complete loss."

There's a pause, and then Dr. Woodall barks out an incredulous, "*What?*"

Baker barely pauses and goes on to inform him of the destruction and the predicament with housing the residents. She explains their temporary setup, and recommends discharging the women. There is no other option.

"They can continue treatments at home through a local health official in their respective towns."

Dr. Woodall says nothing for a moment. Finally, he lets go a deep sigh.

"There will be an inquiry into this event."

"Yes, I know."

"All right. That seems the only plausible thing to do. The jail isn't capable of holding that many, and it's not an appropriate solution. Draw up the paperwork. You have my approval."

Mrs. Maynard, upon hearing this news, throws her hands into the air.

"How can you allow reprobates to go free? They've not completed training! They're not ready to go back to society!"

Baker is oddly disconnected from Mrs. Maynard's rage.

"If you don't like my decision, you call him back and make whatever arrangements you want. I've got other work to do."

"But where are you going? What are you going to do?"

Baker needs to make one more phone call, but it will have to wait, and it's none of Mrs. Maynard's business anyway.

Over the next few days, she completes the discharge paperwork and one by one women trickle out of the Colony, some ecstatic, others disconsolate. Baker is emotionally detached while Stella hovers about her office, nervous and afraid. She's got to decide what to do about her, an important decision, and one she'll have to live with, one way or another. Baker escapes to the cottage, and except for the lingering odor of smoke, which she finds quite tolerable, it's the haven she needs.

Her old friend, Eloise Bell, said to always have a backup plan and Baker took this advice to heart years ago. She makes that important last phone call to Winnifred DeLong. Winnifred has held positions with the North Carolina State Board of Charities, Public Welfare, and the State Board of Health. She's a resourceful and knowledgeable individual with lots of connections throughout North Carolina and the southeast. Also an old friend of Eloise's, and an acquaintance of Baker's, they spend part of the conversation catching up and then Baker tells her about the Colony and what's just happened.

"Good heavens! Again?" Winnifred is incredulous. "What an unfortunate turn. What is it with fire at these facilities? Did you hear about the one in Missouri?"

"No, but maybe word is getting out. I don't know. One of our more deranged residents caused the one here, and may have perished at her own hand. Their behavior can be quite cunning and deceptive at times, resulting in stunts like this."

"I've had one or two like that. One can never be too careful. Her poor parents. I bet they're beside themselves."

"Yes. I told them what I knew, although the investigation is still pending. We're not sure exactly what happened to her."

"Such a tragedy. I'm sorry you're going through this again. As to the question of where to go from there, well, you have choices and that's the good news. There's a facility in Chalkville, Alabama. They need an administrator. It's currently run by an acquaintance of mine, Clara Stiles, who needs to step aside due to health concerns. Maybe it would be a good thing to get away from prying eyes and the stigma of these two unfortunate circumstances under your watch, if you catch my meaning."

Baker has always been impressed by Winnifred's no-nonsense way of speaking even though hearing the facts like this grates.

"I agree, actually."

"I'll call and see if the position is still available."

"Winnifred, could you check into the possibility of me bringing my niece? I'm not sure of this yet, but she seems cut out to work in this field. It might be an opportune time to begin her formal training."

"We can never have enough willing individuals, so yes, I'll be sure to mention it."

For two days, Baker busies herself cleaning up the cottage. The last thing she does is gather her personal effects, of which there are few. The last is the satchel with the Colony's records, and Stella's dress. Frances's last words, *Tell Stella her wish came true,* create a serious question for Baker. Did Frances do it for her? It's a troubling concern. She's back to her doubts as to whether or not she can judge an individual as well as she thought. Later that afternoon, she sits at the kitchen table sipping a cup of coffee and staring out at the scorched trees. She waffles one way and the other over Stella and is almost relieved by a knock at the front door until she pictures Mrs. Maynard wanting something else she seems incapable of figuring out for herself. Baker quietly steps into the living room, and peeks out. As fate would have it, it's her current predicament, Stella, her appearance bedraggled and forlorn. She's twisting her hands in obvious distress. Baker might as well have the conversation. She opens the door and before she has a chance speak, Stella starts with a deluge of words, fast and frantic.

"Mrs. Dot, ma'am, I didn't know Frances was going to do that. I didn't tell her about nothing, except how you come here when them girls at the other school burned down those buildings. Maybe she got the idea when I said I wished I could get revenge on Mrs. Maynard for what she done to us. Please. Wherever you're going, take me too. She's got my discharge papers ready. She's going to send me home. I can't go back there."

Mrs. Maynard comes tromping down the path, a scowl on her face. She points at a petrified Stella, who acts like she's about to run into the cottage and hide behind Baker.

"I figured she'd run over here. She took off as soon as I told her I'd filled out her paperwork to go home."

"I see. Well, all right. She and I will visit for a bit, and then I'll send her back to you."

Baker gives the impression this latest bit of drama has no effect on her. Mrs. Maynard narrows her eyes, her gaze going from Baker to Stella.

"I suppose that's all right."

Baker motions for Stella to go inside. She owes Mrs. Maynard nothing, and follows Stella, shutting the door in the housemother's face.

She says, "All right. Tell me everything, from the beginning."

Thirty minutes later, Baker's decision is made, and Stella is back at the Colony. The timing is perfect because Winnifred calls her later that afternoon.

"I spoke to Clara. She's happy to have you come and see if you like it or not. I told her you were well qualified, and that your niece might be with you."

"Thank you, thank you, Winnifred, I owe you."

"The work is never done and we can't lose a valuable resource such as yourself."

Thank God, for those like Winnifred who understand. Well before the sun is up the next morning, a taxi arrives at the cottage. Baker gets in and in minutes is going down the long drive of the Colony, where, at the end of it, they pick up Stella, who has nothing but the state-issued dress she's wearing. The next stop is the train station, and Baker purchases two one-way tickets to Chalkville. Stella changes into the green dress, and they take on the guise it's a vacation, enjoying the fact it's Stella's first trip out of the state, her first train ride, and so many other firsts. The next afternoon they arrive in Chalkville and take another taxi to the address provided. Baker walks confidently up the sidewalk, while Stella lags a little, gazing around in wide-eyed wonder.

The lawns are well-manicured grounds, and Stella catches up to Baker, exclaiming, "There's even a swimming pool!"

Baker is nervous, but she comes with high recommendations. She presses the buzzer at the main entrance of the building and a moment later, the door swings open. They're greeted by an intensely serious woman about Baker's age.

Baker says, "Hello. I'm Dorothy Baker. This is my niece, Stella Baker. We're here about the administrator's position. Stella here, so I've discovered recently, has a knack for working with the more mentally challenged individuals, and I think she will do well to train here."

Without a word, Clara Stiles opens the door and waves them in with a welcoming gesture. Baker steps over the threshold, and Stella follows.

Chapter 35

Ruth

When something inexplicable takes place, news travels faster than usual. The next day, those still at the Colony and waiting to leave learn of Baker and Stella's disappearance. It's as mysterious as Frances Platt evaporating into thin air, and there's incessant talk and speculation. What happened to them? Where did they go? They were here and now they aren't. The reasonable thing to assume is they left together, but there are no definitive conclusions. Mrs. Maynard tries to find out through her own tactics, expecting to trip someone up. She questions each inmate, holding their release papers as leverage. When it's Ruth's turn, Mrs. Maynard places spindly arms on top of the pages that mean freedom to Ruth, as if she might snatch them. The housemother's curved stature gives the impression of a child sitting at a grownup's desk.

"Tell me what you know."

"If I knew anything, I'd say so."

"You've been a difficult one, Miss Foster."

"Maybe. But I've always told the truth."

There's a sly inference to this reply that Mrs. Maynard chooses to ignore. Her face twists as she hands Ruth her papers and Ruth exits the office as fast as she can. She goes straight out the front door, the very same door she entered almost seven months before. She crawls into the back seat of the waiting taxi and hugs her mother, her body as malleable as rubber and limp with exhaustion. Her mother dabs at her eyes the entire ride home, but doesn't speak because there's plenty of time for talk later. For now, they're both overcome with relief the ordeal is over.

Ruth's days pass in a blur of sleeping and eating, and adjusting to life on the outside. She puzzles over the way it ended. The question is and will always be, what happened to Frances? Did she walk into the fire? Why had she set it in the first place? No one can provide answers as to what was going on in Frances Platt's head, except maybe Stella, but Stella is gone, too. Ruth's high school friend, Patty Campbell, hears she's home and comes to see her, filled with curiosity. She takes hold of Ruth's hand.

"Oh, Ruthie. Look at what they did to you!"

Ruth knows she doesn't look herself. She finally faced the mirror and it's no liar. As she recounts her story, Patty's face fills with horror, not only at Ruth's personal experiences, but about Frances, Baker, and Stella.

"That's so sad. Why would those young girls be there?"

"I'm not sure about Frances, but Stella's father got her pregnant, and the doctor made sure she wouldn't ever be able to have a baby again."

Patty sits back against on the couch.

"If that's what happened, maybe it was for the best."

"What?"

"You know. Think about it. *Her father?*"

"It wasn't her fault."

Patty's voice drops to a whisper, and it's like Ruth didn't speak.

"It's disgusting. That's why these places exist, I suppose. To correct such behavior."

"She's not to blame, Patty. After all, it's not like she wanted it to happen. What if she'd wanted her own family one day? And what about me? What on earth did I do?"

Patty flushes, and begins to open and close the clasp on her pocketbook. It's a nervous habit she's always had.

"There's a certain decorum women should follow. Even a girl, for that matter. I doubt anyone would've married her, not with that sort of past."

She's wise enough not to comment about Ruth, while Ruth is dumbstruck by this reasoning.

"Decorum? What does decorum have to do with rape?" She doesn't want to argue, so she stands abruptly. "I'm feeling tired. I need to go lie down."

Patty has the decency to look a bit embarrassed, but takes the hint. She stands and after a quick hug that Ruth tolerates, she leaves. Ruth watches her from the living room window. What does Patty think of her? Does she think Ruth deserved her time at the Colony? She turns away. Let Patty judge her however she wants; Ruth knows the truth.

As days pass, her mother hovers, cooks her favorite foods, like brown-sugar meatloaf and mashed potatoes, then worries when she picks. Ruth drifts from room to room, wanting to forget, trying to forget, except she can't. Each day as the sun goes down, streaking the sky with lovely peach and pink colors, she ventures outside to share the front porch swing with her mother. Ruth is most at ease at this time of day. The night air is cool, and she dresses in a white cotton shift nightgown. Barefoot, she keeps the swing in a gentle motion as they watch winking stars and fireflies. If it's raining, they listen to the radio and worry about what's going on overseas, and whether or not the United States will get involved. If they talk, it's never about what happened to her. If her mother tries, Ruth turns away, or holds up a hand.

After a month, and when she begins to feel more normal, at least physically, her mother asks her, "What will you do now?"

"I don't know, not anymore."

"Stay as long as you want, dear. No rush."

The truth is, if she leaves the safety of her mother's home, she's constantly on alert expecting to see the sheriff, or a Colony staff member. What would she do if she saw Mrs. Maynard or Baker?

The couple of times she ventures into public results in overheard whispers of "It's her," and "I can't believe she'd be seen in public!"

Stanley Newell calls periodically at first, until Ruth says, "I could use some company."

He starts coming once a week whether he has news or not. If he plans to eat supper with them, Ruth takes over the kitchen and cooks. It's the only time she can clear her mind. Her mother gets her hopes up about these visits and Ruth has to tell her he's already engaged to someone else. One afternoon he drops by with a folder. They've grown comfortable around one another and have switched to first names. She reaches out and pokes the folder he carries.

"Stanley, what'cha got there?"

Stanley has a very serious air about him and a tiny little chill travels down her spine.

"I found information on this case in Michigan involving a woman named Nina McCall."

Ruth gets nervous, then excited at this news, and she steps aside so he can come in.

"Mama's gone for her weekly beauty parlor appointment. She'll hate she missed this visit, especially if you have news."

Across the street, Mrs. Jeffries is watering flowers in the front yard. The woman shoots her a dirty look and Ruth shuts the door a little harder than necessary. Stanley's eyebrows rise, his expression one of surprise.

"Old busybody," she mutters.

He tries to joke.

"I could've gone around to the back door. That'd give her something to talk about."

"I'm sure it would get reported and the sheriff would show up."

She seats him at the kitchen table with a glass of sweet tea, and he opens the folder. Pausing for a second, he moves on to explain what he's found.

"Nina McCall was younger than you at the time she was placed into a detention hospital under the suspicion of having a venereal disease. Her story is strikingly similar to yours except she was on her way to the post office when she was stopped by the local sheriff. If you can believe it, this was in 1918."

"You said this went on during World War One, maybe before, right?"

"I did. She took the government to court because of the treatments she was forced to take not only while she was locked up in the hospital, but after she was released, which was May 1920."

"Did she win?"

He rubs a hand through his hair, which is scant on top, and this action makes it stand on end.

"She didn't. Her lawyers tried to claim there was a conspiracy between the individuals who sent her away along with the woman who continued to harass her afterward to take the shots once she was released. The judge ruled there was no conspiracy. The defense then requested the decision be based on what was allowed at the time. There was a general consensus the doctor was doing his job, so the judge ordered the jury to find 'no cause of action.' Many in the public saw it as a fitting outcome."

"Are there any cases that won?"

There's a strain to Ruth's voice. Stanley shakes his head.

"Not that I'm aware of. Think about it. The fact the Colony even exists means nothing's changed. The federal government organized necessary officials through departments they created, then mandated the social hygiene practices. They sent it down to the states to manage, and most operate in a very similar fashion."

Stanley pulls out another sheet of paper. He slides it across the table. It's an old newspaper article.

"I found it while I was researching. It's about Dorothy Baker. She used to work at a school in Eagle Springs called Samarcand. She was there in 1931, but had to leave. It's very interesting why."

Ruth reads the headline from a paper called *The Moore County News,* which declares in big bold letters, 12 SAMARCAND GIRLS GET PRISON SENTENCES, and NEGLECT OF GIRLS AT SAMARCAND IS PLEA OF DEFENSE.

When she's done reading, she glances up at Stanley.

"Did the girls in this case win?"

"No."

Ruth sits back, dismayed.

"It's an odd coincidence, isn't it, that these girls burned their dormitories too?"

"In reality, it's not that uncommon. Many have been burned in some way or another, across the country. Some are like Lucy, and escaped. A few have jumped from trains as they're being transported. Samarcand continues to operate and is currently overseen by a woman named Grace Robson. These facilities are viewed as doing good for the communities."

"Nothing you've said so far sounds encouraging."

He doesn't argue the point and Ruth gets up to pace around the kitchen.

She stops by the kitchen sink, and with her back to him, she says, "It's not worth it," and turns to look at him. "Is it?"

He raises his hands as if to concede this as a truth or to admit defeat, she's not sure which. He closes the folder, placing his hands on top.

"Have you seen those ads that depict women as dangerous, as if they're solely at fault? It's a campaign, an efficient one that puts a mindset into place, one of good and bad females."

"Fallen women. That's what they called us."

Ruth crosses her arms and drifts around the kitchen. Once, she felt strongly about her independence. How confident she used to be and how certain she was her future could be one she determined freely, without fear of reprisal.

"I don't understand how this happens, but mostly, I don't understand how women can agree this should happen to . . . to . . ." And here, Ruth falters and stops.

Stanley finishes the sentence. "To other women?"

"Yes."

"It's like religion, I think. Everything I've read says those working in this field believe in what they're doing. It's a mission. They belong to many different organizations with many different directives. They don't, or can't, see it for what it is. They simply believe in it." Stanley checks his watch. "I'm sorry, but I've got to get back to the office."

"I appreciate you taking the time to come and tell me."

They walk to the front door, and as she opens it, she says, "I meant what I said. I don't think there's any need to keep trying. Maybe it's best to let it go. I don't want you to waste time on it."

Stanley holds his hat in his hands, poking at the top, reshaping it. He looks apologetic.

"It wasn't a waste of time; I only wish I could tell you something different."

"I'm glad you told me the truth."

"If I learn of anything I think might help, I'll let you know."

"I'd appreciate it, very much. Oh, and please tell Lucy I said hey, and she should come visit me sometime."

"I will."

He sets his hat, touches two fingers to the brim in a gentlemanly farewell, and leaves. Ruth shuts the door and rests her back against it. She doesn't like that her eyes immediately begin to hurt with the pressure of unshed tears. She doesn't like how she feels—lost, aimless, and angry.

Over the next few days, the meeting with Stanley festers and works its way into her head in such a way, she has trouble sleeping. She needs to talk to someone, someone who was there, someone who knows how it was. She goes into her room and retrieves a piece of paper from her top drawer. Back in her mother's living room, she sits in a chair, staring at the handwriting.

When she left the Colony, she'd seen Josephine at the last minute and she'd handed Ruth a phone number and said, "If you need anything, call."

Ruth lifts the receiver and when the operator answers, she reads out the number.

There are the usual clicking noises, and the operator says, "Your call is connected."

Ruth hears a tinny, distant ring, and at last, "Hello? Josephine Littles, here."

At the sound of her voice, Ruth smiles into the phone.

"Hey, Josephine, it's me, Ruth Foster."

"My word, Ruth! I've wondered about you since the day we left. How are you? Where are you?"

"I'm here, at Mama's house. My apartment was rented out to someone while I was gone. I'm . . . I don't know. I'm doing all right, I guess. How about you?"

There's a heavy sigh on the other end of the line.

"It ain't been easy, I'll say that."

"Are you still renting out rooms? Are Melissa, Paula, and Natalie with you?"

"Oh, no, no. I don't dare rent to nobody. They're watching me, you know. I ain't seen the girls since we got let go. I reckon we've scattered to the wind. Nothing's the same. Everything's how it was, yet it isn't. I can't put my finger on it."

Ruth holds the receiver so tight her hand aches.

"It's because we thought we were like everyone else, living our lives, going about our business. What's changed is us."

Josephine's voice is low, subdued.

"I don't know how we get back to how it was, how to get around it, you know?"

"Well, we don't. There's no getting around it. We have no other choice other than to try and move on."

"I suppose you're right."

"Josephine."

"Yeah?"

"If there's any good that came of this it's that I got to know you. You're genuine—you, Lucy, and the rest who went through it too."

"Shoot. That's the nicest thing anyone's ever said to me."

"It's the truth. I'm glad we met."

"Me too, Ruth."

"Take care of yourself."

"You too, Ruth. Come see me sometime, if you're ever in the area."

"I will."

Ruth doesn't move until her mother comes in with a bag of groceries and she gets up to take it from her. After she sets it on the kitchen table, she turns to her and wraps her in a warm hug. Her mother's hair smells of fresh shampoo and crème rinse.

"What's this about?"

Her voice is muffled against Ruth's shoulder.

"I'm glad to be home, Mama."

"I'm glad you're home too, Ruthie. I sure am."

That night, after her mother is in bed, Ruth goes out to the porch swing and sits listening to the night. The tree frogs and crickets are in tune and a full moon bathes her in a pale-yellow light. She rests tucked in the corner of the swing, her face in her hands, but the pent-up tears won't come. Instead, there's a certainty she did nothing wrong and the acceptance she can't do anything about what happened to her. She will, as she said to Josephine, try to get over it and move on. She is different because she endured and now, she's on the other side.

The rumors begin the way all rumors do, with whispers in the community about what took place at the Colony. Initially, there's mystery surrounding the events, and a few of those diminish once the fire department informs the public of the gas canister found inside Dorm B, and that it appears as if it was set intentionally. Frances Platt is still missing and the question of whether or not she purposely walked into the burning building lingers. While it's known there should be something, a bone or bones left behind, none are found.

By this time, Ruth is back at her job with Mr. and Mrs. Buncombe. On her way home after work one day, she passes a newsstand to see the jolting headline THE HEROINE OF THE COLONY. She buys the paper, wondering who on earth they mean. The article is written based on a few individuals who claim to have known Dorothy Baker. They aren't anyone Ruth knows, although most assert she tried to save Frances Platt. Even Ethel Maynard shared stories of her former boss, which are altered, or embellished to the best of Ruth's knowledge. To hear her tell it, they were close, the best of friends. Baker's efforts in reform are hailed as revolutionary since none of those released from the Colony have landed back in a facility. Others, wanting a part of the mystery and intrigue, claim Baker was the one who turned their lives around. Baker, had she known any of this, might have produced that rare smile.

Ruth fumes. Heroine? That evening, she puts pen to paper and writes of her own personal account, a rebuttal to the story. It may not get printed, but the least she can do is try to set the record straight, if for no other reason than her own sense of justice. It takes her hours to tell her version, to outline her experiences, then detail her time in meditation and all she saw while at the institution. She leaves nothing out. She reads it over and over, and finally satisfied, she folds the pages, stuffs them into an envelope, and affixes a stamp to it. The next morning, before she can lose her nerve, she drops it in the mailbox on her way to work. The moment it's no longer in her hands, it feels like a small justice. It will be read by somebody and if anyone wants to know more, they know where to find her.

In the sky, there's not a cloud in sight, and for the first time in a while, her vision of her future becomes just as clear. Next month, she'll turn twenty-five and recently she began a new search for a place of her own. She'll live the way she wants. She won't change a thing. She won't be intimidated. She lengthens her stride and moves along the sidewalk with renewed confidence. The sheriff's car appears, yet she doesn't falter. To him and anyone who observes this moment, they see a young woman with an air of confidence, as if she knows where she's going, and they would be right.

Author's Note

I began this project with an idea of writing about a girls reform school. My searches led me to a book by Karen L. Zipf, *Bad Girls at Samarcand: Sexuality and Sterilization in a Southern Juvenile Reformatory* and this particular book explores what it was like for girls, specifically white, given the segregation laws of the day, to be placed at Samarcand Manor, for reconstituting them back to their "Southern white womanhood." It operated not too far from where I live. There are many facets to reform, including the eugenics movement, which of late is written about with increased frequency. It's a stunning topic, however I wasn't as interested in writing about sterilization; I was curious how these facilities operated, and how girls ended up in them. As I researched, I learned several girls burned down the dormitories at Samarcand because of harsh disciplinary measures. Since I never settle on one source, I continued my exploration of reform to see what else I might find. I'm always looking for a unique angle or history that's unknown or obscure and at some point, I was led to look up the word *prostitution*. This is when it got really interesting. I learned of laws passed by the United States government to curtail venereal diseases, which are now called sexually transmitted infections, or STIs, which then led to a stunning discovery—the mass incarceration of women suspected of these infections—and Scott W. Stern's book *The Trials of Nina McCall: Sex, Surveillance, and the Decades-Long Plan to Imprison "Promiscuous" Women.*

Along with Zipf's work, both gave me valuable information. Collectively, from the conditions at girls reform schools to the knowledge that average, everyday women were stalked, pursued, targeted, and then imprisoned against their will was nothing short of shocking. I learned of another facility, also not too far away, the State Industrial Farm Colony for Women, located in Kinston, North Carolina. Places like this, and other similar facilities, existed across the United States. This history is difficult, if not impossible to find. Even more bizarre, the law that led to the creation of such institutions was once called the American Plan. As per Scott Stern, women like Nina McCall were so stigmatized, they were ashamed to share what had happened to them: "This pattern of silence and marginalization is among the reasons the American Plan is not better known today" (Stern, 2018).

For this novel, I took the liberty of blending these two distinct histories together and highlighted the practices used in reform schools as well as the institutions intended to treat women for STIs because of the parallels with regard to treatment, whether physical or mental. The State Industrial Farm Colony for Women, where most of my story takes place, operated from 1927 until 1945. It was eventually turned over and utilized to house individuals from the State Training School for Negro Girls and became known as Dobbs Farm. The buildings still exist today and since 1985 it's been known as the Dobbs Youth Development Center. Biennial reports from the time period when it was known as a farm colony were utilized for historic detail of how it operated.

How did these mass incarcerations begin? Long before the United States became involved, efforts to manage, control, or eliminate sexually transmitted diseases started in Europe. In England, in particular, during the 1870s, prostitutes were being forced to submit themselves for examinations and were held in captivity to endure treatments. For the United States, it was in the 1900s during World

War I that it was discovered that one out of three servicemen (this is now thought to be incorrect) were infected with some sort of STI. This is when the Chamberlain-Kahn Act, or the American Plan, was born. At first, it was an attempt to control prostitution, but soon scrutiny expanded into local communities and neighborhoods across the United States once it was discovered most men contracted their infections at home. These efforts died down once World War I was over, but with the threat of another possible war, i.e., World War II, the government declared the spread of these types of infections a matter of national security as well as a health threat to society in general.

Eventually, women of all backgrounds, means, and lifestyles became subject to this intense scrutiny. Government officials, law enforcement, and local health officials all participated in routing out suspicious individuals. Some were simply walking down the street. Others might have been eating dinner alone. If a woman was targeted, they were intimidated or forced to submit to invasive, humiliating, and degrading exams. The results of such an exam were often questionable. No matter, all were given ultimatums that gave them little choice but to do as told, which meant going away to a facility and undergoing painful and debilitating treatments. This was before penicillin, so the medicines of the day included mercury and arsenic, and are likened to today's chemotherapies.

This history is dark, disturbing, and unsettling, and while I always write to entertain, I also want to educate, share something rare or unheard of, even if it's difficult to comprehend such events or practices happened. This is a story about women who were held against their will without due process, but it's also a story about women who believed what they were doing was for the greater good. It's an interesting dynamic and one I hope will generate a lot of interesting discussions.

Donna Everhart
December 1, 2024

Acknowledgments

Each time I come to this part of the process, I take some time to reflect about my writing life and those along the way who've lifted my spirits, guided me, supported me, and rooted for my successes, whether big or small. Collectively, each of you are why I still get to live this dream.

Robert Gwaltney, you helped to unlock the emotional treasure chest within this story, suggesting ways to explore the vulnerability of a character's heart. Thank you from the bottom of mine.

Lynne Hugo, I always looked forward to your logical input and suggestions, and can count on you for your quick reading with wonderful notes! Your time and effort are greatly appreciated.

A special shout-out to J. C. Sasser for your wit, sanity checks, and for the great discussions we have about writing, life, and the occasional rant about the silly stuff.

To Scott W. Stern, for writing *The Trials of Nina McCall; Sex, Surveillance, and the Decades-Long Government Plan to Imprison Promiscuous Women*, uncovering a part of history many are unaware of and which gave me the underpinnings for my own story.

To Karin Zipf, for writing *Bad Girls at Samarcand; Sexuality and Sterilization in a Southern Juvenile Reformatory,* another enlightening piece of literature about reform and the harsh methods used. Just when I thought I might be going a little too far, I'd re-read some of Zipf's work, and know I was being conservative.

To my agent, John Talbot, the conversations we have always leave me filled with motivation. Then, there are the shared laughs about random incidents, but best of all is our common bond over the love of southern literature. Altogether, this makes for a true and meaningful connection. Thank you for everything.

To my editor, John Scognamiglio, you have this uncanny knack for spotting what a story needs to make it better. With an eye for the important details, my novels wouldn't be what they are without your insight. Thank you!

To Vida, you're a one-woman cheerleading squad. I know my work is going be positioned in the very best way possible once you get started. Thank you for what you do.

To Alex, and the digital social media team, thank you all for what you do to make my books visible in an ever-growing medium that's become a critical part of showcasing my work to potential readers.

To Kris, for the gorgeous covers that resonate so much with my readers. I'm appreciative of your perception for the story behind the art you so creatively choose.

To the rest of the Kensington team who work behind the scenes, thank you for your part in this author's journey. From copy editors to proofreaders and the rest, without your efforts, the books I write wouldn't be nearly as polished or complete.

To my other writer friends far and wide, too many to name here, you all understand this process, the ups/downs and the in-betweens, and I thank you for your friendships and support.

I remain forever grateful to the independent bookstores and booksellers, libraries and librarians. For one thing, my books wouldn't have a home without your shelves, but as well, my books wouldn't reach readers without your collective voices pitching in to talk about my work.

To my beloved readers, you have my sincere and immense appreciation for your irrepressible enthusiasm for my work. I've listed names in the past and I'd love nothing better than to continue that practice, but, inevitably I leave someone out (only to realize it once it's too late!) and I don't like doing that! Thank you all, time and again.

To Jamie Adkins, of The Broad Street Deli & Market, where I can send the "locals" to get my books. Thank you for sharing your special spot in our little hometown!

Most of all, big love and gratitude to my husband, Blaine, for the conversations as well as your ongoing support and encouragement. You're still making sure I eat, and you never make comments about my "writer's hair." Lots of love to my children, Justin and Brooke, for the individual ways you each show your support. Last, but not least, lots of furry hugs and kisses to the dynamic duo, Daphne and Chloe, who've kept me on my toes, made me laugh, made me get out of the office insisting I accompany them on yard patrol, to include bug investigations, stick chewing, banned digging, poop duty, and so much more. Actually, I'm wondering how I was ever able to finish this story!

A READING GROUP GUIDE

ABOUT THIS GUIDE

The suggested questions are included to enhance your group's reading of Donna Everhart's *Women of a Promiscuous Nature*!

DISCUSSION QUESTIONS

1. Dorothy Baker is passionate about reform, and seeks to transform the women in her charge so they fit into society's views of what's appropriate. Her beliefs are typical of the day, as are the terms used to describe certain individuals. By today's standards, they would be considered unacceptable. Considering the time period, do you believe Baker was cruel, or were her methods a "means to an end"? What similarities do you recognize within these institutions as compared to an actual prison?

2. Stella Temple lives in a highly dysfunctional home with a mother suffering from mental illness and an abusive father. In her case, do you think placement at the Colony was beneficial?

3. Ruth Foster lives independently and doesn't understand why this is a problem. Why do you believe it was?

4. Baker's personal and professional life is filled with triumphs and failures. What did you admire most about her? What did you dislike most? Do you think she got away with too much?

5. Stella's intelligence and eagerness to please win Baker over. What did you think of their relationship? Do you think it was helpful to Stella, or do you wish her outcome were different?

6. Many women, like Ruth, were often scared or intimidated into submitting themselves to these facilities. Sometimes husbands turned their wives in if they felt dissatisfied with their home life. Women didn't receive due process through a court system. Why do you think women were the primary focus of immoral behaviors and not men?

7. The novel is about the mass incarceration of women suspected of promiscuous, immoral, or lewd behavior. Were you aware

of this history? Have you heard of the Chamberlain-Kahn Act, also known as the American Plan? Did you know about "farm colonies," detention centers, etc., where women were forced to stay and endure debilitating treatments? Are there other mass incarcerations you can think of similar to this?

8. Men, whether in the service or not, if found carrying an infection, underwent treatments while going on with their lives. Considering the era, do you find this disparity "normal"? Why?

9. Some of the same laws are still in effect today. Can you think of a recent time period where the law/s allow the government control over individuals?

Visit our website at
KensingtonBooks.com
to sign up for our newsletters, read more from your favorite authors, see books by series, view reading group guides, and more!

Become a Part of Our
Between the Chapters Book Club
Community and Join the Conversation

Betweenthechapters.net

Submit your book review for a chance to win exclusive Between the Chapters swag you can't get anywhere else!
https://www.kensingtonbooks.com/pages/review/